FIRST

FEDERAL SPACE BOOK 1

FLIGHT

ZACHARY JONES

ACKNOWLEDGEMENTS

FIRST FLIGHT WAS written by yours truly, a man who became a science-fiction writer because he didn't know any better.

Because I don't know any better, it's good to enlist help from people who do, starting with a good editor. First Flight was edited by Gary Smailes of Bubblecow.com, who provided the kind of honest and thorough feedback that is essential for turning a raw manuscript into a polished novel.

Speaking of polish, I would like to thank my proofreader, Deborah N. Siegel, for giving First Flight one last pass and making my work look just that much more professional.

As part of my continuing effort to improve the quality of my novel, I enlisted the help of the folks over at Global English Editing to do another proofread to correct errors pointed out by my readers. I greatly appreciate the work they did cleaning up mistakes that my own sloppiness allowed to slip through.

To the reader, I hope you enjoy the adventure waiting for you on the next page. If you enjoy the novel, or think there is something that I can improve on, feel free to leave a review on the novel's Amazon.com page, Goodreads, or both!

Happy hunting,
Zachary Jones

PROLOGUE

OLIVER FERRIS WAS not the kind of captain who commanded starships; he was the kind who built them, and he was damned good at it. Federal Command wouldn't have assigned him to oversee the construction of the most powerful warship ever built otherwise. Not when they went through so much trouble to keep her construction a secret.

The nearly complete starship rested easily inside the 200-meter-deep, 500-meter-diameter tube cut straight down into the ice and dust of Amalthea, a reddish potato-shaped body that orbited close to Jupiter. It was one of the gas giant's inner satellites. The construction chamber was bigger than was needed, even for a vessel as large as *Independence*. That was because the chamber was not officially dug to serve as the construction site of a starship, but as a housing for a pressurized habitat cylinder for the low-orbit luxury resort that would provide the closest place on which to look down upon the bands of Jupiter's upper atmosphere, all the while being protected from the gas giant's deadly radiation belts.

Oliver glanced up as far as his spacesuit's helmet allowed him, the rim of his visor blocking the very top of the starship's pointed bow. Sixteen hundred meters from the tip of her armored bow to the bottom of her five expansive engine bells, the warship stood like an armored tower. Her shape reminded Oliver of the old chemical rockets that had first carried humans into space a thousand years ago. It was largely cylindrical, before tapering down to a sharp point, as was typical of Federal starship design.

Given that starships were still essentially gigantic rockets, powered by nuclear fusion rather than chemical combustion, it was no wonder that their general layout didn't deviate far from the crude contraptions that carried the first intrepid humans into the void. However, the super-firing pairs of massive gun turrets mounted on the dorsal and ventral sides of the ship did make it clear that *Independence* was no simple booster rocket. Each main gun turret sported a pair of terajoule-class kinetic cannons, each capable of hurling kinetic kill vehicles to frightening velocities. They weren't the only weapons on display, merely the most obvious. Small towers, each topped with smaller secondary and point-defense turrets, sprouted like thorns from the battlecarrier's hull. Along the sides, circular hatches for dozens of missile tubes were arranged in neat rectangular blocks, like troopers standing in formation. Just below the main gun turrets were two rings of large doors covering *Independence's* fifty smallcraft bays. Each bay could house one fighter, bomber, or assault shuttle, depending on her mission profile.

She was, in Oliver's humble opinion, the ultimate warship. One that, once he got her off this miserable excuse of a moon and into the fight against the League, would make all existing capital ships obsolete. A smile pulled at his face, and pride warmed his chest. His name was going into the history books.

An icon appeared on his HUD for an incoming call from the command center. When he accepted the call, the voice of his XO piped through his brainset. <"Captain Ferris, the hauler from Starport Gagarin is fifteen minutes out.">

"Understood. I'm on my way up," Oliver said, turning for the airlock.

One airlock cycle later and Oliver was bouncing down the narrow corridors, passing military and civilian workers going about their duties as they got *Independence* ready for launch, the helmet of his space suit tucked under his left arm.

He stopped by his quarters to doff his space suit, take a quick shower, and put on a civilian business suit. As far as the hauler pilots were concerned, the containers their vessel was carrying were filled with polished granite from quarries back on Earth, rather than thousands of rounds of point-defense ammunition, and Oliver intended to keep that fiction intact.

The elevator doors parted at the surface level and he stepped out into a different world. Where the base below was industrial and bare, the lobby was opulent, as befitting the lobby of a luxury resort. The floor was polished tile rather than coarse rubber matting, the walls smooth stone rather than naked insulation foam.

Across from the main elevator was an overly decorated hatch leading to the main airlock. Oliver passed the airlock and followed the signs leading to the hangar bay.

The hauler had already rolled into the hangar and was being off-loaded by the time he arrived. The hauler pilots, a man in a light-red pressure suit and a woman in green, towered over his dockmaster as they spoke to her with pronounced Jovian accents.

The man was taller and darker than the woman. Lanky in build, his thinning black hair cut short. The woman had fair hair flecked with grey, which fell to the nape of her neck, her face so pale it reminded Oliver of snowdrifts.

They noticed his approach. His dockmaster, who was in reality a lieutenant in the Federal Space Forces, moved to salute but stopped when Oliver fixed her with a hard look.

"Well, you look like you're in charge," the male hauler pilot said.

"Administrator Martin, at your service," Oliver said, making a conscious effort not to say "Captain Ferris" by accident. "How was the flight from up orbit?"

"Uneventful, save for all the patrols we had to fly by. Can't imagine what the Space Forces are so worried about this far down the well."

Oliver could imagine just fine, the reason being directly below their feet. He made a dismissive shrug. "It is wartime. I wouldn't put it past the Space Forces if they're worried about a League fleet rising out of the clouds of Jupiter."

The male pilot smiled. "Belts and zones—that would be a sight."

"From high orbit, I would hope, honey," said the female pilot, taking the male pilot's hand and squeezing it.

"You two married?" Oliver asked, noticing the rings on their fingers.

"We just celebrated our thirty-second anniversary," the female hauler pilot said with a bright smile.

The male pilot smiled. "Been co-pilots for just as long."

Oliver nodded. Jovian haulers were often family operations. "Got any kids ready to take over?"

The male pilot grimaced. "Maybe after he finishes his little detour in the Space Forces."

"You have a son in the Space Forces? You must be very proud," Oliver said.

The male pilot was about to say something to the contrary, but his wife interrupted him. "Oh, yes. Though we're also worried sick. War and all."

"Yes, I can understand that." Oliver didn't have anything else to say of the matter. Telling them their son would be fine would be disingenuous. He accepted a dataslate from his dockmaster and signed off on the cargo. "Will your ship require a propellant top off?"

The male pilot shook his head. "That won't be necessary. With your permission, Administrator, we would like to launch as soon as possible. We have other contracts that need to be fulfilled."

"Of course," Oliver said, thankful he wouldn't have to babysit a pair of civilian pilots any longer than necessary. "As soon as we're done off-loading your cargo, we'll return your hauler to the surface for launch."

Both pilots nodded and turned to return to the hangar.

Oliver nodded to his dockmaster to follow them to make sure that the pilots didn't go anywhere that wasn't back to their hauler, and then he returned to the elevator. Halfway down, just after he undid the collar of his business suit, a message prompt appeared on his HUD. It was from his second-in-command, Commander Troyer, down in the command center.

"This is Captain Ferris. What have you got for me, Troyer?"

"Captain, our scopes just detected a large number of unscheduled inbound jump flashes just outside Jupiter's jump limit."

"Send it to my HUD, Troyer," Oliver said.

A constellation of icons showed where the jump flashes had occurred, twenty million kilometers above Jupiter's north pole, but there wasn't a single ship corresponding to the jump flashes. Oliver's brow furrowed. "Commander, patch us into the Jovian TacNet. The radiation belt seems to be interfering with our own sensors."

"I already did, Captain. None of the sensors in the network picked up anything other than the jump flashes."

Oliver stood still for a moment as the elevator descended into the depths of Amalthea. The datalink would've included the powerful sensor suites of both Jupiter Fleet Base and the hundreds of warships orbiting above the reach of Jupiter's radiation belts. There should be something there, he thought. Jump flashes didn't just occur spontaneously. Oliver closed the HUD and waited out the rest of the elevator ride while a cold knot formed in his stomach. The elevator came to a stop at the lowest level, and the doors parted.

An armed trooper walked up and waved a scanner in front of Oliver.

"You're clear, sir." The trooper gave him a crisp salute.

"Thank you," Oliver said, walking past the trooper without paying him any further attention.

The command center was laid out much like the bridge of a starship—a circular room with two raised, concentric rings of consoles centered on a holotank. The room was tense and quiet as Oliver entered, the crew stooped over their stations in rapt attention.

Commander Troyer was perched over the command center's central holotank, which displayed all of Jovian space within the radius of the gas giant's jump limit, including the icons marking the location of the jump flashes.

"Anything new, Commander?" Oliver asked.

"Just waiting for the 9th Fleet's pickets to make their micro jump to the location of the jump flashes," Commander Troyer said. "They should be there in another six minutes." Oliver nodded. "Sir, the civilian hauler is on the pad and ready to launch," Troyer continued.

A scowl pulled at his lips. He almost kicked himself for forgetting about the hauler. "Does Space Traffic Control still have their control systems slaved?" Oliver asked.

"Yes, sir."

"Good. Kill their engines and bring the hauler back inside. While you're at it, begin full emissions control and start evacuating the surface facilities. I want it dark and abandoned before the pickets jump on those contacts."

"Does that include bringing the pilots down here, sir? They're not cleared," Troyer said.

"We'll deal with that problem later, Commander. Carry out my orders."

"Aye aye, sir," Commander Troyer said.

After five minutes, Commander Troyer gave her report. "The moon is on lockdown and we're at full emissions control, Captain."

"Good. Did the hauler pilots give any trouble?" Oliver asked.

"No physical resistance, though they did say that they would lodge formal complaints with both Jupiter's Magistrate Office and the Jovian Hauler Association."

"Fair enough," Oliver said. "ETA to the picket ship's arrival?"

Troyer paused. "Just under sixty seconds and counting, sir. Two minutes when lightspeed delay is factored in."

Oliver nodded, and fixed his eyes on the holotank, waiting for the updates to come in.

A quartet of Churchill-class destroyers appeared in a flash of blue and ultraviolet light. Seconds later, data from the destroyers filtered down the Jovian Tactical Network, and Oliver got the first look at the enemy fleet. On the holotank, the fleet was rendered as a cloud of red icons, the vast majority of which were burning down towards Jupiter, but there were a few that remained near the jump limit, not far from where the picket destroyers had jumped in.

"Sensor AI counts 300 warships, sir. Unknown configuration," Troyer said.

Oliver glanced towards Troyer. "No transponder signals?"

"No, sir."

Oliver looked back at the holotank just in time to see new contacts sprout from the enemy rear guard. The sensor AI classified the contacts as torpedoes, hundreds of them, all converging on the destroyers. From a light-minute away, all Oliver could do was watch as the destroyers attempted to hold off the wave of torpedoes, only to be wiped off the holotank by a wave of nuclear detonations. As soon as the destroyers died, the enemy fleet disappeared.

"God dammit," Oliver said.

"They just kicked up a hornet's nest," Troyer said.

Fighters and bombers started launching from carriers and stations in orbit of Jupiter. Their movements appeared slow on the holotank but, in truth, they were pulling ten gs of acceleration as they moved to gather into a massed formation of angry strikecraft.

Troyer pointed towards a formation in high orbit over Jupiter. "The 9th Fleet's just broken formation with Jupiter Fleet Base."

Ten battleships—*Sirius, Saturn, Jupiter, Charon, Proxima, Ceres, Centaurus, Eris, Liberty,* and *Io*—gathered into battle formation. Two lines of five ships stacked on top of each other, facing their pointed armored bows towards the enemy, and keeping the presumed location of the enemy in the firing arcs of all their main guns.

As they ascended orbit, squadrons of smaller ships moved to join them. Vancouver-class cruisers formed along the flanks of the battleline, ready to add their firepower to that of the battleships. Churchill-class destroyers moved ahead of the fleet to form a defensive picket ahead of the battleships, ready to swat down any torpedoes that came screaming through the void.

"I wish I was up there, sir," Commander Troyer said, her voice pitched low so as not to carry. "I hate just watching."

"We don't have much choice in the matter, Commander," Oliver said.

There was a reason Oliver only wanted to build starships. For all their majesty, a warship was, at the end of the day, a tiny metal bubble in a vast empty void. There were no shortage of tools for breaking open those bubbles and exposing their hapless crews to the dubious mercies of empty space.

Whatever the enemy was using to mask their emissions, dropped as they approached torpedo range. Oliver's stomach twisted as 300 warships popped into existence on the holotank.

Seconds later, thousands of torpedoes erupted from the enemy formations.

"Holy Christ," someone murmured behind him.

"Belay that chatter, spacer!" Troyer barked.

Federal starships replied in kind. But although they launched a world-killing quantity of nuclear munitions, it was barely half as large as that of their enemies.

"Are any of those torpedoes headed our way, Commander?" Oliver asked.

"AI's reading their vector now, sir," Troyer said. "Doesn't look like any of them are headed our way."

"Let me know the moment that changes," Oliver said.

The bombers lit their drives and started burning hard towards the enemy fleet. On the holotank display, Oliver saw the bombers were all carrying free-fall warheads. The bombers would gain speed, drop their payloads, then redline their longburn drives to turn away from the enemy fleet while their stealthy warheads coasted into the enemy fleet and detonated.

They were coordinating their attack to arrive at the same time as the torpedoes launched by the starships, all the better to overwhelm whatever point defenses the incoming hostiles had.

"Doesn't look like the enemy brought fighters," Troyer said.

"Either they are very confident in their point defenses, or there's something we aren't seeing," Oliver said.

Across the enemy fleet, hundreds of contacts started to sprout from the enemy starships. At first, Oliver thought it was another torpedo volley, but the contacts were too big and didn't maneuver like torpedoes.

"Never mind. They did bring fighters," Troyer said. "A lot of them."

The enemy fighters didn't match the configuration of any known fighter design, but Oliver was well past the point of being surprised by that. The enemy fighters outnumbered the Federal Lightnings by a wide margin, forming into a formidable fighter screen ahead of their starships.

"Sir, there's a real risk that this facility won't remain secure. I think we should contact Jupiter Fleet Base to send shuttles down to evac our personnel," Troyer said.

Oliver glanced at the holotank. "No. By the time the shuttle got down here, either the 9th Fleet's won, or Jovian high orbit will be crawling with hostile. Maintain emission protocols."

"But Captain—"

"Those are my orders, Commander," Oliver said.

Troyer relented. "Yes, sir."

Far above, the battle didn't go well for the Federal Space Forces. The massive enemy fighter screen blunted the Federal torpedo attack and turned away the Conquerors before they could drop a single bomb.

Then the emissions from hundreds of enemy ships spiked.

"Jesus!" Oliver said as he read the power output from the guns.

Kinetic kill vehicles, command-guided projectiles that were little more than metal spikes with a few thrusters for course correction, came screaming down towards the 9th Fleet at a higher velocity than Oliver had ever seen out of a starship's gun.

Lightnings and destroyers moved to intercept the KKVs. Interceptors and point-defense guns lashed out, turning hypervelocity projectiles into fast-moving clouds of metal vapor.

In the last seconds before impact, the battleship's point defenses opened fire, vaporizing more enemy KKVs. But not enough.

There were gasps of dismay in the control center as the first Federal battleship died. Three enemy KKVs got through and merged with FSFV *Liberty's* icon. The battleship instantly turned grey on the holotank, marking her as a dead hulk on an escape trajectory out of the solar system.

"Any signs of escape pods launching from *Liberty*, Commander?"

"No, sir," Troyer said.

Others soon followed, the enemy's powerful high-velocity kinetic cannons bombarding the 9th Fleet's battleline, the volume of fire overpowering point defenses and shredding armor.

Before the last battleship, FSFV *Proxima*, died, a general order came from Jupiter Fleet Base. It was a retreat order. Already, the carriers of the 9th and 10th Fleets were burning hard for the jump limit, their decimated strikecraft complements covering their withdrawal.

Civilian ships were also running away. Those equipped with stardrives headed for open space to get beyond Jupiter's jump limit to flee to safety in a flash of red-shifted light. Those that didn't, burned down orbit towards the inner solar system.

"Sir, it looks like the enemy's preparing to board Jupiter Fleet Base," Commander Troyer said. "Why are we just letting them take it?"

"You mean, why aren't we blowing it up, Commander? I would think that would be obvious. Fifty thousand people are on that base, half of them civilians, and there hasn't been enough time to evacuate them all," Oliver said. "I suspect the remaining Federal personnel are doing the very best that they can to ruin every last scrap of intel possible before the enemy takes the base."

"It's pretty clear that there's no escape for us, sir. So, what's our next move?" Troyer asked.

"Any indication that the enemy knows that we're down here?" Oliver asked.

Commander Troyer checked with the Sensor AI. "No, sir. Nothing about the enemy's movements suggests that they do."

"Then we still have options," Oliver said. "Can we send a tightbeam down to Federal Station without the enemy detecting us?"

"There are no enemy ships between us and Federal Station, sir," Commander Troyer said.

"Then send an encrypted message down to Federal Station letting the higher-ups know what our status is," Captain Ferris said.

"It will take awhile before help arrives, sir," Commander Troyer said.

"Which is why we're going to do more than wait, Commander." Oliver tapped a button on the holotank, replacing the carnage around Jupiter with a projection of *Independence*. "We have a mostly complete starship down here, after all. Let's see if we can't make it battle-worthy with the supplies we have on hand."

CHAPTER 1

MASON RESISTED THE urge to squirm in his seat as Wing Commander Kritikos pointed towards a highlighted equatorial crater on the face of the dwarf planet orbiting right on the edge of Ross 128's jump limit.

The briefing room was a small amphitheater in the despun hull of FSFV *Eagle*. Several dozen pilots were strapped into chairs, looking at the holographic projection of a dwarf planet while the commanding officer of the carrier's strikecraft wing sat in front of it.

The dwarf planet in question was an inert sphere of dirty ice, covered in impact craters and high mountains. Evidence of a violent past forever frozen in time.

"Looks like the third time's the charm. Deepscan by *Eagle*'s primary sensor array has found a heat signature consistent with a large surface base." Kritikos said. She was a stout, solid woman with a wide face framed by shoulder-length dark hair.

"What kind of resistance can we expect, Critical?" asked Squadron Leader Adrianna Luca, the 212th Black Hat's Fighter Squadron's, and Mason's, commanding officer. She had short, dark hair and a lean frame, but was of only middling height. Despite her relatively small size, she radiated calm confidence and authority.

"You can expect a lot, Grizzly. The amount of heat we're picking up suggests there are a lot of ships landed on the surface dumping their waste heat into ice," Wing Commander Kritikos said. "So, expect starships, strikecraft, and probably some serious surface defenses as well. Given the power output indicated by the thermals, Captain Iverson's worried about capital-ship class kinetic cannons flinging kinetic kill vehicles at his big delicate carrier, so we're going to jump in when the base is on the dwarf planet's day side."

"You sure about that, sir? The Leaguers could just mount the guns on the poles, where it won't matter what side of the planet's facing us," Squadron Leader Luca said.

"Deepscan doesn't show any evidence of that, Grizzly. And if there are, *Ankara* and the destroyers should be more than capable of keeping *Eagle*'s feathers from getting ruffled."

"They'd better, sir. It's a long flight back home if they don't," Luca said. "What's the mission?"

"The mission is a full strike by all four squadrons." Wing Commander Kritikos nodded to the CO of *Eagle*'s bomber squadron, the Foxhounds. "Wrongway's Conquers will carry the heavy ordinance to deal with the base." She turned to the pilots of the 616th Fighter Squadron. "Fumbles, I want your fighters to carry shortburn torpedoes to deal with any starships in orbit." Her gaze swept over the pilots' 212th and 88th Fighter Squadrons. "Grizzly, Zipper. Black Hats and Ripper Squadrons will carry full interceptor loads."

Mason's wingmate, Flying Officer Tanya Traynor, leaned to whisper into his ear, her ponytail flying weightlessly behind her head. "You think the Leaguers will send fighters after us, Hauler?"

"Critical seems to think so, Skoot," Mason whispered back.

"Good. It would be nice to see some action," she said with a combination of false bravado and very real nervousness.

Kritikos continued the briefing, detailing what she expected of each squadron.

"And, to conclude, precisely none of what I just told you will likely be relevant to what we will encounter out there, so be prepared to adapt to whatever the League throws at you. And, remember, whatever happens, your first job is to stick with your wingmate and watch their six. Understood?"

There was a chorus of affirmatives from the forty-eight pilots assembled before her.

"Put on your hardsuits and mount your fighters. *Eagle* will jump in thirty. Happy hunting."

Mason undid the buckle of his seat belt and floated out, following the line of pilots flowing out of the briefing room like a school of fish swimming out of a tank.

"Hey, Hauler, if Critical says that everything we just went over isn't going to matter once the shooting starts, why go over all those details in the first place?" Traynor asked.

Mason floated through the open door and into the circular corridor, following the pilots in front of him to the suit chamber. "It's because, while plans are useless, planning is essential, Skoot. It reminds you of what you have at your disposal when you're trying to improvise a solution to whatever the enemy throws at you. And, really, that's the whole point of being a pilot."

"What do you mean by that, Hauler?" Traynor asked.

"Exactly that. Combat is a puzzle where you can't see any of the pieces, and those pieces are constantly changing shape. You can't predict it. You can't reduce it to an algorithm an AI can handle. All you can do is try to come up with creative solutions. Solutions that hopefully end with your enemy dead and you still alive."

"Here I thought the job of a fighter pilot was to fly fighters," Traynor said.

"Sure they are, Skoot," Mason said.

The suit chamber was a circular room with alcoves inserted into the walls. In each alcove was a full hardsuit, an essential piece of equipment for mounting a strikecraft. Lightnings lacked their own built-in life-support system. That was the hardsuit's job.

Mason's hardsuit stood in an alcove recessed in one wall of the suit chamber. With a mental command sent through his brainset, Mason opened the hardsuit. The black plates separated with the hiss of broken seals, becoming shorter and fatter as its back opened for him. Mason removed his boots and stowed them in a locker next to his hardsuit. He centered himself behind the hardsuit and shoved his legs through the open back until his feet slipped into the hardsuit's boots. With another command from his brainset, the suit closed around him, plates clicking back together and seals hissing shut. The soft inner gel layer compressed against his body, causing a slight rush of blood to Mason's head. Mason moved his arm around. His hardsuit mimicked the movement so perfectly he barely felt the weight of the acceleration gel and composite plate wrapped around his arm. He plucked his helmet from above and pulled it on. It sealed into place, and his HUD told him the suit was airtight and running on internal life support. He was ready for space. Releasing the clamps holding his hardsuit's boots to the deck, Mason floated free and turned around.

There were eleven hulking armored figures in the room with him, anonymous save for their names stenciled on their chestplates, callsigns stenciled on the front of their helmets, and their names and ranks projected above them by Mason's HUD.

Squadron Leader Luca nodded to him, her face concealed by her polarized visor. <"Check, Hauler. Is your brainset's subvocalization system working?">

<"I hear you in my head loud and clear, Grizzly,"> Mason said.

"Good," Luca said, using her voice instead. "You ready to make some deliveries?"

"Yes, sir. Sixteen interceptors and 2000 rounds of KE shot ready to be dropped right on the League's doorstep," Mason said. "Or thrown through their window."

"Let's make sure that delivery is on time. *Eagle* jumps in twenty," Luca said.

"Yes, sir." Mason turned to his wingmate. "You heard Grizzly, Skoot. Let's mount up."

"Right behind you, Hauler," Traynor said.

They had to pass through an airlock to get to their fighters. As in all carriers, *Eagle*'s hangar bays were usually kept unpressurized. *Eagle* had four primary hangar bays, one for each squadron embarked aboard the carrier. The 212th was in Hangar Bay 2, a broad metal box, two hundred meters across, where two rows of six Lightnings rested, maglocked to docking pads.

Mason floated towards his fighter, firing pulses from his suit jets to guide himself to the open cockpit. The canopy was a curved metal panel that folded flush to the fighter's fuselage. There were no windows to look out of inside a Lightning.

Skoot floated past him and grabbed ahold of her Lightning. She looked toward him. Mason pumped his fist over his head and she nodded, then settled into the cockpit of her fighter.

Pulling himself down into his own fighter, he strapped himself into the gimbaled seat inside and strapped his hardsuit down. The hangar techs had already warmed up his Lightning. Both reactors were running at idle power, and the containment rings of the two longburn drives had already cooled down to operating temperatures. His fighter was ready to fly. After plugging his hardsuit into the fighter's power system, Mason closed the canopy and started pressurizing the cockpit with inert gas. While the cockpit pressurized, Mason connected his brainset to the fighter. Information displays flooded into his HUD, and the fighter became transparent as sensor data was fed into his vision. Lightnings to his right and left glowed with waste heat as they idled on the deck. His eyes followed the glowing tendrils of cooling lines running from the fighters to the deck, transporting the waste heat to *Eagle*'s own radiators.

"Black Hat Nine, ready to launch," Mason said.

"Black Hat Ten, ready for launch," Traynor said.

Squadron Leader Luca piped in over the squadron's channel. "Glad to hear everyone got themselves sorted out," she said. "Keep an eye on your timers. We launch as soon as *Eagle* jumps."

Mason opened the feed from *Eagle*'s own sensors, his attention fixed on the little red dwarf star over a hundred billion kilometers ahead of the ship. A hundred billion kilometers directly above his head. It was little more than a bright point of light among many.

A timer counted down to jump. Mason focused on his breathing, settling down the shaky feeling in his gut. It wasn't the faster-than-light jump that made him nervous. The thought of vaulting across billions of kilometers of space in an instant never bothered him. It was the fact that there was a battle waiting at the end of the jump.

When the time hit zero, a subtle vibration traveled up through Mason's Lightning. The vibration was *Eagle*'s capacitor discharging, dumping energy into the stardrive. There was a flash of light, and Ross 128 grew from a point of light into a proper sun, the thin, silver crescent of the dwarf planet visible to one side.

"All fighters, this is Black Hat's leader. Prepare for immediate launch," Squadron Leader Luca said.

Mason gripped the controls and braced himself for launch.

Luca's Lightning launched first, kicked into space by the launch rails running from the docking pad to the open hangar door. Black Hat Two launched next, followed by Black Hat Three, and so forth, until a sudden acceleration yanked Mason back, and his Lightning flew out of the hangar. *Eagle* fell away behind him, and a few seconds later, the safeties preventing him from lighting his longburn drives disengaged.

"This is Black Hat Nine, my longburn drives are hot," Mason said.

His engines came online at the minimal thrust setting, and a fraction of a g pulled back. He vectored towards the growing formation of fighters, passing the *Eagle's* escorts. The cruiser FSFV *Ankara* and the two destroyers, FSFV *McQuarrie* and FSFV *Yi*, formed a three-ship screen between *Eagle* and the dwarf planet.

Traynor took up formation off his right wing as he passed the escorts.

"Black Hat Nine, in position," Mason said.

The Lightning squadrons formed up abreast of each other, while the bomber squadron flew their Conquers into formation above them. No ship was directly behind another, where they risked getting a blast of hot longburn drive exhaust to the face.

While the strikecraft prepared their attack, the dwarf planet remained quiet. No patrolling fighters, no loitering starships, no wave of torpedoes, and no EM spikes from kinetic cannons launching KKVs. Just the cratered and cracked face of an icy dwarf planet.

"It's pretty quiet, Grizzly," Mason said.

"Won't be for much longer. Prepare for a hard burn," Luca said.

"Roger that," Mason said. His hardsuit started pumping anti-acceleration drugs into his blood, giving him a strong metallic taste in his mouth.

"All fighters, you are clear for cruising burn. Give the Leaguers hell," Wing Commander Kritikos said.

Mason pushed the throttle forward, and his longburn drives came to life. The stiff pull of three gs pulled him back and his seat tilted forward to keep his back facing towards the line of thrust. He gradually increased acceleration, stacking gs on top of his chest like stones. He stopped pushing the throttle forward at ten gs. It felt like the hand of a giant was pressing him down into his seat, but he wasn't in pain. The gel layer of his hardsuit distributed the pressure evenly, and the Federal Space Forces had invested many a taxpayer's FSC into augmenting his body's g-tolerance to the point where ten gs wasn't even all that dangerous. After five minutes, Mason executed the midpoint flip maneuver. He cut the longburn drive, ignoring the disorientation of suddenly going zero-g, and flipped his fighter 180 degrees at the same time every other strikecraft did. He re-lit on his drive, and the giant's hand returned.

There was still no sign of activity from the other side of the dwarf planet. Whatever the Leaguers were up to, they didn't want the incoming Federals to see it.

Mason braced himself for whatever surprises came his way.

The surprise came in the form of four bright flashes in an empty volume of space thousands of kilometers above the dwarf planet. Following the flashes, Mason saw four objects moving fast towards the carrier behind him.

<"Shit. I got KKVs inbound on *Eagle*!"> Mason said.

<"I see them. Anyone spot what fired those?"> Squadron Leader Luca asked.

Tracing back along the path of the KKVs, Mason came across four yellow icons in a volume of space the sensors had shown to be empty seconds earlier. Yellow meant bogeys. Unidentified contacts. Whatever they were, they were big. Sensor AI estimated each vessel was over a kilometer long.

"All strikecraft, emergency burn, vector–" Wing Commander Kritikos' voice was cut off by static as the newly arrived starships activated powerful jammers.

<"All fighters, fall back to *Eagle*; emergency burn."> Squadron Leader Luca said.

<"Roger that, Grizzly. Skoot, stay on my wing and hang on.">

<"I'm with you, Hauler.">

Mason pushed his engines to emergency power, and fifteen gs assaulted him, causing his bones to ache as he was crushed inside his hardsuit. Despite the hard burn, momentum continued to carry the fighters away from *Eagle* as her escorts opened fire on the incoming KKVs.

Ankara, *McQuarrie*, and *Yi* were quick to react. The destroyers lit their longburn drives and vectored straight towards the incoming KKVs. *Ankara* also lit her drive, burning hard towards *Eagle*, moving to put her armored hull between the enemy and the carrier. Though pulling three gs, she couldn't get into position before the KKVs flew by.

Interceptors launched from all four Federal vessels as the KKVs approached. The small, short-range missiles accelerated away from their launch ships before turning to engage the KKVs, over 200 converging on four targets.

Then, all of a sudden, the interceptors lost cohesion as many stopped homing in on their targets.

<"What the hell is wrong with our interceptors?"> Traynor asked.

<"Fuckers are jamming them, Skoot,"> Mason said.

When the scattered interceptors reached the KKVs, there were two bright flashes of kinetic impacts, and two KKVs disappeared while the remaining two continued on toward *Eagle*.

The KKVs zipped past *McQuarrie* and *Yi*, passing through the wall of point-defense fire without issue.

Ankara executed an emergency turn, a gust of hot gas spewing from one of her forward maneuvering thrusters as she turned to bring her broadside to bear against the KKVs.

From thousands of kilometers away, Mason imagined the creaking of structural members as the cruiser's hard turn tried to rip the ship apart.

Bringing the maximum number of point-defense turrets into play, *Ankara* threw up a wall of hypervelocity projectiles ahead of the KKVs, with *Eagle* adding her own meager point-defense fire as well.

In the last second before impact, both remaining KKVs flashed and turned into dense clouds of metal vapor that continued towards *Eagle*, carried by their momentum.

They struck *Eagle* in the drive section with bright flashes of light that momentarily obfuscated the carrier. When the light faded, *Eagle* was adrift, her drive dark and her emissions fading.

<"Oh shit! Oh shit! Oh shit!"> Traynor said, her subvocalized panic echoing through Mason's head.

On the verge of panic himself, Mason lashed out. <"Belts and Zones! Calm the fuck down, Flying Officer!">

It was then Mason noticed huge numbers of contacts rising over the horizon of the dwarf planet that his combat AI identified as forty fighters and hundreds of interceptors.

The combat AI gave him a time to impact measured in seconds.

<"Fuck! Skoot, stay with me!"> Mason said. Despite her panic, the young pilot's Lightning never wavered from his right wing.

<"All fighters, turn to engage!"> Squadron Leader Luca said.

Mason flipped his fighter over, armed his own interceptors, and set his combat AI to the task of computing firing solutions against the incoming missiles. The combat AI picked the interceptors that were most likely to hit and locked one of his own interceptors on them. He had enough interceptors to destroy barely more than half the guided munitions coming his way. Cold, shivering terror ran through Mason's body, overpowering the discomfort from the heavy gs. He was very likely to die in the next few seconds. While he contemplated his mortality, the combat AI started firing interceptors. Eight external missiles flew off the launch rails in a single volley, while the rotary launcher in the belly of his Lightning launched all its interceptors inside of four seconds.

The space ahead of Mason's Lightning lit up like a fireworks display, each interceptor-on-interceptor impact flashing brighter than any star for a bare instant.

Once the light show ended, the combat AI showed more than enough interceptors to kill him several times over.

<"Skoot, get ready to go guns. Stay close on my wing,"> Mason said.

<"Roger,"> she said, her subvocalized response terse and tense.

His Lightning lurched to one side to bring his cannon to bear on an incoming interceptor and shuddered as the combat AI fired the cannon.

The interceptor flashed and disappeared. The cannon continued firing as the combat AI adjusted its aim, sweeping the stream of deadly projectiles across the path of another interceptor. All the while, both Mason's and Traynor's Lightnings hemorrhaged decoys, filling the pocket of space around them with a fireworks display of brightly burning countermeasures.

The volley of interceptors hit like a storm front. Something flashed near his fighter, and then the enemy interceptors were receding in the distance behind Mason's Lightning.

Of the forty-eight fighters and bombers that had launched from *Eagle*, only six Lightnings remained.

Traynor was gone. Mason realized that the flash of light near his fighter had been the death of an eager young pilot on her first combat assignment. A direct hit by an interceptor. Mason had gotten away unscathed, by some stroke of luck.

Squadron Leader Luca had survived as well. Her subvocal commands came through crisp, calm, and clear. <"All fighters, form on me. Prepare to engage the enemy,"> she said.

<"R–roger that, Grizzly. Forming on your wing,"> Mason said. He was the only member of the 212th other than Luca to survive.

Forty enemy strikecraft burned towards them on the heels of the interceptor volley.

Luca continued to issue orders, assigning targets as time to engagement approached zero.

The engagement was brief and decisive. Forty enemy fighters opened fire on the six Lightnings with their kinetic cannons. Squadron Leader Luca disappeared as multiple streams of fire hit her Lightning, shattering the fighter and likely pulping the woman inside.

Something slammed into the side of Mason's Lightning and he went spinning out of control. Alarms hammered his ears while warning icons filled his HUD. Mason relaxed and let go of the controls, waiting for the enemy to finish him off. It took him a moment to realize they couldn't. The swarm of enemy fighters receded in the distance, burning hard to reverse their vector and re-engage Mason. Flight AI corrected the spin, and Mason found himself weightless in the cockpit of his fighter, drifting just short of escape velocity over the surface of the dwarf planet. He checked his damage display. His Lightning was a wreck. She wasn't dead, but she was dying. The left engine nacelle was gone, along with most of the left wing. He just had the longburn drive in the right engine nacelle and the reactor powering it and that reactor was fading. He had only a few minutes of power left.

Mason fired the longburn drive, the flight AI angling the thrust to keep his fighter from spinning, causing acceleration to pull perpendicular relative to the nose.

As he came around to the other side of the dwarf planet, two more large contacts appeared in low orbit. Their emissions were different from the ships that fired on *Eagle*, and they sent no kinetic fire his way, as Mason gently coaxed his strikecraft down to the surface. He guessed the enemy warships didn't want to rob their fighters of one more kill.

The surface grew, revealing details Mason had missed from further away— dormant volcanoes, deep canyons, and innumerable impact craters.

Mason fired his braking thrusters to slow down, cutting his velocity, hoping to bring his fighter to a stop just a few meters above the surface. The reactor died when he was still 100 meters above the flat ground at the bottom of a large impact crater, and his longburn drive went dark for the last time. All Mason had were the maneuvering thrusters. He turned his fighter to align the nose with the direction of travel, and fired both fore and ventral thrusters to slow down his descent as much as possible. The Lightning landed belly-first on the ice and skidded across the surface, metal screaming as momentum dragged the fighter across the ice. The list of damaged systems showing up on his HUD expanded rapidly, until he abruptly lost his link, leaving him staring at the dark control screens in his cockpit as the fighter shuddered around him.

Mason gripped the armrests of his seat, closed his eyes, and held his breath behind clenched teeth until the shuddering stopped. Opening his eyes, Mason took a few shaky breaths, forcing his body to relax. Mason's fist landed on the emergency release and explosive bolts fired, blowing the canopy away. Atmosphere evacuated in an instant. Though small, dim, and far away, Ross 128 was still bright enough to cause the visor of Mason's hardsuit to polarize to protect his eyes. The star hung low over the lip of the crater he had crash-landed in, a disk of light against a black background, hanging above a jagged wall of grey rock and ice, casting long, sharp shadows over the bottom of the crater.

Mason didn't waste time enjoying the sight. He grabbed his survival kit and leapt out of the fighter and started skipping away as soon as his boots touched the regolith. His long shadow ran with him. He glanced over his shoulder, looking back at the broken Lightning lying on the floor of the crater. There was a flash of pure white light and his visor darkened to protect his eyes, but not before the after-image of a white-hot spear puncturing his broken Lightning seared itself into his vision. His foot caught on something and he fell flat to the ground. The ground vibrated like a rolling drumbeat as hundreds of rounds of kinetic fire rained down behind him. Mason curled himself into a ball to make himself a smaller target.

When the sound and vibrations faded, Mason stayed curled up, afraid to move lest it attract the attention of an enemy lurking in the dark sky above him. When he did open his eyes, there was nothing but rock, ice, and empty space above. Mason sat up and turned around. What was left of his fighter was little more than shattered metal and impact craters. He didn't know how he had escaped notice. Maybe the enemy, whoever the hell they were, couldn't distinguish between his body heat and the wreckage of his fighter they had scattered all around the crater. Whatever the case, when he finally stood up, no claw-shaped strikecraft swooped out of the sky to kill him.

Despite the low gravity and the hardsuit empowering his limbs, Mason fell to his knees as the grim reality of his situation dawned on him. Everyone was dead except him. He was stranded on a ball of rock and ice orbiting a star that was close to Sol in astronomical terms, but far, far away when you didn't have access to a stardrive.

"Belts and fucking zones," he whispered.

A sick feeling quivered in his stomach as he looked around. Aside from debris, nothing but dust and ice surrounded him. And it was ice that was as much ammonia and nitrogen as it was water. Ross 128 dipped below the rim of the crater, plunging Mason into total darkness. A shudder ran through his body that had nothing to do with the deep cold outside the dark plates of his hardsuit. It was as if the faceplate of his helmet suddenly became opaque. Only the light of his HUD broke up the black. The only sounds were his shallow breathing and the beating of his heart. He glanced to the survival kit clutched in his hands and couldn't see it in the darkness. He almost activated his helmet lights but stopped.

Mason looked up and glanced around, looking for the glowing drive plumes. What he saw was the shimmering arc of dust and stars that bulged in the center. The Milky Way galaxy. He had seen it many times before, of course. But never quite so clearly, not with his naked eyes, at least. It somehow seemed… bigger and brighter, even though Ross 128 was no closer to the galactic core than Sol. It was beautiful. The kind of beauty that brought a full stop to whatever you were thinking about. Mason rested on his knees and stared at the sky.

When he finally broke his reverie, the paralyzing terror that had gripped him had retreated. Now it was just some slithering thing in the back of his head. Mason activated his helmet lights and turned to the survival kit clutched in his left hand, illuminating the kit with cool light. The contents of the kit would keep him alive. Give him time… time to do what exactly?

Mason hadn't even started to consider his options. It was a good thing his survival instructors weren't there to see him. They'd have a few choice words about him wasting precious time. He chuckled at that. It was a good feeling, even if laughing at one's own doom seemed more than a bit morbid to him.

He closed his eyes and tried to think. Ross 128 was eleven light-years from Sol. Roughly a week's travel using a top-tier stardrive. Jupiter Fleet Base expected *Eagle* back in two weeks. When she didn't return, they'd send ships to investigate systems on her scheduled patrol route. Mason had to keep himself alive for three weeks on an airless dwarf planet.

Mason stood up and looked in the direction of his fighter. It was little more than bits of metal reflecting the light of his LEDs. There wasn't anything in the crater that would keep him alive for that long. There was only one place he could think of that would. The League base he had come all the way out here to destroy. He knew where he was in relation to the base. The dwarf planet wasn't very big, just 1200 klicks across. He had studied the detailed topographical map of the surface from a 150-year-old survey mission Wing Commander Kritikos had provided. The crater he had crash landed in was maybe 200 kilometers east of the base.

Mason looked back up at the sky, not to take in the beauty of the galaxy above, but to let the navigation app on his brainset match the stars above to those in its database. A few stars blinked on his HUD, and a compass showing him the direction of local north appeared at the top of his vision. A green icon showed where the League base was, almost directly west. Mason turned towards the direction of the base, pulled the strap of his survival kit tightly across his shoulder, and started skipping across the surface. These were not the short, hopping skips of a child at play. Mason flew over meters of ice each time his toes touched the surface.

He quickly traversed the kilometer of gentle slope leading up to the nearest crater wall, which he climbed over with ease thanks to the low gravity and the strength-boosting hardsuit. Once out of the crater, a vast desolate landscape stretched out before him. Ice and rock worn by eons of impacts. Mason could feel the age of the dwarf planet he was stranded on. The idea of his frozen corpse becoming a permanent addition to the dwarf planet frightened him into motion.

Focusing on the navigation icon on his HUD, Mason leapt off the crater rim. When his feet touched, he jumped again, aided by his suit thrusters. Each skip became longer and longer as he found the most efficient rhythm to move across the surface, until he was flying over the frozen ground at thirty kilometers per hour.

CHAPTER 2

MASON RECOGNIZED THE biggest of the wrecked spacecraft: a Dragon-class cruiser resting on its side next to a landing pad. The landing legs on the starship's tail pointed into the air like those of a dead insect and its narrow, cone-shaped hull was neatly bisected by a crater in the middle. The launch pad was near a depot of fuel tanks, partially buried in the ice, most of them ruptured. The cruiser must have been on the pad refueling when whoever they were attacked the base. Poor bastards never had a chance.

The irony of his sympathy didn't escape him. If he had attacked the base as planned, he would've loved nothing more than to take shots at a League cruiser caught on the ground. Strange how it was easier to feel sympathy for the enemy when someone else killed them.

Between him and the fallen cruiser was a bone yard of broken spacecraft and fresh impact craters. Billions of stellars worth of military equipment left scattered and ruined across the frozen, airless ground.

Mason jumped and fell slowly into the crater in the light gravity. After about thirty seconds of falling, he fired his hardsuit's cold gas thrusters, slowing his descent enough to land lightly on his feet. He proceeded towards the fallen Dragon.

Skipping across the surface of the crater, Mason passed a neat line of wrecked spacecraft. It took a moment for him to recognize them as Asps, the League's near-equal to the Lightning. Long and slender craft, with reverse geometry wings and a single huge engine nacelle at the rear, they looked like a wasp crossed with a dagger.

Now all these sleek, elegant ships were shattered to pieces, like toys thrown to the ground by an angry toddler.

Larger wrecks he passed looked like destroyers. Based on how many ships seemed to be destroyed as they were being serviced, the only conclusion Mason could draw was that the Leaguers didn't know they were under attack until it was too late to react. Just like *Eagle*. When he reached the wreckage of the League cruiser, its hull loomed over him liked the corpse of the mythical beast it was named after.

One of the habitat modules had broken off and fallen to the ground. A cylinder mounted on a long, folding arm. It was there to provide spin-grav for the ship's crew when she wasn't accelerating, and folded into the hull during periods of acceleration, keeping the decks perpendicular to the line of thrust. Now it lay crumpled on the ice.

Mason approached the module, looking for an entrance. He spied an opening—a rupture in the top of the squat cylinder, near the ground. He stopped just short of entering the tear in the hull when he was taken by a sudden sense of foreboding. There were going to be dead bodies in there.

In two years of war, Mason had both seen and inflicted death, but always from a distance measured in kilometers. He'd never actually seen a dead body in that time. Space warfare was tidy that way. At least for fighter pilots.

There was nothing tidy about the interior of the hab modules. Broken bodies and unsecured equipment littered the corridor the tear led into. As soon as he stepped inside, he almost put a boot through the back of a frozen corpse. The maroon jumpsuit marked them as an enlisted espatier of the League Battlefleet's infantry branch. The body lay face down on what had once been a bulkhead but was now the floor. The man's body lay in a pool of freeze-dried blood, his limbs twisted in unnatural directions. Even in the weak gravity, the hab module must have hit the ground hard enough to kill.

There was something uncanny about the corpse. It didn't look like a body, frozen and robbed of life. It looked like a mannequin, a prop. It just didn't click that the thing lying broken before him had been a person. It did cause his stomach to twist, and a wave of nausea rose. It was quickly forced down, both by Mason's concentration, and a dose of anti-emetic drugs automatically administered by his hardsuit. Once the sick feeling passed,

Mason stepped past the corpse, careful not to look at it. The sideways corridor curved up in both directions.

Mason passed more bodies smashed onto the bulkhead, along with various scattered items: tools, hand computers, and loose personal items. There was even what looked like a packet of juice or soda splattered on the bulkhead Mason walked on, leaving a bright purple smudge. Yet more evidence that Leaguers had been taken by complete surprise.

It didn't make sense to Mason. Any attacking ships should have been detected well before they got in range to open fire. The blue-shifted flash of the ships jumping in would have been more than ample warning. Even ignoring the jump flash, a ship burning towards a target was more than easily detectable, even from billions of kilometers away. It should not have been possible to catch the base by complete surprise, and yet that was apparently what had happened. For some reason, after destroying the League base, they waited for a Federal force to show up and ambush them. Mason had no idea who would be capable and willing to do that. Only the League of Sovereign Worlds was big enough to take on Earth-Fed. Only Earth-Fed was big enough to take on the League.

It turned out League hab modules were laid out like Federal ones. Circular decks stacked atop each other, centered on a bank of elevators. Each deck was sliced into quarters by long corridors that radiated out of the central hub towards the outer bulkhead. One such corridor loomed above Mason, reaching up into the sky at an angle.

With a jump, Mason grabbed a handhold and pulled himself up into the corridor. The angle was too steep for walking, but there were plentiful handholds. Though meant for helping crew move during zero-g, they were just as good for climbing in low gravity. Mason started to ascend, stepping over open doors, trying to ignore the frozen bodies revealed by the twin beams of his helmet lights, focusing instead on every sign he came across. He couldn't read or speak Exospeak, the official language of the League and much of independent space, but his brainset had an app for that. It translated the Exospeak script into Federal and put it up on his HUD. Looking at a sign stenciled on the bulkhead he was climbing, his brainset translated it as "MEDICAL CENTER". Potentially useful, but not what he needed.

Mason climbed to the next compartment a few meters further up. He wiped frost off the sign and stared at it until his brainset translated. "Suit Storage" appeared just under the League sign, projected onto his HUD by his brainset. The door was closed. Mason tried the latch, but it turned without disengaging the bolt holding the door shut. There was a keypad on the door, but Mason didn't know where to find the code and didn't care to look.

Climbing down, away from the door, Mason leaned back and pulled out his pistol. It was a big, ungainly weapon that looked like an oversized revolver, but it wasn't really a gun. It was a rocket launcher, capable of firing small armor-piercing rockets that could punch through a hardsuit's chestplate at close range. Mason aimed for the lock and fired. Even in the vacuum, Mason heard the pop as the shock wave from the close blast hit his suit. The door didn't open, but there was a scorched black hole just below the latch. Holstering his pistol, Mason climbed above the door, braced himself on the doorframe, and gave the door a hard kick. The force was enough to break whatever was left of the bolt, and the door swung inward.

Mason let himself drop down onto the back wall of the compartment. On the walls, laid out like bookshelves, with everything on its side, were lockers containing spacesuits. Mason opened one of the lockers at shoulder level and pulled a suit out, giving it a pull, feeling it stretch in his hands. Then he dropped it and looked inside the locker. There were bottles of air inside, as well as replacement CO_2 scrubbers. There were also some spare power cells. They were long and cylindrical like Federal ones, but not compatible with the ports of his hardsuit. Mason glanced at his HUD's power meter just as it ticked down a percentage point. If worse came to worst, he could use the League suit.

Mason opened the other lockers and pulled out their contents, creating a serious mess inside the suit-storage compartment. He stuffed a spare pressure suit with all the air bottles and CO_2 scrubbers he could fit into it, and then climbed out of the suit-storage room. He had air to breathe and scrubbers to keep him from poisoning the air with his own exhalations.

Mason made his way back to the breach and deposited both his survival kit and the supplies he had salvaged from the wreck. They wouldn't go anywhere on their own, and there wasn't likely to be anyone else on this moon who could take them. Examining the main hull of the cruiser, Mason wrote off searching it. The kinetic strike that had cut the cruiser in half cut right through where the main hull's crew spaces would have been. The rest of the ship would have been dedicated to weapons, sensors, and propulsion, none of which would enable Mason's survival. He opted to move on to the base structures instead. What was left of the central buildings was nothing more than craters and broken debris. The destruction of the central parts of the base had been complete.

There was no shelter to be had there. Mason kept exploring, ignoring his hardsuit's power cells falling to thirty-nine percent.

He counted the wrecks of four League destroyers on the bottom of the crater, located on the remains of smaller landing pads radiating out from the fuel depot. The tanks looked like standardized fuel tanks that would be found attached to a starfreighter. They were all breached—those that had not been completely vaporized, that is.

Near one of the ruptured fuel tanks, Mason found an overturned rover, three wheels sticking into the air, all bent and broken from the explosion that had turned the vehicle on its side. It would never serve as a means of transport again, but it might serve as a shelter. The cabin looked intact.

Mason skipped over to the rover and grabbed a handhold. Aided by the low gravity and the strength of his hardsuit, Mason flipped the rover back onto its wheels. The windows of the cabin on its left side were cracked, but Mason could seal those with sealant from his survival kit. The rover was a box on a six-wheel chassis. At the front of the box was a bubble of ballistic glass around a two-person cabin. The interior was dark, and it was obviously depressurized.

Mason shined his LEDs through the cabin, noting a door in the back of the cabin that led to the compartment in the back. It looked like a personnel transport of some kind, probably for moving people between the central base structures and the parked starships without them needing to put on pressure suits.

Going around to the back, Mason found a hatch. He pulled the latch and it pushed open easily. The interior was unpressurized. Mason climbed inside and looked at the benches. They would make acceptable beds, and there was enough room inside for him to stand at full height, even in his hardsuit. There was even a small bathroom with a toilet. Mason hoped that was still in working order. Moving to the cabin, Mason sat down in the seat and let his brainset translate the controls. He hit a power button, and the lights came on, as did, to his relief, the life-support system. The rover started to pressurize, but then alarms came up on the screen over the central dash: air leaks. Mason glanced at the cracks in the side of the cabin's bubble canopy. No surprise there.

Mason shut down the rover and let it depressurize. Leaving the rover, he returned to the cruiser hab module to collect his survival kit and scavenged supplies.

Upon returning to the rover, he opened the survival kit and pulled out the sealant gun, going over every crack he could find and covering it with a generous dab of sealant. After waiting a few minutes for the golden goo to cure, Mason closed the rear hatch of the rover, then walked to the cabin and started to repressurize it again. Alarms came on and he squelched them, watching as the pressure rose and rose, until he had one atmosphere of air showing on the gauge in his HUD. He shut down the rover's systems and sat still, waiting to see if he had gotten all the leaks.

After five minutes waiting in the rover, the gauge didn't show any change in pressure. Just to double-check, Mason inspected his suit's own atmosphere sniffers. The rover was filled with air. Mostly nitrogen with a large fraction of oxygen. Before even thinking about popping the seals on his suit, Mason examined the life-support system. The rover didn't have an oxygenator like Mason's suit did. It used stored oxygen and CO_2 scrubbers. A cost-saving measure, he assumed. It also meant that the rover used relatively little power to maintain its air supply.

Mason popped the seals on his helmet and pulled it off. The air was cooler than he liked, but fresh. Mason set down his helmet on the rover's console and moved to the cabin in the back, near the hatch. He sent a signal through his brainset instructing the hardsuit to open.

The back plates parted open, giving Mason a clear path out of the hardsuit. He shimmied his arms out of the sleeves and, once he got them out, pulled his legs out of the hardsuit. Mason stretched and moved his shoulders in their full range of motion. Hardsuits were comfortable enough, but they did slightly limit mobility in the joints. As he set it down on the bench seat, the upholstery felt soft and inviting, even though it was still cold from its exposure to the vacuum. Yawning, Mason lay down and fell to sleep.

CHAPTER 3

MASON LEANED BACK in the rover's reclining driver's seat, staring off into the night sky. He told himself he was keeping an eye out for engine plumes but in reality he just wanted to stare off into space. His brainset had gigabytes of entertainment stored in it. But old films and augmented reality games could only hold his attention for so long. His mind inevitably drifted back to the enemy responsible for stranding him on a frigid dwarf planet in an unclaimed system. An enemy that had destroyed a League base, apparently by complete surprise, and then set up an ambush for *Eagle*'s strike group. There were two things Mason could conclude. First, they were hostile to the League. And, second, they knew *Eagle* was coming. Mason sighed. Whoever they were, they were interrupting what had been a nice simple war.

Mason was comfortable in his makeshift shelter. He'd spent the first couple of days gathering enough spare air canisters and scrubbers to make sure he could breathe for the next month, as well as enough food and water to keep body and soul together. After that, it was just a matter of waiting.

A light appeared in the sky, shining brighter than any star. Mason sat there and watched for a moment, noting how the bloom got brighter and brighter and lower and lower. Something was coming in to land. Scrambling out of the driver's seat, Mason ran over to his hardsuit in the back compartment and climbed inside. The suit closed around him, plates merging together, and sealing shut. After locking his helmet over his head, Mason tossed everything that couldn't tolerate vacuum into the crew cabin, shut the hatch, and depressurized the rear compartment.

Mason spent several nervous minutes waiting for the rover's pumps to suck enough of the air away to let him open the rear hatch. He drew his pistol from his holster, checked the ammo cylinder, and holstered it. The sidearm was only a token defense, but it was something.

Pressure dropped enough to let Mason pulled the back hatch open, and he lurched out of the rover.

A sleek, wedged-shaped spacecraft was in front of him, held aloft by thrusters that kicked up a cloud of dust. Mason's heart sank as he recognized it. A League assault shuttle painted in the livery of the League Battlefleet.

A spotlight on the bottom of the shuttle came on, blinding him. When his visor filtered out the glare, he saw five figures fall from the shuttle to land on the ice. They were League espatiers in full combat hardsuits. They leveled their battle rifles at him.

Mason let his sidearm fall out of his hand and raised his arms in surrender. At the same time, he brought up a big red icon on his HUD. A warning prompt came up, asking him if he was sure. He answered yes. It asked if he was really, really sure. He answered yes again. His HUD went dark as his brainset's core module bricked itself, leaving Mason's vision free of overlays and icons.

Mason sat in an interrogation room in a hab cylinder of a Dragon-class cruiser. He knew he was aboard a Dragon because it looked just like the interior of the wreck he had crawled through over a week before. Just without the bodies and everything tilted at an acute angle. One-third of a g pulled him down into his seat, a result of the two RPM of the hab rotor. He was wearing his jumpsuit. The League espatiers had made him remove his hardsuit at gunpoint as soon as they pulled him aboard their shuttle.

They had also surgically removed his brainset. Not dramatic, but inconvenient. Brainsets weren't inside the skull proper but implanted just under the skin at the back of the head. They had just sat Mason down in an autodoc and let it do the delicate work. The only thing he'd felt was the hairs on the back of his head being parted. The Leaguers were probably at this very moment trying to extract what data they could from the implant.

Good luck with that, Mason thought. The kill switch had bricked the device. They'd get more use out of it as a poker chip.

In front of him sat a rather sour-looking man in an espatier's blood-red jumpsuit, dark eyes glaring over a drooping, dark moustache. He had been glaring at Mason for twenty minutes, without speaking a word.

"So, is the silent treatment part of the interrogation process?" Mason said. "Trying to psych me out before the real questioning begins?" The espatier just kept glaring at Mason. "You know what I think?" Mason leaned over the table. "I think you can't speak a word of Federal, can you, Mister Frowny-Face?"

The door to the interrogation room opened, and an officer in a green jumpsuit of the League Battlefleet walked in. A man of middling height and slight build, his shaved head, thin neck, and weak chin made him look like a vulture. Mr. Frowny-Face stood up and snapped a salute towards the officer, planting the knuckles of his clenched fist to his temple like he was punching himself in the side of his head.

The officer saluted back, said something in Exospeak that sounded like a dismissal, then sat down in front of Mason while the espatier departed through the door and closed it behind him.

Glancing at the pins of the officer's uniform, Mason saw that he was a Lieutenant Commander. "I'd salute you, sir, but ah… " He gestured with his cuffed hands.

"Courtesy is always a good sign in an officer, Flight Lieutenant Grey," the League Officer said.

"Rude officers don't get offered for prisoner swaps, sir," Mason said.

The bald officer grinned at that. "Indeed, Flight Lieutenant. My name is Lieutenant Commander Albert Korth. I'm the executive officer of this ship you are currently aboard, LCS *Fafnir*." The way the man pronounced his name made it sound like "court".

"A pleasure to meet you, Commander Korth," Mason said. *Fafnir* didn't have a dedicated intelligence officer aboard, Mason thought. That was the only reason one of the ship's senior officers would take up the task of questioning him.

"Your dossier was quite interesting to read, Flight Lieutenant," Korth said. "You were serving under Admiral Julia Mobius when she started this war at the Battle of Polykastro."

"My carrier at the time was under her command." Mason nodded. "Though I dispute blaming her for starting the war. It was your people who fired first."

"It was your people who invaded a system under League protection," Korth said.

"A system that was harboring pirates," Mason said. "Which is interesting, considering that before then, your people took about as dim a view on piracy as we do."

"And we still take a dim view on pirates. As we do on would-be hegemons who think they can bully independent systems near our territory," Korth said.

"Ah, yes. I guess only the League's allowed to bully their neighbors," Mason said. "But I don't think we're here to debate the causes of our current war, are we?"

"No, we are not," Commander Korth said. "You are here to answer my questions. Starting with how you ended up camping in the ruins of our base."

Federal training was clear when it came to answering questions after capture. Name, rank, and service number. No more. Mason decided those rules didn't apply to his situation.

Mason leaned forward, looking Korth straight in the eye. "I was shot down, and not by your people."

"By whom, then?" Korth asked.

"I don't know," Mason said.

"Any guesses?" Korth asked.

Mason splayed out his cuffed hands. "Someone who doesn't like either Earth-Fed or the League and had the firepower to act on that?"

"There are no shortage of people in this universe who fit the former. But not the latter, Flight Lieutenant," Korth said.

"Well, there's at least one," Mason said. "There were six starships supported by forty fighters. They had some kind of stealth tech that allowed them to avoid detection until the moment they opened fire. They had big guns and a whole hell of a lot of missiles." Mason took in a deep breath, and blew it out through clenched teeth. "They... they killed everyone in a matter of minutes. We never had a chance."

Korth listened, nodded, and clearly didn't believe a word of what Mason was saying.

"So, to summarize. An unknown hostile force snuck up on our base, destroyed it, and then waited to ambush your carrier's strike group?" Lt. Commander Korth held up a finger for each point he made. "Am I correct?"

"You are, Commander," Mason said.

"That is quite the story, Flight Lieutenant," Lt. Commander Korth said.

Mason shrugged. "It's the only story I have, sir."

"A pity you wiped your brainset so we can't verify your claim," Korth said.

Fair point, Mason thought. He spread his cuffed hands apart. "You know it's standard procedure. You'd have done the same in my situation. If you're interested in evidence, there's a wrecked Federal carrier drifting a–" An alarm interrupted him. "Was that battle stations, Commander?" Mason asked.

"No, the hab rotor is about to be despun in preparation for cruising burn," Commander Korth said. "We're leaving the system."

"Wait, you're not going to stay to investigate?" Mason asked.

"Our base was destroyed, Flight Lieutenant. And, if what you say is true, more Federal starships are likely on their way," Lt. Commander Korth said. "We're going home."

"Not directly though," Mason said. "Your ship just came back from a commerce raiding patrol, didn't she? Your base on that ice ball was a refueling station."

Korth didn't say anything.

There was a slight pull to one side as the rotor slowed its spin, and the gs got lighter and lighter. Zero-g training took over, and Mason hooked his feet to the legs of his chair. The chair itself was bolted to the deck. Lt. Commander Korth held himself to his seat when the gravity disappeared as the spin came to a stop. Mason felt a gentle downward pull as the rotor swung like a pendulum towards the back of the ship as the module folded flush with the hull. Moments later, a deep rumble ran through the ship as her main engines lit, and about a tenth of a g pulled down on him. Over the course of several seconds, the pull grew stronger, and the rumble through the ship grew louder, acceleration increasing as *Fafnir's* pilot throttled up her longburn drives. The acceleration topped out at a full standard g. It felt almost uncomfortably heavy compared to the light gravity he had spent the last week in. It could have been much worse. A cruiser like *Fafnir* could push itself to four gs of acceleration.

"I'm not making things up, Commander," Mason said. "If you stay just a little while longer to investigate the wreckage of my carrier, you'd see that."

"And increase the chances of getting caught inside the jump limit when a Federal warship jumps in?" Lt. Commander Korth shook his head. "Captain Ruy isn't going to risk it. There is every chance that this story of yours is just an attempt to stall us from leaving the system before help can arrive."

"Commander, if we did attack your base, why leave me behind?" Mason said. "You know the standard Federal MO for dealing with your commerce raider bases. Why leave the system instead of laying an ambush for returning ships like yours?"

"I don't know, Flight Lieutenant," Lt. Commander Korth said. "But I'm afraid I'm not qualified to ascertain the truthfulness of your claims. We'll just have to wait until we can get you to someone who can."

"You mean a professional interrogator?" Mason said.

"Yes."

Mason gestured with his cuffed hands. "So, is this just a pro-forma interrogation?"

"Hardly pro-forma, Flight Lieutenant," Lt. Commander Korth said. "Military Intelligence requires us to evaluate prisoners as quickly as possible. Separate the cooperative ones from the intransigent."

"I'd say I'm being pretty cooperative, sir," Mason said.

"Or you're attempting to spread disinformation," Lt. Commander Korth said. "I don't know what game you are playing, Flight Lieutenant, but you can trust me that our interrogators will get to the truth of the matter."

"Belts and zones. This isn't some ploy to try and feed you guys bad intel," Mason said.

"You've done it before," Lt. Commander Korth said.

"I haven't... Wait, what?"

"I know of at least one incident where a POW turned out to be a Federal Intelligence agent. She pretended to cooperate, sold a pack of lies to her interrogators." A sneer pulled at Lt. Commander Korth's face. "Her bad intel resulted in a lot of our ships getting caught in a Federal ambush."

"I don't know anything about that, sir," Mason said. "I'm a fighter pilot. I'm not capable of that kind of subtlety."

"If you are indeed a fighter pilot, Flight Lieutenant," Korth said. "Due to past Federal treachery, I'm afraid nothing you say has much credibility. Your treatment will be consistent with the Liberty Accords but, make no mistake, until proven otherwise, we're going to assume you are a spy."

Mason sighed and leaned back in his seat.

⤚

Locked in a cell that just barely met the minimum requirements of the Liberty Accords, Mason had little to do other than lie back in his acceleration couch and listen to *Fafnir*'s capacitors discharge every time she engaged her stardrive and jumped. Each time the ship jumped, *Fafnir* disappeared in a flash of red-shifted emission and reappeared a hundred billion kilometers away in a flash of blue-shifted emissions. It took just under a hundred jumps over a sixteen-hour period for a warship with a mil-spec stardrive to cross a light-year. If Mason's guess about *Fafnir* needing to refuel was correct, then she was probably heading somewhere relatively close. Within a week's travel or less. *Fafnir* was either headed towards a base not unlike the one they picked him up on, or to a forward-positioned tender.

Mason wasn't formulating a plan to escape. Even if he had the means to break out of his cell, which he very much didn't, there wouldn't be anywhere to go. Any base or tender would be in an uninhabited system.

Mason's hosts had been gracious enough to give him a tablet to entertain himself. It looked like it was older than *Fafnir* herself. The plastic bezels were scratched, and the screen had more than a few stuck pixels, but it did have an impressive library of books written in Federal. All of them written by League authors. The League must have thought the best thing POWs could do with their time was sample the League's literature.

Mason settled for a series of historical adventure novels set during the Second League War of sixty years prior. The good guys were Leaguers, obviously, and the bad guys were Federals. The first book was a rather implausible tale about a League destroyer playing a cat-and-mouse game with a Federal battlecruiser out in an independent system, finally emerging triumphant after the destroyer's captain outwitted the Federal ship. There were two problems with the premise of the story, and they had nothing to do with a destroyer overcoming a battlecruiser. The first problem was that Federal battlecruisers never operated alone. Second, no battlecruiser captain would waste time chasing a destroyer. The next book went on from there—the League captain using guile and cunning to outwit more powerful opponents. Mason was pleased that the novels made the point to acknowledge the actual events of the war, even if the destroyer captain's actual achievements were completely fictitious.

Mason was about to start the third book in the series when he noticed something different. It had been more than ten minutes since *Fafnir's* last jump. An alarm warning that the hab rotor was about to spin down sounded, and Mason pulled a strap across his chest to hold him to the bed. There was a brief period of zero gravity after the arms of the hab rotor folded into the hull, then the drives kicked on and a full g pulled Mason into his couch.

Mason held up his tablet to resume reading.

He was two chapters in when another alarm sounded. It was unfamiliar but sounded more urgent than any he heard before. Moments later, the door to his hatch opened, and an espatier entered the cell. His face was concealed by the armored visor of his helmet, but, based on his build, Mason had the distinct impression that it was Mr. Frowny-Face.

The espatier beckoned towards Mason. "Come."

Mason got out of the acceleration cot. "What's going on?"

"Come," Mr. Frowny-Face said.

Mason suspected that the espatier had just used the totality of what Federal he knew. Keeping his hands in view, Mason approached the cell.

The espatier had a pistol holstered at his side, but Mason didn't think about trying to take it from him. He considered himself a good martial artist, the product of being raised by Jovian hauler pilots, but an espatier in a hardsuit, even with rudimentary training, could overpower him with little trouble and, besides, the espatier wasn't alone. Two more in full combat hardsuits waited for him outside of the cell when he walked out.

"Come," Mr. Frowny-Face said.

As Mason did, the other two espatiers fell in behind him. They led him to the center of the habitat module and boarded the elevator. The elevator moved up, and then to the side when it reached the joint in the hab rotor. From there, they made their way further up the main hull of the cruiser until Mason walked through a guarded hatch onto the bridge of the cruiser.

Where the bridges of Federal bridges were circular, this cruiser's bridge was a rectangular box. There were two parallel rows of crew stations facing towards each other, with a holotank and seating for the ship's commanding officers in the gap between the rows.

By the central holotank, Mason spotted Lt. Commander Korth standing next to a shorter woman with dark skin and darker hair, her dark green uniform striped with red. The ship's captain.

She turned to him, her eyes the same shade of green as her uniform. "Flight Lieutenant Grey," she said.

Out of habit, Mason gave her a salute. The sensible kind, with the first two fingers of his right hand just barely touching his brow. None of this pretend punching to the side of the head nonsense the League used. "Reporting, sir."

That amused her, her full lips curving into a smile. "At ease, Flight Lieutenant. I'm Captain Maria Ruy, LCS *Fafnir*."

"A pleasure to make your acquaintance, Captain." Mason cleared his throat and lowered his arm. "Uh... so, what's happening?"

"I was hoping you would tell me, Flight Lieutenant." Captain Ruy nodded to the holotank in the center of the bridge, summoning a projection of the space near her ship. There were three yellow icons representing unidentified contacts. A chill ran up Mason's spine, his body trembling at the sight of them.

"You seem to have a pretty clear idea of what those might be, Flight Lieutenant," Captain Ruy said. "They showed up on our sensors fifteen minutes ago."

Mason locked eyes with Lt. Commander Korth just long enough to think, *I told you so*, before turning back to Captain Ruy. "If those are what

I think they are, then those ships belong to the same guys who destroyed my carrier and your base."

"I see." Captain Ruy turned away from Mason to face the holotank and gestured with a finger to invite him to stand next to her. After glancing at the espatiers flanking him, Mason walked up next to Captain Ruy.

"What can you tell me about them?" Captain Ruy asked.

Mason closed his eyes, digging into his memory of the ambush. "Well, Captain..." Mason opened his eyes, and stared at one of the yellow icons. "If those are the same kind of ships that attacked my carrier, they're going to have a much bigger gun than their apparent size would suggest, a large missile payload, or a complement of fighters."

"Big guns, missiles, and fighters." Ruy nodded to the icons. "Would one of those be a carrier, then?"

"Maybe. I have no way of knowing if they use dedicated carriers, sir," Mason said.

"Fighters could be a problem," Captain Ruy said.

"Captain, far be it from me to tell you what to do with your ship, but I think retreat is the best option," Mason said.

"That is a bit of a problem, Flight Lieutenant," Captain Ruy said. "My ship is short on fuel. If we managed to get through the jump limit and jump out, we won't have enough fuel to make it back home."

"You don't have other refueling stations, Captain?" Mason asked.

Captain Ruy grimaced. "We do, or at least we're supposed to." She gestured to the system ahead of her. "But this is the second refueling station that's turned out to be compromised. I have a feeling all the others have had a similar problem."

Mason examined the holotank. A solitary red dwarf with several small bodies orbiting it. He pointed to a highlighted body. "That your base?"

"Yes, built inside of a comet nucleus in a circular orbit 50,000 kilometers inside the jump limit," Captain Ruy said. "At first, we thought nothing was wrong, but then my communications officer found their IFF codes were out of date. When we sent them a code phrase, they gave the wrong response. So, I ordered the ship to turn around, and then those three ships just appeared out of nowhere next to the base."

"Oh, I was right," Mason said.

"Right about what, Flight Lieutenant?"

"Your base in Ross 128 was taken completely by surprise, Captain," Mason said. "Your people there didn't see the enemy coming until the kinetics started impacting the surface." He gestured to the holotank. "I figured they must have some way of concealing their heat signatures."

"Thermodynamics doesn't allow for that kind of stealth," Captain Ruy said.

"Looks like these guys found a way, Captain," Mason said. "There's every possibility there might be more of them."

Captain Ruy planted her hands on her hips and sighed. "Without the fuel in the base, we can't make it home."

"There's another option, Captain."

"You think we should head for Federal Space," Captain Ruy said.

"That's an excellent idea, sir." Mason said.

Captain Ruy grimaced. "I have no doubt you would think so, Flight Lieutenant. Though the fact that we are at war with the Earth Federation somewhat complicates things."

Mason pointed at the ships burning after *Fafnir*. "They're also at war with you, Captain. And they're not signatories of the Liberty Accords."

"A fair point, Flight Lieutenant," Captain Ruy said. She nodded to an acceleration seat. "Take a seat. We're about to go full burn."

Mason nodded and settled into an acceleration seat near the holotank adjacent to the seats Captain Ruy and Lt. Commander Korth occupied.

Ruy started barking orders in Exo. There was an alarm signaling a high-g burn, and then, thirty seconds later, four gs fell upon Mason like a rock slide. His skin stretched over his face as he sank up to his ears in acceleration gel. The slight incline of the couch allowed him to see the holotank. On the holotank, one of the three ships blossomed with missile icons at the same time as a trilling klaxon sounded. A launch alarm. Contacts broke away from the other two vessels as well, but they weren't missiles. The shape of their icons represented fighters. That was how the enemy carried fighters. Mason counted twenty strikecraft accelerating in pursuit of *Fafnir*, following the wave of torpedoes fired by the third vessel. The missile ship didn't launch any fighters. Mason guessed her missile armament didn't leave room for that.

Mason couldn't read the words on the holotanks, but he figured out the numbers easily enough. There was a timer counting down the time to jump, and a timer counting down the time to impact. The latter was about a minute less than the former.

Dragon-class cruisers were no slouches when it came to point defense. Mason remembered the briefings about the ships. Their main armament was nine gigajoule-class kinetic cannons in three gun turrets mounted radially around the hull, the standard League method of mounting their direct-fire weapons. From destroyers all the way up to battleships. Six smaller turrets carried twelve rapid-fire class secondary guns. Backing those up was a battery of point-defense guns. Along with the guns, the cruiser also had several dozen perpendicular launch tubes containing torpedoes and interceptors.

The standard procedure for attacking a Dragon as a fighter was simple. Don't get close. The point-defense guns had complete coverage from all possible angles of attack, and they were quite capable of completely shredding any fighter or bomber that got too close. Standoff attack with torpedoes and free-fall space bombs were the way to deal with them.

The weight of torpedoes bearing down on the cruiser Mason was riding in struck him as a bit on the light side for dealing with a cruiser. The ship that launched them could throw a much heavier volley. He guessed they were trying to save torpedoes.

No one had spoken since *Fafnir* started pulling hard gs, but that didn't surprise Mason. It was hard to talk with four gs pressing down on you. They had switched to subvocal communications, talking through their brainsets. For not the first time, Mason regretted killing his.

"Share any insights on their missiles, Flight Lieutenant Grey?" Captain Ruy asked, her voiced strained.

"Interceptors seem to work much like anyone else's, sir." Mason spoke slowly, his lips and jaws too heavy for talking at his usual pace. "Can't say what their torpedoes are like, I'm afraid. I only saw them use KKVs to kill our starships."

"Understood," Captain Ruy said.

Mason kept his attention on the holotank as the torpedoes closed on the fleeing cruiser.

Minutes before impact, *Fafnir* launched a volley of interceptors towards the torpedoes. It was an impressive number, fully half of her inventory by Mason's guess.

Fafnir's interceptors flew straight out the sides of the warship and then turned back the way she came, accelerating towards the torpedoes. Several minutes later, icons of interceptors merged with icons of torpedoes, and the result was just over half the incoming torpedoes disappearing from the holotank. Another volley of interceptors left *Fafnir*, half the size of the first volley. Minutes later, most of the remaining torpedoes disappeared from the holotank. League interceptors did better than he expected, but there were still a dozen torpedoes inbound.

"How many of your interceptors did you just use, Captain?" Mason asked.

"Three-quarters, Flight Lieutenant," Captain Ruy said. "Now, please don't distract me."

Secondary guns and point defenses started firing, throwing up a wall of metal between *Fafnir* and the torpedoes. Torpedoes started disappearing one-by-one when they hit that wall. Decoys started flying out of *Fafnir's* sides, and Mason felt the cruiser lurching into a sharp turn.

As the torpedoes neared, an algorithm must have tripped because, as one, they all flashed on the holotank, and Mason felt something slap into the hull. The acceleration couch bucked beneath him, and Mason let out a pained hiss as he was jostled while under high g. A cacophony of different alarms filled the bridge, but the heavy gs still pulled down on Mason. The engines were still burning at full power.

Mason looked up just enough to get a look at Captain Ruy, but her eyes were fixed ahead, probably concentrating on something in her HUD, as she communicated subvocally with her crew. It didn't seem like a good time to pester her with more questions about the state of her ship.

He glanced around the ship, his neck aching from the effort it took to raise his head. The crew all looked calm and focused. No signs of despair or panic. He guessed *Fafnir* had not suffered critical damage.

He let his head fall back into the acceleration gel and watched the enemy fighters approach. It was immediately evident to Mason what the enemy fighters were planning. It was a tactic he seen during the Battle of Polykastro. Torpedoes were indispensable weapons, but they weren't all that efficient when it came to killing starships. Between ECM, interceptors, point defenses, dazzle lasers, and decoys, the chance of an individual torpedo destroying any warship was basically nil. It took massed torpedoes to reliably destroy a target. However, interceptors expended destroying torpedoes were interceptors that couldn't be used on follow-up strikecraft attacks. Mason had flown escort on a couple of bomber attacks following on the heels of a torpedo volley. In both cases, the bombers managed to kill a League battleship that had used most of its interceptors defending itself from a massed torpedo attack.

A part of Mason was curious about what kind of weapons the unknown enemy strikecraft carried. They weren't dedicated bombers, but there was no rule that said only specialized bombers could carry torpedoes or bombs. Mason was pretty sure they weren't using space bombs. The stealthy free-fall weapons were perfect when dropped in large numbers against a lumbering capital ship like a battleship or a carrier. But against a relatively nimble cruiser like *Fafnir*, strikecraft would have to get dangerously close in order to guarantee a hit or drop far more bombs than would be worthwhile to deal with a cruiser. Which probably meant the enemy fighters were carrying torpedoes of some kind.

As they approached, the fighters changed formation into an expanding ring that increased in diameter as they neared *Fafnir*. They were carrying torpedoes, Mason was certain of it. If they had bombs, they would've remained in close formation right up until they released them. The ring of fighters was going to fly by *Fafnir*, and just when the cruiser was in the center of their ring, launch a massed torpedo attack from all directions. It was a familiar tactic for fighters to use against starships. He never used it in combat himself, but he knew pilots who had.

Acceleration stopped. *Fafnir* had crossed the jump limit and had diverted power from engines to the stardrive. The ring of approaching fighters would reach them much sooner.

With no gs pulling him down, Mason sat up and looked towards Captain Ruy. "Captain?"

Her eyes twitched in his direction. "Not now, Flight Lieutenant."

"Captain, you need to listen to me," Mason said. "You need to break up the formation of the enemy fighters before they launch their torpedoes."

"I don't have interceptors to spare, Flight Lieutenant," Captain Ruy said.

"And they know that, Captain," Mason said. "Look, I know you plan on saving your interceptors for when they launch their torpedoes, but that's what they're counting on. You're giving them the chance to position themselves around your ship where they can best overwhelm your remaining interceptors."

"And how would you know that, Flight Lieutenant?" she asked.

"It's what I would do, Captain," Mason said. He pointed to the holotank. "We're dead in the water while the stardrive charges. They can maneuver freely unless you start throwing things at them that they must deal with before they surround your ship."

"We'll run out of interceptors before the stardrive finishes charging, Flight Lieutenant," Captain Ruy said. "Once those are gone, we'll be all but helpless against their torpedoes."

Mason lowered his arm. "Who said anything about interceptors, Captain? You still have torpedoes on this ship?"

"Yes," she said.

"Well, use those. They probably won't kill anything, but if you throw nukes in their direction, they'll have to evade. That will buy you time. Enough that maybe the interceptors can keep them off us until the stardrive finishes charging."

Ruy pursed her lips and looked towards Lt. Commander Korth. They exchanged words in Exo, and the tone of the conversation suggested they were seriously considering it. Ruy nodded, leaned back in her seat, and barked an order.

Torpedoes flew out of *Fafnir's* perpendicular launch tubes and turned towards the fighters. In normal circumstances, using torpedoes against strikecraft was ineffective to the point of being downright wasteful. With their nuclear warheads and fusion engines, torpedoes were far more expensive than simple interceptors. As such, a ship could carry far more interceptors than torpedoes. Since the best way to score a missile hit was to saturate the missile defenses, interceptors were almost always the best choice for dealing with strikecraft. All that being said, longburn torpedoes were a threat that no fighter pilot could ignore.

The enemy fighters scattered, their neat expanding ring breaking apart like snowflakes caught in a gust of wind. Torpedoes, indifferent to the fact they were going after targets they were not designed to engage, continued tracking on the enemy fighters.

The fighters launched interceptors to defend themselves, a wave of fast-moving icons burning hard towards the torpedoes. One by one, torpedoes disappeared from the holotank as interceptors hit them, thinning out *Fafnir's* volley to just a few torpedoes. Fighters that still had a torpedo tracking them made hard turns to face towards the torpedoes, and fired their guns, killing yet more torpedoes before they reached detonation range.

One unfortunate enemy fighter failed to bring their gun to bear in time. There was a discreet flash on the holotank signaling the torpedo detonating its directional nuclear warhead, and the fighter disappeared from the holotank. It was overkill to take out a fighter with a concentrated cone of nuclear death, but damn if it didn't feel good.

The now disorganized enemy fighters launched their torpedoes in a staggered volley as they flew past *Fafnir*, staying outside the range of her point-defense guns.

Ruy barked an order, and the last of *Fafnir's* interceptors launched. While the interceptors flew out to meet the torpedoes, Ruy issued another order, and Mason felt the ship turn. What was she thinking? He looked at the holotank and it dawned on him. She was turning broadside to the torpedoes, bringing as many guns to bear as possible.

Interceptors met torpedoes, icons mutually annihilating each other on the holotank.

Captain Ruy said a word in Exo, and her ship erupted with kinetic fire. Secondary and point-defense guns poured fire towards the torpedoes before they reached effective kinetic range. Torpedoes started disappearing from the holotank as they pushed through the full broadside of the cruiser.

Mason noticed he was trembling. He grabbed the armrests of his seat to steady his hands. It wasn't the first time he had missiles, including nukes, headed in his direction, but all those times, he had been in the cockpit of a fighter, not spectating on the bridge of a drifting starship. He found the total lack of agency more than a little disturbing.

More and more torpedoes fell to kinetic fire, but those that survived were approaching faster and faster, proving to be harder targets for the kinetics. *Fafnir* launched decoys as part of a last-ditch defense, hoping to tempt torpedoes into firing their nuclear blasts into empty space. In the final seconds of approach, the point defenses seemed to find their marks, despite the increasing speed of the torpedoes. Five, then four, then three. A countdown marked by the death of nuclear-tipped missiles.

The ship shuddered and metal groaned. Alarms keened, and people screamed, including Mason. One of the torpedoes got close enough to detonate and spray *Fafnir* with a cone of deadly energy.

Alarms were squelched as *Fafnir*'s bridge crew issued reports. Though Mason didn't understand the words they were saying, he could sense the tension in their voices. He felt more than a bit of his own. The holotank no longer functioned, displaying bright red error messages instead of the space around *Fafnir*. The cruiser had likely lost a lot of her sensors to the blast. If the enemy fighters noticed what bad shape *Fafnir* was in, they would probably close in and finish off the cruiser with their guns.

Mason heard a familiar sound, a buzz traveling through the hull as the ship's capacitors discharged. *Fafnir* had jumped. Mason felt a wave of relief wash over the bridge. The bridge crew, even the Captain, seemed to relax just a bit.

Captain Ruy said something that caused nervous laughter to break out on the bridge. She turned to Mason. "Thank you for your help, Flight Lieutenant."

Mason shrugged with his hands. "My life was on the line too, sir."

CHAPTER 4

MASON HALF EXPECTED Captain Ruy to order him off her bridge, but instead, she and Lt. Commander Korth elected to ignore him while they figured out the condition of their ship. They were one jump out of the system. They were probably safe from pursuit, unless the unknown enemy had some way of getting *Fafnir*'s exact vector when she jumped out. Mason hoped they didn't; he was pretty sure *Fafnir* didn't have any more running battles left in her.

He lay back in his seat and stayed out of the way of the crew. No one seemed to be overly concerned that there was a Federal POW on the bridge.

Captain Ruy floated over to him, her face grim.

"How bad is it, Captain?"

"As is no doubt evident to you, my ship is quite badly damaged," Captain Ruy said. "Twenty casualties, including eight dead. We took two hits from the nukes thrown at us. One minor, one not so. The second hit caused spalling all over the ship. That's where all the casualties came from. It also blew one of the habitat modules clear off the rotor arm."

"I hope no one was in it," Mason said.

"Thankfully, no," Captain Ruy said. "But the habitability of this starship has been severely curtailed."

"I'm sure the battle damage has done nothing to alleviate your fuel situation either," Mason said.

"No, it has not," Captain Ruy said. "We were lucky none of the fuel tanks were breached. Even a moderate leak would leave us without enough fuel to make it to a settled system."

A chill ran through Mason's bones. Stories of starship crews trying to stretch out their supplies for years while they waited for the distress call to travel the distance to the nearest inhabited system at lightspeed were something that always captured the popular imagination. They tended to either be inspiring stories of survival and determination, or horrific tales of cannibalism and mass suicide. If it came to the latter, Mason was pretty sure who would be at the top of the menu.

"So, what's next?" Mason asked. "Am I going back to the brig?"

"The brig was on the hab module that got blown off," Captain Ruy said.

"Oh," Mason said. "Uh… thanks for letting me hang out on your bridge, then."

"It proved helpful in ensuring the survival of my crew," Ruy said. "But now I have a new problem."

"You don't know where to go next, sir?" Mason asked.

"I have two bad choices, Flight Lieutenant," Captain Ruy said. "*Fafnir* can make it to another forward base, but only just. If it proves to be a bust like the last two systems, we won't have the fuel to go anywhere else. The other choice… is to head to the nearest Federal system."

"I vote for the second one, Captain," Mason said.

Ruy smiled. "I thought you would. The thing is, this ship shows up in a Federal system, there's a good chance your people will just shoot and ask questions later."

"That would be an anticlimactic end for us, Captain," Mason said.

"Us?"

"Well, yeah. My fate is kind of tied to that of your ship, sir," Mason said.

"Good point," Ruy said. "I think if we jump into a Federal system, we could put you on the comm. It would encourage your comrades to exercise restraint."

"Using POWs as hostages is against the Liberty Accords, Captain," Mason said.

"You mistake me, Flight Lieutenant," Captain Ruy said. "I don't intend to use you as a hostage. I was thinking about surrendering to you."

"Oh, is that all," Mason said. He glanced around the bridge, seeing that most of the crew were looking in his direction. It appeared she had already discussed the notion with them.

Ruy grimaced. "I'm sure it will be quite a coup for you to have a League cruiser surrender to you, but I'm only considering it because it is the only way I can guarantee the survival of my crew."

"I understand that, Captain," Mason said. "But, I, uh, don't really know how that's supposed to work." Mason looked down at her belt. "I don't see any sword that you can hand over to me."

Captain Ruy gave him an incredulous look. "A sword. Really? No. If you accept my surrender, I'll have it recorded into the log. Then it's done. Me and my crew will be your prisoners."

"I see," Mason said. "I'm sure it's not easy for you to surrender to a Federal."

"I'd hardly be the first League captain to surrender their ship to an Earth Federation officer, Flight Lieutenant," Captain Ruy said. "But it is… galling that I have to surrender to a fighter pilot."

"Hmph… yeah, I can see your point," Mason said.

Captain Ruy straightened her posture. "Flight Lieutenant Mason Grey, I hereby offer the surrender of *Fafnir* and her crew to you."

"I accept your surrender, Captain Ruy," Mason said. "You have my word I'll do everything in my power to get your crew home safely."

"I appreciate that, Flight Lieutenant," Captain Ruy said. "Where would you like my ship to go?"

"What's the nearest Federal system?" Mason asked.

"You don't know?" she asked.

"One red dwarf system looks a lot like any other, Captain," Mason said.

"The one we just escaped from was YZ Canis Minoris," Captain Ruy said.

"Then Procyon's the nearest Federal System," Mason said. "I respectfully request that you order your astrogator to set a course for there."

⇜

Mason floated onto the bridge a few minutes before the last jump to Procyon. Captain Ruy nodded to him as he entered. "You clean up well, Flight Lieutenant."

"Thank you, sir," Mason said. Given what they were about to do, he figured he needed to look his best. His black jumpsuit had been washed, and he had taken the time to shave and get a haircut, courtesy of the ship's barber. He looked far better than the rough-looking prisoner of war *Fafnir* had rescued weeks before. He felt better too. And not just because he was returning to friendly territory.

"You should get that handsome face of yours in front of a camera and record something that will encourage your comrades not to start shooting at my ship the moment we jump in," Captain Ruy said.

"That sounds like a good plan, sir." Mason looked around, and then back to Captain Ruy. "Uh? Where would I do that?"

"Take my seat." Captain Ruy said.

Mason floated into her seat and buckled himself in. Captain Ruy laid a hand on his shoulder and squeezed with surprising strength. "Surrender or not, this is still my seat. You're just borrowing it, so don't let it go to your head."

"Never crossed my mind, sir," Mason said. "*Fafnir*'s too big for my taste, anyway."

"Careful what you say about my ship, Flight Lieutenant," Captain Ruy said. She tapped one of the monitors on the seat, and Mason's face appeared on the screen.

"You're on."

"Uh… yeah, ahem," Mason straightened his jumpsuit. "Procyon Fleet Base, this is Flight Lieutenant Mason Grey, FSFV *Eagle*, 212th Fighter Squadron. I have managed to secure the surrender of this League cruiser and her crew and would very much appreciate it if you didn't shoot at us. Not just because that would ruin my day, but because I have intelligence pertinent to the security of the Earth Federation. Flight Lieutenant Mason Grey, out." He looked up to Captain Ruy. "What do you think?"

"It will do," she said.

Mason nodded to the monitor. "Maybe give it another go, Captain?"

"No. Get out of my chair," she said.

Mason unbuckled and floated out. "You know, Captain, I'm not feeling very surrendered-to right now."

"Would you like me to un-surrender, then?" she asked.

"Point taken, Captain. Thank you for letting me use your seat. It was very comfortable," Mason said.

"Not too comfortable, I hope." Ruy settled back into her seat, buckling herself in while Mason floated next to her. She looked almost at ease, back in her natural environment. She turned to the astrogation station and said words in Exo.

❧

Mason watched, eyes fixed on the icon representing Procyon Fleet Base, waiting to see their response and hoping it didn't involve a spread of torpedoes.

A man's voice, deep, calm, and authoritative, piped through the speakers. "*Fafnir*, this is Procyon Space Traffic Control. You are to hold position until ordered otherwise. Keep weapons powered down and engines cold. Procyon STC out."

Mason let out a breath. "Okay. That's encouraging."

"They're not going to shoot at us?" Captain Ruy asked.

"Not before they figure out what's going on, no, sir," Mason said.

Two Churchill-class destroyers appeared with flashes of blue-shifted light just a few thousand kilometers short of *Fafnir*. Each ship was a 200 meter long cylinder flared out at the rear where the engines were located. Matching dorsal and ventral superstructures mounted the main guns, while smaller point-defense turrets and missile tubes were mounted directly on the main hull.

The destroyers must have been loitering outside of the jump limit as part of the 8th Fleet's picket, ready to use their jump drives to react quickly to any shenanigans going on at the edge of the system.

The accented voice of a young man piped through the bridge's speakers. "FSFV *Mansur* to LCS *Fafnir*, this is Commander George Tobalian. Is Flight Lieutenant Mason Grey on the line?"

"I'm here, sir," Mason said.

"Can you transmit your verification code?" he asked.

"I don't have a brainset to transmit that code, sir," Mason said.

"And why is that, Flight Lieutenant?" Commander Tobalian asked.

"Because *Fafnir*'s crew removed it after I bricked it," Mason said.

"You were captured?" Commander Tobalian said.

"Yes, sir," Mason said.

"So how did you manage to capture a League cruiser all by yourself, Flight Lieutenant?" Captain Tobalian asked.

"I very politely asked her captain to surrender to me," Mason asked. "It, uh… makes much more sense when you know the whole story."

"I'm sending a boarding party over, Flight Lieutenant Grey. And just for the record, if this is a trick, note that I already have torpedoes locked on."

Mason swallowed a lump in his throat. "Understood, sir."

A contact appeared, moving away from Mansur—an assault shuttle, likely loaded with Federal troopers.

"I should probably head to the airlock to greet them," Mason said.

Captain Ruy unbuckled herself and floated off her seat. "Follow me, Flight Lieutenant."

He followed Ruy out of the bridge. At the elevator, Ruy hit the button for the appropriate deck. Mason grabbed the handrail as the elevator started to move.

"So, any idea what your people will do with my crew after they take my ship from me?" Captain Ruy asked.

"Earth Fed likes to keep captured starship crews together when possible, with the same officers in charge. Helps maintain discipline," Mason said.

"So, I'm going to lose command of my ship and gain command of a prison camp," she said.

"Probably on one of the habitat stations in orbit of Procyon A, Captain," Mason said.

Captain Ruy looked down and patted the handrail. "*Fafnir*'s been a good ship to me and my crew. It's a shame to give her up."

Mason wished he could say Earth Fed would take good care of her ship, but that was a lie, and a bad one at that. Earth Fed would tear the ship apart, learning everything they could about modern League ship design. After they took her apart, what was left of *Fafnir*'s hulk would likely be used for target practice.

The elevator stopped at the appropriate level and Mason followed Captain Ruy out. Even after weeks aboard her, he was not yet completely familiar with *Fafnir*'s layout. The inner hatch of the docking port was a seriously beefy rounded plate of metal as wide as Mason was tall.

Captain Ruy had a far off look of someone listening to something from their brainset. "The assault shuttle is positioned over the docking port," Captain Ruy said. "I've just given them permission to dock."

Mason took a deep breath to calm his nerves. Why was he feeling so nervous? It was fellow Federal spacers who were docking, after all.

Deep metallic thumps echoed through the hull as something big, something like a hundred-ton assault shuttle, attached itself to the outer airlock.

"Outer hatch is opened," Captain Ruy said. "Opening inner hatch."

Six metal bolts mounted around the airlock slid out of place, and the heavy metal hatch swung up out of the way until it locked into a catch on the bulkhead.

Inside the airlock was a fireteam of four hulking Federal troopers. They were in full combat hardsuits, each sporting their default drab olive camouflage. The armored faceplates of their helmets concealed their faces, making it hard to tell there were human beings encased under all the articulated plating.

All of them had their battle rifles at the ready, but none pointed in Mason's direction, much to his relief.

The lead trooper, a sergeant, floated up to Captain Ruy.

"Captain Ruy, your ship is now formally in control of the Earth Federation," said the droptrooper, her high voice given a metallic tone by her helmet speakers.

Captain Ruy nodded towards Mason. "I formally surrendered my ship to him, Sergeant. *Fafnir*'s been under Federal control for days."

The droptrooper turned towards Mason. He could see himself in the lenses of her helmet's optics.

"Flight Lieutenant Grey, sir?" she asked.

She sir'ed him. That was a good sign. "That's me, Sergeant."

"I'm Sergeant Glass." She nodded to one of her droptroopers, who had a red cross painted on a white square on his shoulder. A combat medic. "Corporal Yves here will need to examine you."

"Examine away," Mason said.

Sergeant Glass nodded towards Corporal Yves, who floated up to Mason, pulling a device from his belt.

"I'll need to hold you still, sir," the combat medic said.

"Try to be gentle, Corporal," Mason said. "That's all I ask."

A large hand that could collapse his skull cupped the back of his head while Yves pressed the rubber eyepiece of an iris scanner against Mason's eye. There was a flash of red light.

Yves pulled the scanner away and pulled out a thin rod with a bulb on the end of it. "Say ah, sir."

"Ahhh."

Yves ran the rod over the side of his cheek, then pulled it out and cleaned it. The way he held his head suggested he was reading something off his HUD.

"Iris and DNA match, Sarge," Corporal Yves said. "It's him."

At that moment, more troopers came floating in from the assault shuttle, groups of four splitting off in a different direction, shouting commands through their suit speakers as they made their way through.

Mason thought he could hear Captain Ruy's teeth grinding as Federal troopers swept through her ship.

When no more troopers floated in, the sergeant moved up.

"Flight Lieutenant, sir, we'll secure this ship. You are to take our shuttle to Procyon Fleet Base," she said.

"Must be people there who are eager to talk to me," Mason said. He turned to Captain Ruy. "I guess this is goodbye, sir."

"It's been an experience having you aboard my ship, Flight Lieutenant," Captain Ruy said.

"That it has, Captain," Mason said.

CHAPTER 5

JESSICA DIDN'T KNOW much about her commanding officer, despite the two years working under her. All that she could say for sure was that Colonel Dolores Shimura had started her career in the Federal Space Forces as an infantry officer. That was why she held the rank of colonel, wore a drab olive jumpsuit, and had the lean and muscular build one would expect from a ground-pounder. Other than that, all Jessica had were educated guesses about how, when, and why Colonel Shimura gave up commanding troopers to go play spy.

A metallic echo from above signaled the arrival of the assault shuttle carrying the only survivor of FSV *Eagle's* strike group. Shortly after that, the buzz of heavy machinery vibrated through the corridor as the docking pad descended into the Special Purpose Branch's private hangar.

"Colonel, I understand it's very impressive and all that this pilot got a League cruiser to surrender to him all by himself, but why are we debriefing him personally?" Jessica asked as they waited for the hangar of the assault shuttle carrying Flight Lieutenant Mason Grey to repressurize.

They stood in the corridor adjacent to the airlock. Through the large window looking out into the hangar, Jessica could see the landing pad and the assault shuttle atop it descend.

"You're not at all curious how he managed to do it?" Colonel Shimura asked.

"Oh, I'm quite curious. I just don't understand why you insisted that we personally debrief him," Jessica asked. "That's not our usual job."

"That's because you think we're just here to debrief him, Lieutenant," Colonel Shimura said. "And, besides, he's the first person with combat experience with the Ascendency that we have had the opportunity to meet in person."

Jessica relented and asked no further questions. When Colonel Shimura felt like being cagey, there was little Jessica could do to extract further information. She straightened her fleet's blue jumpsuit and waited for the hangar to pressurize. There was a ding and a green light above the airlock door came on, and both the inner and outer hatches swung open.

Colonel Shimura walked through the airlock and Jessica followed. They crossed the black and yellow line that marked the perimeter of the landing pad. The assault shuttle faced away from them, its V tail and folded wings making it look like a gigantic bird roosting in its nest. Looking up, Jessica saw the massive double doors that closed above to seal the hangar from the vacuum environment of the main docking bay.

Jessica took position to Shimura's left, just under the shuttle's tail.

There was a hiss of seals breaking as the shuttle's ramp descended, revealing the tall, slender pilot they were here to debrief. The picture in his dossier had not done him justice. Solid despite his thin frame, with a strong jaw, and high cheekbones, Flight Lieutenant Grey looked like he belonged on a recruiting poster. He walked down the ramp, giving both Jessica and Shimura cautious glances before coming to a stop and giving a crisp salute.

"Welcome to Procyon Fleet Base, Flight Lieutenant," Colonel Shimura said. "It seems you've had quite the journey getting here."

"Yes, sir, you can say that," Mason said.

"I am Colonel Dolores Shimura, and this is my assistant, Lieutenant Jessica Sinclair. We're with Special Purpose Branch. We would like to ask you some questions."

"Though you phrase that as a request, Colonel, I somehow get the feeling that's not optional," Flight Lieutenant Grey said.

"It is not, Flight Lieutenant. Please come with us," Shimura said.

Jessica recognized that she was using the commanding tone she tended to adopt when she wanted to stress out someone she was interrogating. It wasn't a surprise to Jessica. Shimura had done the same to her when she was first assigned to her. It was part of the Colonel's way of sizing up people, seeing how they reacted under a little stress. Flight Lieutenant Grey didn't seem fazed by it. Given what he had survived, Jessica wasn't all that surprised he didn't wilt under Shimura's gaze.

They headed to the tram station adjacent to the hangar, where a single tram car waited for them. The car was shaped like a bullet and hung from a single overhead rail. Large windows revealed a brightly lit interior and brown plastic seating.

Flight Lieutenant Grey did a double-take when he noticed that there was no one else in the tram station beyond him, Jessica, and Colonel Shimura.

"Reserved a ride all for you, Flight Lieutenant. But that doesn't mean you get to delay our departure," Colonel Shimura said.

"Yes, sir," Flight Lieutenant Grey said, before muttering "belts and zones" under his breath.

The tram started rolling as soon as the doors closed. After a few hundred meters traveling through a barely lit tunnel, the tram was greeted by an explosion of light as it entered the main habitable area of Procyon Fleet Base's cylinder. Like all fleet bases, the interior was spartan, but not bare. Neat blocks of rectangular buildings lined the interior, separated by wide roads. Here and there were irregular splashes of color. Forest parks, small artificial lakes, and gardens for growing either flowers or vegetables. Little islands of nature tucked between human constructs to help weary spacers cope with the stress of service. The tram rolled to a stop on the grounds of Procyon Fleet Base's headquarters, a large, circular building surrounded by real grass and a three-meter-tall security fence.

They breezed through the security checkpoint in Colonel Shimura's wake and headed directly for the elevators at the end of the lobby. Jessica hit the button for the level reserved for the Special Purpose Branch and the elevator started descending.

"We're going down?" Flight Lieutenant Grey asked.

"You weren't aware Fleet Base HQs had lower levels, Flight Lieutenant?" Colonel Shimura asked.

"First time in one, sir," Mason said. "Last few weeks have been full of new experiences."

"You likely have more in your future, Flight Lieutenant."

"Good to know, sir," Flight Lieutenant Grey said.

Jessica couldn't help but smile at the exchange. She was already starting to like this pilot.

The elevator came to a stop in the branch's level, so deep they were closer to space than they were to the inner surface of the fleet base. The doors opened to reveal another security checkpoint. A pair of troopers in full combat hardsuits. It was the last layer of security before entering what was likely the single most secure piece of real estate in all of Procyon. After the checkpoint, Shimura led them to a nondescript room with a brushed metal table and three chairs. Two on one side and one on the other.

"Please take a seat over there, Flight Lieutenant," Shimura said, indicating the solitary chair.

Flight Lieutenant Grey sat down. "This looks a lot like an interrogation room, sir."

"That's one of its uses, Flight Lieutenant," Shimura said as she sat down. Jessica took the seat next to her.

<"Observe his reactions, but otherwise remain silent, Lieutenant Sinclair,"> Colonel Shimura subvoked. <"I want your report at the end of this debriefing."">

<"Understood, sir."">

Flight Lieutenant Grey sighed, and sagged in his seat, and for the first time, Jessica got a sense of just how tired he was. Given what he had to have gone through just to now be seated before her, she couldn't blame him.

"Flight Lieutenant Grey, I would like you to begin with *Eagle's* arrival in Ross 128 and move on from there," Colonel Shimura said.

Flight Lieutenant Grey shifted in his seat with clear apprehension. "That's going to be a long story, sir."

"We have time, Flight Lieutenant," Shimura said.

Jessica knew that Colonel Shimura wasn't as cold as she presented herself, but *blimey*, her tone sent shivers down her spine.

Flight Lieutenant Grey retold the story of *Eagle's* destruction in painful detail, pausing when he described the death of his squadron. His voice cracking when he mentioned the death of his young wingmate, a Pilot Officer Traynor.

"You camped out in a League rover for a week?" Colonel Shimura asked.

Flight Lieutenant Grey shrugged. "Yes, sir. Relatively comfortably too."

"And after that, you were captured by the League?" Shimura asked.

"Yes, sir. *Fafnir* was based out of Ross 128 and had arrived for refuel and resupply. All they got was me."

"Describe your time aboard *Fafnir*," Shimura said.

Flight Lieutenant Grey shrugged. "I was treated well enough, though they were more than a bit skeptical when I told them what happened."

"Why is that?" Colonel Shimura said.

"Apparently, there was some fear that I wasn't a genuine POW, but a spy posing as one in an attempt to spread disinformation," Flight Lieutenant Grey said. "Apparently, it's something Special Purpose Branch has done before."

Jessica shot a glance towards Colonel Shimura. <"What is he talking about, sir?">

Shimura didn't so much as flinch in Jessica's direction, but her subvocal response was strong and clear. <"Not your concern, Lieutenant. Pay attention to your task.">

Jessica complied, but when she saw the anger in Flight Lieutenant Grey's eyes, she couldn't help but think his feelings were justified.

"I'm afraid we're not here to discuss Special Purpose Branch's activities, Flight Lieutenant, but yours," Colonel Shimura said. "Suffice to say, you did manage to convince Captain Ruy that you were telling the truth."

"With the help of the enemy, sir, yes," Flight Lieutenant Grey said.

"Ascendency, Flight Lieutenant."

"Is that what we're calling them, sir?" Flight Lieutenant Grey asked.

"It's what they are calling themselves, Flight Lieutenant," Colonel Shimura said, switching to her normal tone.

"I don't follow, sir. Have the... Ascendency made contact?" Flight Lieutenant Grey asked.

Jessica tried to keep her face impassive, but inside she felt great apprehension at what Colonel Shimura was about to tell the Jovian.

"Yes, Flight Lieutenant, after they attacked and occupied the outer solar system," Colonel Shimura said.

Flight Lieutenant Grey became so still and quiet that Jessica thought he'd been frozen in shock. He leaned forward, planting his elbows on the table. "Attacked and occupied, sir? When?"

"About a week before *Eagle's* destruction," Colonel Shimura said. "That included taking Jupiter Fleet Base. It's likely they've been using intelligence gained from there to ambush Federal Starships on patrol. Including *Eagle.*"

Flight Lieutenant Grey leaned back, his eyes thoughtful as he processed what Colonel Shimura said. He ran his hands down his face and let out a heavy sigh. "So much for trying to get the warning out."

"I'm afraid it was us who failed to get the warning out to you, Flight Lieutenant," Colonel Shimura said. "That was on us."

Flight Lieutenant Grey looked down at the table, letting out a long sigh. At the same time, Shimura glanced towards Jessica.

<"Lieutenant, how do you think Flight Lieutenant Grey would do in the Special Purpose Branch?"> Shimura subvoked to Jessica.

<"Is this what it's all about? We're recruiting him, sir?">

Shimura's brow furrowed with irritation. <"Don't answer my question with another question, Lieutenant. Would he do well with Special Purpose Branch—yes or no?">

Jessica looked back at Flight Lieutenant Grey just as he finished gathering his thoughts, apparently oblivious to the subvocalized discussion that had just happened, his attention directed towards Colonel Shimura.

<"Yes,"> Jessica subvoked.

Flight Lieutenant Grey spoke. "What happened to the Jovian civilian stations, sir?"

"All intact and under Ascendency occupation, along with everything else up-orbit of the Belt," Colonel Shimura said. "I'm afraid I can't give you details of any of your family."

Flight Lieutenant Grey nodded. "So, what happens to me now? It's clear there's nothing that I have that you don't already know."

"I wouldn't quite say that, Flight Lieutenant. You're the only person who has faced the Ascendency in combat and lived to tell the tale. That alone makes you valuable. As such," she glanced towards Jessica and then back to Flight Lieutenant Grey, "I'm formally recruiting you into the Special Purpose Branch."

"You're recruiting–" Flight Lieutenant Grey stopped for a moment. "Oh, this wasn't a debriefing, was it, sir?"

"It was not only a debriefing, Flight Lieutenant," Colonel Shimura said. She nodded towards Jessica. "You've made an impression on both me and Lieutenant Sinclair. We think you'd be an excellent addition."

"Do I get a say in this, sir?"

"No, Flight Lieutenant. I'm afraid not."

Flight Lieutenant Grey shot a look at Colonel Shimura that bordered on insolence. "Is this how the Special Purpose Branch normally recruits people?"

"When the situation calls for it, Flight Lieutenant," Colonel Shimura said.

"So, what happens to me now, Colonel?" Flight Lieutenant Grey asked.

"You'll be set up with quarters on-station until I need you again, Flight Lieutenant. An escort will show you there. When you get settled in, I suggest you turn on the news. The Ascendency has, for lack of a better term, been on a media blitz ever since they took Outer Sol. Dismissed."

Flight Lieutenant Grey stood up from his seat, eyeing both Colonel Shimura and Jessica, before opening the door to meet the escort waiting outside. When the door closed, Jessica turned to Colonel Shimura.

"Don't you think it's a bit early to try and recruit him, Colonel? He's only just returned to Federal Space."

"I'm afraid I'm pressed for time, Lieutenant," Colonel Shimura said. "What made you decide he was a good fit, by the way?"

"You didn't seem all that interested in knowing my reasoning before, sir," Jessica said.

"Now I am, Lieutenant."

Jessica shrugged. "He's smart, resourceful, and bold. He'd be a good candidate for training. Just by listening to him speak, and watching him make the connections he did, it's clear he has a good analytical mind. Pity it's being wasted as a fighter pilot."

"It's actually his piloting skills that interest me, Lieutenant," Colonel Shimura said.

"We have the 4th Special Operations Squadron for that, sir," Jessica said.

"Those weren't the piloting skills I was referring to, Lieutenant,"

Colonel Shimura said. "You've seen his record. He didn't start flying in fighters."

"Yes, but I don't see how that's relevant to working with us, sir," Jessica said.

"It does for the mission that we have coming up, Lieutenant," Colonel Shimura said.

"Indeed, sir? Do tell," Jessica said.

CHAPTER 6

MASON LEANED BACK in his bed, watching the interview on his room's monitor. It had been recorded on his home station, Starport Armstrong. The familiar gardens in front of the government center gave a splash of green amid the whites and greys of the space station's interior. He recognized Emilia Delaney of the Outer Planet News Network. She was probably the most famous reporter in Outer Sol, though not exactly a household name across the rest of Federal Space. At least, not before she managed to score an in-person interview with a representative from the Ascendency.

She looked the part of the star reporter. High cheekbones, full red lips, and a delicate chin all framed by long brown hair artfully draped over the shoulders of a charcoal business suit that contrasted well with her fair skin. The Ascendency representative sitting across from her didn't have a single hair on their androgynous body. Just grey skin with strange, almost scale-like texturing. The face was inoffensive, if not bland. They wore a shimmering robe of blue and grey fabric that made them look more like a monk than the spokesperson for an invasion fleet.

"Emissary Jerome, thank you for sitting down with me today," Emilia said, her neutral news-anchor accent completely masking any sign of her native Jovian accent.

"Of course, Emilia. I'm always happy to speak with the press," Emissary Jerome said with a strange accent. Exotic without being difficult to understand.

Emilia kept a pleasant, neutral smile that betrayed nothing of what she might be thinking. "Thank you, Emissary Jerome. As we discussed during the pre-interview, there are two questions that everyone wants to ask of you."

"Yes. Namely, who are we and why did we attack?" Emissary Jerome said.

"In what order would you like to answer those questions, Emissary?"

"I'll start with the first question. We are a post-human species of sapient life adapted to living in space."

"When you say post-human, do you mean that your people started as human and then modified yourselves to the point where you no longer consider yourselves human?"

Emissary Jerome shook his head. "We were never human to start with. We were created by a group of human visionaries, who saw that the basic human platform was ill-suited to life in space, so they endeavored to create a people that is suited to life in space. We are the result of their labors."

"You say that, Emissary, but I can't help but point out that there are hundreds of millions of Federal citizens who live, work, and thrive in space. Some spend their entire lives never setting foot on the surface of a planet. With that in mind, how can you say humans are not suited to life in space?"

"Please forgive me, Emilia, but this," Jerome circled his outstretched finger to indicate the interior of the ring, "is not space. This is a little piece of Earth stuck inside an airtight torus and spun up to create simulated gravity. It's a dreadful inefficiency that extends to your starships as well. Ships that require pressurized crew spaces and spinning modules to maintain the health of their crew. That is part of why your ships are so inferior to ours."

Emilia gestured to Jerome. "Are you saying that you could survive in the vacuum of space?"

Jerome nodded. "I can. Quite comfortably, in fact. But I won't bore you with the details of my biology."

"All right. How about your government?"

"Oh, that's an easy answer. Direct democracy," Emissary Jerome said. "Each and every Ascended gets their own say."

"Including on launching an attack on the Earth Federation?" Emilia asked.

"Yes," Emissary Jerome said. "It was a unanimous vote yes, by the way."

Mason set his cup down. "Really?"

"Indeed? Well, I think that naturally moves into the other big question," Emilia said. "Why did your people decide to start a war with the Earth Federation?"

"To end the current, wasteful conflict between the Earth Federation and the League," Emissary Jerome said. "And then to bring about a permanent peace."

"Don't you think that's a bit ironic, given you have started a war?" Emilia asked.

Emissary Jerome's expression became contrite. "It is tragically ironic. Trust me when I say that if there was any other way, we would have tried it."

"Forgive me, Emissary, but you didn't try," Emilia said. "You never reached out to us. You never spoke to us. You just appeared out of nowhere and started shooting."

"A regrettable necessity, I'm afraid," Emissary Jerome said. "We had hoped to introduce ourselves peacefully, but when your Earth Federation and the League descended into war again, we knew we had no other choice other than to intervene with force."

"So why attack Sol? Was it symbolic?" Emilia asked.

"I understand why you would think that, Emilia. Sol is the origin of humanity, after all. However, the occupation of the outer solar system is for purely strategic reasons. It was the best way to deprive your government of its ability to wage war while minimizing loss of life."

"By depriving Earth Federation access to the fuel sources of Outer Sol?"

"Among other things," Emissary Jerome said. "Hardly a big secret. If your government can't fuel their starships, their ability to wage war is severely curtailed."

"Aren't you worried about the Earth Federation retaliating?" Emelia asked.

"The Ascendency is prepared to repel any attempts by the Earth Federation to regain control of the outer solar system," Emissary Jerome said. "But I can't give any details, for reasons I'm sure you're aware of."

"Of course, Emissary Jerome, but I do have to ask. When the Earth Federation comes to liberate Outer Sol, will you be able to guarantee the safety of the civilians caught in the crossfire?"

"I can't help but notice you use the word 'liberate' to describe the eventual counterattack by your government," Emissary Jerome said.

"Please answer the question, Emissary Jerome. Can you guarantee the safety of the civilian population of the Outer Solar System?" Emilia asked.

"The civilians who live and work in the Outer Solar System are in no danger from us," Emissary Jerome said. "But if the Federal Space Forces were to attempt to retake the outer solar system by force, then the safety of their citizens cannot be guaranteed."

Mason snorted. That was a very circumspect way of threatening to kill hostages.

"So, you intend for the occupation to be indefinite?" Emilia asked.

"We intend to maintain control of the outer solar system for as long as it takes to convince the Earth Federation to demilitarize," Emissary Jerome said.

"That sounds a lot like unconditional surrender, Emissary," Emilia said.

"You can think of it that way," Emissary Jerome said. "Our terms aren't all that strict. We don't wish to conquer the Earth Federation, or any sovereign government. We simply wish to defang them. We have asked President Chopra and the Federal Legislature to disband Federal Space Forces, retire all their warships, and return their crews to their worlds and stations of origin."

"Emissary Jerome, you don't expect the Earth Federation to disband their military after you attacked them, do you?"

"It's true, unfortunately, that your government will likely choose to fight us rather than accept our terms, wasting the lives of their spacers in the process," Emissary Jerome said. "But they will find that they will have little choice in the matter in the end. As demonstrated during the Battle of Jupiter, our warships and strikecraft are superior to those of the Federation and the League." Emissary Jerome shrugged. "The war is over. It's only a question of how many lives your government is willing to throw away before they accept it."

Mason shut down the screen. He got out of bed and put on clothes he had ordered from a local retailer, replacing those that had been lost when *Eagle* was destroyed.

He sat down at the room's desktop computer and composed a video message.

"Hi, Mom. Hi, Dad." Mason opened his hands. "I'm alive. Figured I should lead in with that. I know you two must be very worried. I'm on Procyon, safe and sound, with all the same parts I had the last time you saw me. I hope you both got away from Jupiter okay. I… don't know if you escaped. If not, I hope the Ascendency has been treating you as well as they claim they are.

"I don't know when I'll be able to see you in person again. As you can imagine, things are pretty tense right now. I've, uh, found myself in a strange position. But not an overly dangerous one.

"Hope to hear from both of you soon. Stay safe. Oh, and incidentally, Mom and Dad, I love you."

Mason stopped recording and slumped in his seat and hit send. He didn't bother with editing the message. He just wanted it on its way to his parents. Wherever they were. Hopefully, a few hundred million kilometers from Jupiter, at the least.

After leaving his assigned quarters, an officer's barracks near the headquarters building, Mason turned spinward, for no reason other than he always preferred to move in the direction of spin when he had the option to.

One of the nice things about living on a spinning station, be it a torus like Starport Armstrong or a cylinder like Procyon Fleet Base, was that if you wanted to go on a long walk to clear your head, you could just walk the circumference of the station and find yourself back home without ever having to turn around. Mason intended to do that until he caught the scent of freshly roasted coffee halfway around the circumference of the station. The scent drew him to a coffee shop in a shopping center near a tram station. The perfect location for spacers headed to work to pick up their morning coffee.

A couple of baristas, a man and a woman, stood behind the counter, while patrons filled the seats of the bar and most of the tables both inside and outside the cafe. The mix of people in civilian dress and in uniform was about even, though most of the people in there were likely members of the Space Forces. A glass wall behind where the baristas stood showed where the coffee was roasted. A man was pouring green beans into a roaster as Mason walked in. The din of a dozen conversations competed with the generic pop music playing over the speakers. Most of the conversations were about the Ascendency and their attack on Sol.

Mason walked up to the coffee bar, ordered a large cup of black coffee, and was shocked to find out the price was seven stellars, more than double what he was used to. He paid it anyway. Given the disruption to interstellar trade, it shouldn't have been a surprise to Mason that the coffee cost so much. Taking a seat near the shop's window, Mason sipped his coffee. It was smooth and rich, and likely imported from Sol, considering the cost. Hydroponic coffee tended to all taste the same.

It had been a while since he had the chance to just sit down and relax. The sudden transition from fighter pilot, to castaway, to prisoner of war, then the other way around, and now whatever it was Special Purpose Branch intended him to be... Well, right now he was just a guy drinking coffee and collecting his thoughts.

Eagle's loss was still with him as a tight, sad knot in the pit of his stomach. More than once he remembered Skoot getting shot down and Squadron Leader Luca dying in the middle of giving orders. And yet, he didn't feel guilty, even though he thought he should. Isn't that what survivors were supposed to feel, after all? They got to live even though they didn't do anything better, other than maybe be a bit luckier than their friends. Truth be told, Mason was simply relieved to still be alive. Even if the Earth Federation had been badly, perhaps mortally, wounded, he survived and was sitting down in a cafe enjoying a cup of overpriced coffee. It was a damn sight better than scavenging for supplies amid the ruins of a League commerce raider base.

Finishing his coffee, Mason set his mug down at the cleaning station, left the café and walked the short distance to the HQ building.

The interior cylinder loomed above Mason like an enormous arched roof, but with vehicles and people moving between the buildings on the far side of the cylinder.

Mason took a moment to breathe in the clean air, grateful there were billions of tons of metal around him, keeping air in and radiation out.

As he approached, he saw Lieutenant Sinclair resting on the railing like a lazy college student instead of an officer in Federal Space Forces. In the bright light, her dark skin and hair contrasted sharply with her blue uniform.

When she looked his way, there was a smile on her face and mischief in her eyes.

"We need to get you a new patch now that you're one of us," she said.

Mason looked down at his shoulder patch. It still bore the insignia of his old squadron, the 212th Fighter Squadron.

Lieutenant Sinclair seemed to pick up on that. "Oh, I'm sorry."

"It's all right," Mason said. "Things… well, a lot has happened. More than I feel like I can keep up with."

Lieutenant Sinclair pushed off the railing and walked up to Mason. "I'm afraid your new job won't help much with that. Overwhelmed is kind of the default state in the Special Purpose Branch. Especially now."

"And what would my new job be, exactly?" Mason asked.

A bright smile appeared on her face. "Why, you're going to help Colonel Shimura and me defeat the Ascendency, of course."

"Oh, is that all?" Mason said. "No biggie, then."

"That's the kind of attitude that will take you far in the Branch, Flight Lieutenant," she said with a forced sincerity that Mason couldn't help but laugh at.

It took Mason a moment to force down the chuckle.

"Good one, right?" she said.

"I suppose," Mason said. "You know, you're not as serious as I would expect someone working for the Branch to be."

"Because you've met so many of us?" she asked.

"Well, at least in contrast to Colonel Shimura," Mason said.

"Oh, her? She's not so bad. Just likes to play the stone-cold intelligence officer when it suits her."

"Yeah, I'm sure beneath it all she's just a big marshmallow." Mason started walking up the steps. "So, did she have you wait outside to meet me?"

Jessica took a double step up to catch up with Mason. "No, I waited for you because I wished to speak with you."

"You weren't all that talkative when we first met," Mason said.

"Colonel's orders. 'Observe and analyze, not chat, Lieutenant' were her exact words."

"Is that what all those loving stares with Colonel Shimura were about? Sharing your thoughts via brainset."

"That, and I think her eyes are lovely."

Mason glanced at her. She smiled and giggled at him.

"You are very strange," Mason said.

"Comes with the territory," she said.

"Of being a spy?"

"No, a genius."

"So humble."

"It's true," she said. "Child prodigy and all that. Got a doctorate before I was twenty."

"Should I call you Doctor Sinclair, then?" Mason asked.

"Lieutenant is fine," she said. "Doctor makes me sound old."

"Well, we couldn't have that," Mason said.

They entered the lobby and went straight for the elevators, where one waited to take them down below. When the doors slid shut, Lieutenant Sinclair spoke again. "You know, you're a lot cleverer than most fighter pilots."

"Have you met many fighter pilots?"

"More than you've met intelligence officers, I'm willing to bet," Sinclair said. "I can't say they're dull, but neither do they tend to brim with imagination. They tend not to be too concerned about things that aren't right in front of them."

"That's what I like about being a fighter pilot," Mason said. "Everything's very direct."

"Well, you may like being a fighter pilot, but I think you have the potential to be an analyst, as well," Sinclair said.

"Like you?"

"Oh goodness, no! I'm on a whole other level," she said with a smile. "But you have perspective, and that's almost as valuable as being a genius."

"I hope you're not revealing anything classified in the course of your bragging," Mason said.

Sinclair winked at him. "My genius isn't what's classified about me, Flight Lieutenant."

The elevator doors parted, and Mason walked out. "Cryptic gloating—that's an interesting combination."

"Glad you noticed," Lieutenant Sinclair said.

Colonel Shimura's office was as austere as she was. Her desk was neat and organized, the walls decorated with certificates and pictures of her time as a trooper. The woman sat straight-backed in a kneeling chair, typing something on a keyboard, her fingers landing on the keys with percussive force. She could have done the same with her brainset, but writing via brainset was a pain in the ass. It wasn't faster to use a physical keyboard, but it was more comfortable. That was why fighters still had hand control even though the pilot could directly command the vehicle with their thoughts.

Mason drew in a breath to say he was reporting for duty, but Colonel Shimura held up a finger. "No need for the redundant formality of telling me why you're here, Flight Lieutenant." Shimura's finger came down and she resumed typing. "Please take a seat." Mason sat down and waited for Shimura to finish typing. When she did, she tucked the keyboard under her desk and looked up at him. "How is your new brainset doing, Flight Lieutenant?"

"It's doing fine, sir. Thank you for asking," Mason said. "I got all my preferred settings restored yesterday."

She nodded. "Good to hear. In that case, you should be ready for your new assignment."

"And what would that be, sir?" Mason asked.

"Your record says you did two tours of duty in Fomalhaut during Earth-Fed's occupation of the system," Shimura said.

Mason stiffened at the mention. "Is that where we're going, sir?"

"Yes, Flight Lieutenant," Shimura said.

"May I ask why, sir?" Mason asked.

"Not eager to go back, Flight Lieutenant?" Colonel Shimura asked.

"Not really, sir," Mason said. "Don't have many happy memories of that particular system."

"I've never met anyone who has fond memories of Fomalhaut. Unfortunately, that's where we might find a lead on the Ascendency," Shimura said. "Fomalhaut has more contact with the most distant systems of settled space than any other nearby star system."

"Mostly because the pirates based there raid those distant systems," Mason said. "Federals aren't exactly welcome there after the Occupation."

"No, they're not, but… well, I wouldn't say the Branch has friends there, but we do have contacts," Colonel Shimura said.

"And those contacts say they know something about the Ascendency, sir?" Mason asked.

Shimura nodded to Lieutenant Sinclair. "I think she can explain that for you, Flight Lieutenant."

Lieutenant Sinclair grinned. "For years, going back well before the Occupation, Federal Intelligence has been collecting reports from our contacts in Fomalhaut about encounters with unknown ships in settled space. These reports are mostly second- or third-hand. Easily dismissed. But after searching through the report for particular keywords, I noticed that a plurality of the reports coming out of Fomalhaut matched with what we've seen with the Ascendency."

"Wait, you mean the pirates in Fomalhaut knew about them?" Mason said.

"I wouldn't go that far. They simply have been hearing things," Lieutenant Sinclair said. "Encounters with ships that matched the descriptions of the ones that conquered Jupiter. Of meeting with people with unusual cybernetics."

Mason turned his seat to face Sinclair. "You mean there are people who met members of the Ascendency in person?"

"Yes, but the exact nature of who, or what, they are is unclear," Lieutenant Sinclair said. "All that I'm sure about is that they are human in origin."

"Human in origin, but not necessarily human," Mason said.

"Well, that would get into what you define as human, Flight Lieutenant," Lieutenant Sinclair said. "There are–"

Colonel Shimura interrupted. "That is a philosophical question that falls outside the purview of our mission, Lieutenant." She turned to Mason. "Thanks to Lieutenant Sinclair's analysis, we think we might know who to ask in Fomalhaut that might give us a lead."

"And you're sure there are people in Fomalhaut willing to talk to us, sir?" Mason said. "We didn't make a lot of friends during the Occupation."

"It's a good thing we won't be going as Federals, then," Sinclair said.

Mason glanced at Lieutenant Sinclair. "So, we're going to be disguised; is that it?"

"In effect, yes, Flight Lieutenant," Colonel Shimura said.

Mason turned back to the Colonel. "Sir, this sounds like spy stuff. I'm not a spy. I don't have any training in that regard."

"But you do have a quite a bit of training as a hauler pilot, Flight Lieutenant," Colonel Shimura said.

Mason paused for a couple of seconds. "You want me to fly a hauler, sir?"

"Can you think of a better way to dock with an independent station without drawing attention?"

"The Branch doesn't have hauler pilots of its own, sir?" Mason asked.

"Not on this station," Colonel Shimura said. "And since we are in a serious scramble, I don't have time to find and vet one. Lucky for me, I have you. And since you have actual combat experience against the Ascendency, I think you will be a valuable addition to the mission."

"I'm assuming we're not flying all the way to Fomalhaut in a hauler," Mason said. "Because that might take a while."

Jessica chuckled at that.

Colonel Shimura gave him the barest hint of a smile. "Not to worry, Flight Lieutenant. I already have that covered."

CHAPTER 7

THE GENERIC PASSENGER shuttle was a small thing compared to the cavernous assault shuttle that had carried Mason from *Fafnir*, but he didn't feel at all cramped inside the shuttle's cozy passenger compartment, largely because, with his new brainset, he could patch into the shuttle's sensor system and see the universe around him.

The space around Procyon Fleet Base buzzed with activity. At either tapered end of the station, a steady stream of haulers, shuttles, and fighters flew in and out. In a parking orbit, 20,000 kilometers retrograde from Procyon Fleet Base loitered the bulk of the 8th Fleet, the icons representing their ships forming a dense constellation against the backdrop of space. The shuttle was not flying towards the 8th Fleet, but to a designated parking orbit prograde of the station.

MR-5 waited alone in the parking zone, well away from the traffic moving about the fleet base. Mason could only guess what MR-5 meant, but he suspected it didn't mean anything. Just a generic alpha-numeric designation meant to let the ship hide in plain sight should League spies, or worse, curious legislators, start poking through a list of the Federal Space Forces' starship inventory. You could learn a lot about a ship just by reading its name, especially given the Space Forces' rock-solid naming conventions. A Federal Space Forces starship named after a person was probably a destroyer. If it was named after a city, it was a cruiser. An animal meant a carrier. If it was named after a cosmic body like a star, planet, or moon, it was a battleship. A name like MR-5, which tellingly didn't have the FSFV prefix for Federal Space Forces Vessel, was a clear indicator that her owners didn't want anyone to easily guess what the vessel's true nature was. Mason's hunch was that she was some kind of spying ship. Probably a converted starfreighter or something similar. That's what he would use if he were trying to go incognito into Fomalhaut.

When the shuttle got close enough for Mason to see the details of the hull, he saw neither of those things. MR-5 looked like a small carrier—a long cylinder, with a rectangular module at the front, covered in large hatches for smallcraft docking bays. Seven hundred meters in length, and north of half a million tons, at a guess, she was about the size of a Vancouver-class cruiser.

She had a spinning hab rotor that looked good for the 0.3 g minimum standard that the Federal Space Forces required of its ships.

The forward section of the ship stretched out ahead of the spinning hab module like a flattened brick. As the shuttle maneuvered over the forward section, he saw twelve rectangular doors stacked one on top of the other. Each large enough for one full-sized smallcraft such as a Lightning or an assault shuttle. He was willing to bet that there were twelve matching bays on the opposite side of the forward module. MR-5 was not a frontline warship. Her weapons consisted of scattered point-defense turrets and clustered interceptor tubes. Rather than proper armor, she was covered in strange panels that gave her hull a fractal look.

The shuttle didn't fly into one of the hangars. Instead, it mated to a docking tube near the center of the ship, just forward of the spinning hab rotor. There was a chunky metallic sound as the docking clamps secured the shuttle to MR-5.

A strong hand jostled his shoulder and Mason broke his connection with the shuttle and pulled his head back into the passenger compartment.

Colonel Shimura floated next to his seat. "What do you think of *Mervie*, Flight Lieutenant?"

"*Mervie*, sir? Oh, wait. I got it. M, R, and then roman numeral five," Mason said. "It must have taken whole minutes for someone to come up with that name."

"Is that all you noticed about that ship?" she said.

"She looks like a small carrier, sir," Mason said. "Of course, Earth-Fed doesn't have any carriers that small. At least, not officially."

"And, officially, *Mervie's* not a carrier," she said. "But close enough, functionally."

"I am curious why she's covered in panels the way she is, sir," Mason said. "That's not the most efficient use for the outer hull real estate. If those are radiators, it's usually better to mount them perpendicular to the hull rather than flat on top of it."

"Only if the purpose of those radiators was to evacuate heat," Shimura said.

"I don't follow, sir," Mason said. "There are other uses of radiators?"

"For *Mervie*, yes. For example, changing her emissions signature to look like another ship," Colonel Shimura said.

"You're saying that *Mervie* can disguise herself as other ships, sir?" Mason asked.

"Exactly, Flight Lieutenant," Colonel Shimura said.

"And what disguise are we wearing when we arrive in Fomalhaut, sir?" Mason asked.

"I actually don't know. Captain Vann hasn't informed me yet," Colonel Shimura said. "Something inconspicuous, I would hope. Let's get aboard. I think the airlock has equalized by now."

Mason gathered his duffle bag and floated free of his seat. Shimura did the same. Lieutenant Sinclair had two bags—one strapped across her back, and one across her chest. It looked awkward, but it didn't seem to interfere with her ability to maneuver in zero g.

They floated up the well-lit tunnel of the docking tube, where a tall woman with cropped blonde hair waited for them. Colonel Shimura stopped just short of the threshold between the docking tube and *Mervie's* pressure hull and gave the starship's captain a salute.

"Permission to come aboard, Captain Vann?"

Captain Vann nodded. She was a tall, lean woman, her short, blonde hair fading gracefully into dusky skin. There wasn't the hint of a wrinkle on her blue jumpsuit.

Mervie's captain glanced at Mason. "I see your retinue has expanded, Colonel."

"You know me, Captain; always picking up strays," Colonel Shimura said.

Vann turned to face Mason. "Welcome aboard MR-5, Flight Lieutenant."

"Thank you, sir," Mason said.

She turned to Lieutenant Sinclair. "And it's good to see you again, Lieutenant."

"Thank you, Captain. I've always liked spending time on *Mervie*."

"Your quarters have already been assigned. I'll give you all time to stow your belongings and get settled in," Captain Vann said. "Colonel Shimura, can you and Lieutenant Sinclair show the Flight Lieutenant the way?"

"We can, Captain." Shimura turned to Mason. "This way, Flight Lieutenant."

They moved down the hull of the ship, towards the engines, deck after deck, passing by floating spacers moving through circular corridors like fish in a pipe. Mason noted how thin the structure partitioning each deck was. *Mervie* was not built for taking punishment.

They stopped at a large, circular room dominated by a slowly rotating torus. They had arrived in the hub where the spinning hab module met the static hull of the ship.

They entered the torus and, in the minute gravity, boarded an elevator that took them down one of the two rotor arms that sprouted from *Mervie's* hab rotor. At the end of the elevator ride, a little over 0.3 of a g pulled them all to the deck. Enough to give Mason's duffle bag some real weight, though not difficult to manage.

Lieutenant Sinclair managed to hold both her duffle bags with little trouble, holding them by their handles rather than the shoulder straps. Even accounting for the low gravity, those bags still had to be heavy, and yet she didn't seem at all encumbered by them. It seemed Lieutenant Sinclair was stronger than she looked. Mason could see the outlines of her toned shoulder muscles under her blue jumpsuit. For an analyst, she looked like she took physical training seriously. Lieutenant Sinclair seemed to notice he was staring at her and looked up to him.

"Uh... so, what's with all the gear?" Mason asked.

"Oh, these?" Lieutenant Sinclair shrugged her shoulders. "Sundries. I like to pack light."

"I see," Mason said.

They stopped in a corridor. Shimura pointed at one of the doors. "That's yours over there, Flight Lieutenant. Lieutenant Sinclair will be the next door down. I'll be at the end of the corridor."

Mason pushed open the door and glanced inside. There was a gel bed up against one wall, a small folding desk and chair on the opposing wall and, between them, a door that led into a private head. "I'm getting a full cabin?"

"I could reassign you to something more cozy if that's too big for you."

"Oh, no, that won't be necessary, sir." Mason pushed the door open and tossed his duffel bag onto the bed. A lifetime of living in spin-gravity had taught him to compensate for the Coriolis effect, and his bag landed right in the middle of the bed.

"Good. Glad you approve," Colonel Shimura said. "But before you settle in, I want you to touch base with Wing Commander Cade. His pilots, elite as they are, don't have any combat experience against the Ascendency. You do."

"In that case, where would I find him, sir?" Mason asked.

Colonel Shimura pointed down the corridor. "Pilot country is down that way, on the other side of this deck, Flight Lieutenant. Wing Commander Cade will be waiting for you in his office."

⌇

Mason found that the door to Wing Commander Cade's office was open. Inside was a tiny compartment dominated by a little desk, where a small man with black hair, dark complexion, and a gaunt face was hunched over, tapping away at a keyboard. He didn't seem to notice when Mason entered.

"Wing Commander Cade, sir?" Mason snapped a salute as Cade's grey eyes looked up from his monitor and locked onto Mason.

"You must be Colonel Shimura's hauler pilot," Wing Commander Cade said. "Which is interesting given your callsign is Hauler."

"Something I picked up in Flight School, sir. Instructors kept referring to me as 'the hauler pilot' due to my background. That got shortened to Hauler by the time I graduated and got assigned to an active fighter squadron."

"And now you are flying a hauler."

"Hopefully, just for this mission, sir," Mason said.

69

"Not a fan of flying haulers?"

"I like them just fine, sir, but if I wanted to fly them professionally, I would've remained a civilian pilot. Pays better."

"Fair enough." Cade pointed to the chair in front of his desk. "Please, take a seat, Hauler. They call me Zero around these parts."

"Thank you, sir." Mason sat down. Even in the mild spin-gravity of the hab rotor, the lightweight plastic seat creaked under his weight.

"If your record is anything to go by, you've had a very eventful last few months."

"That's one way to put it, sir," Mason said.

"I suppose 'eventful' doesn't really do it justice. *Eagle*'s loss must weigh on you."

"I'm hardly the only spacer to survive the loss of their ship, sir."

"Very true, that. Hopefully, this mission Colonel Shimura has cobbled together will go a ways towards evening the score with the Cendies."

"Is that what we're calling the Ascendency now, sir?" Mason asked.

"The nickname's been gaining traction ever since the Cendies took Jupiter. I admit to a certain fondness for it. It is condescending and petty."

"The making of a fine derogatory nickname, sir," Mason said.

"Well, speaking of the Cendies, I cannot ignore the fact that you are the only pilot on this ship with actual combat experience against them."

"Does getting shot down count as combat experience, sir?"

"It does when you can walk away from the crash site, Flight Lieutenant. I also can not overlook the fact that you helped a League cruiser fight its way out of a Cendy ambush."

"Well, sir, they wouldn't have been able to surrender to me if I let the Cendies blow them up."

A smile pulled at the corners of Cade's mouth. "I suppose not. So, tell me, Hauler, what insights from your first-hand combat experience with the Cendies can you share?"

"Uh, well, sir, uh…" Mason sighed and scratched his temple. "I would say they strongly favor quantity over quality. The way they took down *Eagle*'s fighters, including mine, the way they dealt with our fighters around Jupiter—all by use of overwhelming numbers of fighters, combined with the stupendously heavy interceptor volleys launched by their arsenal ships."

"You think their fighters are inferior to our Lightnings?"

"On a one-to-one basis, yes sir," Mason said. "Their performance is about the same—maybe a bit better—but they don't appear to carry as many weapons as a Lightning can. Nor is their ECM as good. Their power output isn't enough for that. Which isn't to say they're not dangerous."

"No, not if their results are anything to go by," Wing Commander Cade said. "I'll want you to meet with my pilots during the flight to Fomalhaut; go more in-depth about your experiences."

"I can do that, sir," Mason said. "But I feel I should mention that if you want me to share my experience, the best place would be in the cockpit of a fighter."

Cade chuckled at that. "I was wondering when you'd get to that."

"Seemed like a good time to broach the subject, sir."

"Well, unfortunately, Hauler, the simple fact of the matter is, I have all the fighter pilots I need right now. Which I don't mean as a slight against your flying skills. Your record would make you a fine addition to any regular fighter squadron."

"Which the Void Knights aren't, sir. I understand. I'm aware of the training Spec Ops pilots have to go through."

Cade nodded. "Good. But I wouldn't fret too much about it. Participating in a special ops mission, even when flying a humble hauler, looks good on the service record. Once this mission is complete, I'm sure you'll have your pick of assignments. Might even get a squadron of your own."

"Something to look forward to, sir."

"Indeed. If you have the time, you should head to Hangar Bay 12. That's where the hauler Colonel Shimura wants you to fly is. I'll have *Mervie's* chief hangar tech meet you there."

"With your leave, sir, I'll head there now."

"You have it, Hauler. I do hope you like what you find waiting for you in Hangar Bay 12."

The hauler Mason was supposed to fly rested on the docking pad, held in place by magnetic locks. The hangar bay was just a metal box with a large door on the far side, leading out into empty space. The squat hauler, resting on its six landing legs, looked like a spider that was frozen still after just realizing it had been spotted.

A short man with dusky skin and dark hair, wearing the utilitarian orange jumpsuit of a hangar tech, floated around the bottom of the hauler, examining its single engine bell. Mason grabbed a rung on one of the hauler's landing struts to bring himself to a stop.

"Chief Rabin?"

The tech turned around. "Ah, sir, you must be Flight Lieutenant Grey." He pushed off the hauler's hull and floated towards Mason, grabbing the landing strut with his left hand to float in front of him. He held out his right hand. "Welcome aboard *Mervie*, sir."

Mason took Rabin's hand and shook it. "Thanks, Chief." He nodded towards the hauler. "What can you tell me about my new ride?"

"Oh, *Buttercup*? She's a gem," Rabin said.

"Who named her that?" Mason asked.

"Dunno, sir. Not a bad name, though."

"She got any special Federal Intelligence gadgetry I should know about?"

"Nope, nothing like that, sir," Chief Rabin said. "She's just a stock Kolar 125P high-endurance hauler. Though she does have the premium trim option."

Mason nodded. "I always did like heated seats."

"You ever fly one like this, sir?"

"Did my last certification flight on a 100-series Kolar," Mason said. "Though that was a few years ago."

"You'll have plenty of time to get acquainted with *Buttercup*, sir," Chief Rabin said. "This girl's had a long history. Been all over settled space. Passed through a lot of hands."

"I see the Branch has spared no expense," Mason said.

Rabin chuckled for a moment, then cleared his throat. "Yes, well, sir, used spacecraft dealers tend not to ask too many questions, which makes it convenient for the Special Purpose Branch when they need to buy a ship on the down-low. Especially on short notice."

"I see," Mason said. "You seem pretty fond of her, Chief."

"Used to do a lot of work on haulers like this in my civilian life. Before the war with the League started and I got activated."

"You're a reservist?"

Rabin nodded. "Yes, sir. It's how I paid for technical school. Spent ten years working on haulers like Buttercup on Federal Station during the week. Then one weekend a month, I'd help keep the station's Lightnings running."

"How did you get roped into working on a Special Purpose Branch reconnaissance vessel?" Mason asked.

"What? You don't think reservists get recruited by the Branch?" Rabin asked.

"Frankly, I haven't a clue how the Branch picks their recruits," Mason said. "I just kind of fell into it myself."

Rabin nodded. "Much the same with me, sir. I think when they were looking to fill out the crew, my name came up, and *boom*, here I am, chief hangar tech on a secret starship that can disguise herself as other ships."

"Funny how things work out," Mason said.

"You got that right, sir," Rabin said. "If you don't mind me asking, sir, where does a fighter pilot learn how to fly haulers?"

"Jupiter, Chief," Mason said. "Both parents are hauler pilots."

"Ah. Should have guessed by the accent," Rabin said. "Did your parents get caught up in the invasion, sir?"

"Maybe? Probably," Mason said. "I haven't actually heard anything."

"Sorry to hear that, sir," Chief Rabin said.

"Thanks, Chief." Mason cleared his throat. "So, you maintain all the smallcraft on this ship, or are you just here to keep *Buttercup* running?"

"Oh, my main job's keeping the Void Knight's eighteen fighters running," Rabin said. "Everything else I do is a side job next to that."

"Eighteen fighters? Last I checked there were sixteen pilots," Mason said.

"Mervie can't make spare parts for her fighters like a real carrier can," Chief Rabin said. "So, we take a couple of complete Lightnings along to serve as a source of spare parts."

"I see," Mason said. "So, anything fancy about the fighters you can tell me about?"

"Not really, sir," Rabin said.

"Too classified, I take it," Mason said.

"No, just nothing fancy about special-ops fighters," Rabin said. "The idea that special-ops squadrons get fancier ships than frontline squadrons is a myth perpetuated by the media. Fact is, regular fighter squadrons get priority on new fighters. Special-ops tend to get older birds."

"That's news to me, Chief."

"Not like the Branch advertises their procurement practices, sir."

"I suppose not," Mason said. "Well, if Wing Commander Cade has a couple of spare Lightnings, maybe I could try again to convince him to let me fly on occasion."

Rabin shook his head. "I'm sorry to burst your bubble, sir, but I wouldn't hold out much hope for that. Those two extra Lightnings will be the only spare parts for his active fighters during our mission, and he's not going to risk them in the hands of an unproven pilot."

"I hardly have an unproven flight record, Chief," Mason said.

"You haven't gone through the Special Operations training pipeline, sir," Chief Rabin said. "That's what matters to Wing Commander Cade, I'm sorry to say. I know that flying haulers is probably a downgrade for you."

"It's not what I would call ideal, Chief," Mason said. "So, you mentioned older strikecraft. Does that mean the Void Knights venture into danger flying worn-out fighters?"

"Old doesn't mean worn-out, sir," Rabin said. "Every fighter on this ship's been recently rebuilt and upgraded. Hey, tell you what, sir. How about I show my favorite Lightning? She's just a deck up from this hangar."

"That would be like asking a starving kid to look through the window of a cake shop," Mason said. "But, sure, let's take a look."

Rabin smiled, like he was about to show off one of his kids. Which was kind of the default for crew chiefs. The only people who loved fighters more than the people who flew them were the people who kept the temperamental beasts working.

"Follow me, sir," Rabin said. "The hangar's pressurized, so you won't need a pressure suit."

"Not too often I get to interact with a Lightning in shirt-sleeves," Mason said. "Lead the way, Chief."

⋙

Rabin floated straight into Hangar Bay 10. Mason followed him inside and saw the Lightning resting on the landing pad, held in place by maglocks on her landing gear. A long, thin fuselage was flanked by large engine nacelles, with her wings folded up and over them.

Rabin launched from handhold to handhold until he was floating next to the fighter. Mason followed. The Lighting's cockpit canopy, internal weapons bay doors, and every conceivable access panel were open, exposing the fighter's internal components. As Mason followed Chief Rabin to the fighter's nose, he saw the words *"Magnificent Seven"* stenciled over the nose, just short of the gun port. Rabin was right about special ops getting older fighters. If a smallcraft or a strikecraft, be it a bomber, shuttle, or fighter, survived more than ten years of service, it usually earned a nickname of some sort. In contrast to pilot callsigns, which were usually embarrassing in origin, spacecraft almost always got endearing nicknames. It probably said something about the men and women of the Federal Space Forces that they thought better of their equipment than their comrades in arms.

Mason thought of the first Lightning he ever flew. It was named *Gunslinger*, mostly because, at the time, the fighter had the most gun kills of any Lightning in active service. During his first tour in Fomalhaut, Mason flew a Lightning named *Beehive*. Her name derived from the unusually loud buzzing sound the fighter would make when fully throttled up, due to poorly installed noise insulation that, for one reason or another, was never corrected.

"Isn't she a beauty, sir?" Rabin asked.

"She would be if her guts weren't exposed for all to see, Chief." Mason moved handhold to handhold to the open canopy, peering into the cockpit, where two acceleration seats mounted in tandem rested inside. The second seat was not for a co-pilot, but for a passenger who valued speed over comfort.

Glancing at a panel inside the cockpit, Mason checked the fighter's registry number. It was a solitary 7 preceded by line of zeros.

"Belts and zones," Mason said. "Never seen a Lightning built back in 2920 before. This bird must have seen a lot of service."

"That she has, sir," Chief Rabin said. "Saw five tours during the Occupation of Fomalhaut and a few missions against the League before she was brought in to get rebuilt as a Mark V. Picked up thirteen kills along the way."

"I am very, very impressed, Chief," Mason said. "She must be the oldest fighter in the system."

"Yeah, she's got the next oldest fighter I can think of beat by two years," Rabin said. "Only fighter on this ship that started life as a Mark I. Can't be too many of those still in service."

"No, probably not," Mason said. "She can't have much more than five years left on her service life; probably saw her last upgrade."

"I'm sure she's got more than that in her, sir," Chief Rabin said. "If there was one thing Xi-Mac got right when they designed the Mark Is, it was the strength of their fighter's space frame."

"Who's her pilot?" Mason asked.

"She's one of the spares, sir," Rabin said. "She doesn't have one."

"Explains why you got her all opened up." Thirty-five years of service and now she's just spare parts. He patted the fighter. "Lightning with that kind of provenance should be flown."

"No argument here, sir," Chief said. "Unfortunately, Wing Commander Cade's not all that sentimental."

"Yeah, I got that impression when I met him." Mason sighed. "Well, thank you for showing *Magnificent Seven* off to me, Chief. I can tell why you like her so much."

"Any time, sir," Rabin said. "In the meantime, I'll make sure *Buttercup's* in perfect working order. She might not be the hottest ride on the ship, but she'll treat you well."

"I'm sure you will and I'm sure she will, Chief," Mason said. "I think I'll head back to the hab rotor. Got to get my quarters squared away."

Rabin nodded. "Good meeting you, sir."

"Likewise, Chief," Mason said.

With a gentle kick off the side of Magnificent Seven, Mason launched himself towards the airlock, floating straight through both hatches without touching the sides. From there, he floated down a deck, and got the elevator to take himself back to the habitat rotor. He was about to dial for the rotor hub when a group of people in drab olive jumpsuits floated around the corner.

"Hold the elevator, flyboy," said a square-jawed man leading the group, the four bars of a major pinned to the collar of his dark green jumpsuit.

"Uh… yes, sir," Mason said, holding down the open button.

The major nodded over his shoulder, and a full squad of troopers started floating into the elevator, duffle bags the same color as their jumpsuits strapped to their backs.

By the time the last floated in, Mason had to press himself against the elevator's control panel.

The lantern-jawed major floated inside, hooking his feet through toe holds on the elevator's floor. "Spin hub."

Mason hit the button for the spin hub, feeling a bit mortified that he was playing elevator operator. It took two years of training and augmentation surgery to allow him to operate a Lightning. He had logged almost ten thousand hours of flying time in the last eight years. Now he was flying an elevator carrying a bunch of grunts. A bunch of grunts who acted like he wasn't there. Mason supposed that was his ego getting the better of him. He glanced at the trooper next to him, a woman who looked like a younger, darker version of Colonel Shimura. Her jumpsuit did little to conceal the muscles underneath. On her shoulder was her unit patch. A silver dagger on a black background. These weren't typical troopers. Mason only had marginal familiarity with the various infantry units in the Federal Space Forces, but he knew of these guys by reputation. Everyone did. They were from the Raider Regiment. Emphasis on the article. No numbers needed because there was only the one. The Special Purpose Branch's own troopers, specialized in covert operations. They were one of those units that often popped up when the question of "most elite" came up.

"Can I help you with something, sir?" the sergeant asked, her dark brown, almost black eyes glancing towards him.

"Oh, uh… " The elevator stopped and the doors opened. Mason gestured. "After you, Sergeant."

"Thank you, sir," she said. She floated out, following the major, and the rest of the troopers floated out after her, leaving Mason holding the door.

Mason let out a long sigh, then left the elevator.

The corridor outside the elevator was clogged with Raiders. Almost completely obscured by the collection of bodies was Colonel Shimura, who was speaking with the major.

"Thanks for getting a team together on short notice, Major," Shimura said.

"It's our job, sir," the major said. "Better than spinning our wheels waiting for Federal Command to decide what to do about the fleet occupying Outer Sol."

Shimura nodded, and then noticed Mason in the back. "I see you met one of my team already."

The major, and his squad of Raiders, including the sergeant who noticed Mason staring at her, all turned their attention to Mason as he floated in the corridor.

"That flyboy over there? He showed real excellence in operating the elevator, sir," Major Hauer said.

"I'm glad you're impressed, Major. He'll be the one who will fly your team to Dagon Freeport when we arrive in Fomalhaut," Shimura said.

"He is?" the major said.

"Uh, yeah, that's right, sir," Mason said.

"Our assault shuttle already has a pilot," Major Hauer said.

"We won't be using an assault shuttle to fly to Dagon Freeport, Major," Colonel Shimura said. "I'll brief you during the flight to Fomalhaut."

"Understood, sir," Major Hauer said. "Come on, people. Let's get settled."

The troopers floated away, leaving Mason and Shimura alone.

"Huh, so I take it they're going to be my passengers?" Mason asked.

Shimura nodded. "Along with me and Lieutenant Sinclair, yes."

"Guess that explains why we have a hauler outfitted for passengers," Mason said. "So, are we expecting trouble in Fomalhaut, sir? Because the presence of both a special ops fighter squadron and now a squad of Raiders leads me to believe that there's trouble waiting for us."

"Dagon Freeport is a wild place. Even more in the years since Earth-Fed withdrew," Colonel Shimura said. "And even if it turns out there is no trouble waiting for us in Fomalhaut, there's every possibility that what we learn there will lead us to trouble."

"Ah," Mason said. "Good to know we have something to look forward to, sir."

CHAPTER 8

MASON'S ARMS BURNED something fierce as he finished his last set on the resistance bands. He set the handles back into their holders and wiped the sweat off his brow with a towel. Strong muscles were just as important in improving a pilot's high-g tolerance as reinforced connective tissues and a boosted cardiovascular system, and unlike the latter two, Earth-Fed did nothing to strengthen Mason's muscles. They left that to him. Not that he would likely to put his g-tolerance to the test. *Buttercup* could do two gs maximum, and that was only if she were lightly loaded. For hauling cargo or passengers, one g of acceleration was more than enough. In contrast, a fighter pilot was expected to be able to sustain up to ten gs for days and tolerate up to twenty gs in bursts.

He exercised mostly to fight off boredom. There just wasn't that much to do on a starship traversing the vast emptiness between stars, especially on a mid-sized one like *Mervie*.

"You done with that, or are you just taking a breather?"

Mason looked up to find Jessica standing over him, dressed in the standard tshirt and shorts of the Federal Space Forces' exercise clothing.

"Uh, yeah, I'm done." He surrendered the exercise machine to Jessica.

Jessica smiled. "Thank you." She stood between the handles.

The resistance bands were connected to the floor and were designed to simulate free weights. They didn't do that great a job of it, but unsecured weights could become deadly projectiles during maneuvering, so resistance bands had to do. Jessica pinched the weight-setting dial between her thumb and forefinger, and turned it a quarter-turn clockwise, increasing the weight by a significant margin.

"Huh."

Jessica glanced at him, a delicate eyebrow arched. "Huh, what?"

"That's a lot of weight," Mason said.

Jessica arched an eyebrow. "You think it's too much for me?"

"I don't think anything. That's just a lot of weight."

Jessica grabbed the handles and started doing bicep curls with them. "Arms won't exercise themselves."

"Guess not," Mason said. She didn't seem to have much trouble, but though well-toned, her arms just didn't look big enough to take the weight she was pulling. She probably had some kind of muscle enhancement, the kind that increased strength without adding mass. Why an analyst would need that was beyond Mason, but it wasn't really his business. He was just a glorified chauffeur.

"So, tell me, Mason, what do you think about visiting Dagon Freeport again?" Jessica asked.

"Uh... I can't say I missed the place."

"Not a lot of good memories, I take it."

"Oh, there were. I'd be lying if I said I didn't look forward to taking leave there. But even under Federal control, that place was pretty damn grungy. And the vehicular traffic there was downright dangerous. I somehow doubt that's improved in the years since we left."

Jessica continued to work her set, building a sweat, but showing no apparent signs of fatigue. "Not a fan of grunge?"

"Nope. I like nice clean space stations. I take it you've never been there yourself?"

"No, this is my first time going to Fomalhaut," Jessica said.

"What did you do during the Occupation?"

She smiled "That's need-to-know and you don't need to know."

"Other than the fact that whatever you did, it wasn't in Fomalhaut."

"Exactly."

"Well, I hope you like the smell of garbage, then."

"Dagon smells like garbage?"

Mason nodded. "When Dagon was built, its builders didn't include the kind of waste management systems that modern Federal stations do. They collect garbage in dumpsters and they use trucks to transport those dumpsters to a centralized area. It's archaic."

"Sounds normal for a city."

"Not one in space," Mason said.

"I take it you haven't spent too much time planet-side."

"All that sky with nothing but gravity to hold it down?" Mason shuddered. "No thanks."

"Gravity has a reliable track record for keeping atmospheres where they belong."

"I'm not claiming I'm being logical. I'm just saying that the favorite parts of my planet-side assignments were their endings."

Jessica finished her first set, and placed the handles back in their holders. Her dark skin glistened with sweat. "You're serious? What about oceans?"

Mason shrugged. "I like Europa's oceans better."

"What does Europa's oceans have that Earth's don't?"

"A ceiling."

"But there's no life in those oceans."

"Another thing I like about them. Sea life creeps the hell out of me."

"Blimey, you've really internalized the sterile life of a space station."

"Life is hardly sterile on a space station. Birds, bugs, plant life. Even a mid-sized station like Starport Armstrong has all that. I just don't like stuff that swims."

"Even dolphins?"

Mason shrugged. "Eh."

"What do you mean, 'eh'? They're bloody dolphins."

"I take it you're fond of dolphins."

"Got to swim with them when I was young. It was a magical experience."

"I got to swim in a methane lake on Titan when I was a kid. That was also magical. No aquatic mammals required."

"I bet you looked adorable in your little environment suit."

"My mom thought so. She recorded the whole thing." Mason's smile faded when he realized what he was talking about.

"Sore subject?"

Mason sighed. "Just remembered most of my childhood is under enemy occupation."

"That has to be rough."

"It's not great. But what can you do?"

"Well, I didn't mean to dig up painful memories."

"They are all very pleasant memories," Mason said. "It's the present that's not so much fun."

"Well, in that case, I have a question."

"Shoot."

"If you don't like going outside, then how could you enjoy swimming on Titan?"

"I like going outside just fine. So long as I'm wearing something with an oxygen supply."

⁓

Mason sat in *Mervie's* largest briefing room with both Major Hauer's Raiders and Wing Commander Cade's spec ops pilots. On the large screen that dominated the wall behind Colonel Shimura were two pictures. One of a dark-haired man in his mid-thirties, and the other of a horribly scarred, bald man with solid black artificial eyes replacing those likely lost to the same incident that ruined his face. At first, Mason thought they were pictures of different people, but he then realized that they were, in fact, pictures of the same person.

"This is Oren Marquez, former pirate captain turned pirate lord," Colonel Shimura said. "The before image is what he looked like before the Federal Occupation, when he was just another pirate captain operating under the command of one of his cousins, the late pirate lord Carter Marquez. Today, he goes by the name Mister Cordial, and he's now the most powerful pirate lord in Fomalhaut. You all are probably no doubt curious what happened to his face. Well, to be blunt, we did. When FSFV *Trieste* attacked his cousin's base, Oren got caught in a fire and was broiled inside his pressure suit, which resulted in severe burns over his entire body. It was a miracle that he managed to survive. It was an even greater miracle that he didn't hold it against us."

The image shifted, changing to what looked like the front of a nightclub with "The Philistine" written in glowing blue LEDs over the heavy double doors.

Colonel Shimura pointed at the image. "This is Mister Cordial's base of operations. Though still a pirate lord, he's branched off into several legitimate and not-so-legitimate enterprises. Both in Fomalhaut, and all around independent space. Prostitution, drugs, extortion and, of course, piracy. He's also been Earth-Fed's most important contact in Fomalhaut since the end of the Occupation."

Mason held up his hand. "Pardon me, Colonel, but why is this guy working with Earth-Fed if we're the ones who killed his cousin and turned his face into a potato?"

"I would avoid saying that within earshot of him, Flight Lieutenant," Colonel Shimura said. "And to answer your question, the reason is that Oren blames his cousin and the other pirate lords who ruled Fomalhaut before the Occupation for what happened to him. He believed that raiding Federal Space would attract too much heat. Literally, in his case."

"And then he decides to become an informant for the Branch, sir?" Mason asked. "I don't follow."

"The Occupation resulted in the death or capture of much of Fomalhaut's old pirate lords, creating a power vacuum. We helped Mister Cordial partially fill that vacuum. In return, he agreed never to raid Federal Space and share intelligence with us. Because of Fomalhaut's unique position within independent space, and Mister Cordial's unique position within Fomalhaut, he's the perfect person for us to ask about the activities of the Ascendency," Colonel Shimura said.

Major Hauer raised his hand. Shimura nodded to him.

"Sir, can we trust him?" Major Hauer asked. "He is a criminal, after all."

"He is a criminal, but he's a criminal whose interests align with ours," Colonel Shimura said. "But, no, I don't trust him. Which is why I'm bringing your Raiders along. Your people will adopt the guise of mercenaries and stand by in case something goes wrong."

"After which, we kick down the nice double doors to Mister Cordial's little club and pull you out," Major Hauer said.

"Me, Lieutenant Sinclair, and Flight Lieutenant Grey," Colonel Shimura said.

"Wait. Me, sir?" Mason asked. "Isn't it a bit risky to bring your only hauler pilot along?"

"Worse comes to worst, *Buttercup* can fly herself back, if necessary, Flight Lieutenant," Colonel Shimura said. "You'll be coming along because Mister Cordial is an avid pilot, who feels a sense of kinship with other pilots. He takes all the chances he can get to meet with accomplished pilots, be they Federal, League, or Independent."

"So, I'm supposed to try and become his buddy or something, sir?" Mason asked.

"You're to share your story with him, Flight Lieutenant," Colonel Shimura said.

"Uh… which parts?" Mason asked.

"The parts relevant to his interests, Flight Lieutenant. Like your childhood aboard Haulers, your training as a fighter pilot, even your kill record during the Occupation of Fomalhaut. And, yes, your encounter with the Ascendency. The fact the last part is not yet part of the public record will be particularly appealing to him."

"So, I'm supposed to trade war stories with a pirate lord, sir?" Mason asked.

"That's right," Colonel Shimura said.

"Sir, you realize I might have killed some of his friends during the Occupation," Mason said.

Colonel Shimura shook her head. "I checked your kill record against our intelligence, Flight Lieutenant. You never operated in the parts of Fomalhaut where his clan was active. The chances you killed anyone he knew is essentially nil. Like I said, he doesn't hold the Occupation against us."

"So, you're saying I should be open and honest, sir?" Mason said.

"In this instance, yes," Colonel Shimura said. "I know honesty might seem incongruous with intelligence work but, even in our industry, honesty is sometimes the best policy."

"If frankness is what's called for, I can do it, sir," Mason said.

"Excellent," Colonel Shimura said. "Lieutenant Sinclair will come along to provide technical support, and on-point analysis of any data Mister Cordial shares with us."

CHAPTER 9

THE BRIDGE WAS quiet while *Mervie* prepared to make the last jump to Fomalhaut. Mason sat next to Colonel Shimura, as she, Jessica, and Captain Vann surrounded the holotank of *Mervie's* small bridge. The bridge crew surrounded him from their stations like a silent audience.

They were technically already inside Fomalhaut, well inside the orbit of the main star's stellar companions. It would be after this jump that *Mervie's* vaunted mimic array would be put to use. Mason hoped it lived up to the hype. *Mervie* had assumed the identity of the independent starfreighter *Surface Tension*, complete with a registry and flag of convenience that Mason suspected were genuine. Flags of convenience were, by definition, easy to get.

Capacitors discharged, and planet Dagon appeared twenty million kilometers away, its huge rings edge-on and practically invisible. After two minutes, more than enough time for the light of *Mervie's* jump flash to reach Dagon Freeport, an incoming transmission icon appeared on the holotank as a man's voice echoed through the speakers.

"Merchant vessel *Surface Tension*, this is Dagon Freeport STC. State your business."

"Okay, Colonel Shimura, this is your show," Captain Vann said.

Colonel Shimura, seated facing the holotank, nodded. "Dagon Freeport, this is merchant vessel *Surface Tension*. My ship's here to drop off passengers on our way to Tien Kang."

"What kind of passengers, *Surface Tension*?"

"The armed kind, Dagon Freeport," she said.

"Mercenaries. Got it. Your shuttle has permission to approach. Make sure it follows the assigned vector."

"Roger that, STC; *Surface Tension* out." Shimura closed the connection and turned to Captain Vann. "I still can't believe you went with 'Surface Tension', Captain."

Captain Vann shrugged. "It was available, Colonel."

"Of course it was," Colonel Shimura said. "Lieutenant Sinclair, Flight Lieutenant Grey, follow me. It's time to get our disguises on."

Mason headed to his quarters to put on his disguise. He had already spent the last few days growing a beard, trying to look more like a scruffy cargo pilot than a clean-cut Federal Space Forces officer. After he changed, he walked out of his quarters wearing a utilitarian jumpsuit that reminded Mason of the kind his parents wore when they were at work. Dark blue, with a black stripe running down the side of each sleeve, it was tailored to fit his lean frame, so it could be easily worn under a spacesuit.

Colonel Shimura walked out of her quarters wearing a beige jumpsuit. Her normally neat hair now a spiked tousle that, he had to admit, looked good on her. Lieutenant Sinclair's transformation was even more impressive. She wore a worn purple jumpsuit with grey highlights, spotted with stains. She looked every inch a civilian engineer. Her hair hung loose, with a simple headband holding the strands away from her face. Her suit was also very snug, showing off the curves of her body.

Sinclair smiled up at him. "You like what you see, Flight Lieutenant?"

"Uh... well, no one's going to mistake you for a Federal Officer," Mason said.

"Fantastic," she said.

"Let's head to Hangar Bay 24. Major Hauer and his team will meet us there," Colonel Shimura said.

Major Hauer, Sergeant Cane, and the dozen other Raiders waited for them outside the airlock to Hangar Bay 24. They were fully armed and armored, but not with standard Federal equipment. Their weapons and gear looked like it came from all over settled space. They all wore matching dull-brown armor, each with bits of personal decoration that would never be tolerated in a regular trooper unit.

Major Hauer saluted Colonel Shimura as they approached, the chest-plate of his armor sporting a stenciled skull. "You look every inch the indie starship captain, sir."

"And you look every bit the two-bit merc, Major Hauer," she said.

"Thank you, sir," he said.

"You got our guns?" Shimura asked.

Major Hauer nodded. "Yes, sir." He nodded to Sergeant Cane, who came forward holding three holstered pistols.

"Excellent." Shimura accepted a holstered pistol from Sergeant Cane and pulled it out to examine it. It was a block of metal and polymer with an ergonomic grip and a small-diameter muzzle. Cane handed the second pistol to Jessica, and the third to Mason.

Mason took the opportunity to draw the pistol out and look at it. The weapon was unloaded, an empty hole in the grip where the magazine would go. Mounted on either side, in easy reach of his thumb, was a fire selected with three different positions.

"You ever use a burst pistol before, Flight Lieutenant?" Colonel Shimura asked.

"No, sir," Mason said. "Only ever practiced with equalizers."

"There's not too much to it. Just set the weapon to burst fire and aim for center mass," Colonel Shimura said. "The rate of fire is so fast that the burst will feel like one shot."

"Ouch," Mason said. He holstered the gun, and clipped the holster to his belt. "Hopefully, we won't have to use these, sir."

"A wise sentiment," Colonel Shimura said.

"Well, just in case you do need to use them, you might want to take a few of these, sir," Sergeant Cane said, holding out a magazine holster with three mags.

Mason accepted the magazines and clipped them to his belt opposite his pistol. "Not much point in an empty gun."

"No, sir," Sergeant Cane said.

"Let's mount up," Shimura said. "Flight Lieutenant Grey, you know what to do."

"Yes, sir," Mason said. He launched himself through the airlock and into the hauler's open cargo hold without touching the deck in between.

Buttercup was typical of haulers carried by starfreighters all over settled space. Big as an assault shuttle, she was a squat, rectangular craft resting on short landing struts that kept the nozzle of her single longburn drive half a meter off the docking pad. The hauler was a tail-lander, with the cockpit at the top. Mason floated up the ladder that ran up the middle of the ship, bypassing the main galley and crew quarters before entering the cockpit. Unlike a Lightning, *Buttercup* sported a full bubble canopy, giving Mason a clear view of the outside without having to link his brainset to the hauler's sensors. He strapped himself down into the seat and started powering up the hauler's systems.

Colonel Shimura had floated up into the cockpit by the time he got the main reactor online.

"How long until we're ready to launch?" she asked.

"Another five minutes until the containment rings for the longburn drive are ready," Mason said.

"Right on schedule," Colonel Shimura said. She strapped herself into the copilot's seat to Mason's right.

"Sir, you're sure no one's going to take offense to me speaking Federal when we get there?" he asked.

"They'll just think you're some merchant pilot far from home, Flight Lieutenant," she said.

"As opposed to a spy, sir?" Mason said.

"Exactly," Colonel Shimura said.

"What about my accent, sir?" Mason asked.

"Nobody is going to care about your Jovian accent out here, Flight Lieutenant," Colonel Shimura said. "You'll be fine. If you're really nervous about giving away your identity, you can always limit your communications to your brainset."

"I'm sure Flight Lieutenant Grey could pull off being the strong silent type," Jessica said as she floated up into the cockpit, taking a seat behind Mason and Shimura.

"I've never known a fighter pilot who didn't like the sound of their own voice," Shimura said. "Major, are your people ready?"

"We just buttoned up the airlock, sir," Hauer said.

"All right, Flight Lieutenant, time to earn your pay," Colonel Shimura said.

"Roger that, sir." Mason opened a connection with *Mervie*. "*Buttercup* to bridge, reactors are hot and drive rings are cold. Requesting permission to launch."

"We read you, *Buttercup*," Captain Vann said. "Depressurizing the hangar."

The external pressure gauge fell as powerful pumps sucked the air out. *Buttercup's* pressure hull popped as the external pressure dropped. A few minutes later, the hangar was evacuated, and the heavy doors separating the hangar from open space swung open.

"You're clear to launch, *Buttercup*."

"Disengaging maglock," Mason said, shutting down the electromagnets holding the hauler to the docking pad. *Buttercup* floated off the docking pad. Mason fired maneuvering thrusters to steady the hauler and ease her out of Hangar Bay 24. It was slow, steady, and with none of the alacrity he was used to when launching a Lightning. Memories of the first time he flew a hauler with his parents out of one of Starport Armstrong's many hangar bays flashed in his memory. *Buttercup* drifted out of the hangar, and away from *Mervie*. Mason fired the maneuvering thrusters to increase the hauler's departure speed.

"Okay, we're far enough away to engage the longburn drive."

Shimura nodded. "Major, are all your people seated?"

"Yes, sir. Upright with the tray tables up too."

Shimura nodded to Mason. "Hit it."

"Igniting longburn drive now," Mason said.

He opened the throttle, and *Buttercup* pushed gently against his back. He gradually increased power to the longburn drive until, thirty seconds after ignition, the hauler was accelerating at 1.5 gs.

Mason locked in the autopilot. "We'll reach Dagon Freeport in eight hours."

Mervie, herself, could have made the trip in similar time, but the lumbering starfreighter she was pretending to be could not. Most starfreighters her size barely had the engine power to do much more than enter a parking orbit. They relied on smaller ships like *Buttercup* to ferry supplies to and from stations. While *Mervie* could mimic an indie starfreighter's EM signature, she couldn't make herself look like one. Getting close would only increase the chances of someone with a telescope spotting *Mervie* and taking note of the fact that she didn't look anything like what their sensors were reporting. She would have to remain where she was, loitering near the jump limit.

Mason spent much of the acceleration burn doing what hauler pilots usually did at such times—babysitting the autopilot broken up by trips to the head. At the halfway point, he took over to flip *Buttercup* over for her braking burn, restored the autopilot, and then got up to get his third packet of coffee from the hauler's galley. After he finished his coffee and tucked the empty packet into one of the many pockets of his jumpsuit, a priority message arrived from *Mervie*, sent via tightbeam. That couldn't be good. They were supposed to be exercising radio silence.

"*Buttercup*, we just got an ID on one of the ships loitering near Dagon Freeport. It's an Ascendency battlecruiser," Captain Vann said. "Target information should be uploaded to your ship now."

"Shit," Shimura said.

The Cendy warship appeared as an icon projected against *Buttercup's* cockpit canopy, right next to Dagon Freeport.

"Well, that's not good," Mason said, grabbing the controls.

"Captain Vann, did that ship just appear out of nowhere?"

"Negative. It was there the whole time. We just had trouble identifying it with all the traffic flying around Dagon Freeport," Captain Vann said. "We only got a firm ID after it fired its station-keeping thrusters."

"Is there anything you can do, Flight Lieutenant?" Colonel Shimura asked.

"Well, it's too late to try and reverse our vector," Mason said. "We'll just come to a stop right in front of them before we start burning back for *Mervie*. What I could do is turn back around, start picking up speed again. We can slingshot around Dagon and run for the jump limit."

"That'll get the attention of the Cendies," Shimura said.

"Not to mention Dagon STC. If either launches fighters to intercept us, they'll catch us before we reach the jump limit," Mason said.

"You can't get more thrust out of the engines?" Shimura asked.

"I can coax more acceleration if we dump most of our propellant," Mason said. "But *Buttercup's* hull's only rated for two gs."

"Right. I'll call in the 4th and get their fighters to escort us out," Shimura said.

"Wait," Jessica said.

"What is it, Lieutenant?" Shimura said.

"With respect, Colonel, I think you're acting a bit hastily," Jessica said. "Look at the traffic around the station. Do you notice something?"

Mason looked, and noticed the steady flow of small ships moving to and from the station, paying the Ascendency warship no mind. "Seems as far as the locals are concerned, it's business as usual."

"Exactly," Jessica said. "I don't think we've blundered into an Ascendency ambush. I think that they might just be here coincidently."

"Why would an Ascendency warship be loitering so openly by an independent station?" Shimura asked.

"That's something we should find out, sir," Jessica said. "We're intelligence officers, after all."

Shimura nodded and turned back to Mason. "Maintain current vector, Flight Lieutenant. If the local traffic isn't reacting to the presence of the Cendies, we shouldn't either."

"Right. I'll just keep it casual," Mason said.

"Captain Vann, be advised we're proceeding with the mission as planned," Shimura said.

Mervie's reply came in via tightbeam. "Understood, Colonel. I have Wing Commander Cade on alert. His pilots can launch as soon as we get the word."

"Acknowledged, Captain. Hopefully, we won't end up needing them. Shimura out."

Buttercup coasted the rest of the way to Dagon Freeport. Mason approached from above the plane of the station's orbit around Dagon, vectored for the docking bay on the top of the central spine. The station orbited inside a gap in Dagon's enormous rings carved out by a small moon in an opposing orbit. The station had a long, thin spine that ran parallel to Dagon's poles, with six spinning habitat rings stacked one atop the other.

Mason was only sparing a part of his attention towards the station.

Most of his attention, and all the attention of Colonel Shimura and Jessica, was focused on the Ascendency battlecruiser loitering near the station.

"I knew I should have had better sensors installed on this thing," Shimura said. "We're probably the first Federals to get this close to one of their ships without getting shot at."

"I wouldn't lament about that too much, sir." Jessica hunched over the sensor station, as if to help her absorb the raw data more easily. "We're getting a pretty good look at that thing, as is."

The Ascendency battlecruiser was a long, almost spike-like pyramid, with engines at the base and the muzzle of the spinal gun sticking out of the apex. It was north of a million tons at least, a full kilometer in length, but the starship lacked a spinning hab module that most large warships had. If Emissary Jerome was to be believed, the crew didn't need it. Towards the rear of the ship, mounted on racks on the side of the hull, were claw-like Ascendency fighters. Each Cendy fighter had three reverse-geometry fins, each tipped by an engine nacelle. The three wings met at a central nacelle, which Mason suspected housed the pilot. If it had a pilot, that is. There was so much they didn't know about the Ascendency, he was hesitant to assume their fighters were manned.

"It's really quite ingenious how they designed their ships," Jessica said.

"What do you mean, Lieutenant?" Shimura asked.

"That long spinal gun gives them an advantage in effective range over our battleships. And the way they carry their fighters—a few on every ship instead of stuffing them all in a carrier—really allows them to bring massed strikecraft to bear."

"I see your point, Lieutenant," Shimura said. "It's almost like they designed their ships specifically to counter ours."

"Well, it's pretty clear they've been planning to attack the Earth Federation and the League for some time," Jessica said. "It would make sense that they designed their ships specifically to kill ours."

"But who are they? Where did they come from?" Colonel Shimura asked. "And how in the hell did they get the resources to build so many ships?"

"Well, the resource question is pretty easy to answer," Jessica said. "You have basically unlimited resources out in space. All you need is an industrial base big enough to exploit it."

"And without getting detected by the people you're about to attack," Colonel Shimura said. "That couldn't have been easy."

"Hopefully, our little sojourn here will help us find some answers, sir," Lieutenant Sinclair said. "It's almost tempting to try and get closer to the Ascendency ship. Perhaps we could try to sneak some of Colonel Hauer's troopers aboard?"

"And how do we do that without getting shredded by point defenses?" Mason asked.

"No idea," she said.

"Let's focus on the mission at hand," Colonel Shimura said. "The presence of one of their ships might just be a good sign, and an indication that Mister Cordial has an idea what the Ascendency is up to out here."

Mason nodded, but his attention was focused on the Ascendency warship, and he felt something hot burn in the pit of his stomach. If only he had a few torpedoes that he could drop on an intercept trajectory, but he didn't have any. He just had the hauler and its passengers who expected him to safely convey them to Dagon Freeport and then back home after their business there was complete.

Buttercup flew past the Ascendency warship, which paid no more mind to her than she did to the dozens of other smallcraft flittering through the space around the station.

"*Buttercup* to Dagon STC, requesting permission to dock," Mason said.

"*Buttercup*, take position in the queue lining up to enter the Northern docking bay."

"Roger that, STC," Mason said.

A marker appeared on the screen where STC wanted him to fly his ship. Following it, Mason tucked the hauler behind a fuel hauler, presumably emptied from a trip out to one of the starfreighters loitering near the edge of the jump limit. Twenty smallcraft were ahead of him, including passenger haulers like *Buttercup*, tanker haulers like the vessel before them, container haulers lugging boxes of cargo larger than *Buttercup* herself, and various passenger shuttles. Towards the front of the line, near the entrance to the station's docking facilities, was a yacht with an ivory-white hull and golden trimming. The kind of garish decorations that served no purpose other than to look impressive in dock. The line moved at a deliberate pace.

An hour after slipping in behind the fuel hauler, they neared the northern entrance to the station, more ships behind them than were in front of them when they first got into the docking queue.

Mason considered himself lucky they arrived when they did.

"*Buttercup*, you may proceed into the Northern Dock. Proceed to Docking Pad 31."

"Docking Pad 31. Acknowledged, STC," Mason said. He pulsed the maneuvering thrusters and coasted *Buttercup* inside.

The northern docking bay was a large cylinder, lined with docking pads all along the interior, most of them occupied with a ship of some kind. Docking Pad 31 was towards the back of the massive chamber. Mason let inertia carry *Buttercup* to the back, before pulsing the maneuvering thrusters again to arrest the hauler's motion, then pitched the craft up to face her tail towards the docking pad and lowered the landing gear. With one last push of the maneuvering thrusters, Mason backed the hauler towards the docking pad. The landing gear contacted the docking pad and the electromagnets engaged, securing the hauler.

"Okay, we're here," Mason said.

"Good flying, Flight Lieutenant," Shimura said.

"Thanks, sir," Mason said.

"It's almost too bad you decided to become a fighter pilot instead of getting a real job," Shimura said.

"Yes, sir, a real shame that," Mason said, but Colonel Shimura had already drifted down the ladder, Jessica close behind.

Mason sighed and unbuckled himself from his seat. He pushed himself to the ladder and floated down into the main hold. Major Hauer's troopers were already out of their seats, floating about with weapons and equipment secured to their armor.

Colonel Shimura was speaking with Major Hauer.

"Locked 'N Loaded is not far from Mister Cordial's club," Colonel Shimura said. "It's a merc bar, so your squad won't look out of place there. In fact, you'll probably have more than a few shady types try to hire you."

"In which case, I'll break out the standard response, sir," Major Hauer said.

"Good. I would encourage your troopers to order drinks," Shimura said. "Just don't go overboard. Light beer. No spirits."

"I'll make sure my people don't overindulge, sir." Major Hauer nodded towards Mason. "You think the flyboy and your analyst will be enough? I can have a couple of my Raiders go with you."

"That'll send the wrong message," Shimura said. "Flight Lieutenant Grey and Lieutenant Sinclair should be enough."

"Understood, sir," Major Hauer said. "If things go sour, we'll come running."

"I expect you to," Shimura said. She turned to Mason. "Ready, Flight Lieutenant?"

"Ready, sir," Mason said.

"Follow me," Shimura said.

Mason and Jessica followed her down the docking tube, and into the pressurized part of the station. From there, it was an elevator ride towards the spin hub of the Red Ring. Another elevator ride, and they stepped out into the sultry red lights of the Red Ring itself.

The beats of dance music throbbed through the hazy air. Holograms advertising various bars, bordellos, massage parlors, and strip clubs shimmered above tightly packed buildings. It all had the effect of concealing the fact that Red Ring was a big tube wrapped around itself. It had more the feel of a crowded city street than a space station.

"Wow." Jessica turned around, taking it all in.

"Impressed?" Mason said.

"Yes. This place is grand." She returned her attention to Mason. "How many times did you visit?"

"Red Ring? Just the once," Mason said. "During my first leave on this station."

"Only once?" Jessica said with disbelief.

"Once was enough," Mason said.

"How ever did you manage two tours of duty in this system and only visit the Red Ring once?" Jessica asked.

"I never needed to pay for what this place offered," Mason said.

"Focus, you two. There will be a lot of eye-candy all around, but remember we're here on a mission," Colonel Shimura said. "Remember to play your roles."

"I'm an engineer who has been cooped up in a starship for weeks. I am playing my part," Jessica said.

"Fair enough, but please don't forget to watch my back while you window-shop," Shimura said.

"Good thing I can do both," she said.

Mason shrugged. As he walked, he felt the weight of the pistol hanging from his jumpsuit's utility belt. It was clear that openly carrying a gun was not an unusual sight on Dagon Freeport. It seemed most of the patrons browsing the Red Ring were packing heat, even some of the prostitutes dancing in the windows of the brothels they passed. Some wore gun belts and nothing else.

"I feel like I'm in a candy store," Jessica said as they walked by a nude woman covered in glowing pink body paint.

"Some of them are probably named after candy," Mason said.

"You're probably right," Jessica said. "What would be your name?"

"Pardon?"

She nodded to a man gyrating in another glass booth as they passed it. "If you were like him."

"Eh… you know, I've never really thought what my stage name would be," Mason said.

"Think of one," she said.

"Why? Are you suggesting I take up the guise of a prostitute?"

"There's an idea," Colonel Shimura said.

Not her, too. Mason sighed. "Fine. Thruster."

"Thruster? Oh, because you're a pilot. Double entendre; I like it," Jessica said.

"And what would your stage name be?" Mason asked.

"Easy," she said, smiling. "Wires."

"Wires, huh?" Mason said.

"Yep," Jessica said with a broad smile. Then she saw something ahead and scampered up to a shop, its windows showing all kinds of elaborately decorated prosthetic limbs. Arms with golden inlays, reverse-articulated legs ending in polished silver talons, glowing prosthetic eyes that changed color every couple of seconds.

"Oh, wow," Jessica said. "Now, those look fancy."

"And expensive," Mason said.

"Also, not relevant to the task at hand," Colonel Shimura said. "So, get moving. You can go shopping on your own time."

"Yes, sir," Jessica said.

Mason's curiosity was piqued by Jessica's interest in rather garish cybernetics. She didn't seem to sport any herself, though the Federal Space Forces had pretty strict regulations on the shape and appearance of any prosthetics a Spacer could have installed. That would have to be a question he'd ask later, after the mission. He continued to follow Colonel Shimura until she came to a stop.

"This is the place," Colonel Shimura said, standing before an establishment that stood out as an island of restrained taste among a sea of garish lighting and tacky decor. There were no windows in the front of the building. It was just a facade of matte basalt blocks trimmed with grey granite. A pair of large double doors was the only entrance. The two burly men standing outside the doors made it clear that the place was not meant for the general public.

"Uh, you sure I can't wait outside?" Mason asked.

"Just follow my lead and we'll be fine," Colonel Shimura said. "We'll be safe enough in there."

"Uh, right," Mason said.

As they approached the club, the two immaculately dressed guards gave them blank stares from behind their shades. Their hands rested at their sides, in easy reach of the weapons they no doubt had hidden under their jackets. The hands of the guard on the left were rugged grey polymer, the fingertips covered in darker grey grip pads. Mason's gaze went up the guard's arm, wondering where the machine ended and the meat began.

It was robo-hands who spoke first. "You have an invitation?"

"Cordial's expecting us," she said.

The man didn't answer. Probably speaking with someone in the club subvocally. Robo-hands and his partner stepped aside, clearing the way to the entrance. "You can go in," he said in brainset-translated Exospeak. "Leave your weapons with the receptionist."

The receptionist sat behind a large black metal desk like a queen sitting on her throne. She had a strange asymmetrical haircut and an artificial left eye that was an unnatural shade of blue. A wave of black hair fell from the top of her head and hung just short of her left shoulder. The back and sides of her head were shaved. She wore a finely cut black vest with a high collar that exposed her marble-colored cybernetic arms up to the shoulders. A stylized dragon in relief coiled around each arm, the whiskers of their nostrils stopping just short of her wrists.

"You can leave your weapons with me," she said in Federal with just a hint of an accent. "You can claim them after your meeting with Mister Cordial."

Colonel Shimura removed her holstered weapon from her belt and set it onto the reception desk. A mechanical hand grabbed the weapon and pulled it under the desk.

The receptionist's eyes, one dark brown, the other inhumanly blue, fixed on Mason.

"Uh, here you go," Mason said, depositing his pistol on the desk. The receptionist nodded and collected the weapon.

Jessica set her pistol on the desk. "I love what you've done with yourself."

The receptionist blinked in surprise. "Oh?"

"Oh, yes. I love what you did with the arms," Jessica said. "The polished marble goes great with your hair."

The receptionist smiled. "Well, thank you for noticing. It's always nice to meet someone with good taste."

"Don't mention it," Jessica said.

The receptionist turned to Colonel Shimura. "Mister Cordial will be waiting in the second-floor lounge." She gestured with a marble-colored hand. "Take the stairs on the right past that door."

Shimura nodded. "Let's not keep him waiting."

"Yes, sir," Jessica said, following behind Shimura.

Mason followed behind Jessica and Shimura. They passed through the door into a foyer. On the floor was a large carpet with an artistic interpretation of the Fomalhaut system sewn into it. He noted a couple more cybernetically enhanced guards flanking the stairs the receptionist had indicated.

"I'm sensing a theme here," Mason said.

"The security firm Mister Cordial uses likes to hire visibly augmented people," Colonel Shimura said. "Helps up their intimidation factor."

"It certainly does that," Mason said.

They climbed up the stairs, past a black door with "Private" stenciled in gold leaf lettering across its face. Inside, there was a lounge filled with black leather furniture and black tables. Two guards and a bartender occupied the room, but it was devoid of guests.

"So, I guess we wait?" Mason asked.

One of the guards gestured towards an open door with a metal hand. It was where the singing was coming from. "Mister Cordial is waiting for you on the balcony," he said in Federal.

They followed the guard's direction out onto a balcony overlooking the main floor of the club. Well-dressed guests sat at round tables as they watched a woman in a sparkling blue gown with shimmering white hair and pale skin sing to the beat of the band seated behind her. Waiters and waitresses in tuxedoes flowed between the tables with trays of drinks.

Mister Cordial sat in a high-backed chair with his back towards them, watching the performance, hand dancing to the beat of the song. The back of his head was a mass of pale scar tissue.

"Mister Cordial?" Colonel Shimura said.

"Federal Intelligence is always so punctual," Mister Cordial said, a slight trill accenting his Federal. He rose from his seat and turned around. His face was a scarred mask, both eyes replaced by solid black prosthetics. "I hear your people have been having trouble as of late. Losing Jupiter, along with the rest of Outer Sol. How do you manage a thing like that?"

"By not knowing what we need to about our enemies," Colonel Shimura said. "I understand you could help us with that."

Mister Cordial gestured as if he was pointing at something outside his club. "I take it you saw the curious starship loitering outside this station."

"It didn't escape notice," Colonel Shimura said.

"Curious bunch, the Ascendancy," Mister Cordial said. "I'm not sure what madness has possessed them to attack both the Earth Federation and the League but, I must say, their results thus far have been most impressive."

"Do you know why they're here?" Colonel Shimura asked.

"To make introductions, it seems," Mister Cordial said. "One of their emissaries is here to meet with the station's government. It seems they wish to contact the leaders of the various organizations that call Fomalhaut home."

"You're the leader of the biggest of those organizations, Mister Cordial," Shimura said. "Have you met with them?"

"Not directly, no," Mister Cordial said. "They're still speaking with the station's official government. Those people are so desperate to make themselves relevant, they've tied up the Ascendency's emissary for the whole week they've been here."

"So, they arrived a week ago?" Shimura said. "That would have been after you sent your message."

"Yes, it seems events are proceeding faster than either of us anticipated," Mister Cordial said. "Let's return to the lounge so we can discuss what's going on in quieter surroundings."

They followed Mister Cordial back through the lounge, his bodyguards leading the way, opening the door and taking position to either side. Cordial walked over to the bar while his bodyguards closed the doors behind Mason, cutting off the singing from the dance floor. Shimura and Jessica sat on one of the large couches. Mason went to join them and settled into the impressive cushions of the couch. Cordial walked up with a shot glass of some amber liquid in one hand, and a slate in the other.

He handed the slate to Shimura. "These are the reports of unusual activity my associates have informed me of—encounters with ships much like the one loitering outside our station, visiting independent systems far outside either Federal or League space."

Shimura handed the slate to Jessica, who immediately got to reading it.

"Already getting to work, I see," Mister Cordial said.

"She's an analyst; it's her job," Shimura said.

Cordial's black eyes locked on Mason. "And what of this one?"

"I'm the pilot, sir," Mason said.

Cordial chuckled. "He actually called me sir, like I'm a general or something."

"General Cordial doesn't have the same ring to it," Mason said before he could stop himself.

Cordial chuckled again. "No, it doesn't, but it doesn't always stop my peers. So many style themselves as general this, admiral that, or lord whatsit. I never quite understood what it is about pirate lords needing to adopt such prefixes."

"Uh, you're a pirate lord too, sir," Mason said.

"True, though I prefer to think of myself as a businessman," Mister Cordial said. "You'd be surprised how much of my income comes from legitimate businesses such as the one you're sitting in today."

"But you still do piracy," Mason said.

"Yes, but not directly anymore," Mister Cordial said. "That's the nice thing about being a pirate lord." He waved around the room with his empty hand. "I can stay in a nice place like this, while I have someone else take the risk of bushwacking some starfreighter in deep space."

"Seems like quite the setup," Mason said.

"It is, isn't it?" Mister Cordial said. "And it's one that I would like to maintain."

"Is that why you're helping us?" Mason asked. "Because you want to maintain your position?"

"Of course. I didn't catch your name."

"Mason Grey, sir," Mason said.

"Mister Grey," Cordial said. "As a businessman, I like stability. The Ascendency represents a disruptive force that I would like to keep out of Fomalhaut, if at all possible."

"But you got in power because of the Federal Occupation disrupting the status quo," Mason said.

"Yes, disruptions are good when you're looking to climb to the top," Mister Cordial said. "But when you're at the top, you don't want things to shake too much. It can be a very long fall should you lose your footing."

"So that's why you're helping us?" Mason asked.

"Yes," Mister Cordial said. "And I also owe Colonel Shimura a favor."

Mason glanced at Shimura. It all fell into place. She had been the one who had helped Mister Cordial become the most powerful pirate lord in Fomalhaut. He was the reason why, since the Occupation ended five years ago, there had been no attacks by Fomalhaut-based pirates against Federal shipping lanes. It occurred to Mason that he didn't really know how long Colonel Shimura's history with the Special Purpose Branch was.

"Jessica?" Shimura asked.

"This is fantastically thorough, Colonel," she said. "They've been having encounters with unknown ships that match the Ascendency going back four years."

"Four years?" Shimura asked. "Why is this the first time I've heard of this, Cordial?"

Cordial shrugged. "Because I didn't know the significance of it. I thought they were just tales, stories. God knows I've heard my share of fanciful rumors from pirates and spacers who have been away for too long. It wasn't until the Ascendency started showing itself that I began giving them a second look."

"Sir, I'm seeing a pattern in these reports," Jessica said.

Cordial glanced at Jessica, eyebrow arched. "She works fast."

"She's a very good analyst," Shimura said.

"I'm chuffed you think so, sir," Jessica said. "A lot of the encounters reported by Mister Cordial's associates take place in systems with mineable gas giants. Some quite recently."

"You mean for fuel?" Mason asked.

"Is there another reason to mine a gas giant?" Jessica asked.

"Does it point to which systems?" Shimura asked.

"Yes," Cordial and Jessica said at the same time.

"Then I think we have an idea of where to go next," Shimura said.

"One of the systems the Ascendency uses for gas mining?" Jessica asked.

"Yes." Shimura stood up. "I'm sorry to cut this visit short, Mister Cordial."

Cordial smiled, a disturbing sight with his scarred face. "I knew this wasn't a social call. I assume this means we are now even."

"If Earth-Fed survives this, then, yes, I would say so," Colonel Shimura said. "Though I expect you to abide by our previous agreements."

"Any pirate from Fomalhaut who preys upon Federal shipping will answer to me," Mister Cordial said. "I will not make the same mistake my predecessors did." He touched his scarred face. "It's a lesson I'm reminded of every time I look in a mirror."

Shimura nodded. "Good." She turned towards the exit. "Let's go."

Mason got up to follow. He noticed Jessica had not yet sat up.

Shimura tapped her shoulder. "Jessica?"

Jessica looked up from the slate. "Just another minute, sir. I haven't finished downloading everything."

"Well, then," Cordial turned to head to the bar, "would you like Keith to fix you something while your analyst finishes up?"

Shimura shook her head. "That won't be–"

A sharp, high-pitched note echoed through Mason's head before cutting off in an instant.

"What the hell was that?"

"Jamming," Colonel Shimura said.

Mason noticed Jessica was doubled over, her head clutched in her hands.

"You okay?" Mason asked.

"Jamming caught me mid-download. Zapped me pretty good," Jessica said. "Felt like a hot spike went through my brain. Scrambled my HUD in the process, too."

Colonel Shimura walked up next to Mason and put a hand on Jessica's shoulder. "We need to move, Lieutenant. Can you get up?"

Jessica looked up to Colonel Shimura, blinking her eyes as if she was having trouble focusing. "Ah, okay. I just did a reset. Didn't get to finish the download."

"We'll just take the slate with us," Colonel Shimura said. "Get up. If there's jamming that means–"

Screams and gunshots drowned out the music from the dance hall.

The two bodyguards standing at the balcony door reacted in an instant, producing short-barreled carbines from beneath their jackets. Just as they shouldered their weapons, the door leading to the balcony exploded. The concussion knocked Mason to the floor. When he got up, there were three faceless figures forcing their way through the broken door. They had slender, muscular bodies, with armored plating bulging beneath their skin. But it was their blank faces that seared themselves into Mason's mind.

Despite standing right next to the blast, neither bodyguard was stunned. The one on the right rammed his shoulder into one of the faceless grey things, knocking them into their comrades before they could bring their weapons to bear. The bodyguard on the left brought up his carbine and fired three bursts at point-blank range into the intruders. The faceless attackers dropped to the ground, their torsos perforated by close-range bursts of automatic fire, ooze leaking from the holes.

The bodyguards moved to cover the door, but not before an object came flying in. Jessica snatched it out of the air and immediately threw it back through the balcony door. A sharp bang stung Mason's ears while a flash of light burned a rectangular after-image of the door in his vision. Blind, he crawled behind the couch and rubbed his eyes, the staccato of full-auto gunfire almost drowning out the ringing in his ears. A strong hand grabbed Mason's jumpsuit and pulled him to his feet.

"Get out of the line of fire," Colonel Shimura shouted over the gunshots.

By the time Mason's vision cleared, he was crouched behind the bar with Colonel Shimura and the bartender, who was flat on the floor, hands covering his head.

"Well, this is a bad time to be caught without a gun," Shimura said.

"Where's Lieutenant Sinclair?" Mason said. He tried to look over the bar, but Colonel Shimura pulled him down.

"She's on the other side of the lounge, keeping her head down. You should do the same," Shimura said.

"What the hell are those things?" Mason said.

"Some kind of Ascendency assassins, I would think," Colonel Shimura said.

"Belts and zones, the surprises never end with those fuckers, does it?" Mason said.

Someone leapt over the bar, and almost landed on top of the cowering bartender.

"My apologies, Keith," Mister Cordial said, patting the man on the shoulder with his left hand while his right clutched a gilded burst pistol. His ruin of a face turned towards Mason and Shimura. He did not look happy. "I don't appreciate it when people bring trouble to my home, Colonel."

"I don't think this is a good time to start assigning blame, Mister Cordial," Shimura said.

"On the contrary, I thin–"

A faceless thing, muscle and armor plating bulging under its grey skin, jumped over the bar and landed right among them. Up close. Mister Cordial tried to bring his burst pistol to bear, but a long, thin arm lashed out, and the weapon went flying out of reach. Mason got up to try and tackle it. The thing spun about, and Mason caught a blow on the side of his head. Stars exploded in his vision as he crashed into glasses and bottles on the back wall of the bar. As the stars faded, Mason saw Colonel Shimura wrestling with the faceless thing's weapon, a pistol of some kind. Using the weapon as a lever, she executed a perfect trip, and the thing fell to the ground with Shimura landing on top of it. While she fought for control of the weapon, Mason got up to try to help her, but the ground lurched, and he stumbled to one knee. Strangely, no one else seemed to take notice of the floor tilting to one side.

Shimura managed to pry the weapon away from the thing. Rather than try to figure out how to use the exotic weapon, she simply used it as a club, striking the thing's featureless face. That only seemed to annoy it. It brought its legs up and got its feet under Shimura's armpits and launched her off its body. Shimura managed to land her feet and turned to face the thing, just in time to catch a kick to the knee. There was a wet pop, and Shimura went down, hissing through clenched teeth. The thing was on top of her in an instant, trying to recover its weapon from her.

The room had stopped tilting from side-to-side just enough for Mason to get his feet back under him. He stumbled into the thing, knocking it off Shimura and landing on top of it. He managed to catch the thing's arm and pivoted around, trapping it between the shoulder and elbow with his knees while he leaned back to try and break its arm. It was like trying to pull a bent metal bar straight—the thin muscles were as taut as a coiled rope. Mason pulled back as hard as he could, but the thing continued to pull its arm back despite his leverage advantage.

Mister Cordial stumbled over, put the muzzle of a small pistol up against the thing's head, and fired. The arm suddenly went limp, and Mason fell back.

Cordial's black marble eyes gazed down at him. "I do hate being interrupted."

Mason realized the shooting had stopped, replaced with a tense silence.

The receptionist appeared out of nowhere, holding an impressive looking battle rifle.

Mister Cordial looked to her. "Status?"

"Security shutters are closed, and all hostiles are dead, boss," she said. "They killed Ax and Morgan at the entrance."

"And how did they get past you, Miss Cynth?" Mister Cordial asked.

"Couple of them pinned me down behind my desk, boss," Cynth said. "Got here as soon as I dealt with them."

Jessica rushed over and knelt above Colonel Shimura. "How bad is it?"

"Pretty sure my ACL popped," Colonel Shimura said. "That Cendy sure knew how to throw a kick."

Jessica looked up to Mason. "How about you?"

"The room's stopped moving," Mason said.

"He took a hard blow to the head," Colonel Shimura said. "He's lucky he didn't get knocked out."

"Thank goodness impact protection is standard-issue enactment for the Space Forces," Mason said.

"Yes, very fortunate for you," Mister Cordial said. Mason noticed that the small-bore barrel of the pirate lord's pocket pistol was pointed at him. Cynth's battle rifle was leveled at Shimura.

"Now that the distractions are out of the way, I think I can go about expressing my displeasure at the sloppiness of the Federal Space Forces' Special Purpose Branch."

CHAPTER 10

IT WAS AN odd feeling looking down the barrel of a gun. Mister Cordial's pocket pistol was not a large weapon, but from Mason's point of view, its tiny barrel may as well have been a tunnel with a train barreling towards him.

"It wasn't us they were after, Mister Cordial," Shimura said.

"The timing of your arrival and the Ascendency's attack suggest otherwise, Colonel," Mister Cordial said, never taking his eyes off Mason while he talked to Colonel Shimura. "They saw you enter The Philistine, my home, and moved to attack you here."

"Uh, Mister Cordial, sir, I think you might be jumping to conclusions," Mason said, trying not to think too hard about what Cordial's pistol could do to his skull.

"Am I now, Mister Grey?" Mister Cordial said. "Please enlighten me, then."

Mason tapped the dead Cendy with his foot. "Because this thing didn't kill you when it had the chance, sir. It disarmed you rather than just shoot you."

"Your point?" Mister Cordial said.

"It didn't take interest in either me or Colonel Shimura until we got in its way," Mason said. "My guess? These things came here to capture you."

The barrel of Mister Cordial's gun tilted away from Mason. "So, you're stating that their attack and your arrival are coincidental."

Mason shrugged. "We're just lucky that way, I guess."

"Well, we'll find out what the truth of the matter is. Miss Cynth, can you contact my people in security?" Mister Cordial said.

"I've already tried, boss, but the jamming's blocking all calls out of the club," Cynth said.

"What about the hardline?" Mister Cordial said.

"Dead, boss," Cynth said.

Mister Cordial stopped pointing his gun at Mason. "Indeed? Hmm, you might be correct about my jumping to conclusions, Mister Grey. Do accept my apologies."

"I'll accept them if you promise not to shoot me, or Lieutenant Sinclair and Colonel Shimura," Mason said.

"I second that," Jessica said.

"Thirded," Shimura said.

"Fair enough," Mister Cordial said. "Cynth, help attend to the Colonel's injury."

"Yes, boss." Cynth walked around the bar, but paused, her eyes distant. "Boss?"

"What is it, Miss Cynth?" Mister Cordial said.

"Station security on the cameras. A lot of them," Cynth said.

"Ours?"

"No, boss," she said.

"Curious," Mister Cordial said.

"Uh, is it bad that the cops are showing up?"

"It is when they're not my cops," Mister Cordial said. "Tag, Styles."

The two bodyguards who had guarded the door walked up. Their suits were a total loss, but neither of them looked injured, even though more than a few of the holes in their suits were clearly caused by bullets.

"Yes, Mister Cordial," one of them said. Mason's brainset translated from Exospeak.

"Secure the escape tunnel," Mister Cordial said.

"We bugging out, Mister Cordial?"

"No, we're going to pay a visit to Red Ring's Security Chief," Mister Cordial said. "Find out why he's letting someone else's security in his turf."

"You got it, Mister Cordial. Come on, Styles," said the bodyguard Mason presumed was Tag.

Cynth pulled open a panel in the bar's wall and hauled out a large medkit. She set it down next to Colonel Shimura and opened it.

"So, I take it not all of security is loyal to Mister Cordial?" Mason asked.

Cynth chuckled. "That's not how things work in Dagon Freeport, or anywhere in Fomalhaut for that matter. Not since you guys pulled up stakes and headed home." She pulled out an injector. "This will take the edge off."

"Thanks," Colonel Shimura said.

The injector hissed, and Shimura relaxed. "That's much better."

"That kit have a pair of scissors?" Jessica asked.

"Right here." Cynth pulled out a pair of scissors and handed them to Jessica.

"Thanks," Jessica said.

"Anything I can do to help?" Mason asked.

"I appreciate the sentiment, Flight Lieutenant, but I saw the hit you took to your head. I'd rather not have someone suffering a concussion render first aid," Colonel Shimura said.

"I'm feeling fine now, sir," Mason said. He stood up and was happy to see the floor only wobbled a little.

"Find a comfortable seat, Flight Lieutenant. Let Lieutenant Sinclair take a look at you after she's finished with me," Shimura said.

Mason sighed. "Yes, sir."

Seating wasn't as easy to find as Mason hoped. The well-upholstered furniture inside Mister Cordial's lounge had not fared well in the firefight. Fluffy white foam spilled out of gaping holes in the leather, making it look like a cloud had exploded inside the lounge. Mason opted to sit on an undamaged bar stool and rest his elbows on the bar.

He noticed the bartender still sitting down in the corner, arms wrapped around his legs.

"Hey, you okay?" Mason asked.

"Eh?"

"Are you hurt?" Mason asked.

"I, uh…" The young man looked himself up and down, like he wasn't sure if he was hit in the first place. "I do not think so." His Federal was passable.

"Think you could get some ice? I can feel a bruise coming on," Mason said.

"Uh, ice. I can do that," the bartender said. He produced a ball of ice likely intended to cool a glass of whisky and wrapped it in a napkin before handing it to Mason.

"Thanks." Mason pressed the wrapped ball of ice on the spot where the Cendy assassin struck him.

Jessica helped Colonel Shimura up while Cynth repacked the medkit. Her jumpsuit's right leg was cut above the knee, which itself was wrapped in a black fabric brace. Shimura also had some seriously toned legs, if the exposed right leg was any indication.

Mister Cordial walked up. "Can you walk?"

Shimura nodded. "I can, but not quickly."

Shiny black eyes turned to Mason. "And you?"

Mason got up from the barstool, still holding the ice to his cheek. The floor remained rock-steady. "I'm mobile. Where are we going?"

"To the local security headquarters, Flight Lieutenant," Mister Cordial said. "We need to find out what's going on, and I can't do it while this club is cut off from the rest of my properties on this station."

Mason looked to Colonel Shimura. "Shouldn't we try and contact Major Hauer's team, sir?"

"Got to get out of this jamming, first, Flight Lieutenant," Colonel Shimura said. "We could also use the security station's network access to try and contact them." She turned to Mister Cordial. "Assuming your people there will let us."

"I'm more than willing to enlist the services of any backup you brought, Colonel," Mister Cordial said.

"Then let's head out," Colonel Shimura said. "You think you could give us back our guns by any chance?"

"Miss Cynth, please go recover our guests' weapons and meet us at the escape tunnel," Mister Cordial said.

Cynth tightened the sling of her battle rifle. "On it, boss."

Mason moved to help Jessica carry Shimura, but Jessica bore the weight of the larger woman easily.

"I've got this, flyboy."

They followed Mister Cordial down the stairs. The lobby was an unholy mess. The reception desk was pitted and dented in a hundred places. Two grey bodies lay on the ground, and the main entrance was blocked by a slab of segmented metal.

Cynth walked out from behind her ruined desk, holding three gun belts. "Here you go," she said.

Mason took the gunbelts and handed one each to Jessica and Shimura, before belting on his own.

They proceeded to follow Mister Cordial down another, much more austere, flight of stairs leading to the sub-surface level of his club. It was all exposed piping and tile flooring, with none of the opulence of the club above.

Tag and Styles waited near the entrance to the narrow escape tunnel, carbines at the ready.

"Sent drones into the tunnel, Mister Cordial," Tag said in Exo that Mason's brainset translated and turned into text on his HUD. "Looks clear."

"Good," Mister Cordial replied in Exo. "You two lead the way." He turned around and spoke in Federal. "Colonel Shimura, your people should follow behind me. Miss Cynth will take up the rear."

"Where does this tunnel go?" Colonel Shimura said.

"To the sub-surface maintenance tunnels that make up the bottom levels of the Red Ring," Mister Cordial said. "From there, we head about a thousand meters anti-spinward towards Red Ring's security headquarters."

"You think that will be safe?" Colonel Shimura asked. "Escaping into the sewers isn't the most original method of avoiding detection."

"And, yet, it is still effective, provided one takes the necessary precautions," Mister Cordial said. "Tag's drones will keep an eye out for trouble long before we run into it, be it hostile security or more Ascendency assassins."

"In that case, Mister Cordial, lead the way," Colonel Shimura said.

Mister Cordial nodded and turned to enter the escape tunnel.

Shimura, with Jessica propping her up, followed. The tunnel was barely wide enough for the two of them to walk next to each other. Mason followed behind Jessica and Shimura, while Cynth backpedaled into the tunnel, and closed the door behind them. She continued walking backwards down the incline of the tunnel the whole way, holding her black battle rifle in her marble arms. A glint of something on the shaved back of Cynth's head caught Mason's attention, and when he squinted to get a better look, he realized they were camera lenses.

"Yes, I have eyes on the back of my head," Cynth said, her voice echoing down the tunnel.

"Oh, that's brilliant," Jessica said.

"I know, right? Had them installed a couple years ago. Saved me from getting shot in the back twice since then," Cynth said.

"Sounds like your investment paid off," Mason said.

"Yeah, replacing cracked sub-dermal plates is a pain," Cynth said.

As they neared the end of the tunnel, Mason detected a faint but growing odor of raw sewage.

"Belts and zones," Mason said. "I should have brought a pressure suit."

The tunnel ended in a utility room of dull-grey metal. The floor was metal grates covering exposed piping that clicked with every step, the sound echoing down the corridors. After a thousand meters of echoing footsteps and bad smells, they arrived at a ladder.

"Tag, make sure the top is clear," Mister Cordial said.

"Yes, Mister Cordial," Tag said. He climbed up the ladder. There was a faint buzzing noise as a trio of drones flew up the ladder after him.

Mason walked up to see Tag lift the hatch at the top of the ladder just enough to let the fist-sized drones fly through.

"Alley's clear," Tag said.

"You and Styles secure the top," Mister Cordial said.

"On our way up, Mister Cordial," Tag said.

While the two bodyguards ascended the ladder, Mister Cordial turned to Colonel Shimura. "Once my men give the all-clear, we'll head directly towards the security headquarters."

"And how do we get inside?" Colonel Shimura asked. "Because I hope it doesn't involve walking through the front door."

"We'll use a back entrance. I have the codes to disarm the lock." Mister Cordial's expression became distant for a moment. He smiled. "Ah, my men say it's all clear up top." He grabbed a rung of the ladder. "Please follow me. Miss Cynth will cover us while we climb."

Mason looked to Colonel Shimura. "You think your knee can handle the climb, sir?"

"I can climb using one leg, Flight Lieutenant," Shimura said. "You follow Mister Cordial up."

"Yes, sir," Mason said.

Mason followed Mister Cordial up the ladder, stealing the occasional glance down to make sure Shimura was making her way up. She didn't seem to have too much trouble, letting her injured leg hang free while she relied on her arms and good leg to pull her up. When he reached the top, Mister Cordial held out a gloved hand for Mason. Mason took it and pulled himself through the open hatch. He emerged into the permanent twilight of the Red Ring in a filthy alley between the bare, dirty, white walls of two squat buildings. He helped Colonel Shimura up, and Jessica after her.

Cynth declined assistance and pulled herself out of the manhole with little trouble. While Cynth closed the hatch, Mister Cordial pointed in the anti-spinward direction.

"Security station's two blocks that way. We can get there without going out into the street."

"Have your man's drones spotted any trouble?" Colonel Shimura asked.

"Not as of yet, Colonel," Mister Cordial said. "Mister Tag has sent some of them to scout the security headquarters itself."

"Right. So, should we wait here until they finish searching the head-quarters?" Colonel Shimura asked.

"I think we should keep moving. The drones should be finished scouting the headquarters by the time we walk there," Mister Cordial said.

They proceeded down the alley in the same order as they had in the tunnels below. Tag and Styles in the front; Mister Cordial behind them. Mason, Shimura, and Jessica in the middle. Cynth watching the rear.

Tag came to a stop.

"What is it, Mister Tag?"

"I'm seeing some weird stuff from my drones, Mister Cordial," Tag said. "There are grey-suits manning the checkpoints at the front, but there's no one going in and out of the building itself. All the doors are locked tight."

"Are the grey-suits manning the checkpoints anyone we know?" Mister Cordial asked.

"Drones don't recognize them, Mister Cordial," Tag said. "They're not from the Red Ring."

"That sounds awfully ominous, Mister Cordial," Colonel Shimura said.

"Trust me, Colonel, I share your feelings," Mister Cordial said. "Is the back entrance still clear?"

"It is, Mister Cordial," Tag said.

"Then have your drones form a lookout," Mister Cordial said. "It's time we found out what happened to Chief Rowe and his people."

"Moving the drones now, Mister Cordial."

Mister Cordial turned to Colonel Shimura. "There's a good chance we might be getting into a firefight, Colonel. Keep your heads down and let my people handle it."

"Wait, if you think your security headquarters are compromised, then why are we still going there?" Mason asked.

"Because we can access the Red Ring's security network from there," Mister Cordial said. "Get a better idea of what's going on. Maybe contact my people on other parts of the station."

"If you need help with the security station, Mister Cordial, Lieutenant Sinclair has a full hackware suite," Colonel Shimura said.

Mister Cordial turned to Jessica and nodded. "Indeed? I thought she was an analyst."

"You learn to wear a lot of hats when working for the Special Purpose Branch, Mister Cordial," Jessica said.

"She's right on that count," Mason said.

Mister Cordial glanced towards Mason, then turned his attention back to Jessica. "In that case, let's see if there is anything that requires your talents in the headquarters, Miss Sinclair."

The back entrance wasn't hard to spot. It was a solitary door in the otherwise featureless white wall of the security headquarters. A single LED above the grey metal door illuminated it with a lonely cone of light.

"Not big on windows around here," Mason said.

"Not exactly a lot to see around here, Flight Lieutenant," Mister Cordial said.

Mason looked around the empty alley. "Fair point."

"Indeed," Mister Cordial said. He handed a card to Cynth. "See what's inside."

"On it, boss," Cynth said.

Cynth walked over to the door and waved the card over the scanner. There was a click as the bolt released. Cynth leveled her battle rifle and pushed inside.

"Is anyone going to watch her back?" Mason asked.

"I think she watches her own back just fine," Jessica said.

"Indeed, she does," Mister Cordial said. "Any trouble that runs into Cynth is going to regret the experience."

"So, we just wait until she clears the building by herself?" Mason asked.

"Yes," Mister Cordial said.

After ten minutes, Cynth reappeared, her face grim. "It's ugly in there, boss. Entire headquarters is a slaughterhouse."

"Let's get inside," Mister Cordial said.

Shimura nodded to Mason and, with Jessica's help, hobbled through the back entrance.

They were immediately greeted by the dead bodies of two security personnel, a heavyset man and a middle-aged woman, lying where they had been gunned down. They had been shot in the back, likely while they were fleeing from whomever killed them. Mister Cordial crouched next to the man and flipped him onto his back. His body was so stiff it looked like Cordial was flipping over a board.

Colonel Shimura hobbled up to the body. "You know him?"

Mister Cordial set the man's head down. "This is Sector Chief Javier Rowe, the head of security for the Red Ring. He worked for me." Cordial gestured to the stiff body. "This would explain why no one answered when Cynth called. He's been dead for hours. Long enough for rigor mortis to set in."

"That would have been before we arrived on the station," Mason said.

"You're right, Mister Grey." Mister Cordial stood up and turned around. "It appears I did jump to a conclusion. It seems I owe you all an apology."

"Apologies can wait, Mister Cordial. Let's focus on finding a way out of this mess," Colonel Shimura said.

"Indeed," Mister Cordial said. He nodded to Cynth. "Miss Cynth, please relieve Chief Rowe of his head. We'll need his eyes to open the biometric lock on his console."

"Wait a moment; wait a moment." Jessica extracted herself from under Shimura's arm. "No need to go cutting off anyone's head."

"I wouldn't feel too squeamish, Miss Sinclair," Mister Cordial said. "It's not like he's using his head anymore. Didn't use it that much in life, either."

Jessica knelt over Chief Rowe's body and pulled open his eyes. "It's not that, Mister Cordial. I just have a more efficient way of getting Chief Rowe's eyes on that scanner."

"Uh, what are you doing?" Mason asked.

"Scanning his irises. My eyes can mimic them," Jessica said.

Mason twisted a little. "That is creepy."

"What it is, is useful," Mister Cordial said. "Follow me, Miss Sinclair. We can use the console in Chief Rowe's office. Miss Cynth, with me. Mister Styles, guard the front. Mister Tag, guard the back entrance."

Mason took over helping Colonel Shimura walk, while Jessica followed Mister Cordial to Chief Rowe's office.

There were a lot of bodies in grey security uniforms littering the hallways of the station, and Mason had to help Colonel Shimura step over them. Only the second time in his life he had seen dead bodies, Mason's stomach twisted at the sight of them. He noted that most of them didn't have their weapons drawn.

"The Cendies hit this place," Mason said.

"I was thinking the same, Flight Lieutenant," Colonel Shimura said. "Striking the enemy unawares. That fits their MO."

"Yes, I'm starting to appreciate how your people must be feeling right now, Colonel." Mister Cordial stopped at an open door. "This is it."

Mason followed Jessica inside with Colonel Shimura.

Jessica walked around the desk and sat down in the late security chief's chair.

Mason noticed a coffee mug on the floor, complete with spilled coffee staining the cheap carpeting. Written in Exo on the mug, translated by Mason's brainset, was "Red Ring's Top Cop". Looked like Chief Rowe was about to enjoy a cup of coffee when his station was murdered.

"Poor guy," Mason said.

Colonel Shimura glanced at him. "What?"

"Nothing, sir," Mason said. He helped Shimura settle in the chair in front of the chief's desk.

"And I'm in," Jessica said. "Curious that this station uses biometrics for authentication. That's rather outdated."

"By design. None of the powers that be in Fomalhaut, myself included, would allow this station's security to have up-to-date hardware."

"Yes, it shows," Jessica said. "The coverage on the Red Ring is spotty as hell."

"Also by design," Mister Cordial said.

"Right, right. It wouldn't do on a station run by criminals for security to be able to easily track down said criminals."

"Exactly," Mister Cordial said.

"So, good news and bad news," Jessica said.

"Start with the bad news, if you please, Lieutenant," Mister Cordial said.

"Good, because it's mostly got to do with you," Jessica said. "There's a station-wide security alert ordering the arrest of you and all your known associates, Mister Cordial." She turned the screen around so Mister Cordial could see. "They've got your face plastered on every notification going through the system. From what I can tell, every location on this station that belongs to you is getting hit by security forces not loyal to you, with the assistance of the Ascendency."

Mister Cordial's jaw tightened, flexing the scars covering his face. "It's a coup, and I didn't see it coming."

"I wouldn't be too hard on yourself, Mister Cordial," Mason said. "The Cendies have a talent for blindsiding people."

Mister Cordial leaned close to the screen, his black prosthetic eyes glistening with reflected light. "It appears this is far worse than I thought. Any ally that I thought I could call upon for help is either dead or under attack. Looks like they've put all the ships I own, or are owned by my allies, under lockdown."

"Well, there are two pieces of good news," Jessica said. "First, it looks like security wants to take you alive, Mister Cordial."

"Likely as a hostage to get the rest of my organization in line," Mister Cordial said.

"A fair plan, if true," Jessica said. "Also, based on what I'm reading off the security feeds, there's no sign anyone is aware that there are Federal personnel active on this station."

"So, you're saying that you, me, and Colonel Shimura can move around the station without drawing suspicion?" Mason asked.

"If we're careful, yes," Jessica said.

"So, we just need to find a safe place for Mister Cordial to lie low while we find Major Hauer's squad," Mason said.

Colonel Shimura nodded. "Seems like a logical next step. We should get out of this building before someone takes notice of the fact a dead man just logged into his console."

Mister Cordial's eyes became distant. "Too late."

Jessica put an exterior camera feed onto the security chief's monitor. On it, dozens of security personnel formed a grey wall in front of the Red Ring's security headquarters. Peppered among them were the sleek, faceless forms of Ascendency soldiers.

"They must have been expecting I'd come here," Mister Cordial said. "Seems I've become predictable."

"We need to get out of here before they storm the building." Colonel Shimura held out her hand and Mason took it, putting his shoulder under hers.

"Agreed," Mister Cordial said.

"You coming?" Shimura said to Jessica.

"Just a moment. I'm almost finished," Jessica said.

"With what?" Shimura asked.

"Creating a new profile. I'll explain later," Jessica said. "Done."

"All right, let's move," Shimura said.

CHAPTER 11

TAG AND STYLES were waiting for them when they reached the back entrance, the hulking bodyguards crouched with their backs to each other, holding their carbines at their shoulders.

"We've got movement in the alleys, Mister Cordial," Tag said. "We're going to have to shoot our way out."

"Take the lead, Miss Cynth," Mister Cordial said. "Plow us a path."

"On it, boss," Cynth said. She turned to Tag and Styles. "Time to earn our pay."

Mister Cordial drew his pistol. Shimura did the same. Mason would have drawn his gun, but he was busy helping hold Shimura up. He didn't complain too much. As a trooper, Shimura would be a better shot. Jessica took up the rear with her pistol ready.

The three cyborg bodyguards led the way, guided by Tag's drones, presumably giving early warning to movements from the alley.

Cynth lifted her assault rifle into the air and fired a burst. A faceless body landed on the ground limp. Mason looked up just in time to see a rain of grey faceless figures descend on them, some falling to the ground dead as Cynth and the other bodyguards shot them down, but more landing on their feet, weapons ready.

In the close confines of the alley, the roar of the battle rifle was deafening. A faceless grey body crashed into the ground to Mason's left, causing him to lose his balance. He and Shimura went tumbling down as more landed on their feet. As bodies fell to the ground and the alley filled with the sound of close-quarters automatic fire, Mason scrambled for his gun. Tag knocked over a faceless Cendy and planted a boot on their chest before unloading a burst into their face, but then was dropped by a burst to the back by a Cendy who landed behind him.

Styles fired his carbine in full auto as he swept it across the alley, catching two Cendies, before the third dropped him with a shot to the head. Mister Cordial brought his weapon up and then spasmed, dropping his gun as he fell to the ground. A Cendy landed in front of Jessica and shot her in the stomach. Unperturbed, Jessica grabbed the barrel of a Cendy's rifle and yanked it, pulling herself close as she placed the barrel of her burst pistol under the chin of the Cendy and squeezed the trigger, sending a spray of blood and brains out the top of the Cendy's head.

By the time he pulled the gun out of his holster, the fight was done. Long faceless bodies littered the floor of the alley, along with Tag, Styles, and Mister Cordial. The only ones left standing were Jessica and Cynth, and neither was uninjured. Cynth's left arm was severed above the elbow, exposing wires and broken strands of artificial muscle. Jessica had a hole in her stomach.

Mason got up. "You're hit."

Jessica looked down and probed the wound with her hand. "I am, aren't I?"

Cynth crouched over Mister Cordial and set down her battle rifle with her functioning arm to look over him. Shimura sat up, her pistol at the ready.

"You should sit down," Mason said to Jessica. "I'll get the medkit from Cynth."

"It's not that bad," Jessica said.

Mason spared a moment to glance at the hole in her side, then back up to her face. "That looks pretty bad to me."

Jessica held up a reassuring hand, showing no signs that her very serious-looking bullet wound was causing her any pain. "I know what it looks like, and I'm telling you that it's not that bad for me. Help me pick up Colonel Shimura, so we can get out of here."

Mason noticed Cynth reach under Mister Cordial's body and load him onto her shoulder one-handed. "What are you doing?"

"He's not dead. They hit him with a stun dart," Cynth said. "You were right about them wanting him alive."

"Where do we go?" Mason asked.

She nodded towards a barely lit alley that didn't seem to lead anywhere. "How about that way?"

Mason didn't know why she picked that particular direction but didn't feel he had the time to ask questions. He and Jessica hooked their arms under Colonel Shimura's shoulders and carried her between them.

"We're not going to make it," Shimura said.

"We can if we hustle," Mason said, picking up his pace.

Cynth came to a stop. "No, she's right, I can hear them closing in around us."

Mason came to a stop behind her. "What do we do?"

"Set me down, both of you," Shimura said.

They set Shimura against a grey plastic wall, footsteps and voices echoing through the alley and growing closer by the second.

"Lieutenant Sinclair," Shimura said.

"Yes, sir?"

"You take Flight Lieutenant Grey and find Major Hauer," Shimura said.

"You can't ask us to abandon you, sir," Mason said.

"I'm not asking, I'm ordering. And you're not abandoning me," Colonel Shimura said. "You're going to find Major Hauer and get him and his raiders to rescue me, Cynth, and Mister Cordial."

"Mister Cordial would appreciate a rescue," Cynth said. "As would I."

"And how do we find you after we take you?" Mason asked.

"I managed to create a backdoor account while using Chief Rowe's identity," Jessica said. "I should be able to access the security network without anyone noticing and track down wherever security takes the colonel."

"See? We already have a solution to that problem," Colonel Shimura said. "Security shouldn't be on the lookout for you two, but only if you get out of here and find a place to hide. Right now."

Jessica took Mason by the shoulder. "Come on, we need to go."

Mason sighed, nodded, and followed Jessica down the alley.

She ran up to a dumpster and lifted the lid. "In here."

"Seriously?"

"This is not the time for an argument," Jessica said. "Get in!"

"Ah, belts and zones," Mason said. He pinched his nose and climbed inside. Jessica followed right behind and closed the lid.

The garbage was soft and moist in ways Mason didn't want to think about, inspiring him to keep his nose pinched tightly shut. A thin line of reddish light leaking through the dumpster's lid was the only illumination. Barely enough for him to see Jessica lying in the trash in front of him.

She held her finger to her lips.

The thumps of boots—lots of boots—echoed outside the plastic walls of the dumpster. Voices shouted out in Exo, too muffled by distance and the dumpster to make out. His brainset couldn't translate, but the tone was easy enough to read. It sounded like they were commanding someone to surrender. The echoed shouts and lack of any weapons fire seemed to indicate that Shimura and Cynth had complied. There were more footsteps, more voices, and maybe the sound of handcuffs clicking together. Mason assumed those were for Shimura and the unconscious Mister Cordial. He wasn't sure what the procedure was for restraining a one-armed cyborg. The boots and voices faded away, some moving right past the plastic dumpster Mason and Jessica were hiding in. Mason felt the grip of his pistol as he saw shadows break up the thin line of light, and then relief as the sound of the boots faded out of hearing range.

After several minutes, Jessica opened the lid to the dumpster and looked out.

"I think we're clear," she said.

Mason climbed out of the dumpster. There was nothing in the alley other than pools of condensation and loose garbage. He took a preliminary sniff of his forearm and recoiled.

"Not a fan of the smell of wet garbage?" Jessica asked.

"Not especially, no." Mason took another sniff and sighed. "Well, it's not that strong. Just remind me to take a shower when we get back aboard *Mervie*."

"Not before I do, but let's find those Raiders and see if we can't use them to sort out this mess, yeah?" Jessica said. She gestured for him to follow and walked down the alley.

After a couple of turns, they walked out of the alley onto a deserted street. Mason didn't know if he should be grateful or concerned that there wasn't anyone in sight.

A vehicle came barreling around the corner. Mason almost leapt back into the alley until he saw that it was an automated garbage truck, moving far faster than Mason thought safe as it passed by them.

"Well, that thing's in a damn blood hurry," Jessica said, more annoyed than surprised.

"Yeah." Mason let out a long sigh. "Belts and zones."

"You all right there?" Jessica asked.

"Yeah, just a bit on edge." Mason grunted to clear his throat. "So, we find Raiders, rescue Colonel Shimura and her pirate lord not-friend as well. Then escape the station without getting shot down by either the Cendies or the station's own defenses."

Jessica walked up to the curb and turned around to face Mason, crossing her arms in front of her. "You think you could fly us out of here?"

"I mean, *Buttercup* could push 1.5 gs at maximum burn. Totally adequate for evading weapons fire," Mason said.

"It's a poor craftsman who blames his tools," Jessica said.

"I'm not saying *Buttercup* is a bad tool. She's just the wrong one for escaping a hostile station," Mason said. "At least, not without help."

"So, we'll need to contact *Mervie* and see about getting Wing Commander Cade and his pilots to give us some cover."

"Yes, that would help," Mason said.

A smile broke out on Jessica's face. "Sounds like we have everything we need."

"Does that include luck?" Mason asked. "Because I think we're going to need heaps of that."

Jessica turned around. "Trust me, Mason—we'll make our own luck. You'll see."

She turned around to cross the street just as another automated garbage truck came barreling around the corner. The vehicle didn't so much as slow down as it plowed over Jessica. There was a sickening wet crunch as the wheels rolled over her.

"Jessica." Mason ran to her and grabbed two fistfuls of her jumpsuit, dragging her out of the road and back into the concealment of the alley, noting with queasy unease the way her head flopped around limply. He laid her down and went to check her vitals and stopped. Her chest had a tire-width divot carved into it, and her neck bent at an unnatural angle. Her eyes stared sightlessly up at him with a surprised expression on her face. She was dead.

Mason sat down on the ground in shock. She was there just a few seconds ago, planning a daring escape. Mason buried his face in his hands. Mason got up and turned to leave. He paused and looked back at Jessica. He thought he should say something, but the words didn't present themselves.

Sighing, he turned away and started to walk.

He got maybe five paces when Jessica's subvocalized voice popped in his head.

<"Mason, come back!">

Mason paused in his tracks and turned around. Jessica lay on the ground where he had left her, her head still bent at an unnatural angle.

<"Don't you bloody dare leave me here!">

Mason walked back over to Jessica and knelt down. Her body didn't so much as twitch, but her eyes were moving, and her face had a relieved expression on it.

"You were dead just a moment ago," Mason said, horror turning into bewilderment while he spoke to Jessica's not-so-dead body.

<"What? Last thing I remember was starting to cross the street, and then I found myself lying on the ground,"> Jessica said. <"What happened?">

"You got ran over by an automated garbage truck," Mason said.

<"Oh,"> Jessica said. <"How bad?">

"Uh… your neck is broken and your chest is caved in," Mason said.

<"Well, bollocks,"> Jessica said.

"Would the fact that you're not dead have anything to do with what's classified about you?" Mason asked.

Her eyes glanced away, then locked back on him. <"Yes, this actually has everything to do with what's classified about me.">

"So, what are you? Some kind of android?" Mason asked.

She rolled her eyes, her expression impatient. <"No, you dolt. I just have a full-body prosthesis.">

"Full-body? Like you have your brain in a jar?" Mason asked.

<"My brain is in my head, just like yours,"> Jessica said. <"It just so happens that the braincase includes an emergency life-support function. It'll keep me alive for the next hour or so. After that, I'll die for real.">

"So, we need to get you to a cyberneticist before it runs out," Mason said.

<"A good idea, but there's something you can do to buy me a lot more time,"> Jessica said. <"You're going to need to detach my head from my body. I'm afraid it's not good for much anymore.">

"Okay," Mason said. "How do I do that?"

Her eyes went to his belt. <"See that multi-tool on your belt?">

"Yeah."

<"Take out the knife and cut my head off,"> Jessica said.

"What?"

Her expression became annoyed. <"Take out your knife and cut away the last bits of synthetic flesh attaching my head to my broken body. The truck already took care of the bone.">

Mason looked around the alley to make sure no one was looking before pulling his multi-tool out and flipping out its small knife blade. He looked at the clean steel, then up towards Jessica's body. It might be a prosthesis, but it looked indistinguishable from the real thing.

<"Come on, chop, chop. Get to the decapitating.">

Mason kneeled over Jessica's body, knife in hand. He looked down at Jessica's bent and crushed neck. "Oh, I think I'm going to throw up." A burning mass started working its way up his esophagus.

<"Not on me, please. I'd rather not have to clean sick out of my hair,"> Jessica said. <"Which I can't do right now, on account of the fact that I can't move my arms. Or anything else below the chin, for that matter.">

The pre-packaged meal he had eaten in *Buttercup's* cockpit splattered onto the ground next to Jessica's immobile body.

<"Thank you.">

Mason wiped his mouth with the back of his sleeve. "Don't mention it."

<"Now, don't dally,"> Jessica said. <"I'm on the clock here.">

"Oh boy." Bile was rising in Mason's throat again, as he held the knife over Jessica. He dry heaved but didn't let anything out.

<"Are you going to need to throw up again?"> Jessica asked.

"No, just give me a moment," Mason said.

<"I don't have many of those to give right now,"> Jessica said.

"Yeah, I know—one hour before you're dead for real," Mason said. "Uh… are you in any pain, by the way?"

<"Thank you for asking, but no,"> Jessica said. <"I shut down my pain receptors.">

"That must be nice," Mason said.

<"It's quite convenient, yes,"> Jessica said.

"Okay." Mason lowered the knife. "Here goes." He started cutting, the ragged flesh giving little resistance. Stomach churning, he looked away.

<"Hey. Eyes on the task,"> Jessica said. <"I don't want you to cut anything you don't have to.">

"Ah, belts and zones," Mason said, forcing himself to look at what he was doing. He gritted his teeth and started slicing through Jessica's flesh in earnest. The multi-tool's knife blade and his hand became covered in warm blood. It looked and felt real, though it didn't have the coppery scent of true blood. With a last cut, Mason got through an artificial tendon and Jessica's head rolled to the side.

<"Pick me up.">

"Yeah, just a sec." Mason wiped the blood off his multi-tool using Jessica's uniform. The way that her head had turned, she couldn't see what he was doing. Replacing the multi-tool, Mason wiped his hands clean and picked up Jessica's head with both hands.

<"Wow, this is a weird feeling."> Her eyes narrowed and shifted side-to-side.

"Never been a disembodied head before, I take it?" Mason asked.

<"Not while awake,"> Jessica said. <"It's like being a hand-held camera with very poor stabilization. But never mind. We need to find a place that sells external life-support modules.">

"Know of one that's nearby?" Mason asked.

<"Uh, well... "> Jessica said.

"What?" Mason asked.

<"Remember that shop I was staring at?"> Jessica asked.

"The one with the garish cybernetic limbs in the window?" Mason asked.

<"Yeah, that one,"> Jessica said. <"I'm willing to bet they have an external life-support module.">

"Any idea how much they cost?" Mason asked.

<"I'm not versed in what cybernetic accessories go for on this station, but they're not generally cheap,"> Jessica said.

<"Will the money I have on me be enough?"> Mason asked.

<"You might want to take my currency card from my wallet,"> Jessica said.

Mason looked down at the headless broken body. "Which pocket?"

<"Right front pocket,"> Jessica said.

Mason reached into the pocket and found it. After cutting off Jessica's head, rummaging around in her body's pocket didn't feel as surreal as it probably should.

"Okay. Guess it's time we go shopping." Mason tucked Jessica's head under his arm.

<"Could you adjust how you're holding me? My face is in your armpit.">

"Oh, sorry." Mason turned Jessica's head around, so her face looked forward.

<"That's better,"> Jessica said.

"It occurs to me that I should stuff your head in something," Mason said. "Walking around with a woman's severed head will attract attention I'd rather not have to deal with."

<"Yes, I suppose you're right,"> Jessica said. <"Not exactly the most dignified method of transport. I don't suppose you have any bags handy?">

"No," Mason said.

<"Oh, I know! You can use my old jumpsuit. It's not like anyone's using it.">

"It's got bloodstains on it," Mason said.

<"Let me take a look,"> Jessica said.

Mason held up Jessica's severed head so that she could get a better look at her own body.

<"Wow, that is gruesome,"> Jessica said. <"But enough of the suit's unsoiled you could just stuff the bloody bits on the inside.">

"Oh, good. As if this day wasn't awkward enough."

<"Oh, please, this is nothing compared to severing my head,"> Jessica said. <"Now stop whining and get my jumpsuit off. With luck, it'll just look like you're carrying some rolled-up clothing instead of a head.">

"So long as none of the blood seeps through," Mason said.

He set Jessica down on the side of her head, keeping the stump of her neck off the ground. He didn't know if she could get an infection, but it seemed prudent not to let dirt and debris get into her neck. He reached up and grabbed the zipper of Jessica's jumpsuit.

"Man, this is so weird."

<"What, never undressed a woman before?"> Jessica asked.

"This is a bit different," Mason said.

<"Is it? I know how you looked at me,"> Jessica said. <"I would think you'd relish the chance to take my clothes off.">

Mason felt his cheeks heating. "Not even close to what I had in mind."

<"Oh, so you *were* thinking of me?">

Mason pulled down the zipper of Jessica's jumpsuit, trying and failing to not notice the lacy black bra underneath. He felt like a serial killer disrobing a body before disposing of it. Pulling off the body's boots, Mason pulled the jumpsuit down and off Jessica's body, keeping his eyes averted. He was no prude, but the sight of Jessica's headless body, artificial or not, made him very uncomfortable. Folding up the jumpsuit to hide the blood, he picked up Jessica's head.

"Okay, in you go," Mason said.

<"Oh, yay,"> Jessica said.

Mason wrapped the jumpsuit around Jessica's severed head until she was completely covered. He then tucked Jessica under his arm and walked out into the street.

<"Well, this won't do,"> Jessica said.

"What?" Mason asked.

<"Can't see a thing,"> Jessica said.

"You're surprised?" Mason asked.

<"No. Not by the blindness, at least,"> Jessica said. <"This is just more claustrophobic than I expected.">

"I'm not sure how I can solve that problem without negating the whole 'keeping your severed head out of sight' thing," Mason said.

<"You could create an audio-visual link between your brainset and mine so I can see and hear what you do,"> Jessica said. <"That might help.">

"I'm not sure I feel comfortable with that," Mason said.

<"You're not a head wrapped up in a bloodied jumpsuit,"> Jessica said.

"Fair point," Mason said. He made the connection, and an icon appeared in his HUD indicating that there were now two people looking through his eyes.

<"Weird,"> Jessica said.

"What now?" Mason asked.

<"Never been this tall before. Never really occurred to me what 190 centimeters looks like from the top,"> Jessica said.

"Well, glad I could give you a new perspective," Mason said. "How much time do you have left?"

<"Forty minutes until emergency life support fails,"> Jessica said.

Mason broke out into a jog. "In other words, we need to hustle."

It was a long jog spinward, heading towards the spoke where they had first entered the Red Ring. Mason spotted more than a few security patrols, accompanied by the tall, lanky form of a Cendy soldier. None of them paid any mind to the tall man carrying a bundle under his arm.

The cybershop looked exactly the same as it did before, a squat rectangular building with large windows displaying the latest in prosthetic technology and fashion.

"So how long will this life-support module keep you alive?" Mason asked.

<"It depends, but your typical module can probably keep me alive for a couple of days or more,"> Jessica said.

"Enough time to fly back to *Mervie* to get a more permanent solution," Mason said.

<"That's the idea,"> Jessica said.

"Is the language barrier going to be a problem?" Mason said.

<"Probably not,"> Jessica said. <"This is a high-end place. The staff should know Federal, and if they don't, their brainsets can translate just as well as yours does.">

"High-end means expensive," Mason said. "You think the cash we have on hand's going to be enough to cover the asking price?"

<"There's one way to find out.">

"Right. One big learning experience," Mason said. He made sure Jessica's head was concealed by the jumpsuit wrapped around it before walking through the door.

The shop was full of artificial body parts, all organized by what part of the body they were meant to replace. There was an aisle for legs, an aisle for arms, and an aisle with cases full of artificial eyeballs. There was even a novelty aisle with inhuman prosthetics. From wolves' heads, to insect-like legs, to tentacular arms.

The shopkeeper, a middle-aged man with a glossy-white left arm and matte-black right arm greeted him. "How may I help you, sir?" he asked in Exo translated into Federal text on Mason's HUD.

"I need an external life-support rig," Mason said. "You guys wouldn't happen to have one?"

The clerk arched an eyebrow. "No offense, sir, but you don't look like someone who would need that kind of equipment," he said in excellent Federal.

"Oh, I'm not here for myself," Mason said. "Friend of mine is having some trouble with her systems and she needs something to act as a backup in case her body fails."

<"Or, in actuality, gets run over by a truck,"> Jessica said.

"Friend, of course," the clerk said. He pointed down the aisle. "You'll find the utility-oriented stuff over there, at the other end of the prosthetic-arms aisle. It's not much, but it might have what you're looking for. If not, I'd suggest going to the Orange Ring."

"I'll keep that in mind," Mason said.

He carried Jessica through the prosthetic-arm aisle, passing arms made to look like Damascus steel, or polished jade, or even hardwood. At the back of the store, Mason found the store's small utility section. Mason scanned the area, letting Jessica see through his eyes. All he saw were boxes of unfamiliar equipment stacked without apparent order on the shelves.

<"See what you're looking for?">

<"Not yet... not yet. There,"> Jessica said. <"Bottom shelf, lower right-hand side.">

Mason kneeled down and grabbed the box.

<"This has some heft to it,"> Mason said.

<"Takes a lot to keep a brain alive.">

<"Apparently."> Mason checked the price tag. <"Yikes. We don't have enough money for this.">

<"Just haggle the price down,"> Jessica said.

<"You are exceedingly optimistic about my ability to haggle,"> Mason said.

<"Well, how about your ability to steal?"> Jessica asked. <"Just nick the thing and get out of here.">

<"This thing weighs at least ten kilos, Jessica. I'm not sure I'll be able to run away carrying both it and you.">

<"Well, think of something. You're a smart guy,"> Jessica said.

Mason sighed and looked towards the clerk. <"Is bartering a thing here?">

<"I mean, I would think so, given that it's a major port,"> Jessica said.

<"You don't know? Aren't you supposed to be some kind of super analyst?"> Mason asked.

<"That doesn't mean I know everything, Mason. The microeconomics of Dagon Freeport is not an area that I've given much study,"> Jessica said.

<"Well, I guess you're about to witness an example of it first-hand,"> Mason said.

<"If I still had hands, I'd be taking notes,"> Jessica said.

Mason walked over to the clerk and set the box on the counter.

"Found what you're looking for?" the clerk asked.

"Right where you said it would be, thanks." Mason pulled out his and Jessica's currency chit. "Unfortunately, I don't have the cash on hand to pay the sticker price."

"I'm afraid we're not doing any sales today, sir," the clerk said.

"I wasn't asking for a discount," Mason said. "But along with the money on the cards, I'm willing to trade an item on my person."

"I see," the clerk said. He looked Mason up and down, then glanced at the bundle under his arm. "What are you holding there?"

"Not something I'm willing to trade," Mason said.

The clerk's eyes drifted down to Mason's belt. "Is that a Triumph Munitions Hornet II?"

Mason glanced at the burst pistol holstered at his side. "Uh… yes. Yes, it is."

The clerk scratched his chin with matte-black fingers for a moment.

He picked up the currency chits and looked at them. "How about this? I'll take the balance of one of your chits, and the gun, and its magazines."

"Done," Mason said. He pulled the holster weapon and magazines off his belt and deposited them on the counter, while the clerk drained the money from the currency chit. Mason recovered the remaining chit and the external life-support module. "It was a pleasure doing business with you."

The clerk was already examining the pistol. "I hope your friend appreciates what you're doing for them."

"You and me both, friend," Mason said before leaving.

<"For the record, I do appreciate everything you're doing,"> Jessica said. <"Now, let's find somewhere quiet to get this thing attached to my head. Like that alley up ahead.">

Mason ducked into the alley and set the box and Jessica down. He took out his multi-tool and used the knife to cut the tape holding the box shut before pulling off the lid to reveal the mobile life-support module resting in the box's foam interior. Out of the box, it looked like a backpack, complete with a pair of straps.

"Okay, how the hell do I attach this thing?" Mason asked.

<"My head has a couple of ports behind my right ear,"> Jessica said. <"That's where you can plug the module in.">

"Right," Mason said, unwrapping Jessica's head and setting her down on her left side, giving him clear access to the right of her head. He pulled back her hair, exposing the smooth skin beneath. "I don't see the ports."

<"If you pull the skin away from my ear, it will open along a vertical seam,"> Jessica said. <"You'll see the ports then.">

With his thumb, Mason pulled on the skin, and a dark line appeared on Jessica's brown skin. Pulling the skin further apart, Mason exposed one rectangular port and two round ports.

"The rectangle looks like a standard power port," Mason said. "But what are those two round ones?"

"They're for my brain's blood supply," Jessica said. "You should take care not to get those crossed. I'd die in seconds if you did."

"Right. Don't cross the blood tubes," Mason said. "Any handy way to make sure which one is the right one?"

"I'll walk you through it," Jessica said. "Start with the power cable."

"Okay, easy enough." Mason reached for the power cable but noticed someone approaching from deeper inside the alley. A tall, muscular youth with glowing tattoos and a pistol tucked into his waistband.

<"Uh-oh,"> Jessica said.

Mason stood up, hand drifting to his pistol, only to find it missing. The young man spoke in Exospeak, his speech translated in text across Mason's HUD.

"What's going on here? You lost, friend?" he asked, glancing at what lay next to Mason's feet.

<"Nope, nothing to see here,"> Jessica said.

The punk's eyes widened in shock, and he drew a pistol. "What the fuck is this, sicko?"

Mason held up his hands. "It's not what it looks like."

"What did you say?"

It seemed the punk didn't speak Federal or have a brainset to translate.

Another voice in accented Exospeak spoke behind him. A shorter young man with thick arms and a rotund belly stood in the alley entrance where Mason had come from. His tattoos matched those of the other.

"Oh, dude, is that a severed head?"

"Yeah, man. We got ourselves some sicko cutting the heads off whores," the punk in front of Mason said. "I think we interrupted him."

<"I'm not a whore,"> Jessica said, as if the punks could hear her.

"Good thing, too. I don't want to know what he had planned," the punk behind Mason said.

<"A little help here,"> Mason said.

<"What do you expect me to do?"> Jessica asked. <"Blink my eyelashes at them?">

<"Can you hack something to make a distraction?">

<"Not lying on the ground here, no.">

<"What's the point of all that hackware you were bragging about, then?"> Mason said.

"Hey, let's just rob this guy and go," said the one behind Mason. "We let him keep his head."

<"You can't let them take the power pack, Mason,"> Jessica said.

<"I'm not sure I'll have a choice,"> Mason said, eyeing the gun the

punk was holding. Glancing over his shoulder, he saw the other one was holding a knife.

<"If you let them take that power pack, I'm dead,"> Jessica said.

<"If I get shanked or shot, you're dead,"> Mason said.

<"So don't let either of those happen.">

"Check his pockets."

Knife-punk walked up behind Mason and started rummaging through his pockets while gun-punk watched, pistol held at the hip.

"Found a chit on him. Got some cash on it," knife-punk said.

"What about that thing on the ground?" gun-punk said.

"I'm not touching that," knife-punk said.

"Not the head, dipshit; the other thing. Looks expensive," gun-punk said.

Knife-punk reached down and picked up the power pack with his off-hand. "It's heavy. Must be worth something."

"Looks like one of those backpacks they sell to cyber-jobs," gun-punk said.

Neither seemed to be focusing their attention on Mason. He shifted his weight, getting a boot behind Jessica's head.

<"How's the integrity of your skull's impact protection?"> Mason asked.

<"The truck didn't damage it, if that's what you're asking.">

Mason kicked Jessica's head towards gun-punk, sending her arching towards him. Mason turned towards knife-punk, who was still holding the power pack, and kicked him in the knee. Something popped, and knife-punk went down screaming. Gun-punk was juggling Jessica's head, horrified, when Mason turned his attention towards him and charged. Slamming into gun-punk before he could bring his weapon to bear, the gun went off, stinging Mason's ears as he drove gun-punk into the ground.

The punk started shooting in a panic as Mason got control of the arm holding the gun, further assaulting his hearing as he put the arm into a lock and twisted. The punk's shoulder broke. The punk screamed, and the gun fell out of his hands. Mason grabbed the gun. Its slide was locked back, empty.

"Shit," Mason said.

He struck the punk's nose with the grip of the pistol. While the punk covered his nose with his uninjured arm, Mason checked his pockets and found a magazine.   Dropping the spent magazine, Mason loaded the fresh one and drew back the slide to chamber a round.

By this time, knife-punk had gotten back on his feet, favoring one leg, knife held in his hand. Mason stepped away from gun-punk and trained the pistol on knife-punk, who dropped the knife and put up his hands. Mason pointed down at gun-punk, who was moaning on the ground, then towards the alleyway behind knife-punk. Knife-punk nodded and limped up to his friend, Mason backpedaling to keep his distance. Knife-punk helped gun-punk up to his feet, then leaned against gun-punk as they both left the alley.

"Man, we should've kept to Yellow Ring," said knife-punk. "Red Ring's always had too much crazy."

Mason let out a breath and looked to Jessica's head. She rested on the ground facing towards him, her eyes not moving.

"Oh God." Mason kneeled down. "Hey, Jessica, say something. Are you all right?"

For a couple of agonizing seconds, she was completely still. Then her eyes locked onto him and her face contorted into a furious sneer.

<"You absolute bastard. You fucking kicked me.">

Mason picked her up, keeping her face towards him. "It worked, didn't it? You should have seen the look on the guy's face."

Jessica's sneer faded into a sour grimace. <"I did see his face.">

"Right. I suppose you did." Mason walked up to the power pack knife-punk had dropped. "Let me get you plugged in."

<"Please do,"> Jessica said.

Mason picked up the power back by the strap, slinging it over his shoulder, then inserted the power cord and two blood tubs into the port behind Jessica's ear, then flipped it on.

<"And there we go. I'm getting external power and circulation,"> Jessica said. <"They didn't keep the battery topped off. I got just over twenty-five hours of power.">

"That's still plenty of time," Mason said. He set Jessica down and sat on the floor of the alley, resting his back against the wall.

<"Need to take a breather?">

"Yeah, I've had a long day."

<"Tell me about it.">

Mason glanced at Jessica's head, connected by wires and tubes to the life-support module. "Yeah, sorry."

<"Oh, that's not your fault.">

"I'll spare you the 'I told you so'."

<"Thank you. I'd say that I've learned my lesson. Good moves, by the way. You took down those thugs in seconds.">

"Just a couple of kids looking for an easy score."

<"So modest. A trooper would've had trouble taking down two armed men.">

"You saw the martial-arts training on my dossier. Shouldn't be that big a surprise."

<"It's one thing to read a line of text, another to actually see it in action. Where does a fighter pilot learn to fight like that?">

"The Outer Sol Hauler Pilot Association requires a minimum of five years martial-arts training from its members," Mason said. "It's a precaution against hijackers overpowering the pilots and using their craft as a weapon. And a rebuttal to advocates for drone haulers."

<"How so?">

"A hauler manned by a pilot with combat training is, in theory, more secure than a drone hauler. Drones can't fight off hackers as effectively as a pilot can fight off a hijacker. At least, that's the argument. Both Mom and Dad took martial-arts training almost as seriously as pilot training."

<"Looks like it paid off.">

"Yeah, I guess it did. So, how are you holding up? Your present condition can't be fun."

<"You mean now that I'm just a head?">

"Basically, though that phrasing does present the temptation for some truly awful puns."

<"I'm grateful that you're restraining yourself. And, no, my 'present condition' is not fun at all. Spent too much of my life like this.">

"Do you mind elaborating? I don't think you spent most of your life as a disembodied head."

<"I might as well have been. My parents were very... conservative. Pretty much rejected all forms of modern pre-natal care. Didn't even get a

bloody ultrasound because they didn't want to know my sex until I popped out, which was too bad, otherwise they would've noticed the rather serious birth defects caused by a recessive gene carried by both my parents, which was never corrected because their parents were also very conservative. The end result was that I was born with Tetra-Amelia Syndrome, meaning I had neither arms nor legs. I also had a host of other health problems as a bonus.">

"They didn't fix that post-natal?"

<"Conservative, remember?">

"Sounds more irresponsible than conservative."

<"No argument from me.">

"Well, I can understand why you opted for full-body replacement." Mason stood up and pulled the mobile life-support module onto his back.

<"You're not interested in the rest of my story?">

"Oh, I am, but I don't think we really have time for it," Mason said. "Let's continue this talk after we connect with Major Hauer and rescue Colonel Shimura."

<"Fair enough. So, how do you plan on finding Major Hauer?">

"Locked 'N Loaded is the last place we knew where they were. Might as well start there."

CHAPTER 12

LOCKED 'N LOADED was a squat, nondescript building that stood out amid the colorful buildings that loomed over it. Just a simple sign above the door, illuminated by a white LED, marked the bar.

"Well, here we are," Mason said.

<"An island of tasteful austerity among all the tacky glamour,"> Jessica said.

"My kind of place," Mason said. "Kind of reminds me of the pubs that served Hauler pilots back home. Just more militant."

<"With luck, we'll find Major Hauer and his troopers sitting around a table sipping beers and chatting about whatever Raiders chat about.">

"That would be a change."

Mason pushed open the door, hearing the dulcet tunes of a guitar from inside. The pungent smells of tobacco, marijuana, and various flavors of vapor were so thick it stuck to his skin. The interior was as austere as the front facade. Just a wide, open room filled mostly with circular tables occupied by men and women, all armed and armored with a diverse selection of gear. The bar was on the far side from the entrance, a metal slab with a bartender and racks filled with colorful bottles on the other side. The dull-brown armor of the Raiders was nowhere to be seen.

"They're not here," Mason said.

<"Too much to hope for, I guess,"> Jessica said.

"You said that the security on this station was spotty, right?" Mason asked. "Would the Raiders know that?"

<"Well, of course they would. Shit,"> Jessica said. <"I didn't think of that.">

"You've had a lot on your mind."

<"They didn't pop up on any security feeds while I was plugged in.">

The bartender looked at him and said in Exo, "Hey, pal, no loitering. Buy a drink or get out."

Mason shrugged and walked up to the bar.

"What are you doing?" Jessica asked.

"Getting a drink," Mason said.

<"Now?">

"Need to think. Don't feel like going outside," Mason said. He planted Jessica's wrapped head on the bar and glanced at the drink offerings.

<"Really?" You're just going to prop me on top of the bar? Just fantastic.">

<"There's a method to my madness,"> Mason said, gesturing to the bartender.

The bartender walked up. Bald and with the build and complexion of a brick. Thick muscles bulged through his thin, white t-shirt.

"What will it be?" he asked in Exospeak.

Mason read the selection scrawled in chalk on the wall and noticed that it was written in both Exo and Federal.

Mason looked back at the bartender. "You speak Federal?"

"Yeah," the bartender said in Federal with a familiar accent. "Been awhile since I've heard a Jovian accent."

"Good ear," Mason said. "You don't sound local yourself. You from Rain?"

"Born 'n raised," the bartender said. "Name's Nick."

"Mason."

"So, what will it be, Mason?"

"I'll take a pint of the house brew," Mason said.

The bartender nodded and filled a glass with a frothy dark-brown liquid and set it on the bar before Mason.

<"He's a deserter,"> Jessica said.

Mason glanced towards the bundle resting next to him.

The bartender noticed. "So, what's that you got wrapped up there?"

Mason looked back at the bartender and smiled. "A severed head."

<"Really?"> Jessica subvoked.

"A what?" the bartender asked.

"A head, sans body." Mason drew a line across his neck with his finger. "That's generally what a severed head means."

"Right. If that's the case, don't leave it on top of my bar. It's unsanitary," the bartender said.

Mason took Jessica's head off the bar and rested her in his lap, while the bartender planted a glass in front of him and started filling it with something dark and frothy.

"So, you a bounty hunter?" bartender asked. "You don't really have the look."

"Didn't realize there was a look," Mason said.

"Not enough scars or tattoos," the bartender said.

<"Former Sergeant Nicholas Canul, Federal Military Police,"> Jessica said from his lap. <"Spent six years with the troopers before transferring over to the MPs. Went AWOL during Earth-Fed's final withdrawal from Dagon Freeport five years ago.">

Mason picked up his beer. <"You're really going to read me this guy's dossier while I drink?"> He sipped his beer. "Yum."

<"Just thought you should know who's serving your drinks,"> Jessica said. <"Also, I need something to do while you drink on the job.">

<"You're just sore that I didn't order you a drink.">

<"That is generally the thing to do when you drag a girl to a bar.">

<"I didn't drag you; I carried you."> Mason took another sip of his beer.

<"Thank you for rubbing that in.">

Mason set down his glass. <"I could order you a drink if you want.">

<"You realize I can't swallow, right?">

<"Just open your mouth and I'll pour it in,"> Mason said. <"We'll have to do it in a sink, of course. Wouldn't want to make a mess.">

Jessica sighed over the subvocal. <"I can't tell if you're serious or not.">

<"It's good beer—you should try it.">

<"Maybe later.">

Mason noticed the bartender, Nick, was still looking at him with an expectant expression. Setting down his beer, he said, "So, uh… Nick, I was wondering if you could help me with something."

"Let me guess—you're not done collecting heads?" Nick asked.

"Oh, this is just a one-off." Mason patted Jessica's head, hoping very much that was true. "I'm actually looking for a group of mercenaries. A dozen or so men and women in brown armor. Their leader is a man with a jaw that could crack a rock."

Nick arched an eyebrow. "I hope there's more than just you if you're looking to take them down."

Mason shook his head. "Not what I'm after. I was supposed to meet them here."

"Looking to hire them? Must cut into your bounty-hunting income," Nick said.

"I never said I was a bounty hunter," Mason said.

"Right, well, I don't know where they went. All I know is that they went out the back door, probably to avoid surveillance," Nick said.

"What makes you say that?" Mason asked.

"Because that's the way people usually exit the bar when they want to avoid surveillance," Nick said.

Mason finished his beer and pulled out the remaining currency card and paid for the beer, along with a generous tip for Nick. "Thanks for the beer."

"Be sure to visit us again if you get the chance," Nick said.

Mason headed to the back exit and pushed open the door into a dark alley, a stretch of bare pavement flanked by unpainted polymer walls glistening with condensation. There seemed to be a lot of those on this station, or at least in the Red Ring. The builders of this place really wanted that old-style city feel.

"So, any ideas where our Raiders would have gone?" Mason asked.

<"To The Philistine club, I would assume,"> Jessica said. <"Major Hauer probably found our silence alarming and went to investigate.">

Mason scratched his chin with his free hand. "Seems logical. Think you could narrow it down?"

<"Not sure. Like I said, I didn't see them when I was connected to the security network,"> Jessica said.

"So that means we know where they weren't, assuming they moved to avoid surveillance coverage."

<"Oh, yes. Very clever, Mason. It's good to know you brought your brain with you.">

"I try not to leave home without it." Mason looked towards the alley. "So, if I were a team of elite special-forces troopers, and I wanted to move from Locked 'N Loaded to Mister Cordial's without getting spotted on camera, where would I go?"

<"I got something that might help us find out,"> Jessica said. <"I saved the coverage map to my brainset. I'll upload it to you.">

On Mason's HUD, a map of the part of the ring between Locked 'N Loaded and Mister Cordial's appeared. The main street was shaded in green, indicating where there was camera coverage, black indicating buildings, and yellow indicating sections where there was no camera coverage.

"Wow, did you just make that?" Mason asked.

<"I wish I could say so, but it was actually the late Chief Rowe who made this," Jessica said. <"He was aware of the weaknesses in his security system.">

"But never took steps to correct them. I wonder why? I don't suppose you could draw the most direct route between here and Cordial's that avoids surveillance?"

<"Done. That, incidentally, was all me.">

"Good work," Mason said. He started walking, following the directions Jessica laid out.

He kept his hand on his gun as he followed the path through the damp alley, glancing up in case any Cendies tried to fall on him from above, and behind him in case some lowlife tried to rob him again.

<"Can you keep your eyes on the ground?">

"Why? I'm kind of busy looking out for danger."

<"And I'm trying to see if Major Hauer and his team made it through here.">

"Okay, what should I look for?" Mason asked.

<"I don't know. Anything.">

"How about we head to The Philistine," Mason said. "With luck, we'll run into them there."

At the last turn in the alley, Mason backed up against the wall and glanced around the corner. The Philistine's front lights shone through the end of the alley, silhouetting security personnel loitering in front of it.

<"I don't see any sign of Major Hauer or his raiders,"> Jessica said.

"Maybe they came through here and moved on when they saw Security," Mason said.

<"This was our only lead. If they're not here, then I'm not sure how we're going to find them in time."">

"I don't suppose you could broadcast something?" Mason said. "Try and find them that way."

<"The Raiders will be under strict radio silence,"> Jessica said. <"And, besides, if I broadcast, Security, Ascendency, or both, might pick it up. That would likely bring a lot of trouble down upon our heads."">

"That would be especially rough since—"

<"I'm just a head, I know. Very droll."">

"You got a leg up on me on that one," Mason said.

<"I... you're horrible,"> Jessica said.

Something scraped behind him, and Mason turned around to find half a dozen figures in dull-brown armor facing him, their weapons held ready, but not leveled at him.

"I've been looking for you guys," Mason said. Major Hauer, are you there, sir? I can't tell you guys apart under all that armor."

One of the Raiders lowered his weapon and flipped up his visor, exposing Major Hauer's lantern jaw. "Where the hell have you been? What happened?"

"We might have stumbled upon a coup, sir," Mason said.

The Raiders pulled back, clearing a path for Mason to approach Major Hauer.

Major Hauer gestured. "Get back here before you're seen."

Mason nodded and marched around the corner, finding more troopers covering the other direction of the alley.

Hauer stepped in front of Mason. "Colonel Shimura?"

"Captured, sir. Along with her contact and one of his bodyguards," Mason said.

"And Lieutenant Sinclair?" he asked.

<"Oh, he's going to be in for a surprise.">

Mason glanced at the bundle tucked under his shoulder. "He doesn't know?"

<"He didn't need to know.">

"What's in that bundle?" Major Hauer said. "And, more to the point, why are you talking to it?"

Mason took Jessica's head and started unwrapping. "Uh, so about Lieutenant Sinclair." He let Jessica's jumpsuit fall to the ground and held up Jessica's head. "It's not nearly as bad as it looks."

Hauer's eyebrows shot up. "Why are you carrying her head?"

"As I said, sir, it's not as bad as it looks," Mason said. "She's still alive."

"That doesn't look very alive to me, Flight Lieutenant."

Another Raider stepped up and lifted their visor. It was Sergeant Cane. "Sir, she just rolled her eyes."

"There's a lot more to Lieutenant Sinclair than either of us realized, sir," Mason said. "If you can open a brainset connection with her, she can explain everything herself."

Hauer's eyes narrowed, his wide jaw shifting from side-to-side. "It's open."

<"Hello, Major.">

"Lieutenant," Major Hauer said. "What happened to the rest of you?"

<"Died, sir.">

"So, I take it you're a full-body replacement cyborg?" Major Hauer said.

<"Correct, sir.">

"Hmph." He looked to Mason. "You said Colonel Shimura's been captured. What exactly happened?"

Mason jerked a thumb back towards The Philistine. "Well, sir, it seems we got caught in the middle of a coup instigated by the Cendies. They started jamming everything other than near-field communications and moved in to try and capture Mister Cordial with the assistance of station security not loyal to him. Colonel Shimura was injured in all the excitement and ordered Lieutenant Sinclair and me to leave her to be captured along with Mister Cordial when we got cornered."

"How did you avoid getting captured?"

<"We jumped into a dumpster to hide,"> Jessica said.

"That would explain the Flight Lieutenant's smell," Major Hauer said.

"Uh, yeah." Mason cleared his throat. "So the plan was for us to find you, sir, so you can rescue Colonel Shimura and Mister Cordial."

"Why does she want us to rescue the pirate too?" Major Hauer asked.

"It seems Mister Cordial's responsible for directing Fomalhaut's pirates away from Federal shipping," Mason said. "Our guess is that the Cendies are trying to take him down so that they can get those pirates to start raiding us again."

"Well, we can't have that," Major Hauer said. "Do we know where they are now?"

<"Not yet, but if you reconnect me to the security network, I should be able to find out where they were taken.">

"So how do we go about doing that?" Major Hauer asked.

<"Well, another security headquarters would work,"> Jessica said. <"Perhaps in one of the other rings.">

"We might have a hard time getting past the checkpoints leading into the other rings," Mason said. "Especially whichever one they took Colonel Shimura to."

<"Good point. Which actually brings up another problem. Getting to them once we've found them. Security and the Cendies will expect Mister Cordial's people to try and break him out.">

"So, we hit them from an unexpected direction," Major Hauer said.

"What are you suggesting, sir?" Mason asked.

Major Hauer looked down at Jessica's head. "Could you access the security network from this station's Space Traffic Control?"

<"I think so, Major,"> Jessica said. <"And I think we can bypass most of the security. Just get me to a biometric scanner and I can requisition a tram to take us directly to the STC room for the northern docking ports.">

"Then that's where we're headed. Sergeant Cane?"

"Sir?"

"Find something more comfortable to put Lieutenant Sinclair's head in."

CHAPTER 13

MASON HELD JESSICA up to the biometric scanner, and a moment later, the doors to the STC center opened. The troopers flowed in, shouting for everyone to get down.

The control center was a glass-enclosed cupola filled with traffic controllers hunched over consoles facing towards the line of traffic flowing into Dagon Freeport's northern docking port.

Located in the despun spine of the station, there was no gravity holding anything down, so when the troopers started flowing in, the stunned controllers inside floated about the compartment in random directions, dropping whatever they were holding as the troopers started restraining them. Within a minute, the traffic controllers were bundled into an adjacent room to get them out of the way, and locked inside.

Mason floated out of the large window that dominated the front of the STC room and gave a wide view of the entry into Eridu's northern docking port. The voices of confused pilots echoed from unattended speakers.

"They don't sound happy," Mason said.

<"Let's not dally then. I need a hardwire connection. Look around, and I'll catch it.">

Mason panned his vision across the consoles that lined the huge windows looking out into space, overviewing the traffic moving in and out of the station's northern dock.

<"Right, there, near the center. Get me plugged in quick.">

Mason floated over to the console. With a strip of tape, he secured Jessica to the console, along with her life-support module.

Jessica's eyes examined the strip of tape across her forehead with a bemused expression. <"This isn't big on dignity.">

Mason pulled out more tape to secure Jessica's power pack in place. "At least I'm not using your hair to tie you down."

<"How very kind of you."> With Jessica's head and the life-support module secure, Mason pulled a wire from a spool in the console and attached it to the port behind her left ear. <"Okay, here goes.">

A man's voice piped over the speaker in Exo, the voice of the controller that had directed Mason when he docked.

"Sorry about that, everyone. We had a power surge on our end."

"Whatever you say, STC. Just get us our docking clearance. My passengers are going to start eating each other if we don't dock soon."

Jessica's disguised voice barked out instructions, and the flow of ships into Dagon Freeport's docking bay resumed.

<"All right, that particular crisis is averted,"> Jessica said after spending ten minutes speaking with the pilots waiting to dock. <"Now, to look for the colonel... Ah-ha!>

"That didn't take long," Mason said. <"Where is she?">

<"Security headquarters in the Orange Ring. Looks like she's being kept there with Mister Cordial. Local security assumes she's one of Mister Cordial's bodyguards like Cynth.">

"Good. We know where to go then," Major Hauer said. "Have you contacted *Mervie* yet?"

<"I've relayed a tightbeam through the satellite network. We should hear a response from Captain Vann in about four minutes.">

Mason sighed. Even in an era defined by the stardrive, which allowed vessels to leap billions of kilometers in an instant, the tyranny of lightspeed delay still reigned wherever massive objects bent spacetime too much for stardrives to function.

"Assuming the 4th launches as soon as Captain Vann gets your message, it'll take two hours at a ten g cruising burn to get here," Mason said.

"Can they handle that, Flight Lieutenant?" Major Hauer asked.

Mason nodded. "Easily, sir. Fighter pilots are supposed to tolerate that kind of acceleration for days at a time."

Major Hauer grunted. "I forgot how much abuse you flyboys have to deal with."

"Eh, that's what the enhancements and hardsuits are for, sir," Mason said.

<"I've got a reply,"> Jessica said. <"Captain Vann acknowledges. She had ordered Wing Command Cade's fighters to launch immediately.">

Jessica summoned a projection on the STC center's window, showing *Mervie's* position on the far side of Dagon. After a few minutes, icons of fighters appeared launching from the starship. Only they weren't coming up as Federal Lightnings.

<"I've given each fighter a false ID and have retroactively altered the logs to make their appearance look scheduled,"> Jessica said.

The fighters started their burn, and the numbers of their icons indicated their ten g acceleration.

"Won't someone think their hard burn is unusual?" Major Hauer said.

"Probably not, Major," Jessica said. "Everyone knows fighter pilots are an impatient bunch. A hard burn will be seen as normal."

"Nice to see stereotypes about my profession are proving helpful," Mason said. "You know what loadout they're carrying?"

"Captain Vann didn't give specifics, but she indicated that the fighters would be fully loaded," Jessica said. "They'll attempt to strike the Cendy battlecruisers when they come around the planet. Once they show up on Cendy sensors, there's nothing that's going to keep them from noticing they're Federal fighters."

"It's times like this I wish the Legislature didn't ban exporting the Lightning back in the day," Mason said.

<"The false IDs I gave them should hold up until they fly around the planet Dagon,"> Jessica said. <"Once the Cendies spot them, the fighters will already be positioned to make a torpedo run on the starship.">

"Then let's spring Colonel Shimura and her contact before that happens," Major Hauer said. "Sergeant Cane and her fireteam will hold the STC while the rest of the squad heads to the Orange Ring. Flight Lieutenant Grey?"

Mason nodded. "Right. Back to the *Buttercup*." He turned to Jessica. "Stay safe while I'm out there."

<"You stay safe, yourself. I'm going to feel really silly going through all this trouble if you end up crashing into the side of the station.">

❧

MASON DONNED A spacesuit before floating up to *Buttercup's* cockpit. If things went as planned, then hopefully no one would shoot at his hauler, but there was no guarantee that wouldn't happen. Major Hauer's Raiders waited below, strapped into the seats as they waited for Mason to do his job.

"*Buttercup* to STC, requesting permission to launch," Mason said.

"STC to *Buttercup*, you have priority clearance to launch," Jessica said, her voice disguised to match that of the male controller who was supposed to be on duty. Giving Mason priority clearance meant he could skip the line out of the station, but it also increased the chances of someone getting suspicious. But they couldn't waste time. The 4th would fly around Dagon in less than two hours. He felt an odd sense of envy when he thought about the 4th. They were about to take a Cendy warship by surprise, and Mason was stuck playing bus driver. Well, he shouldn't complain too much. Trying to land on a spinning ring was going to be no easy feat.

Disengaging the maglocks, Mason lifted *Buttercup* off the docking pad with a pulse of the maneuvering thrusters. *Buttercup* drifted into the long tube of the dock. With another puff from the maneuvering thrusters, Mason set the hauler drifting towards the open exit. Over the radio, pilots of other ships were complaining, clearly outraged that Mason's ship bumped back their launch times. Jessica, with her disguised voice, calmly told them to settle down and let the priority launch through. When *Buttercup* slipped out of the dock, Mason fired the maneuvering thrusters again, turning the hauler to start moving perpendicular to the spine of the station.

"We're supposed to be headed for Orange Ring, Flight Lieutenant," Major Hauer said. "Not open space."

"I know what I'm doing, sir. Just hold on," Mason said. He hated backseat drivers, especially when they outranked him.

After several minutes drifting away from the station, Mason fired the maneuvering thrusters again to kill *Buttercup's* velocity next to the station and turned around.

"Jessica, give me a real-time feed on Orange Ring. I need to see it spinning," Mason said.

"One live feed coming up," Jessica said.

A feed from one of Dagon Freeport's external cameras showed Orange Ring spinning around the central spine. Orange Ring looked identical to all the others spinning about the station's central spine, except for the thick, orange stripes marking it.

"Highlight where the security headquarters is," Mason said.

A section of the station not far from Orange's Ring's number five spoke started glowing yellow. Mason did some quick calculations, noting the tangential velocity of the ring. He would have to match it when he landed. With the assistance of the flight AI, Mason calculated the window for his burn. *Buttercup* would have to be moving at over 350 kilometers per hour relative to the station when she reached the landing zone on the Orange Ring.

"Okay, beginning approach burn in five... four... three... two... one... start."

The maneuvering thrusters fired, and a tenth of a g pulled Mason down into his seat.

"I still don't understand why you didn't pick a more direct route, Flight Lieutenant," Major Hauer said.

"Taking the direct route would require me to burn more fuel, sir," Mason said. "It would increase our chances of detection. Approaching like this requires much less fuel. It's not entirely unlike a runway landing."

He wasn't approaching parallel to Orange Ring, but at a slight angle to clear the near side of the ring and get inside. It would require one short burn to turn *Buttercup's* vector parallel to the spinning ring.

Dagon Freeport grew and the spin of the station's rings seemed faster than before.

Mason let out a breath. Though 350 kph was peanuts compared to the velocities he was used to dealing with, it was quite fast for docking. Dangerously fast, in fact.

<"Your vector looks good, *Buttercup*,"> Jessica said, using her voice in the subvocal.

"One minute to contact," Mason said.

The near side of Orange Ring slipped past Mason's right. Now came the tricky part. Mason pitched *Buttercup* up until her nose was perpendicular to the line of travel, and, at a preplanned point, he fired the lateral thrusters, turning the hauler's vector parallel to the ring's rotation. In the rear camera, the ring's inner surface appeared to stop moving, belying the fact that *Buttercup* was moving as fast as a bullet train. The point where *Buttercup's* vector almost, but not quite, intercepted with the Orange Ring neared. Mason's thumb hovered over the maneuvering thruster stick while he waited for just the right moment, then he fired the reverse thrusters. *Buttercup* shook as her landing gear touched down on the upper surface of the Orange Ring, her shock absorbers sagging as a full g of spin-gravity pulled the ship down.

"Contact. We're down," Mason said. "Has anyone noticed that I just landed a hundred-ton hauler on the roof of the Orange Ring?"

"Yes, I'm quite impressed," Jessica said.

"Thanks, but I meant the locals," Mason said.

"Oh, right. No, it doesn't appear so."

Mason sighed. That was tenser than he'd hoped. Unbuckling his seatbelt, he climbed down the ladder to the hold. The Raiders were already out of their seats, getting ready to disembark. Checking their weapons, making sure their suits had good seals.

Major Hauer walked up to Mason. "Good job not splattering us over the side of the station, Flight Lieutenant. You should switch over to flying assault shuttles. Put your skills towards honest work."

"Glad you approve, sir, but I like flying Lightnings just fine."

"I'm sure you do, Flight Lieutenant. Just remember to keep the engine warm. There's a good chance that we'll have to find an alternate escape route once this is all said and done. You think you'll be able to pluck us out of space if that happens?"

"You've seen my work, sir," Mason said. "I'll pick you up, no matter what route you decide to take off the station."

"Good attitude, Flight Lieutenant," Major Hauer said. "Now, if you'll excuse me." The Raider officer turned towards his squad and barked an order. They all started marching towards *Buttercup's* airlock. Along with their weapons, two of the Raiders carried spare pressure suits in bags strapped to their armor. Whatever way they ended leaving the station, the people they rescued would be in for a spacewalk.

Mason returned to the cockpit, while the airlock depressurized.

"Jessica, the Raiders are disembarking. How do things look on your end?" Mason asked.

<"All quiet so far, despite the whining of a few impatient pilots,"> Jessica said. <"Sergeant Cane's got the STC center locked down tight.">

"Can you set up a security feed from the Orange Ring?" Mason asked.

<"Sure thing,"> Jessica said.

Real-time footage of the interior of the Orange Ring appeared on Mason's HUD. It showed the security headquarters building, a three-tier structure sitting amid a well-manicured lawn and neat rows of trees.

"Can you see what's going on inside?" Mason asked.

<"I can. Do you want me to send that to you?"> Jessica asked.

"Not yet. I just need to know when to get this thing ready to take off," Mason said.

<"Understood,"> Jessica said.

"How's the 4th doing?" Mason asked.

<"So far no one's taken issue with sixteen Lightnings doing a hard-braking burn below Dagon's horizon,"> Jessica said. <"Looks like the false IDs I gave them are holding.">

"Hard to believe the Cendies aren't reacting," Mason said.

<"They probably weren't expecting Federal ships this far out,"> Jessica said. <"Means they're complacent.">

Mason felt something of a relief at that statement. As inhuman as the Ascendency seemed to be, the fact that they could become complacent meant they weren't invulnerable. They could make mistakes. If they could make mistakes, then they could be beaten.

On *Buttercup's* external monitors, twelve armored figures marched across the surface of the Orange Ring, moving towards a maintenance airlock a hundred meters spinward from where Mason landed.

"Lieutenant Sinclair, we're approaching the airlock," Major Hauer said.

<"I've already disconnected it from the network and unlocked it, Major,"> Jessica said. <"No one should notice you using it.">

"Good work, Lieutenant," Major Hauer said.

The first fireteam got to the airlock. One pulled open the outer hatch while the other three moved inside with their weapons at the ready.

"Clear," Corporal Tiller said.

"Everyone inside," Major Hauer said. "Once we open the inner hatch, we make our way straight for security headquarters. Lieutenant Sinclair, you have a clear route for us?"

<"You'll be entering the upper maintenance corridors, sir," Jessica said. "There's minimal civilian activity and nothing in the way of armed opposition. I don't think they ever expected to be infiltrated in the way we're about to.">

"Good. I like having surprise on my side," Major Hauer said. "If we run into civilians, hit them with the stunners and move on."

The airlock finished pressurizing and the Raiders opened the inner hatch.

Jessica gave Mason a view of the security feed from the upper maintenance corridors. The corridors were narrow and cramped, with just enough space for a couple of technicians to go about checking ventilation and the lighting system for the roof of the ring. It meant there was barely enough room for the Raiders to move single file. They made their way to the most direct access to the surface level; in this case, a scaffold hanging over a public park spinward of security headquarters.

"We're in the main interior," Major Hauer said. "Lopez, get a scope on the headquarters."

"Roger that, sir," she said.

"What do you see?" Major Hauer asked.

"I count two dozen security, and four of those skinny Cendy soldiers standing at the front entrance," Lopez said.

"Make the Cendies your first targets," Major Hauer said. "Lopez, Kongrel, Grills, and Kisri. Each of you pick a Cendy and drop them on my order. Grills, set up your kinetic barriers. This position is exposed, and I'd like some cover for the shooters."

There was a chorus of affirmatives. There was no security camera overlooking the scaffold, so Mason couldn't see what was going on, but he knew enough about Federal trooper tactics to be able to guess. Corporal Grills was attaching composite plates to the railing and floor of the scaffold, making a little fort hanging from the roof of the Orange Ring for the four marksmen who would take the first shots, and likely be the first targets of any return fire.

"Ready to fire, sir," Lopez said.

"Wait for my order," Major Hauer said.

Mason watched the feed of the front of the security headquarters, seeing the four lanky Cendy soldiers loiter out front of the main entrance. He noticed how the security personnel kept their distance from them, clearly creeped out by their inhuman visitors.

"Switch on active camo. Prepare to jump on my mark," Major Hauer said. "Mark."

The scaffold was not directly over the headquarters building, but slightly spinward of it, to compensate for the Coriolis effect. Mason didn't see the troopers as they fell, thanks to their active camo.

"Open fire," Major Hauer said.

There were four sharp cracks, and the four Cendy soldiers dropped to the deck, much to the surprise of Dagon security, who promptly started shooting into the air. Major Hauer and his troopers landed on the roof with the blast of their descent thrusters slowing them down enough to land lightly on their feet. The sound of the rockets drew the attention of the guards on the ground level, but before they could do anything, they started getting picked off by rifle fire from above.

"We've got you covered, sir! Get inside," Lopez said.

"I'm counting on it," Major Hauer said. "Everyone, move."

CHAPTER 14

<"MASON, WE HAVE a problem,"> Jessica said.

"What is it?" Mason asked.

<"Locals have taken notice of my dummy account and are working to lock me out. Worse, they know something's up with the STC, and we've got security teams converging on our location. Too many for Sergeant Cane and her fireteam to hold off.">

"So, you're going to need a pickup; is that it?" Mason asked.

"That's right," Jessica said. "We have five minutes before security gets here."

"Major Hauer, did you get that?" Mason asked.

<"I heard, Flight Lieutenant,"> Major Hauer said, subvocalizing, probably because it was hard to talk over the sound of gunfire. <"You're clear to go and pick up Lieutenant Sinclair and Cane's fireteam. Just make sure you come back here to pick us up after you take care of that.">

"Roger that, sir," said Mason. "I'll be back in a jiff."

<"Back in a jiff? Who talks like that?"> Jessica asked.

Mason prepared to lift off the ring. "I do."

<"I'm going to have to revise the ETA downward. Security's here, and they have help,"> Jessica said.

"Cendy soldiers?" Mason asked.

<"Yes. Cane and her troopers are holding them off, but they're expending their ammunition too quickly to do it,"> Jessica said.

"Belts and zones," Mason said. "I'm about to take off. I'll be there in a moment. The spin-gravity is too strong for the maneuvering thrusters to push *Buttercup* off the ring. I'll have to use the main drive."

<"Which will get the attention of the Cendy warship,"> Jessica said. <"As if we need more trouble.">

"Yeah, tell me about it. Taking off now," Mason said. "How long do you think it will take for you guys to reach a dock?"

<"Oh, don't bother with that," Jessica said. <"Just fly close to the STC cupola and get ready to pick us up.">

Mason fired up the main drive, throttling to full power and lifting Buttercup off the roof of the ring. The drive exhaust left a circle of red-hot metal behind. Mason suspected he just caused some very expensive property damage. He cut the drive as soon as he lifted off, hoping he didn't get the attention of the Cendies. When he directed one of *Buttercup's* long-range cameras toward the Cendy battlecruiser, he saw a pair of fighters slip off the racks on its side.

"Oh, belts and zones!"

Mason turned *Buttercup* towards the northern dock, and lit the long-burn drive. There was no point in stealth anymore. A hauler pilot who lit a longburn drive near a station would face an immediate revocation of their pilot's license and five years in prison in Federal Space. Reckless maneuvers around a station, such as flying through the spinning rings, would add even more charges. But Mason wasn't in Federal Space and, besides, the Cendies were about to try and kill him anyway.

A proximity alert flashed in his HUD as one of the spokes of the Blue Ring swung through his path. He weaved around it with less than a dozen meters to spare before flying through the Green Ring and the bare spine of the station beyond it.

Once clear of the rings, he flipped *Buttercup* over and fired the longburn drive in a full-power burst to stop the hauler a couple hundred meters away from the STC cupola. With the fine adjustments of the maneuvering thrusters, he closed to within a few meters.

"I'm here, Jessica. What's your status?"

<"Cane's troopers are falling back to the cupola,"> Jessica said.

"I have fighters incoming from the Cendy warship," Mason said. "They'll be here in a few minutes."

<"Won't be long now. We're about to blow the windows.">

"Well, that's one way to make an exit," Mason said.

Through the cupola's windows, Mason could see armored figures huddled against the far wall of the STC center. There was a flash, and the window blew out, sending sparkling shards of glass out into space. Figures started floating out of the hole as atmosphere gushed out. Mason opened the outer airlock's outer hatch and turned it to face the troopers.

"Jessica, you there?" Mason said.

<"I'm here,"> she said. <"Sergeant Cane's carrying me.">

"Aren't there supposed to be four troopers?" Mason asked.

<"One of them didn't make it,"> Jessica said.

The three troopers, one carrying a container likely holding Jessica's head, floated into the airlock. Mason closed the outer hatch as soon as they entered, starting the repressurization cycle. The enemy fighters were incoming at a hard burn. Mason turned towards the Freeport, intending to use it as cover. It was then that the lanky, armored figure of an Ascendency soldier landed on the canopy of *Buttercup's* cockpit, their blank face locking onto Mason.

"Oh shit!" Mason said.

The soldier brought its weapon to bear—a long, wicked rifle that looked more than up to the task of punching through the double-paned ballistic glass of the cockpit. He'd be dead before the troopers in the hold could help, so Mason did the only thing he could. He fired the longburn drive. The sudden acceleration threw off the soldier's aim, and the first shot went through the glass and flew past Mason to impact the deck behind him. The soldier regained their balance and aimed their weapon at Mason, while collision alarms blared and flashed in the cockpit. The soldier seemed to notice that, because their blank face turned around to see the side of the Dagon Freeport approach.

There was a loud crunch and a groan of metal as the impact threw Mason into his restraints. *Buttercup* bounced off the side of the station and drifted back. The twitching body of the Cendy soldier with a caved-in chest floated just outside of *Buttercup's* cracked cockpit. All the armored plating that covered the thing didn't seem to provide much protection against a hundred-ton hauler ramming into the side of a large space station. There was a steady hiss of air escaping from the bullet hole in the canopy.

"Flight Lieutenant Grey, what the hell was that?" Sergeant Cane asked.

"I just rammed the station," Mason said

"By accident?"

"Deliberately," Mason said. "Now there's a bullet hole in the cockpit."

"Bullet hole?" she asked.

"That's directly related to why I just rammed the station," Mason said. "If someone could come up to the cockpit to patch the hole, that would be great. I'm a little busy flying the ship."

Sergeant Cane floated into the cockpit. She still had her helmet on, so he couldn't see her expression, but he had a good guess based on her body language as she saw the damage to the cockpit.

"What happened up here?" she asked.

Mason pointed towards the figure drifting outside the cockpit. "That thing happened."

"Ouch," she said.

"Assuming those things even feel pain," Mason said. "Where's Lieutenant Sinclair?"

<"I'm right here, with Sergeant Cane, Mason,"> she said.

Cane pulled a container from behind her back.

"I didn't realize they made boxes just for carrying talking heads in space," Mason said.

"They don't, sir," Cane said. "It's for holding food. Keeps it from drying out or freezing in a vacuum."

<"You didn't have to explain that to him, Sergeant,"> Jessica said.

Mason pointed at the hole in the cockpit. "Please plug that hole, Sergeant."

Sergeant Cane locked Jessica's container under a cargo net, then worked on sealing the hole. With dexterity that belied the bulk of her hardsuit, Sergeant Cane opened a sealing kit and put a patch over the bullet hole in the cockpit.

While she did that, Mason maneuvered *Buttercup*, putting the station's central spine between the hauler and the approaching fighters. "Jessica, I don't suppose you know what Major Hauer's status is?"

<"I'm afraid not. Even if I didn't lose my connection when I went off station, I crashed both the security network and the STC system,"> Jessica said.

"Well, at least the locals won't be able to use them," Mason said. "What about the station's fighters?"

<"The doors to their fighters' hangar bays are locked tight. It'll take hours for them to launch,"> Jessica said.

"One less thing to worry about," Mason said.

Mason moved directly for the Orange Ring, keeping an eye on the sensors for the enemy fighters. The two craft flew around the side of the station just a couple hundred kilometers away. A pair of interceptors rocketed away from each of them, burning straight for *Buttercup*.

"Evading. Hold on," Mason said, wishing he wasn't flying a stock hauler.

Mason had no real defense against the interceptors burning towards him beyond the cover provided by the immense bulk of Dagon Freeport. Mason flew *Buttercup* as close to the hull of the Dagon Freeport as he could, putting the station between him and the incoming interceptors. If he were flying a Lightning, there would be a dedicated AI calculating the course of the interceptors, giving him a projected course and time to impact. He had none of those things with *Buttercup*.

"Next time, Special Purpose Branch needs to budget in some countermeasures for their haulers," Mason said.

<"I'll be sure to make that point in the mission report if we survive this,"> Jessica said.

Two interceptors flashed through space past the station, their motors burned out.

Mason sighed in relief but didn't let himself relax. Those fighters would be repositioning themselves to take another shot. Checking the timer, Mason realized that the 4th should have come around the side of Dagon by now. He flew around the station, revealing an Ascendency battlecruiser burning hard away from the station, toward the sixteen Lightnings rising up from the horizon.

"The 4th is here," Mason said.

<"I'm sending a message now letting them know what's happening,"> Jessica said.

Mason tucked *Buttercup* into an alcove in the side of the spine, thinking it might be a good hiding spot.

Thousands of kilometers away, the fighters of the 4th Fighter Squadron ascended from Dagon at a hard burn, on a direct vector for the Ascendency battlecruiser.

The Cendy battlecruiser launched their remaining fighters, which formed a screen between their mothership and the approaching Federal fighters. As soon as the Lightnings entered range, the Cendy fighters launched a heavy volley of interceptors at the Lightnings. The 4th replied with an even heavier wave of their own, throwing several dozen more interceptors into space.

As the time to impact counted down, Mason felt his stomach twist with anxiety. With so many interceptors in space, there would be losses on both sides. Then he saw more interceptors launch from the Lightnings, hundreds more. Far more than they should have been able to carry. The enormous second wave of Federal interceptors crashed into the Cendy interceptors and erased them from the sensor's display well before they reached the 4th's Lightnings.

"What the hell was that?" Mason asked.

<"Oh, the 4th's carrying experimental weapons called stilettos," Jessica said. "I'm pretty sure you just witnessed their first use in combat."

"I could've used a few of those not too long ago," Mason said.

The Cendies didn't have a similar counter to the Federal interceptors. Instead, they used more conventional tactics, scattering before the incoming missiles while dropping decoys. Five Cendy fighters disappeared from the sensors as the wave of interceptors washed over them. The remaining three continued to burn for the Federal fighters, clearly intent on getting into gun range despite being outnumbered. The fighters sent to kill him flew into view, but not to pursue Mason. They were burning hard away from the station, heading back to their ship. It looked like they had decided *Buttercup* was no longer a priority target.

Mason let out a long sigh.

"Major Hauer's probably making his exit from the station now, assuming he's keeping to the mission schedule, sir," Sergeant Cane said.

Mason pushed *Buttercup* out of the alcove and flew her back in the direction of the Orange Ring. "Let's make sure we're there when they show up."

Flying inside the circumference of the Orange Ring, Mason scanned the landing zone. All he saw was the large splotch of blackened plating left behind by his emergency launch. "I don't see any sign of them," Mason said.

"Drop me and my fireteam off on the station, sir," Sergeant Cane said. "We can reinforce Major Hauer."

"We don't know where they are, Sergeant," Mason said.

"Then we'll find them, sir," Sergeant Cane said.

Mason shook his head. "Not good enough, Sergeant. We need to know what's going on in there. Jessica? Anything you can do to reestablish contact?"

<"I'm afraid not, Mason," Jessica said. "The radios the Raiders have aren't strong enough to transmit through the hull of the station.">

"Let my troopers onto that station and we'll find Major Hauer, sir," Sergeant Cane said.

"Just hold on, Sergeant," Mason said. "They might be headed for an alternate escape route. I can't occupy myself dropping you off if I need to pick them up in a hurry."

Sergeant Cane sighed. "Fine. But I'm going back into the hold to get my team ready." She unbuckled herself and floated down out of the cockpit, into the hold below, leaving Mason and Jessica alone.

<"You're doing the right thing not letting Sergeant Cane go onto the station,"> Jessica said.

"I know," Mason said. "But if she had to choose between her people and following my orders, I don't have much doubt she'd pick her people. That's what I would do if those were my squadron-mates in there."

<"No, you wouldn't,"> Jessica said. <"You'd wait to see what the best thing you could do to help them was, not run off half-cocked with no plan.">

There was an explosion out the side of the ring, gas and debris blowing out the hole. Figures started jumping out, falling away from the station with considerable speed as the angular momentum of the spinning ring carried them away.

"This is Major Hauer. *Buttercup*, you out there?"

"I'm here, sir. I have eyes on four groups floating away from the station," Mason said. "What's your status?"

"We got Colonel Shimura, Cordial, and his surviving bodyguard. What's the status of Sergeant Cane and her team?"

"I'm here, sir. Wiles didn't make it," Sergeant Cane said.

"Understood," Major Hauer said. "I've got two wounded drifting in space. They're part of the first group to jump from the station."

"I'm moving to intercept them, sir," Mason said. He fired his drive, setting *Buttercup* on an intercept.

The first group of four troopers all huddled together. Mason couldn't tell the state of their injuries, but he assumed they must be serious if Hauer wanted them picked up first.

"Sergeant, I could use some people in the airlock to help the wounded in," Mason said.

"Already done, sir," Cane said. "We're ready."

A light appeared in the HUD, indicating the inner hatch had closed and the airlock was depressurizing.

"Get ready. We'll be on them in a minute," Mason said

Mason flipped on *Buttercup's* running lights, so the troopers could see him approach. They were all huddled around each other, forming a ring with their arms like skydivers falling together. Mason fired braking thrusters to slow his velocity, careful to make sure the blasts were aimed away from the ring of interlocked figures.

"*Buttercup*, is that you?" asked Sergeant Lopez.

"I understand you have a couple of wounded," Mason said.

"That would be me and Corporal Grills, sir," she said. "We both took hits after the ballistic barrier broke. I got a hole in my thigh, while he's got a stomach wound."

"How bad?"

"I'll live, but Grills is in bad shape, sir," Lopez said.

"We're coming to get you, Janney. Just hold on," Sergeant Cane said.

"We're not going anywhere," she said.

Mason maneuvered on a very slow-speed collision vector with the troopers, facing *Buttercup's* open airlock at them. The troopers drifted into the airlock at half a meter per second. Sergeant Cane's fireteam pulled them inside and closed the outer hatch. While the airlock repressurized, Mason moved to the next group, made up of the prisoners the troopers had rescued. By the time Mason positioned *Buttercup* to scoop them up, Sergeant Cane had brought the first group inside and returned to the airlock alone. She had left her other troopers behind to tend to the wounded.

"Colonel Shimura, I'm one minute out from you. Can you see my running lights?" Mason asked.

"I see them, Flight Lieutenant," Shimura said.

"Sergeant Cane's in the airlock waiting to grab you, sir."

There was an energy spike on the sensors, and something bright flashed in the side windows. By the time Mason turned his head to look, the flashing was over, leaving just an after-image in his peripheral vision. He knew what the flashes meant. The 4th had just used nukes on the Cendy warship.

Mason scanned the sensors and saw what was left of the Cendy battlecruiser. Bright spots on the thermal imagining marked where the blast cones of the torpedoes' directional warheads had struck the Cendy warship's hull.

"*Buttercup*, this is Void Knight Leader. Do you copy?" Wing Commander Cade said.

"This is *Buttercup*. Thanks for the save, sir," Mason said.

"You're welcome, *Buttercup*. We're moving towards your position to give you cover," Wing Commander Cade said.

"Roger that, Void Knight Leader," Mason said.

"This is Cane. We just pulled the rest inside," Sergeant Cane said.

"Good job, Sergeant. Tell everyone to secure themselves to the deck. I'm going one g in thirty seconds," Mason said.

"We're getting everyone strapped down right now, sir. Thanks for the heads-up," Sergeant Cane said.

Mason turned *Buttercup* until Mervie's icon was in the center of the cockpit, and throttled the hauler up to full power. The hauler's rugged powerplant throbbed with a deep growl as Mason opened up the throttle, and the pull of full gravity bit down on him.

The sixteen Lightnings of the 4th formed around *Buttercup* in a loose escort formation as Mason opened the distance with Dagon Freeport. An almost overpowering sense of relief filled him as he saw the station grow smaller in the rear sensors. He very much hoped he would never have to visit the place ever again.

Thirty minutes after he started his burn, more contacts appeared, fighters launching from Dagon Freeport itself.

"Looks like the locals managed to unscramble their systems enough to launch fighters," Mason said. "Void Knight Leader, can you handle them?"

"With ease, *Buttercup*. Maintain your present course."

"Roger," Mason said.

Twelve Lightnings peeled off to intercept the fighters from Dagon Freeport, leaving four to provide close escort for *Buttercup*.

There were almost three times as many Dagon fighters as there were Federal, but the fighters from Dagon were a disparate collection of old League and independent fighter designs. All likely bought surplus.

Wing Commander Cade's Void Knights launched a wave of interceptors at the incoming enemy fighters. When the enemy launched their own, their old, second-hand interceptors proved no match for the ECM systems of the Lightnings and none were able to maintain lock.

The Federal interceptors maintained lock just fine, and the space far behind *Buttercup* flashed with a dozen impacts. A third of the enemy fighters dropped off the boards.

The remainder disengaged, scattering each and every direction their drives could push them. Wing Commander Cade let them go and returned to escort formation with *Buttercup*.

After completing the midpoint flip, Mason heard someone climbing up the ladder into the cockpit. He turned to find Colonel Shimura. Her face was bruised and her nose looked like it had been broken and then reset.

"Flight Lieutenant," she said while pulling herself up.

"Sir," Mason said. "Was that the Cendies who did that, or the Dagon security?"

"Security," she said. "They didn't survive."

"Good to hear that, sir," Mason said.

Shimura limped heavily over to the seat next to Mason and dropped into it. "Thanks for picking us up, Flight Lieutenant."

"My pleasure, Colonel," Mason said.

"So, where's Lieutenant Sinclair?" Shimura asked.

Mason nodded to the container holding Jessica's head. "Right there, sir. She went to sleep to conserve her life-support module."

Shimura turned from Jessica's container back to Mason. "I understand you cut her head off."

"Seemed the thing to do at the time, sir," Mason said.

"You might be the only person in the universe who has ever saved someone's life by decapitating them," Colonel Shimura said.

"You know, that never occurred to me, sir," Mason said.

"Just wait until I write it in the mission report," Colonel Shimura said.

"I do not envy you, sir," Mason said. "How's Mister Cordial and Cynth doing?"

"They beat him harder than me, but I think he'll be all right. Frankly, he looks better for it. The bruises help hide the scars," she said. "Other than missing an arm, Cynth is in decent shape."

Mason nodded. "Sounds like we got lucky today, sir."

"That we did, Flight Lieutenant," Shimura said.

Mason turned to Jessica's container. "So, I've been meaning to ask. Do you guys keep a spare body for her lying around?"

"Doctor Cole will have something for her," Colonel Shimura said. "But she's probably going to hate it."

CHAPTER 15

MASON SLIPPED *BUTTERCUP* back into Hangar Bay 24, settling the hauler on the docking pad, maglocking the landing gear, and idling the reactor. As soon as the hangar doors closed, the hangar pressurized and *Mervie's* medics came aboard to collect the wounded. Jessica was the first the medics took off *Buttercup*, bundled away by Doctor Cole himself, who tucked the container under his arm and floated out of the hangar with impressive speed. The wounded troopers, then Mister Cordial, Colonel Shimura, and Cynth followed them, each accompanied by at least one medic. When Mason followed Major Hauer and his remaining troopers out of the hangar, a power surge traveled through the ship. *Mervie* had jumped.

"I wonder where we're going?" Mason asked.

"Probably just a precautionary jump in case more Cendies show up," Major Hauer said. "You did good today, flyboy."

"Uh, thanks, sir," Mason said. "I have to say, it was good to see first-hand that the Raiders' reputation is well-earned." He sighed. "Um… I'm sorry about Corporal Wiles."

Major Hauer nodded. "So am I, Flight Lieutenant. But given what we were up against, I am grateful I only have one letter to write to a grieving family. Your parents did a good job teaching you how to fly haulers."

"Helps they're among the best in the business," Mason said. "Though I was hardly the only pilot who earned their pay today."

"Hmm, maybe," Major Hauer said. "I'm sure the Void Knights are feeling quite proud of themselves."

"They did take out a League starship and its fighters without suffering any casualties," Mason said. "Those are results to be proud of."

Major Hauer grimaced. "Yeah, but it gives them more ammunition to puff-up their egos. Not something I like about fighter pilots. No offense, Flight Lieutenant."

"None taken, sir," Mason said.

<"Flight Lieutenant Grey, please report to the bridge.">

"What is it, Flight Lieutenant?" Major Hauer asked.

"I just got an order to report to the bridge, sir," Mason said.

"Ah, I guess, as the last intelligence officer standing, Captain Vann's selected you for the debriefing," Major Hauer said.

"I'm not an intelligence officer, sir," Mason said.

"Looks like you are today, flyboy," Major Hauer said.

As Mason made his way to the bridge, *Mervie* jumped again.

Mervie's circular bridge buzzed with the chatter from the various bridge stations as their crews went about the business of operating the starship. Captain Vann floated parallel to the deck in front of the holotank in the center of the compartment, her hands grasping the base of the holotank while her boots hung in the air. She gazed into a representation of the entire Fomalhaut system.

"Reporting, Captain," Mason said.

"Welcome back, Flight Lieutenant." Captain Vann pulled her feet to the deck and hooked them through a pair of footholds. "I understand things got interesting in Dagon Freeport."

"Too interesting for my taste, sir," Mason said.

"I can imagine," Captain Vann said. She turned away from Mason and locked her dark eyes on him. "More than a little disturbing that the Cendies would help overthrow Fomalhaut's most powerful pirate lord. Do you think they know he works with us?"

"I'd say they do now, sir. That said, the Cendies didn't know we were there. I think that's why we're still alive."

"Did Mister Cordial give you any useful information?" Captain Vann asked.

"Yes, sir," Mason said. "He gave us a collection of reported encounters by pirates and independent ships with the Ascendency in several unclaimed systems. Lieutenant Sinclair copied everything onto her brainset."

"Colonel Shimura will want us to investigate those systems," Captain Vann said.

"She mentioned something to that effect, sir," Mason said.

"I'll have to speak with her once Doctor Cole clears her."

Mason glanced at the holotanks past Captain Vann, noting the icon representing *Mervie*. The two jumps had taken them beyond Fomalhaut's outer debris disk.

"We holding position here, sir?" Mason asked.

"Yes. At least until we figure out what to do next," Captain Vann said. "There is the question of what to do about Mister Cordial."

"Are we taking him with us, sir?" Mason asked.

"That depends on him, Flight Lieutenant," Captain Vann said. "But it's premature to discuss these things." She glanced back at him. "You should head to your quarters. You must be exhausted."

Mason's sleep had been deep and dreamless. When he woke up, he had a bad taste in his mouth, and a feeling of weariness, despite the long hours of sleep. Both were side effects of the stimulant cocktail Mason had used while flying *Buttercup*. They were mild symptoms. The pilots of the 4th were going to be an order of magnitude more hungover than him. None of the drugs used to keep pilots functional in high-g flight were addictive, but they could still make their absence felt in the hours after they wore off.

After showering and getting dressed, he headed to the wardroom and fixed himself a large packet of coffee. The go-to cure for post-flight hangovers. The strong flavor washed away the bad taste in his mouth, and the caffeine drove away weariness. Of all the substances Mason used to remain functional, coffee was his favorite by a parsec.

A message appeared in his HUD before he was even halfway finished with his coffee. It was from Colonel Shimura.

"Good morning, sir," Mason said.

<"Likewise, Flight Lieutenant. You rest well?">

"Like the dead, sir," Mason said. "How are you recovering?"

<"Quickly, Flight Lieutenant. Doctor Cole already got my knee mostly fixed up,"> Colonel Shimura said. <"I need to speak with you in person. Head over to my office as quickly as you can.">

"I'm on my way, sir." He got up and grabbed a breakfast burrito from a dispenser, tearing open the edible wrapper and scarfing it down as he walked down the corridor.

He washed down the last of it, wrapper and all, with a swig of his coffee before knocking on Shimura's door.

"It's open," Shimura said from the other side.

Mason pushed open the door and entered Colonel Shimura's austere office, ready to salute her, but stopped in his tracks at the sight of Mister Cordial's scarred scalp and the artificial eyes on the back of Cynth's head.

The pirate lord turned his horrible face to Mason and stood up, holding out his hand. "Ah, Flight Lieutenant Grey, it's good to see you again."

Mason took Cordial's hand without thinking about it, giving it a firm shake. The pirate lord's hand squeezed back with confident strength. His expensive suit was gone, replaced by a utilitarian jumpsuit of durable grey fabric. It seemed more natural on him than the suit ever did. Cynth stood up, though she didn't offer a hand to shake, which Mason didn't blame her for—she only had the one. Doctor Cole had removed the damaged remains of her forearm, and her right arm ended in a bandaged-wrapped stump that hung just below the rolled-up sleeve of her jumpsuit.

"I must thank you for helping save my life and the life of one of my bodyguards, Flight Lieutenant," Mister Cordial said. "You did a remarkable job surviving on your own."

"I'm a big boy, sir," Mason said. "And I wasn't on my own. I had Lieutenant Sinclair with me."

"Yes, I was quite impressed by both the quality and quantity of Lieutenant Sinclair's enhancements." Mister Cordial pointed at his ruined face. "Might consider getting something like that done for myself when I get older. Fix this face of mine in the process."

"You'd get no objection from me, sir," Mason said.

Cordial chuckled. "Honest? I like that. Not something I'm used to from the Federal Space Forces Special Purpose Branch."

"To be fair, I've not been a part of the Branch for very long," Mason said. "And besides, I'm basically a glorified chauffeur."

"Well, be that as it may, I wanted to thank you in person before I departed," Mister Cordial said. "If you're ever back in Fomalhaut, remember that Mister Cordial owes you a favor."

"That is a very open-ended promise, sir," Mason said.

"I tend to give those to people who save my life," Mister Cordial said. He nodded to Cynth. "She's lined up a serious bonus, for example. And a new arm at my expense."

Cynth flexed her undamaged left arm. "Might as well replace this one too. I hate it when my parts don't match."

"I don't know, Miss Cynth. I think a bit of asymmetry would go well with your hair," Mister Cordial said. He turned back to Mason. "Now, if you'll excuse me, Flight Lieutenant, I need to get *Buttercup* ready to fly. Colonel Shimura was gracious enough to give her to me to fly to one of my bases in Fomalhaut."

"She's a good ship, sir," Mason said.

Mister Cordial chuckled. "No doubt. Goodbye, Flight Lieutenant." He turned to Shimura. "Until we meet again, Colonel."

After Mister Cordial and Cynth departed, Mason turned to Colonel Shimura. "So, I guess my skills as a hauler pilot are no longer needed."

"You have other skills that might come in useful, Flight Lieutenant," Colonel Shimura said.

"So, is Mister Cordial staying on our side, sir?" Mason asked.

"He's on his side, as always, but at least for the duration of the conflict with the Ascendency, his interests and Earth-Fed's align," Shimura said. "He'll do his part to limit their influence among the pirate groups in Fomalhaut, and he'll continue to feed us intel on what's going on in unclaimed space. You did a good job recovering the mission from the disaster it turned into. I cannot overstate how important it was that we got Cordial out of that mess alive. I also appreciate you helping with my own rescue."

Mason nodded. "You're welcome, sir. So, what's next for us? Is Lieutenant Sinclair still recovering?"

"She is. Doctor Cole has set her up with a mobility rig, but she's still acclimating to it," Colonel Shimura said. "As for what's next, as soon as Mister Cordial launches, we'll jump out to meet with a refueling station near Fomalhaut. Then we'll proceed to one of the systems Mister Cordial listed for us."

Mason's stomach quivered. "Sir, I feel the need to point out that when I was a prisoner aboard *Fafnir*, they had some difficulties with their forward refueling bases. Namely, that the Ascendency always got to them first."

"This isn't a forward base. It's just a cache dropped off by a Federal Intelligence ship years ago," Colonel Shimura said. "If the Cendies know about it, then we're in bigger trouble than I thought."

"That's not very comforting, sir," Mason said.

"Oh? That was supposed to be a bit of a joke," Shimura said. "It we will be fine, Flight Lieutenant. I'm more worried about what we're going to find in the unclaimed systems."

"Expecting trouble there?" Mason said.

"Hoping for it, Flight Lieutenant. That's the point of this mission," Colonel Shimura said. "The question is, will it be more trouble than we can handle?"

After an uneventful resupply at the Special Purpose Branch's secret cache, *Mervie* jumped out, leaving Fomalhaut behind. Mason was glad of it. There was not anything that made him want to go back, including the favor of a pirate lord.

With *Buttercup* no longer aboard, Mason was once again a pilot without a ship to fly. The hauler wasn't much, but at least, with her, he didn't feel superfluous. As it was, he mostly only served as an assistant to Colonel Shimura and Jessica. Not exactly putting his expensive training to use.

Jessica's quarters, which doubled as her office, sported large photos of London landmarks on each wall, along with a stack of diplomas and certificates. The bed, rather than the standard drab sheets, had a thick and beautifully embroidered blanket and a large pillow in a crimson pillowcase. Jessica herself was seated at her desk, stooped forward with the faraway look of someone reading something on their HUD. The collar of her blue jumpsuit was zipped all the way up to conceal where her neck interfaced with the mobility rig Doctor Cole had attached her to.

Mason carried a coffee packet in one hand and a vial of nutrients in the other as he joined Jessica in her quarters. The coffee was for him, fresh from the Special Purpose Branch supply cache, and the nutrients were for Jessica. Jessica looked up from her desk.

"Ah, I see you brought lunch," Jessica said with a forced smile. She held out a skeletal hand of dark grey polymer tipped with lighter grey at the fingertips. Mason placed the vial in Jessica's hand and, to his surprise, she immediately unzipped her jumpsuit down to where her navel would have been, exposing the smooth, dark-grey polymer beneath, and inserted the vial into a port in her chest. There was a quiet hiss as the mobility rig's digestive system sucked out the vial's contents. Jessica stared at him, as if challenging him to look away. He didn't. Instead, he made an effort not to gaze at the rig's flat polymer chest, or where the flesh of her neck interacted with the collar of her rig. Instead, he kept his gaze fixed on her large, dark eyes.

"Uh, so, find anything interesting about that Cendy ship?"

Jessica relaxed a bit. "Yes, surprisingly. *Buttercup's* sensors might have been stock, but we still got a full passive scan of the ship. The people back in Procyon are going to be in for a treat when the courier drone arrives."

"There anything in particular?" Mason asked.

"Well, at least while idling, the Cendy battlecruiser's emissions fall inside the range that *Mervie's* mimic array can emulate," Jessica said.

"I suppose that could be useful."

"More than useful, Mason. I mean it's clear that the Ascendency doesn't know that we have ships that can alter their signatures to look like other vessels. That's an advantage we need to exploit to the fullest if we want to turn this war around."

"Ships? You mean *Mervie's* not the only ship of her kind?" Mason asked.

Jessica's eyes shifted around as she played back what she just said. "Oh, I did just let that slip. Huh. Well, you are technically authorized to know. *Mervie's* not the only ship with a mimic array, but she is the largest. So, she is unique in that regard. All the others are about the size of destroyers, meant for passive surveillance."

"They got the same naming scheme?" Mason asked.

Jessica nodded. "Just an arbitrary alphanumeric that their crews use to come up with a nickname. You can imagine what B-1-R's nickname is."

"There's a B-1-R?" Mason asked. "How does the Branch come up with these names?"

Jessica shrugged. "They're randomly generated by a computer. Sometimes that computer is feeling cheeky."

"So, are these other ships out there trying to find out about the Ascendency?" Mason asked.

"Probably? I don't think even Colonel Shimura knows what the other Special Purpose Branch ships are up to. Each operates independently."

"So, if *Mervie* can disguise herself as a Cendy warship, how are we going to use that?" Mason asked.

"Don't really know just yet," Jessica said. "Something ambitious, I hope."

"Ambitious?" Mason said. "That's the same as saying risky."

"Big rewards usually are," Jessica said.

A ding from Jessica's mobility rig signaled that it had finished draining the vial. She pulled the vial out and zipped up her jumpsuit. Jessica held up the empty vial, turning it in her fingers. "Hopefully, what we learned from Mister Cordial will be worth all the trouble." She let go of the vial and watched it fall to the deck, then continued to stare at it where it rested.

"You okay, Jessica?" Mason asked.

Her gaze shifted from the vial on the deck to Mason. "I'm... I'm... You know, you're not the first person to ask me if I'm okay, but you are the first I can't say I'm okay to."

"You asked me to cut your head off," Mason said. "Yeah, it saved your life, but I doubt that's something you can feel okay about."

"No, I suppose not." Jessica looked at her polymer-covered mechanical hand and opened it up, spreading the fingers out. "Blimey, this body is a downgrade. Still, it's a step up from being carried around in a jumpsuit."

"And, as a bonus, when we get back home, you'll be able to get a whole new body at the taxpayer's expense," Mason said.

"True." Jessica rested her chin on her right hand and tapped her lips with one finger. "Maybe I'll try something taller. Seeing things through your eyes gave me an appreciation for height."

"Glad I could give you a new perspective," Mason said.

"It's not an experience I will soon forget. Though I could happily forget the part where you used my head as a football," Jessica said. "I'm still annoyed with you about that."

"Sorry," Mason said.

"You better be," she said, her smile playful. She chuckled.

"There something on my face?"

"No, no. I just had a dreadful thought."

"Dreadful, you say? About what?"

"My body. The one we left behind," Jessica said.

"The one I left headless and half-naked?"

"The one and only. They must have found it by now. I bet they think they've got Jack the Ripper loose inside the Red Ring now."

"Belts and zones, I never thought of that until now," Mason said. "After everything they're likely dealing with, I bet we gave someone in Dagon's Security ulcers thinking about it."

CHAPTER 16

"THERE'S SOMETHING HERE," Jessica said, pointing at the projection of the system hovering on the holotank.

Mervie was a couple jumps out from the edge of a red dwarf system Mister Cordial had marked as a place where independent ships had encountered Ascendency starships. A lone star barely massive enough to exist on the Main Sequence smoldered in the middle of a not-to-scale representation of its three-world planetary system. The two inner planets were tidally-locked worlds. The innermost one was an airless ball of silicate rock and iron. The next one out was a pressure cooker with a thick, cloudy atmosphere of carbon dioxide. The third planet was the largest, and the only one of real military value in the system. A Neptune-mass world the same color as Jupiter's dark belts. Orbiting it was a collection of small moons, each an airless body of rock and ice whose combined mass was less than that of Luna. Ships were also there. As befitting a spy ship, *Mervie* had some very large and sensitive scopes on her, and after a few hours fixed on the gas giant, they picked up the emissions that could only come from longburn drives.

Colonel Shimura walked up next to Jessica, her bruises faded to near invisibility, her limp all but gone. She crossed her arms at the projection. "So now it's just a question of if that's the Cendies or an independent gas mining crew looking for a quick buck."

"In either case, Colonel, we'll need to jump in close to find out," Jessica said.

Mason loitered behind the two intelligence officers, leaning against the wall, thinking about how *Mervie* would attack, assuming there was a Cendy gas mining operation in the system. The radius of the star's jump limit was tiny, smaller than the distance between the Earth and the Sun. On a hard burn, Lightnings could fly from the jump limit to the gas giant in less than a day. Twelve hours if they just wanted to do a flyby. As fast a strike as one could hope for in space combat. That was assuming the icons on the holotank were, in fact, Cendies, and that Colonel Shimura planned on launching a strike.

Colonel Shimura glanced over at Mason. "I hope that silence of yours is of the thoughtful variety, Flight Lieutenant."

Mason straightened his posture. "Ah, yes, sir. If we're planning a simple strike, then we won't be in the system for too long. It'd take maybe… forty hours for the Void Knights to fly into the system, blast the Cendies, and get back to *Mervie*. Of course, that's assuming this is a simple strike, which I have my doubts about."

"Yeah, we don't do simple in the Special Purpose Branch," Jessica said. "Clever and daring are our MO."

Mason glanced at Colonel Shimura. "So, what are you planning that's so clever and daring, sir?"

"We need to find out everything we can about the enemy," Colonel Shimura said. "Which means we can't simply destroy every Cendy ship we see. If we get a chance, we need to capture one."

Mason's right eyebrow twitched upwards. "Capture, sir? That's a vastly more complicated undertaking."

"And, yet, that's what we need to do," Colonel Shimura said.

The Void Knights launched as soon as *Mervie* jumped into the edge of the jump limit, above the local plane of the ecliptic. The Lightnings shot out of the hangar, turned to face the distant gas giant, and lit their longburn drives at a hard burn. It would be several minutes before the light from *Mervie* jumping in and launching fighters reached the enemy. By then, the Void Knights would be well on their way.

As soon as the last Void Knight launched, *Mervie's* engines lit and three gs pulled down on Mason. His acceleration couch tilted back and his body sank into the gel cushions. The pull of acceleration gravity wasn't heavy by Mason's standards, but it wasn't light either. Walking around was possible, but dangerous. Captain Vann had made sure the whole crew had one last visit to the head before the jump. If the call of nature came visiting under burn, you'd have to wait until Mervie throttled back or make use of a maximum absorbency garment.

Mason glanced over at Jessica. The skin of her face was pulled taut, but her eyes were focused, either looking at the screen or staring off at something only she could see through her HUD.

Mason's own HUD showed a tactical display of the space around Mervie, while the monitor attached to his couch displayed telemetry from the fighters of the Void Knights. Each of the Void Knight's Lightnings was fully loaded. Eight interceptors loaded internally, four shortburn torpedoes and four of those impressive stiletto pods mounted on the external hardpoints. They were ready to deal with anything the Cendies threw at them, or at least Mason hoped they were.

Fifteen minutes after Mervie's arrival, the Cendies responded, the lone warship launching her fighters and lighting her longburn drive to break orbit from the planet. The two utility starships were also burning, attempting to escape from the Federal fighters bearing down on them.

Mason watched and waited.

For several hours, the developing battle was just icons moving on a screen. The Void Knights burning hard for the Cendy warship, Mervie burning after them, and the Cendy warship and its halo of ten fighters burning up to meet them. The two presumed tanker ships burned down towards the star, trying to get as much distance between themselves and the incoming Federal fighters as they could. There was nothing surprising about the Cendies' tactics. Facing a fighter force larger than their own, they had elected to keep their fighters close to the parent starship, hoping to support each other when the Federal fighters engaged. The Lightnings hit the midpoint and flipped in one coordinated movement to start their braking burn, though at a lower acceleration so they could catch up to the fleeing transports. They intended to fly by the Cendy starship and their escorts.

Still in their braking burn, the Void Knight launched half their interceptors and all their torpedoes at the Cendy warship and their fighter escorts.

The Cendy fighters launched interceptors of their own and accelerated to engage the Federal fighters. The stiletto pods did their job protecting the Void Knights, clearing the Cendy interceptors without a single Lightning getting hit.

The Cendies weren't so lucky. The heavy barrage of interceptors knocked them all out before they could do anything about the torpedoes bearing down on their home starship. The Cendy starship itself lit up with point-defense fire in the last moments before detonation, knocking out several of the incoming Federal torpedoes, but not enough of them. As the Cendy warship put up a wall of point-defense fire, the torpedoes split up, missiles slewing sideways, both to evade the point-defense fire, and to get shot at the warship's flanks before detonating.

They exploded not with the flash of nuclear fire, but instead the EM spike of a kinetic cannon going off. The recoil shattered the torpedoes, but not before each fired a kinetic slug into the sides of the Cendy warship. Slugger torpedoes lacked the raw killing power of a nuclear-tipped torpedo, but that was by design. They were surgical weapons, meant for taking out a critical subsystem, rather than blasting a starship into a glowing wreck.

<"Direct hit on target. Outgassing detected. Looks like we got her on the first shot,"> Wing Commander Cade said, still accelerating too hard to speak into his microphone.

"We see it, Wing Commander. Good shooting," Captain Vann said.

"Thank you, Captain," Wing Commander Cade said after a few minutes of delay. "Proceeding to secondary targets."

"Understood, Wing Commander," Captain Vann said. "Helm, drop acceleration to one g."

"Roger that, sir," *Mervie's* primary pilot said.

Acceleration dropped, and Mason felt a weight come off him as his acceleration couch tilted forward and the gel cushion pushed him out of its embrace.

"Eight Ball 1, Eight Ball 2, you're clear to launch," Captain Vann said.

The assault shuttle pilots acknowledged and launched. Only one assault shuttle, Eight Ball 1, carried troopers. Eight Ball 2 was in full gunship configuration. It would be its job to take out the Cendy ship's point-defense turrets before Eight Ball 1 moved in to deliver the troopers.

The assault shuttle's engines flared to life, pushing ahead at their maximum acceleration of five gs. *Mervie* resumed her three g burn not long after, yanking Mason down into his seat. The midpoint flip came and went, the assault shuttles nearing the end of their braking burn while the Void Knights pursued the gas miners.

Though only a spectator, Mason felt something warm bloom in his chest that the acceleration gravity couldn't squeeze away, the pride of a mission going according to plan, and the excitement at getting to see an intact example of enemy tech up close.

Assuming, of course, the Cendies didn't scuttle their ship before the assault shuttles arrived or, worse, after the Major Hauer's Raiders boarded them.

An alarm sounded, shrill and familiar, which drove away the warm pride and replaced it with ice-cold fear.

"Jump flashes near the ecliptic. Three contacts."

Mason saw the contacts appear tens of millions of kilometers off to *Mervie's* side. Two battlecruisers supported by an arsenal ship. Probably thirsty warships looking to top off, just as *Mervie* was in the middle of her attack. One of the icons, the arsenal ship, flickered and a staggering wave of longburn torpedoes started burning towards *Mervie*.

"Wing Commander Cade, break off your attack and start burning back to *Mervie*. We're going to need your support!"

<"Roger that, *Mervie*. Beginning return burn.">

The Lightnings flared their engines, and their acceleration rose to fifteen gs, the maximum acceleration Lightning pilots could sustain for more than a few minutes. It wouldn't be enough. The enemy torpedoes would reach them well before the fighters did.

Following on the heels of the torpedo launch, the two battlecruisers launched their fighters, which started burning after the torpedoes. All three enemy starships were also burning into the system, their vectors locked onto *Mervie*.

A feeling of dread filled Mason's stomach. They were stuck inside the jump limit, with their fighters too far away to help, and a wave of at least two hundred torpedoes bearing down on them.

"Gunnery, can you take down that many torpedoes?" Captain Vann asked.

"Not likely, sir," the gunnery officer said.

"Then we'll need to figure out something clever before those torpedoes reach us," Captain Vann said.

From her acceleration couch, Jessica spoke up. "Captain, I might have an idea."

"Give it to me, Lieutenant," Captain Vann said.

"*Mervie's* mimic array can match the emissions we recorded from the Cendy starship loitering in Fomalhaut," Jessica said. "If we do that and start transmitting a false transponder signal, it might trick the enemy torpedoes into thinking we're friendly and disarm."

"How do you know they have that kind of failsafe, Lieutenant?" Captain Vann said.

"I don't, sir," Jessica said. "Just seems worth a try."

"Get to working on it, Lieutenant, but I would rather not risk the ship on that assumption," Captain Vann said.

"Captain, sir. I could take one of the 4th's spare Lightnings out to try and thin out those torpedoes," Mason said.

Captain Vann nodded. "Do it. Helm, reduce acceleration to 1.5 gs."

The pull of gravity lightened to just a bit over half-again Earth gravity, and Mason unbuckled himself from his acceleration couch and got to his feet. As soon as the soles of his boots touched the deck, he was running for the nearest elevator.

The doors closed behind him and it started climbing before he had a chance to hit the controls.

<"Flight Lieutenant, I've routed the elevator to the appropriate deck. I've instructed the hangar bay to get Lightning 007 equipped up with a full load of stiletto pods and ready to launch,"> Captain Vann said.

"I've never used stiletto pods before, sir," Mason said.

<"Then I hope you're a quick study, Flight Lieutenant. The lives of my crew depend on it,"> Captain Vann said. <"As does yours.">

"Uh, yeah, no pressure," Mason said. "I'll figure it out, sir."

<"You do that, Flight Lieutenant. You launch as soon as you get buckled in,"> Captain Vann said.

The elevator opened to the hangar. Waiting just outside the elevator were a pair of hangar techs with an open hardsuit between them. The hardsuit faced away from the elevator, its open back beckoning to Mason. He all but jumped inside, shoving his legs through and letting the suit's plates close around him. A tech placed a helmet over his head, and as soon as it sealed, he ran towards the airlock leading to *Magnificent Seven's* hangar bay. At the airlock, Mason hit the emergency cycle, blowing out the air rather than pumping it out. *Mervie* had air to spare, not time.

Magnificent Seven rested in the middle of the hangar, her wings folded up and out of the way. Hangar techs in orange pressure suits crawled around her like ants over a discarded lollipop. All eight external hardpoints, four on top and four on the bottom, had a stiletto pod mounted.

Chief Rabin marched up to Mason, encased in an orange and white pressure suit. "I've got *Magnificent Seven* almost ready, sir."

"How ready is 'almost ready', Chief?" Mason asked.

"Should be ready for space as soon as you've stuck your butt in the pilot's seat, sir," Chief Rabin. "Probably before, now that you've stopped to gab with me."

"Point taken, Chief," Mason said, running past Rabin and jumping up to grab the handhold to pull himself up to the cockpit. He dropped into the acceleration couch, pulling on straps, while he synced his brainset with the fighter's systems. The fighter was already started, her reactors humming at idle power, containment rings for both longburn drives cooled to operating temperature. Combat, sensor, and flight AIs all reported ready to execute the pilot's commands. Mason finished strapping in and unlocked the acceleration couch's gimbal. The seat tilted letting back with the pull of acceleration.

"This is Hauler. I'm strapped in and ready to go."

"Hangar crew is headed to the shelter now, Flight Lieutenant," Captain Vann said. "Prepare to launch in sixty seconds."

Mason settled into his seat, savoring the feeling, despite the danger, of finally being back in the cockpit of a fighter. It had been too long. It felt like a mix of coming home and getting a hit of a drug after a long period of abstinence.

"Ten seconds to launch. Good Hunting, Flight Lieutenant," Captain Vann said.

That's right; he was a hunter. His Lightning was both his mount and his weapon. The wave of long-range torpedoes bearing down on *Mervie*, his prey. Hopefully, that was true of the fighters following behind them as well.

The catapult kicked *Magnificent Seven* out of the hangar with a jolt. Mason immediately pushed down on the stick, pointing the Lightning towards the wave of incoming torpedoes. Their icons clustered together like a deadly constellation, with the Cendy fighters and starships in the distance behind them.

Mason shoved the throttle forward until it hit the first stage of resistance and lit the engines.

Magnificent Seven slammed into his back, and *Mervie* fell away behind him. The ten gs weren't just a pressure squeezing down on him. It was an ache he felt in his eyes, his jaw, his balls, and across his back. It was physically torturous, and he loved it. Not due to masochism—the pain was just the price of admission. It was the feeling of raw power that Mason reveled in.

The sensor AI highlighted the enemy contact ahead of him, showing the two hundred torpedoes and twenty fighters behind them as easy-to-digest icons. Combat AI had already started plotting firing solutions for both his interceptors and the stiletto pods. With the increasing relative speed, the engagement windows for the interceptors were short, and even shorter still for the stilettos. The little interceptors only had seconds of burn time in their motors. Just enough to position themselves ahead of the incoming torpedoes, and that was assuming the torpedoes stayed close together. At some point, they'd split apart during final approach to try and attack *Mervie's* flanks with their directional warheads. He wasn't sure when the Cendy torpedoes would do their terminal flanking maneuver, but he figured he'd need to engage them as soon as possible, so he pushed the throttles to the second stage of resistance, and the gs pushed up to fifteen. The ache turned into a burn as he pushed his Lightning towards the maximum sustained acceleration.

The gel layer of his hardsuit felt like stone against his back, and the suit itself fell into the supporting gel layer of the acceleration seat. His hands were barely able to move under the strain as he pushed them past the third stage. Acceleration crept up to eighteen gs, and Mason's vision narrowed as the blood was pulled from his eyes. If he survived this, he'd have some nasty bruises on his back, and inside his body, his g-tolerance implants barely able to keep him conscious.

Flight AI threw up warnings at the same time his suit's medical system did. The old fighter's frame was nearing overstress, and the engines were generating more heat than the cooling system could pump out. He couldn't keep up this kind of acceleration for long. He'd overheat the engines, a structural member would snap, or he would simply die from one of a potential multitude of acceleration-included traumas. A clot could form in his brain, a heart ventricle could collapse, or perhaps a floating rib would snap off and stab into his liver, bleeding him out from the inside. The options were endless.

Mason neared the launch range of the stilettos. The launch window was too narrow, the approach speed too fast, for Mason to try to fire the weapons on his own. He left it up to the combat AI. A whump Mason felt as much as heard echoed inside the cockpit as 160 stilettos launched all at once. A fraction of a second later, space lit up around the Lightning. Behind him, *Magnificent Seven's* sensor AI tracked the remaining torpedoes. Of the 200 that the Cendies had launched, 50 remained. *Mervie* would have to deal with the remaining torpedoes herself. *Magnificent Seven's* combat AI made it clear there was no firing solution that would bring his conventional interceptors into contact with the torpedoes.

Mason jettisoned the empty stiletto pods. Captain Vann had probably expected him to bring them back, but he didn't need the extra mass weighing *Magnificent Seven* down. With just the eight interceptors, Mason had to pick between saving them to shoot down interceptors the attack craft launched or firing them all in the hopes of inflicting attrition on the enemy ships. While the combat AI presented Mason with potential firing solutions, the sensor AI alerted him to another launch from the Cendy arsenal ship. Another wave of 200 torpedoes. Mason forced the torpedoes out of his mind. They wouldn't matter if the fighters killed him.

He kept up the acceleration, unconcerned about the strain he was inflicting both on *Magnificent Seven* and his own body. When heavily outnumbered by an enemy force in open space, the best chance of survival was to maximize relative velocity.

The attack craft changed vectors, splitting into four groups of five. They were paying Mason and his lone fighter no mind—they were focused on *Mervie*. The rate they were splitting apart, Mason would only be able to engage one group, the other three slipping by to fire torpedoes into *Mervie's* flanks. Mason picked the group above and to the right for no reason other than he had to decide and commit to it. He wouldn't be able to stop their torpedo run, but he could reduce the number of torps *Mervie* would have to deal with.

Mervie started firing interceptors at the incoming torpedoes as Mason neared the interceptor range of Cendy fighters. The launch window would be short, barely enough time for the rotary launcher to discharge all eight missiles before flyby. Mason aimed to pass right through the center of the five Cendy fighters, leaving it to the combat AI to fire the weapons. As he burned in on them like a meteor in its final descent through the atmosphere, the fighters didn't fire any interceptors at him. There was only one reason they wouldn't launch interceptors at an attacking fighter—they didn't have any. He guessed the Cendies wanted to kill the starship, leaving the fighters stranded in the backwater system. A cruel but effective way to eliminate a squadron of enemy fighters.

The rotary launcher started kicking interceptors into space, and the last interceptor fell from *Magnificent Seven's* belly four seconds after the first. The combat AI had highlighted a target that would fall into kinetic range. Mason selected it and let the AI aim his cannon. Four attack craft dropped off the board after getting hit by two interceptors apiece. A fraction of a second after that, *Magnificent Seven's* cannon barked. The fifth attack craft went dark, drifting towards *Mervie* amid a cloud of gas and debris. The remaining fifteen receded away faster than Mason could possibly reengage before they launched on *Mervie*.

Mervie's point defenses swatted down the last of the first wave of torpedoes, just as the attack craft dropped their own torpedoes. The sensor AI tallied 135 shortburn torpedoes vectoring on *Mervie*. There was nothing Mason could do but watch.

The torpedoes converged on *Mervie* from three directions, unopposed by defensive interceptors. The starship must have expended them dealing with the first wave. Mason's heart sank to his stomach, and it had nothing to do with the punishing acceleration as he finally managed to kill the last of his velocity and start moving back towards *Mervie*. The sensor AI helpfully marked the radius the torpedoes were expected to detonate.

The icon representing *Mervie* morphed into a hostile icon representing a Cendy battlecruiser. The torpedoes crossed into detonation range and kept on going without detonating. *Mervie's* point defenses continued swatting down disarmed torpedoes by the dozen until the icons of the torpedoes merged with the starship, and then the flashes of kinetic impacts, as the remaining torpedoes smashed into the hull. Behind him, the second wave of Cendy torpedoes approached. Mason doubted *Mervie's* disguise would work on them. The Cendies were likely already reprograming the warheads to keep them from disarming. But they wouldn't reach *Mervie* before the Void Knights arrived, just in time to take down the second wave of torpedoes with their interceptors, letting the Cendy fighters slip by as they did their own braking burn to return to their ships.

"Hauler, I see you've helped yourself to one of my fighters," Group Captain Cade said. "Form up with *Mervie* and dock to rearm. You'll be flying with us until we figure out a way out of this mess."

So, that's what it takes to fly with Wing Commander Cade's little squadron. <"Roger that, Zero. Vectoring on your position.">

CHAPTER 17

"WELL, THE GOOD news is that Major Hauer's boarding operation was successful," Jessica said.

"For all the good that will do if we can't escape the system," Captain Vann said.

Mason tried to ignore the deep ache permeating his body. The high gs he pulled left him feeling like he had been worked over with a tenderizer. Withdrawal from the drugs that kept him alive and functional left him feeling like he had been marinated, too.

"We managed to accomplish our mission objectives, Captain," Colonel Shimura said. "This is just a complication. One that we can adapt to and overcome."

"We'll have to adapt and overcome fast, then," Captain Vann said. "We detected the jump flash of a courier drone. The Cendies are calling in reinforcements."

Colonel Shimura turned to Wing Commander Cade. "It'll be your people who will have to make us an opening, Wing Commander. Do you think you can take on three Cendy starships?"

"With sixteen..." he glanced at Mason, "seventeen fighters, maybe, sir. The stiletto pods are proving to be very effective, but we're low on missiles."

Colonel Shimura leaned forward. "We could make more."

"Yes, sir, but I'm not sure we have time to wait long enough to replenish our inventory," Wing Commander Cade said.

"A fair point," Shimura said.

Jessica held up a polymer finger. "We could see what we can salvage from the Cendy starship we captured. Perhaps there's something we could use."

Shimura sighed. "I wished some of the crew survived. We might have been able to negotiate the release of the crew in exchange for letting us go."

"Major Hauer made it pretty clear that the crew weren't interested in surrendering, sir," Jessica said.

Shimura shook her head. "I didn't mean that as an indictment of Major Hauer or his people, Lieutenant. But you're right. We should see what we can salvage from the ship."

"I don't suppose we could try to repurpose their guns?" Mason asked.

Shimura shook her head. "Sluggers took out the main reactors. We'd have no way to power them."

"Their shortburn torpedoes might be useful," Group Captain Cade said. "Major Hauer's people found 180 of them stored on the ship."

"That could be a start. God knows we'll need all the firepower we can scrounge up if we try to fight our way out of the system," Shimura said.

"Hopefully, we can figure out how to disable the failsafes that disarm their warheads when they're close to a friendly target," Jessica said.

"They still did a number to my ship, even without their warheads detonating," Captain Vann said. "Several of the hull-mounted radiators were damaged, and we can no longer mimic the signatures of other starships. Not to mention all the bits of broken torpedo lodged into the hull."

"Well, it's pretty clear we have our work cut out for us," Colonel Shimura said. She turned to Mason. "Flight Lieutenant. I'm putting you under Wing Commander Cade's command until we manage to fight our way out of the system."

"Understood, sir," Mason said.

"After seeing him in action, I'm happy to have him augmenting my squadron," Group Captain Cade said.

Colonel Shimura stood up. "Then, that concludes our meeting. Lieutenant Sinclair and I will go over what Major Hauer's team has found on the ship. Captain Vann, once we rendezvous with the captured warship, we'll need to assemble a salvage team to get to work removing everything of either intelligence value or useful for fighting the Cendy taskforce."

"A lot of my crew are champing at the bit to get a close look at Cendy tech," Captain Vann said. "And Doctor Cole is insistent that he get his hands on one of the enemy's bodies for dissection."

Cade stood up and nodded to Mason. "Follow me, Flight Lieutenant. We have some planning to do."

"Yes, sir," Mason said.

Mason followed Cade out of the corridor, gravity pulling him straight down without the slight sideways pull of the Coriolis effect. *Mervie* was making 1.5 gs braking towards the captured Cendy warship.

"That was a good trick you pulled with the stilettos, Flight Lieutenant. Shame you didn't bring those pods back," Wing Command Cade said.

"I admit dumping them might have been a bit hasty, sir," Mason said.

"It was expedient. If I were in your position, I would do the same," Wing Commander Cade said. "Or, at least, I hope I would. You did good."

"I wasn't the only one to save the ship, sir," Mason said. "Lieutenant Sinclair's trick was just as important in keeping *Mervie* in one piece."

"Yes, but she's not a pilot who I've been keeping grounded," Group Captain Cade said. "You're not an official part of the Void Knights, but as far as I'm concerned, you can be a—"

"A squire?" Mason said.

"An associate. Or assistant. I don't know," Group Captain Cade said.

"I suppose we can figure out where I stand with your squadron after we survive this," Mason said.

"Yes. There is that. Though effective, those tricks you and Lieutenant Sinclair pulled won't work again, now that the Cendies have seen what we can do," Wing Commander Cade said. "We'll have to find something else to surprise them with."

Mason followed Cade into the elevator and leaned against the wall while the Wing Commander selected the deck.

"In that case, we should probably wait until we know what exactly the Cendy warship the troopers captured has. I'm already thinking of things we can do with their torpedoes, assuming we can get them to work, but there's one piece of Cendy tech that I'm really curious about."

"Their stealth technology," Wing Commander Cade said.

"Yes, sir," Mason said. "If we can figure out what it is and get it to work, we wouldn't have to fight our way out. Just flip it on and sneak past the Cendies."

"Assuming their stealth tech works that way, or that the ship in question carries it."

"Like I said, sir, until we know what exactly we have, it's premature to try and formulate a clever escape plan," Mason said.

∽

When *Mervie* pulled alongside the crippled battlecruiser, engineering teams went to work transferring as much equipment and gear over as possible. Instead of assisting Jessica and Colonel Shimura catalog and examine gear, Mason was put on rotation for alert launch, in case the Cendies launched another longburn torpedo strike. Thus far, they seemed content to loiter outside of the jump limit, holding *Mervie* in position until an overwhelming force arrived so they could destroy or capture her. Mason suspected capture was their objective, or at least to leave an intact enough wreck to examine the systems that allowed *Mervie* to disguise herself as other ships.

The embarked fighters were the only thing *Mervie* had with any real offensive punch, but there just weren't enough of them to deal with the entire Cendy force.

It was the arsenal ship that was the real problem. The huge load of interceptors it carried could overwhelm any fighter attack, even with the edge stiletto pods provided.

So Mason spent his days loitering near the suit chamber on ready-five alert. If the Cendies pulled something, he was expected to suit up, jump into his idling fighter, and launch in the space of five minutes.

As the odd man out, Mason mostly filled in for pilots who needed an extra break.

"Good to see you managed to find new work after Colonel Shimura gave away your hauler," Flight Lieutenant Landing said.

"Wasn't my hauler to give away," Mason said. "But thanks. It's nice being a fighter pilot again."

Landing nodded. "Yes, really exciting job right now. Just the right mix of anxiety and boredom."

"I don't know; this feels pretty familiar to me," Mason said.

"Familiar? I didn't realize you were ever blockaded by the Cendies before," Flight Lieutenant Landing said.

"Well, not this specific situation, no, but the long hours waiting for something bad to happen. That you knew was going to happen but didn't know when," Mason said. "That's something I'm pretty familiar with. Aren't you?"

Landing looked up as she searched her memory. "Not too much of that in the last couple of years. Nice thing about doing special operations work is that you're usually on the offense. You know when shit's about to hit the fan. Fomalhaut, though—that's what this feels like the most. Waiting for some stim-crazed pirate flying in a home-made bomber to pop out from behind a comet and make a run on your carrier." She tsked and shook her head. "Man, that got the adrenaline going. Trying to strap yourself into your fighter while a wave of cobbled-together torpedoes come burning down on you."

"Happy memories," Mason said.

"Yeah, thanks for that." Landing gave him a sour smile. "So, what do you think our chances are?"

Mason shrugged. "Honestly, these aren't the worst odds I've faced."

The hatch to the suit chamber opened and Squadron Leader Vasquez and Flight Lieutenant Quinn floated in.

"Crash," Vasquez said to Landing, then nodded to Mason. "Hauler."

Mason nodded back. "Growler."

"You here to relieve us, sir?" Landing asked.

"Yep, looks like it's our turn to wait for the Cendies to start shit," Squadron Leader Vasquez said.

Landing undid the straps holding her to her wall-mounted seat. "Well, I've got a nice warm seat right here for you, sir."

"Thanks, Crash," Vasquez said.

Mason floated out of his seat, letting Quinn take his place.

"By the way," Vasquez said, "word is they found some interesting tech inside the Cendy ship. They pressurized the Hangar Bay 12 to store a lot of it. Group Captain Cade's headed there now to check out some of the stuff."

"Huh. Maybe we'll head over there and check it out." Landing glanced at Mason. "You still in good with Colonel Shimura to get a look?"

"Worth a try," Mason said.

They floated one deck up to Hangar Bay 12, vacant since *Buttercup's* departure. A pair of armed spacers stood guard outside the airlock. Beyond, Mason could see that both the inner and outer hatches were open.

"Sorry, sirs, but only authorized personnel can enter," said one of the spacers.

"I work with Colonel Shimura," Mason said. "Maybe let her know I'm here."

"Colonel Shimura's in a meeting with the Captain, sir," the spacer said. "You'll have to wait for her to finish."

"Hmph, I hate waiting," Landing said.

Jessica's head popped up on the other side of the airlock. "Oh, I thought I heard your voice. Pop on in. There's something cool I need to show you."

Mason gestured to the guards. "These guys might get the wrong idea if I try to float inside."

"Oh?" Jessica floated through the airlock. "Why aren't you letting them in?"

"Colonel Shimura's orders, sir," said the spacer. "Not supposed to let unauthorized personnel in."

"Well, consider these two authorized," Jessica said.

"But, sir—"

"Colonel Shimura's placed the contents of this hangar, including its security, under my supervision," Jessica said. "Let them through."

"Yes, sir," the spacer said.

"Excellent." Jessica turned to Mason and Crash. "Well, come along. We found out how they hide their ships."

"Holy shit, what is it?" Landing asked.

"I'll show you," Jessica said. "Mason here was right about the Cendies having stealth technology."

"Mason, huh?" Crash said, floating into the hangar after Jessica.

Mason sighed and followed them inside.

Nets stuffed with bits of debris covered the deck of the hangar while engineers and techs went over them with various hand-held implements.

"So, where's this stealth tech?" Crash asked.

"Patience, Flight Lieutenant. We got a sample of it over here," Jessica said. She floated to a workbench bolted to the deck. She stuck her feet through the foothold to stand next to it. Attached to the top of the workbench, held to it by clamps, was a featureless black square. It was like there was a hole cut into the bench, leading into a universe where light never existed. It hurt Mason's brain just looking at it.

"Okay, that's weird," Mason said. "Is that what they use to hide their ships?"

Jessica undid one of the clamps. "It's half of what they use." With her mechanical hand, she folded a corner of the square over. The other side was a perfect mirror.

"Shiny," Mason said.

"It is, isn't it?" Jessica said. "And not just visible light. This side reflects the full em spectrum."

"And the dark side fully absorbs the full spectrum," Mason said.

"That's right," Jessica said. "And the two working together totally blocks the emissions of anything behind it."

"Damn," Mason said. "It's a literal cloak."

"Yes, it is," Jessica said.

"I assume they use more than just that to hide a battlecruiser," Landing said.

"Oh, yes. Much, much more. The Cendy warship had almost 10,000 square meters of the stuff. I got a look at the mechanism during a spacewalk. Works a lot like a solar sail."

"So, when the Cendies want to hide their ship, they unfold that, and become invisible to anything on the other side?" Mason asked.

"To an extent, but it does have limits," Jessica said. "It won't hide engine exhaust, so the ship would have to keep her drives cold to avoid detection."

"So how do they hide their jump flash?" Landing asked.

"You know, I've been thinking about that and I have a theory," Jessica said.

"I'm all ears," Mason said.

"I don't think they have any special way of hiding their jump flashes," Jessica said. "I think that before their last jump, they burn their drives in deep space to build up velocity, then jump a long distance out. In a high-traffic system, like Sol, it would be hard to detect a distant jump flash amid all the much closer ones going on around the system."

"And what about low-traffic systems?" Mason asked.

"You mean like in Ross 128?" Jessica said. "Simple. They come out of the sun. The star's emissions will do all the work of hiding any jump flash. In either case, once they jump in, they deploy their cloaks and let momentum carry them into the system."

"That explains the braking burn when they were first detected," Mason said. "Belt and zones, the Cendies sure are patient."

"Could we use this stuff to hide *Mervie*?" Landing asked.

"That's why Colonel Shimura's meeting with Captain Vann," Lieutenant Sinclair said. "They're brainstorming ways to use the Cendy cloak against them."

"The Cendies are going to know what stuff we could find on their ship," Mason said. "They're probably thinking of ways to counter any tricks we pull using their tech."

"Yes, that's the problem," Jessica said. "Anything we're likely to pull, the Cendies will likely expect."

Mason reached to touch the cloak, but Jessica grabbed his wrist to stop him.

"This stuff is thin enough to give you the mother of all papercuts." She wriggled her mechanical hand. "I can get away with touching it on account that I don't have flesh to cut at the moment."

Mason withdrew his hand and looked down at the cloak. One corner was still folded over, creating a contrast between perfect darkness and perfect reflectivity.

"So, you think Colonel Shimura and Captain Vann are open to suggestions?" Mason asked.

"Probably. Why? You have any suggestions?" Jessica asked.

"Well, I was thinking. Maybe we don't try to hide *Mervie* behind the cloak," Mason said. "Maybe we use it to hide our fighters."

"So, you want to try and use the Cendy cloak to conceal a fighter strike?" Colonel Shimura said.

"That's right, sir," Mason said. "The Cendies would expect us to try and sneak past using the cloak. They might not be prepared for us to try and attack them."

"We can't assume they haven't thought of that," Colonel Shimura said.

"They'll probably notice the absence of our fighters and do something to counter it."

"Yeah, that's the rub," Mason said. "I'm not sure quite how to fix that issue. I'm hoping that someone smarter than me will find a solution."

"Well, good thing I'm here, then," Jessica said.

"You have a suggestion, Lieutenant, or are you just taking the opportunity to show off how smart you are?" Shimura asked.

"Both, sir," Jessica said. She turned to Captain Vann. "Captain, how functional is the mimic array?"

"Only partially," Captain Vann said. "The inert missiles knocked out several panels. We can no longer fully conceal *Mervie's* signature. Why?"

"Well, sir, how about instead of trying to alter *Mervie* completely, you instead use the array to create false contacts?"

"You mean generated phantom Lightnings?" Captain Vann said.

"That's right, Captain. We use the cloak to hide our fighters like Mason suggests, but we use what's left of the mimic array to make it look like the fighters are in close formation with *Mervie*," Jessica said.

Thoughts played out over Captain Vann's face. "The array was never designed with that in mind, but it may work. I'll have to consult with engineering. If it is possible, it will only work from a distance. The Cendies will probably notice the ruse once we get inside a light-second."

"We don't have to use all our fighters, sir," Mason said. "Just a few fully loaded with torpedoes to knock out the arsenal ship."

"If they spot us, that arsenal ship's interceptors are going to tear us apart," Wing Commander Cade said.

Mason shrugged. "This is probably the best chance we have of getting past the Cendy ships, sir. We should probably see if we can't find a way to put the Cendy torpedoes we salvaged to use."

CHAPTER 18

<"ONE MINUTE TO release,"> Wing Commander Cade said over tightbeam.

<"Roger that,"> Mason said.

<"Ready to light them up, Zero,"> Crash said.

Five Lightnings hid behind the jury-rigged cloak that the engineering team had put together from what they recovered from the captured battlecruiser. Mason had eight torpedoes loaded on the internal rotary launcher, four more mounted externally, along with four stiletto pods filling the remaining external hardpoints. The pods contained some of the last of *Mervie's* inventory of the little interceptors.

Once the Lightnings broke cover and launched their torpedoes, assuming the Cendies didn't detect and destroy them before they launched their weapons, the stilettos were their only hope of surviving the arsenal ship's retaliatory volley of interceptors. When Wing Commander Cade had laid out the mission to his squadron, all sixteen pilots of the 4th Special Operations Fighter Squadron tried to volunteer for a mission that required only five pilots.

Cade took the lead, because that's what leaders did, leaving Squadron Leader Vasquez to command the remaining twelve fighters. Instead, he picked four of the most junior and, therefore, most expendable members of his squadron for the potential suicide mission.

He also saved a spot for Mason, since it was partly his idea. Mason had been stupid enough at the time to accept.

Now he was about to face the full wrath of a ship that could throw a thousand interceptors at any strikecraft dumb enough to blunder into range. Which they already were. They had drifted inside interceptor range a while ago.

Mervie glowed like a star behind them, still canceling out speed from the approach burn when she released the five Lightnings of the strike.

Seventeen Lightnings escorted her, even though five of them were fake. False contacts generated by what was left of *Mervie's* mimic array. If they could fool Mason's sensors, then hopefully they were fooling the Cendies as well.

Facing a superior force of Lightnings, the Cendy fighters opted to stay close, well inside the protection provided by the arsenal ship. He couldn't see through the back of the cloak. The concave, perfectly reflective surface just gave him a funhouse-mirror reflection of *Magnificent Seven*, the four other Lightnings, *Mervie*, and the rest of the universe behind him. His only view of the universe on the other side of the cloak was provided by *Mervie*, relayed over tightbeam.

The Cendies, Mason learned, had sensors mounted on masts that could peek around the edge of the cloak like a periscope. *Mervie's* engineers didn't have time for anything like that, so Mason had to deal with the light-lagged information fed from *Mervie*. Everything he saw of the Cendies was on a five-second delay. If the Cendies detected them and launched a wave of interceptors at them, it would be five fewer seconds he'd have to react. Life and death could be decided by much smaller slices of time.

<"Thirty seconds,"> Wing Commander Cade said.

"Belts and zones," Mason whispered. His thumb tingled, ready to release his torpedoes, his left hand poised over the throttle, ready to light his engines and burn like hell as soon as the torpedoes were away. *Magnificent Seven's* Combat AI had done the work of calculating a firing solution, correcting for the light-lag of *Mervie's* targeting data. All Mason had to do was launch his weapons and survive the consequences.

<"Fifteen seconds.">

They were really close now, just a few hundred kilometers away.

<"Ten seconds.">

Belts and zones, they were too close.

<"Five seconds.">

Too late to back out now. Mason prepared to fire, trusting in the plan and the combat AI's firing solution.

<"Fire!">

Mason's right thumb came down on the firing button on the back of his control stick and held it down. The belly doors opened, and the rotary launch pushed out torpedoes at half-second intervals. After four seconds, the torpedoes mounted on the ventral hardpoints cold-launched, drifting under the impulse of the ejectors. Mason waited, teeth clenched, for the Cendies to detect the cold-launched torpedoes. Six seconds after the order to fire, the last of the torpedoes drifted past the edge of the cloak.

<"Turn and burn,"> Cade said.

Mason fired maneuvering thrusters, pushing *Magnificent Seven* clear of the cloak, and lit the longburn drives at full power. *Magnificent Seven* slammed into his back as she leapt forward at eighteen gs. Crushing pain settled over his body, and he almost let go of the controls as his hand jostled the control stick, trying to hold on. The Flight AI correctly interpreted the inputs as a mistake and ignored them, keeping the Lightning flying straight and true. This close, it would be suicide to try and reverse course. The only way out was through. As the torpedoes bore down on the arsenal ship, Mason followed the four other Lightnings through the gap between the Cendy arsenal ship and one of the battlecruisers. The hulls of all three Cendy starships flashed with point-defense fire as they threw up a cloud of metal between them and the torpedoes.

Missile alarms sounded as interceptors flew into space, directed, he hoped, at the torpedoes and not their launching spacecraft. The combat AI started launching stilettos, but Mason didn't keep track of what their targets were. All he knew was that it was bad news. If the stilettos were launching, that's because there were interceptors homing in. All worries for incoming interceptors, crushing gs, or the sharp pain in Mason's side was washed aside by a staccato of powerful, blinding flashes somewhere ahead of Mason. Radiological alarms went off as the outer hull was bombarded by x-rays.

When the sensors came back, and Mason could see again, the arsenal ship was a hot glowing wreck surrounded by an expanding bubble of rapidly cooling gas. There were no interceptors burning after him, nor fighters in close pursuit. There weren't even point-defense guns firing at him. There were engine glows from the twelve remaining Lightnings of the 4th, now clear of the danger of the arsenal ship's interceptors, moving to engage the Cendy battlecruisers.

The maneuvering thrusters of the two battlecruisers burned hard, turning the long hulls of the warships until they faced towards open space. The remaining Cendy fighters latched onto their hulls. There was a red-shifted flash, and one Cendy ship disappeared, followed seconds later by the second flash as the last Ascendency warship jumped out.

Mason killed his engines, relief washing over him in the sudden weightlessness. He pumped his fist in the air and shouted where the Cendy battlecruisers had disappeared.

"Ha! You motherfuckers don't much like the taste of your own medicine, do you?"

"Flight Lieutenant, who are you talking to?" Group Captain Cade asked.

He realized he still had an open tightbeam link with the four other Lightnings.   "Uh. Sorry, sir."

"Get your fighter turned around and start the return burn to *Mervie*," Wing Commander Cade said. "You can celebrate all you want once we dock."

"Yes, sir," Mason said. He flipped *Magnificent Seven* over and started braking at a leisurely three gs.

⁂

Mason boarded the elevator, and Wing Commander Cade joined him, the smaller man's head barely coming up to Mason's shoulder.

Wing Commander Cade hit a button on the command console, the doors closed, and the elevator started to move down the rotor arm towards the hab module.

He then turned to Mason. "Well, Flight Lieutenant, that plan of yours worked."

"Yeah, that was nice of the Cendies to cut and run," Mason said. "We're lucky they didn't feel the need to get even for blowing up their arsenal ship."

"I'm not sure the Cendies are big on revenge," Wing Commander Cade said.

"Well, good. Means I don't have to worry about them hunting us down to get even," Mason said.

"It also makes them harder to manipulate, Flight Lieutenant," Wing Commander Cade said.

"Always looking for the silver lining, aren't you, sir?" Mason said.

Cade smiled, with all the warmth of a stone. "I suppose I do. The 4th's going to celebrate our victory. Consider yourself invited as the guest of honor."

"I've never partied with Special Ops pilots before. Should be interesting," Mason said.

"Well, one of these days, you should consider applying for Special Ops duty," Wing Commander Cade said. "You've shown yourself to possess the right combination of resourcefulness and reckless disregard for personal safety."

"I'll consider it, sir," Mason said.

"Not interested?" Wing Commander Cade asked.

"Oh, I'm interested, but my brain's past the point where I can make decisions," Mason said.

"Understood, Hauler. I'll talk to you about it after you get some rest," Wing Commander Cade said.

"Thank you, sir," Mason said.

The elevator stopped at the deck where their quarters were located. Cade headed spinward towards the 4th's quarters and Mason went anti-spinward, straight for his quarters. Waiting for him in the corridor leading to his quarters were Jessica and Colonel Shimura. Jessica bounded over to him and wrapped him into a hug while Colonel Shimura walked up behind her.

"It worked! It worked. Blimey, it bloody worked." Her mobility rig made it feel like he was being hugged by a mannequin, but Mason hugged her back regardless, sharing his relief at surviving.

"Yeah, it did," Mason said. He looked over Jessica's shoulder to Colonel Shimura. "So, we're headed home?"

Shimura nodded. "We're headed back to Procyon, Flight Lieutenant. We've recovered more than enough intelligence on the Cendies to make this mission fruitful."

"Took out three of their warships and sent another pair running," Mason said. "Pretty good results, I'd say."

"Yes, very good," Colonel Shimura said. "Expensive, though."

"What do you mean?" Mason said. "We haven't taken that many casualties."

"Which I am grateful for," Shimura said. "But the Cendies now know about the existence of ships with mimic arrays. We won't be able to pull tricks like this again."

Mason shrugged. "I'd say this was worth it, sir."

"Probably," Colonel Shimura said. "If we can take advantage of what we've learned."

"Oh, come now, Colonel," Jessica said. "There's no reason to be so dour. We triumphed against some truly abysmal odds. They'll make movies about what we did!"

Shimura tsked. "Not for another fifty years at the least, probably longer."

"Right. Can't forget about the Branch's obsession with keeping its accomplishments secret," Jessica said. "There go my dreams of fame."

"You're in the wrong career for fame, Lieutenant," Colonel Shimura said.

"Oh, bother," Jessica said. "I knew I should have taken theater classes."

"Hey, just look on the bright side, Jessica," Mason said.

"You mean other than the whole victory thing?"

"Yeah." Mason pointed down at Jessica's skeletal replacement body. "You'll finally be able to exchange that spare for the real deal."

"True," Jessica said. "You don't know how uncomfortable it is to try to sit without a proper ass."

CHAPTER 19

THE BODIES OF four dead Cendies, recovered from the captured battlecruiser, lay on the tables in the medical bay. Only one looked like the soldiers encountered in Dagon Freeport. A lanky frame covered in textured grey skin, armor plating, bulging muscle. The head was utterly faceless. Just a smooth dome of grey skin over an armored plate where the face would have been.

Doctor Cole, in a full pressure suit, had already opened the Cendy's chest like an old-school doctor's bag and was busy pulling out familiar organs, handing them off to an assistant who bagged and labeled them. Mason stood near Colonel Shimura and Jessica, all three in full pressure suits. A precaution in case the Cendy bodies had toxins or contagions waiting for anyone who cut them open.

The organs were laid out on a table next to them. Heart, lungs, liver. All shiny, fresh, and inhumanly black, like they had been dipped in ink. Apparently, where human organs were made of collagen, Cendy organs used carbon fibers.

Doctor Cole handed a grizzly mass of glossy black intestines over to his assistant, who bagged and deposited the entrails in a pan.

"So, Doctor Cole, what can you tell us about Cendy anatomy?" Colonel Shimura asked.

"Well, this is a theory, but based on what I'm seeing, I'm pretty confident that the Cendies are, for the lack of a better word, *born* the way they are."

Mason glanced down at the armored figure. "I'd hate to be that thing's mother."

"I said 'born', Flight Lieutenant. I never said this thing had a mother," Doctor Cole said.

Jessica started ticking off points on her gloved fingers. "So, they have black hearts and might literally be motherless. Blimey, they're like the perfect villains."

"They seem to think of themselves as the good guys," Mason said.

"Most bad guys think that way," Colonel Shimura said. "So, when you say 'born'," she gestured towards the Cendy body, "do you mean they popped out of the womb, or whatever serves as the Cendy equivalent, looking like that?"

Doctor Cole shrugged. "Probably."

"Any insight as to how?" Colonel Shimura asked.

Doctor Cole brought his hands together. "Well, not unlike how human bodies are grown." His hands separated. "Cell division."

Jessica turned her attention away from the organs, walked over to the opened body, and looked down into the soldier's open chest cavity. "Does that include the bones?"

"Yes," Doctor Cole said. "There are growth rings like you would find in human bone tissue."

"Bollocks," Jessica said.

"What is it, Lieutenant?" Colonel Shimura said.

"I'm just a bit jealous," Jessica said. "They have more advanced cyberware than I ever had."

"I'm not sure I'd go so far as to say it's more advanced—just different," Doctor Cole said. "What's lying on the table here may not represent a great advance in cybernetics, but rather the product of a different development path."

"Can you elaborate, doctor?" Colonel Shimura asked.

"Well, our technology has focused on enhancing existing biology," Doctor Cole said. He gestured towards Mason and Shimura. "We've gotten very good at producing major performance gains in human anatomy with relatively little artificial material. You're both ninety-nine percent meat, bone, and guts by mass." He gestured towards Jessica. "In Lieutenant

Sinclair's case, it's to replace non-functioning or defective biology with parts that are externally indistinguishable from the real thing." He pointed down at the corpse. "The Cendies? They're not humans who've been enhanced. They're a purely artificial form of life."

"Like they claim. So, who created them?" Mason asked.

"Humans, probably, given how closely their bodies follow the conventions of human anatomy," Doctor Cole said. "Beyond that? No idea. I think that's a job for your intelligence people to find out."

"Yes," Colonel Shimura said. "But that's a question that we're not going to be able to answer on this ship with the resources at hand." She nodded towards the other two corpses. "What can you tell us about these two?"

Doctor Cole walked over to the next table, which featured an androgynous corpse much shorter and stouter than the soldier. The only remarkable feature of it, other than the black organs and colorless blood exposed by its open chest, were its hand-like feet. "I'd say this one's role was pretty clear."

"Some kind of specialized zero-g worker," Mason said.

Doctor Cole nodded. "Yes. That's a sound theory. Most of the crew were made up of these."

"So, they're like ants?" Jessica gestured towards the largest of the three. "Soldier." She pointed at the next. "Worker." She pointed to the last. "Emissary."

"One for fighting, one for keeping their ships running, and one for interacting with people," Colonel Shimura said.

"Specialization," Mason said. "Makes me wonder what their pilots look like."

"If their fighters are manned," Colonel Shimura said.

"That would be my bet, sir," Mason said. "There's nothing to suggest they have the technology to protect a drone from getting subverted. They need a brain in there making decisions, commanding their mount's AI systems. Their drones would face the same problems as ours if they didn't."

"Yes, light-lag is what makes remotely operated combat craft impractical," Jessica said. "It doesn't matter how smart your drone is. After all, the AI on a starship is always going to be smarter. When you factor in light-lag, then you have a situation where the enemy can more readily communicate with your drone than you can. Unless you have someone sitting inside it, making decisions in real-time."

"Well, whatever their pilots look like, we can assume it's geared towards tolerating high gs," Colonel Shimura said.

"Yeah, that would be interesting to look at," Mason said.

His body required both substantial internal enhancement and external support from his hardsuit. He could only speculate as to what a body that had all those capabilities rolled up into a single package would look like.

Jessica scratched her helmet as if she were trying to rub her chin.

"What is it, Lieutenant?" Colonel Shimura asked.

"I was just thinking, sir. They all seem to have human brains—same shape, presumably the same cognitive ability, if not more so."

"Your point?"

"Well, the analogy to ants might not be entirely applicable. Ants don't have much in the way of intellect, just instinct programing. They're basically little biological robots. But the Cendies? They're people. People who, by all appearances, are born into their jobs."

"Interesting," Colonel Shimura said. "What do you think it means?"

'Well, if I were to take a stab in the dark, I would think their society is caste-based."

Mason spent most of the return flight to Procyon parsing through the overwhelming amount of data collected during *Mervie's* encounters with the Cendies. Helmet-cam footage from the troopers fighting Cendy soldiers, flight data from the Void Knight's battles, reports from the engineers examining Cendy tech, and Doctor Cole's autopsy report.

Mason even got a chance to help take apart a Cendy torpedo. It was a lot like the ones carried by Federal fighters. A seeker head at the front, a directional fusion warhead behind that, and the rest a tube of solid propellant ending at a gimbaled nozzle at the back. Even the seeker head had familiar components. A multi-spectral sensor designed to home in on the emissions of a target, while ignoring any decoys that said target might drop.

Compared to everything he saw of the Cendies, including their almost human anatomy, the fact that the torpedoes carried by their fighters were largely the same as those carried by his fighter just struck him as strange. Though he supposed there were only so many ways to deliver a nuclear warhead against a maneuvering target.

Their interceptors were very similar as well. Just a seeker head, a short-burn motor, and programed desire to make physical contact with the target.

The main item of interest when it came to weapons, of course, was the spinal gun carried by the battlecruisers—the weapon that proved so effective against the Federal starships. The guns ran the full length of the hull, the back of the gun nestled between the engines at the rear. A detailed examination of the ship's hull explained why the Cendy battlecruisers didn't have an organic missile armament beyond those of its embarked strikecraft. The main gun and its supporting equipment simply didn't leave room. That also explained why their fighters were carried outside the hull on racks, almost like an afterthought. Like the Cendies knew they needed to bring strikecraft, but didn't want to go through the trouble of designing and building a dedicated carrier.

That probably explained why their fighters had somewhat limited capabilities. They were there to be good enough, not to be the kind of cosmos-beating strikecraft Lightnings were.

"I have a thought," Mason said.

"I'm listening," Jessica said.

"The Cendies have two kinds of warship, and one kind of strikecraft," Mason said.

"Yes, which would make for a very streamlined logistics system," Jessica said.

"Yeah," Mason said. "Perhaps as a matter of necessity."

"You mean, like they only have a limited industrial base to support their military," Jessica said. "And if we work backwards from there…"

"We could maybe get an idea of their strategic capabilities," Mason said.

"The invasion and occupation of Jupiter shows that they're considerable," Jessica said.

"But not unlimited," Mason said. "They didn't proceed down orbit to attack Earth, or the industrial base on Luna, or the Inner Sol orbital habitats. At least, not before we departed, anyway."

"Right," Jessica said. "Likely because they're at their limit, logistically.

Either because they don't have the reserves, or they do have the reserves but don't wish to commit them unless absolutely needed."

"And you saw the results of Doctor Cole's autopsy. The Cendies are adapted to living in space like no human is. They don't suffer muscle atrophy or bone density loss. They don't need to bother with creating artificial gravity for the comfort and health of their crews."

"Which might imply that they don't hold any planets," Jessica said.

"What if we're not dealing with a fixed power like the League, who have territory and planets to defend," Mason said. "What if... what if we're dealing with a nomadic power, with a mobile industrial base?"

"Blimey," Jessica said. "The entire Space Forces was built around fighting an enemy with territory they'd have to defend."

"Yeah," Mason said. "That's why the Space Forces have had so much trouble dealing with the pirates in Fomalhaut. Every time we found one of their bases, they'd just pack everything they need onto their ships and burned hard for the jump limit, then set up shop somewhere else. Either in another part of Fomalhaut or in a nearby system."

"All the recipe for a long occupation that doesn't go anywhere," Jessica said.

"Which the Cendies might be capable of, only on a far larger scale than even the largest pirate group," Mason said.

Jessica sighed and lay back in her seat. "If that's true, then the Cendies have a serious advantage over us—over all humanity, really. We can't beat them by taking away their territory and destroying their industrial base. Not when it could be distributed all over unclaimed space and able to flee at the first sign of trouble. But they can do that to us."

"Yeah, our fixed industrial base does present a disadvantage, but also an advantage."

"You mean in terms of raw output? Yes, I suspect the Cendies wouldn't be able to match the Earth Federation at that. But that means the only way to beat them..."

"Is through a war of attrition, the likes of which we've never seen before."

Jessica steepled her mechanical fingers, eyes downcast. "It wouldn't be a matter of simply material destruction. It would be a matter of who broke first.

And we don't know if the Cendies are capable of being broken on a psychological level."

"Yeah. That's one more thing we're going to have to learn about them. Likely the hard way."

CHAPTER 20

MERVIE COMPLETED HER braking burn and entered a parking orbit 200 kilometers prograde of the station, pulling up next to the repair ship FSFV *Clydesdale. Clydesdale* already had its retractable spacedock deployed into a rectangular scaffold of metal beams covered in reflective Mylar sheets far larger than *Clydesdale* herself. It was more than large enough for *Mervie* to slip inside the confines of the space dock, out of view of any external observers.

As soon as the Special Purpose Branch starship came to a stop, heavy docking clamps unfolded from the sides of the scaffold to grasp the starship and hold her fast. Drones and figures in hardsuits started floating towards the ship.

Mason glanced over to Colonel Shimura. "Is the Branch always this prompt about repairing battle damage to ships, sir?"

"No, not usually," Colonel Shimura said. "Something's up."

"You're right, Colonel," Captain Vann said. "I just got a priority message from Procyon Fleet Base. There's a shuttle on its way here to pick up you, Lieutenant Sinclair, Flight Lieutenant Grey, and me."

"They give you any hints as to why, Captain?" Colonel Shimura asked.

"They weren't very forthcoming, Colonel," Captain Vann said.

"I guess we have a flight to catch." Colonel Shimura released her seat buckles and floated free from her seat.

✍

A tall, handsome officer in the sleek blue uniform of a fleet officer waited to greet them as they left the shuttle. He snapped a salute to Colonel Shimura and Captain Vann. "Welcome back, sirs. I'm Lieutenant Wu and it is my pleasure to escort you to the headquarters building."

"I know the way, Lieutenant. I have an office there," Colonel Shimura said.

"I know, sir, but it's not your office we're going to. You, Captain Vann, and your two assistants are due for a meeting."

"A meeting with whom, Lieutenant?" Colonel Shimura asked.

"Admiral Mobius, sir," Lieutenant Wu said.

"What's the commanding officer of the 1st Fleet doing out here, Lieutenant?" asked Captain Vann.

Wu turned to address her. "She's no longer commander of the 1st Fleet, sir. President Chopra appointed her supreme commander of the Federal Space Forces.

"Seems a lot has been going on since we left for Fomalhaut," Colonel Shimura said.

"There has, sir, and the Admiral will be more than happy to fill you in." Lieutenant Wu beckoned them to follow. "Now, if you please, sirs, the Admiral's orders were pretty clear that I convey you to her without delay."

"Convey away, Lieutenant," Colonel Shimura said.

Lieutenant Wu led them to the same tram station that Colonel Shimura and Jessica had used to take Mason to Procyon Fleet Base's headquarters building when he had arrived aboard *Fafnir*. Like before, there was an empty tram waiting for them.

"That isn't a good sign," Jessica said as the tram left the station and started descending towards the surface level.

"I know. Last time I had a private tram waiting for me, I ended up flying haulers for the Special Purpose Branch," Mason said.

"Yes, I'd say that decision has paid off pretty well, wouldn't you agree, Flight Lieutenant?" Colonel Shimura said.

"I don't know, sir," Mason said. "Is the payoff going to come in the form of another dangerous mission?"

"Most likely, Flight Lieutenant," Colonel Shimura said.

"Hooray," Mason said as the doors slid shut and the tram started moving.

The tram arrived at the station adjacent to Procyon Fleet Base's head-quarters building, where Lieutenant Wu quickly led them inside, passing through the security checkpoints without so much as breaking step, stopping only when they reached a conference room on the highest level of the HQ building. A pair of armed guards flanked the door. After a quick exchange of salutes and words with the guards, Lieutenant Wu opened the door and gestured for them to go inside.

A long conference table dominated the room, with a solitary woman in a heavily decorated blue uniform seated at the head of the vast expanse of polished wood. Admiral Julia Mobius, the woman who started the Third League War. Everyone snapped a salute.

Admiral Mobius smiled. "At ease." Mason's hand dropped to his side. Admiral Mobius stood up and walked around the conference table with long, deliberate strides. She stopped before Colonel Shimura and Captain Vann.

"Colonel Shimura, Captain Vann. It's good to see you two. I started reading your mission report as soon as it arrived. Seems *Mervie* had quite the harrowing mission."

"Yes, sir, but also a very productive one," Colonel Shimura said.

"More productive than you know, Colonel." Admiral Mobius turned to Jessica. "What happened to you, Lieutenant?"

Jessica nodded to Mason. "He cut off my head, so it could be grafted onto a mobility rig."

A dark eyebrow rose on Mobius' face as she turned her attention to Mason. "Really now?"

"To be fair, sir, what was left of her body wasn't much use for her," Mason said.

"The report I got didn't mention that," Admiral Mobius said, directing her attention to Colonel Shimura. "It mentioned casualties, but not… therapeutic decapitation."

"I left that out for the sake of brevity, sir," Colonel Shimura said. "I can go into more detail if you like."

"No need, Colonel. I already know what I need," Admiral Mobius said. "If you could all please take a seat at the table."

Mason sat down between Shimura and Jessica while Admiral Mobius resumed sitting at the head of the table. "So, the most pertinent news is that President Chopra, with the advice and consent of the Federal Legislature, has signed an armistice with the League Interstellar Council." She nodded to Mason. "Flight Lieutenant Grey helped with that, incidentally."

"I did, sir?" Mason asked.

"Indeed you did, Flight Lieutenant. By 'capturing' that cruiser, you inadvertently helped expedite the peace process. It gave us a way to propose an armistice and show our good faith at the same time."

"Huh. I never thought of myself as a peacemaker, sir," Mason said.

Admiral Mobius nodded. "Yes, your career has become quite eclectic of late."

"Well, it's good we have put our little dustup with the League to bed," Jessica said. "I assume, given that you're speaking with us, that there is something in the works that requires *Mervie*, Admiral?"

"That's a good piece of conjecture right there, Lieutenant. And you are correct," Admiral Mobius said. "If you will join me at the table, I will brief you on what is in the works for you and MR-5."

A holotank descended from the ceiling, until it hovered over the top of the table. A projection of Jupiter and all the planet's moons appeared over the table. The sight sent a twinge of homesickness through Mason's chest.

"The Ascendency has spent the last couple of months fortifying their position in Jupiter. They've taken full control of Jupiter Fleet Base's facilities, as well as those of all of the starports orbiting Jupiter."

Mason leaned forward. "What about the civilian population?"

"The Ascendency has been distributing humanitarian supplies set up from Inner Sol," Admiral Mobius said. "Thus far, they've been content to simply leave the civilians be, so long as no one attempts to enter or leave Jovian space that isn't either an Ascendency vessel or an approved humanitarian transport."

"I take it now that the war with the League is over, Federal Command's gearing up to oust the League from Jupiter?" Colonel Shimura asked.

"Yes, but not just yet," Admiral Mobius said. "With the loss of the 9th Fleet's battleships, Earth-Fed's months away from having the forces needed to push the Ascendency fleet out of Jupiter."

"The League's not helping, sir?" Mason asked.

A sour grin appeared on Admiral Mobius' face. "There's only so much help they're willing to offer, Flight Lieutenant. We're still arch-enemies, after all. Right now, Earth-Fed and the League's going to see to their own defenses. Hopefully, enough Ascendency warships will be tied up by the Leaguers to prevent them from reinforcing their position in Outer Sol."

"But you are still planning for some kind of major operation in Jovian space, aren't you, Admiral?" Colonel Shimura asked.

"I am, Colonel," Admiral Mobius said. "As soon as *Mervie* returned from her mission carrying a functional piece of Cendy stealth technology, I immediately saw an opportunity to use it against the Cendy forces occupying Jupiter."

"I thought you said we don't have the ships to drive the Cendies out of Jupiter, sir," Mason said.

"We don't, Flight Lieutenant. And that's not what I have in mind. The 1st Fleet will be launching a sortie against the Ascendency in Jovian space, but only to serve as a distraction."

"A distraction for what, sir?" Colonel Shimura asked.

"Operation Autumn Fire, Colonel," Admiral Mobius said. She nodded to the holotank, which zoomed in on a reddish, potato-shaped moon in low orbit of the gas giant.

"Amalthea, sir? There's nothing down there but a half-built resort," Mason said.

"There is no resort being built on Amalthea, Flight Lieutenant. There never was," Admiral Mobius said. "It was all a cover for the construction of a secret shipyard."

"One that the Cendies have not detected yet, I assume, sir," Colonel Shimura said.

"Correct. The cover seemed to have fooled the Cendies just as well as it fooled everyone else, no doubt aided by the heavy radiation present in low Jovian orbit," Admiral Mobius said.

"So, what will our job be, sir? I assume Earth-Fed plans on destroying the shipyard before the Cendies get their hands on it?" Colonel Shimura said.

"Destroying the shipyard is one of our objectives, Colonel, but not the primary one," Admiral Mobius said. "The primary objective will be the recovery of the warship that the shipyard in Amalthea almost finished constructing when the Cendies invaded. Along with rescuing the shipyard's personnel."

"Must be a hell of a warship to warrant the resources we're committing to recovering her, sir," Colonel Shimura said.

"She is indeed, Colonel," Admiral Mobius said. The holotank further zoomed in, focusing on the part of Amalthea the moon always kept pointed towards Jupiter due to tidal locking. A cutaway of a tunnel appeared superimposed over Amalthea. Rather than the spinning resort, the tunnel contained a complete starship. The ship looked like a battleship, with the typical Federal layout. A long, cylindrical hull that tapered to a pointed, armored prow. Pairs of large superfiring turrets mounted on squat towers on the ventral and dorsal sides, and the five engine bells of the main drive. The tunnel measured 2000 meters deep, and the length of the warship filled most of it. It dawned on Mason he was looking at the representation of the largest warship ever built.

"Meet FSFV *Independence*, the first battlecarrier," Admiral Mobius said.

Battlecarrier—a hybrid of a battleship and a carrier, designed to replace both. It was a concept that had been discussed among the Space Forces for decades, but never actually built. Until now, it seemed.

Jessica chuckled. "Oh, wow. They actually did it. They actually built a battlecarrier, and in secret, too."

"What can you tell us about *Independence*, sir?" Colonel Shimura asked. "How are we supposed to get her out of Amalthea?"

"Under her own power, Colonel," Admiral Mobius said. "*Independence* is fully space-worthy."

"How do we know that, sir?" Colonel Shimura asked.

"Because Amalthea's commander, Captain Oliver Ferris, has been communicating with Earth-Fed over a secure tightbeam connection," Admiral Mobius said. "The flash messages he's been sending have confirmed that *Independence* is complete and capable of flying out of Amalthea under her own power. She just needs a crew to do it."

"Admiral, as soon as a ship that big lights her drives, every sensor in the solar system is going to pick her up," Captain Vann said. "The Ascendency are not going to ignore a massive warship appearing deep inside what they consider secure space."

"Fortunately, Captain, *Independence* isn't just flight-worthy, she is battle-worthy too," Admiral Mobius said.

"That would be quite the feat for a ship that's never flown before, sir," Captain Vann said.

"A valid concern, Captain, but Captain Ferris' report says that the ship-yard workers have spent the last few months getting *Independence* ready for just such an event," Admiral Mobius said. "The original plan, before MR-5's return, was for him, the space forces personnel under his command, and the civilian shipyard workers who built her, to fly *Independence* out during the 1st Fleet's attack. Now, with the stealth technology you helped steal, we have a chance to bring more crew down, thus increasing the chance of success."

"I hope you don't plan on having me fly that thing, sir," Mason said. "My hauler license doesn't cover anything over a thousand tons."

Admiral Mobius chuckled at that. "We have no shortage of talented starship drivers available, Flight Lieutenant. Though, if you wish, you can participate in the mission as part of the fighter escort."

"Sure thing, sir," Mason said. "What's one more highly risky mission?"

"There's a positive attitude," Admiral Mobius said.

"Well, it's good to know what Flight Lieutenant Grey's role in the mission will be, sir, but what about me and Lieutenant Sinclair?" Colonel Shimura asked.

Admiral Mobius turned to Colonel Shimura. "You will have overall command of the mission, Colonel. The 4th Special Operations Squadron will provide a fighter squadron, while Raiders under Major Hauer's command will provide groundside security."

"I believe they will both be eager to participate, sir." Colonel Shimura glanced at Jessica. "I'm sure you're eager to get a new body, Lieutenant Sinclair. So it's up to you if you want to come along."

Jessica sighed and looked down at her hands, opening and closing them with the subtle mechanical whir. "I admit, this loaner body grew old weeks ago, but given the nature of the mission you're about to engage in, Colonel, you will probably need me to come along in case we need to improvise a solution."

"Well, good, Colonel. It looks like you have your team," Admiral Mobius said. "It should take one week for *Clydesdale* to complete repairs to MR-5. That's how long we have to get all the pieces into place."

CHAPTER 21

COLONEL SHIMURA STOOD in the center of the auditorium filled with the officers and senior enlisted spacers participating in Operation Autumn Fire. She gestured to what looked like an umbrella missing its handle, the convex side an abyssal shade of black, the concave side completely reflective. It was a larger, much more refined version of the cloak they had used to launch a surprise attack on the Cendies that had blockaded *Mervie*.

"The engineers from *Clydesdale* have put together this cloak from most of the remaining material we recovered from the Ascendency battlecruiser we boarded. It's large enough to provide effective cover for seventeen fighters and one assault shuttle."

Holographic representations of eighteen smallcraft appeared, crowding behind the protection of the cloak.

"The cloak won't hide longburn exhaust, so *Mervie* will need to accelerate to 500 kps prior to her last jump to give the strikecraft enough speed to drift down to Amalthea in a timely fashion. Unfortunately, if the Cendies see *Mervie* jump in moving that fast, and then jump out, it will be easy for them to guess that something is up."

The holotank zoomed out to empty space, where a flotilla of warships flashed into existence.

"Therefore, *Mervie* won't be jumping in alone, but as part of a task force, which itself will be one of several jumping in around the jump limit."

The holotank zoomed out beyond the orbit of the Galilean moons until the bubble of Jupiter's jump limit was visible. All around it, icons marking

Federal task forces popped into existence around Mason's homeworld. Icons representing torpedoes spawned from the taskforces, burning down towards Jupiter.

"In order to conceal *Mervie's* activities, several taskforces made up of cruisers and destroyers of the 8th Fleet will jump into the edge of the system moving at high closing velocities and launch all their longburn torpedoes before jumping out. The Cendies should see this as a hit-and-run torpedo attack against their ships, and not pay attention to *Mervie* deploying the cloak and launching fighters."

The taskgroups flashed out of existence, and the holotank zoomed in to the cloak and the strikecraft huddled behind it.

"While the torpedoes burn towards the Cendy fleet, our ships will follow a ballistic trajectory down towards the orbit of Amalthea until it is time for them to begin the braking burn."

The holotank zoomed back out to the full Jovian system, including a line reaching almost straight down from twenty-three million kilometers above the planet's north pole until Jupiter's gravity started to bend the line. A dot on the line marked where the braking burn was supposed to begin, ending just short of Amalthea.

"We'll be on the drift for twelve hours, letting the momentum from *Mervie's* pre-jump burn carry us down into low Jovian orbit. Then, just over a million klicks out from Amalthea, we will begin an eight-minute hard burn to match velocities with the moon and begin the recovery operation. Should things go as planned, the Cendies will only notice us when we begin our burn and, by then, they will be too engaged with the 1st Fleet to react before we reach Amalthea."

She nodded to a pair of officers seated at the front. They stood up—a man in blue and woman in a black uniform like Mason's, but instead of wings, she had a stylized rocket pinned to the front of her uniform. A starship driver.

"Commander Gustav Peeters is a weapons officer who will control *Independence's* weapon systems. Flight Lieutenant York will fly her," Colonel Shimura said. "It will be the job of the Raiders to make sure they get aboard *Independence* alive."

Major Hauer nodded. "You can count on us, sir."

"Good." Colonel Shimura said. "The fighters' jobs will be simple enough: provide close escort for the assault shuttle, hold off the Cendies from reaching Amalthea until *Independence* launches, then escort her to the jump limit, where *Mervie* and her escorts will jump in to provide support when *Independence* crosses the jump limit."

She closed the display and turned to face her audience, her lean face composed. "This will be the most dangerous mission any of us have participated in, which I know you're all aware of. I've heard the term 'suicide mission' mentioned more than once. I personally hate that term. It's defeatist, even if our chances of survival aren't what any of us would prefer. There will be deviations from the plan. Things will go wrong, quite possibly in ways that we can't survive. But I expect everyone to keep trying, even in the face of certain death. Success will mean the recovery of the most powerful warship Earth-Fed has ever built, something the Space Forces desperately need after the losses the Cendies have inflicted on us. And, perhaps more importantly, it will show the Cendies that they have not won. The war they started is not over yet, but is only just beginning."

"Quite the speech Colonel Shimura gave, wasn't it?" Jessica said as they walked together on the white concrete walkway that ran around the perimeter of an artificial lake surrounded by pine trees and tall grass, where indolent ducks floated about, ignorant and apathetic to the fact that they were light-years from their homeworld.

"Yep, very inspiring. She should consider politics at some point," Mason said.

"Could you imagine her holding a press conference? Or, blimey, at a debate? She'd melt her opponents with a hard stare," Jessica said.

"Vote for me or I'll melt you with my eye-lasers," Mason said. "That's a campaign I could get behind."

"Not sure I liked the part where she mentioned our dubious odds of survival," Jessica said.

"Well, she was just being honest there," Mason said. "Trying to sugar-coat the mission isn't going to do anyone any favors."

"I don't know. I hear sugar's great for helping the medicine go down," Jessica said.

"Good reference. We even have a flying umbrella. Does that make Colonel Shimura Mary Poppins?" Mason said.

"Probably. But I wouldn't mention that to her if you value your life," Jessica said.

"Noted," Mason said. "So, you feel ready?"

"No. And I'm unlikely to change that during the flight to Sol," Jessica said. "This is way out of bounds of anything I expected when I joined the Special Purpose Branch. I mean, I thought I'd do a bit of risky fieldwork in exchange for a spiffing body. But, well..." Jessica rapped the chest of her mobility rig. "It's only gotten more dangerous, and I have the body that has all the sex appeal of a crash test dummy."

"Still got a nice face; it's not a total wash," Mason said.

"Yes, thank you very much for not cutting off anything above the larynx. I'd have had to throw out all my mirrors," Jessica said.

"You really own a bunch of mirrors?" Mason asked.

"Yes, for applying make-up," Jessica said. "What? Don't look at me like that. Of course, I put on make-up. It was one of the first things I learned how to do when I finally got a useful pair of arms to apply it with."

"Huh. I just thought, well, what with the perfect face and all that," Mason said.

"Oh? You think just because I have an unblemished, perfectly pro-portioned face, that it couldn't be improved by a discreet application of make-up? So little you know, Mason."

Mason squinted. "Are you wearing make-up now?"

Jessica grimaced. "No, I'm afraid not." She held up the hands of her mobility rig. "These are dexterous enough to fit the basic requirements, but they're rubbish when it comes to applying make-up by hand." She let her arms drop to her sides.

"Well, after this mission, I'm sure they'll have a shiny new body waiting to graft that well-designed head of yours on," Mason said.

Jessica chuckled. "Assuming we survive. Blimey. Come to think of it, my body-image problems aren't likely to last much longer, either way."

"That's rather pessimistic," Mason said.

"I'm British. Pessimism is an ancient tradition for us," Jessica said. "What about you?"

"Pessimists don't try to colonize radioactive gas giants," Mason said. "Jovian is pretty much a synonym for obstinate."

"I suppose that trait has worked out well for you." Jessica's eyes became distant as they fixed on a mallard splashing the water with its wings. "I never understood why they have ducks here."

Mason looked out over the lake. "What's wrong with ducks?"

"It's just rather inefficient. Jessica pointed at the mallard. "That feathered bastard is a solid kilo of perfectly good biomass doing nothing but floating around eating pellets tossed into the water by bored spacers. A kilo that's not used for food, or for organs, or anything else."

"Looks nice, though," Mason said.

"Yes, they are nice," Jessica said. "Mason?"

"Yes, Jessica?"

"Whatever happens, could you promise me not to die doing something heroic, yeah?" She looked up at him. "It would be a real let down, you know, if you didn't come back."

Mason turned to face her. "I'll do my best. You do the same, all right?"

Jessica nodded and then walked up and pulled Mason into a quick hug. Before Mason could do anything, she pushed away.

"I've got to meet with the Colonel. Thank you for walking with me."

"No problem," Mason said as Jessica departed.

Mason turned to look out over the lake, just as a duck scurried across the water, leaving a wake behind as it gathered speed before taking off, flying to who knows where.

❧

One fact became abundantly clear as Mason prepared for Operation Autumn Fire. The seventeen Lightnings that were to escort the assault shuttle down orbit to Amalthea were expendable. Simulating the mission with the Void Knights, Mason had died with them a dozen times over. Both in scenarios where the mission was a total failure, and even when *Independence* was recovered and escorted out of Jovian space. After all, it would be up to seventeen Lightnings to hold off whatever the Cendy occupation fleet sent their way.

It was a grim thought, dying with a group of special-forces pilots, many of whom he barely knew. He imagined his name carved into a monolith in Memorial Park on Federal Station. One of hundreds of thousands of names for every Federal spacer who had died in combat. He wondered if anyone would visit him.

When he wasn't flying a simulated Lightning, he was working on a real one. *Magnificent Seven*, opened like the time he first saw her, had been transferred to Procyon Fleet Base with the rest of *Mervie's* fighter complement while the reconnaissance ship underwent emergency repairs. Every time he stepped into the maintenance hangar, the seventeen Lightnings that filled it were swarmed with techs in orange jumpsuits, both Chief Rabin's people and Procyon Fleet Base's own techs.

It seemed the techs were examining every system of each fighter three times over, making sure to minimize any chance of a mechanical failure jeopardizing an already risky mission. During his last visit to the maintenance hangar before *Mervie's* departure, Chief Rabin handed Mason a pad with the maintenance report for *Magnificent Seven*.

"Congratulations, sir. Your fighter needed the most man-hours of maintenance," Chief Rabin said.

"Do I get a prize, Chief?" Mason asked.

"Yes, sir. You'll get one Lightning that you know will work when you drop over Jupiter."

Mason smiled. "Can't ask for better than that."

"Well, I could ask you to go easy on the old girl, sir," Chief Rabin said. "Makes my life easier."

"If you're referring to the hard burns I had to do in our last fight, I'd like to point out that neither of us would be having this conversation if I didn't push *Magnificent Seven* for all she was worth," Mason said.

"Fair enough, sir, but you're not the one who has to crawl through her space frame with a scanner looking for microscopic fractures every time you break twelve gs," Chief Rabin said. "Look, sir, I'm not saying you should risk your life just to make life easier on some technicians, but *Magnificent Seven's* an old ship. At least try to treat her gently if you can get away with it."

"I'll take good care of her, Chief," Mason said. "She's taken good care of me, after all."

"And she will for this mission as well, sir. Trust me," Chief Rabin said.

Mason placed a hand on the chief technician's shoulder. "I do, Chief."

Chief Rabin nodded, but his face turned grim as he looked over the collection of fighters preparing for Operation Autumn Fire.

"A lot of these birds aren't coming home, sir," Rabin said.

Mason sighed. "No, probably not, Chief. But you and your people are doing everything within your power to make sure that they do."

"Hardly seems fair, sir," Chief Rabin said.

"What does?" Mason asked.

"I like to grouse about you flyers as much as the next tech, but the truth is, sir, I have one of the safer jobs in the Space Forces," Chief Rabin said. "I just fix strikecraft. You have to climb into one and fly it into combat."

"War isn't fair, Chief," Mason said. "All we can do is play our chosen roles as best we can. That's something you've done without fail. Hopefully, I'll play mine just as well."

◆

A line of shuttles and fighters snaked towards the newly refurbished *Mervie*. A pair of cruisers and four destroyers had joined *Mervie* while the recon ship had engaged her mimic array to appear as a third cruiser on his scope. Any Cendy intelligence ship loitering at the edge of the system would just see a small task force being assembled.

Mason slotted *Magnificent Seven* into Hangar Bay 12 and disembarked from his fighter as soon as the engines cooled. After storing his hardsuit in an alcove in the suit chamber, he proceeded to the habitat module, passing the ship's crew as they moved about the ship, getting her ready to depart.

"Mason," Jessica said. It was the first time he'd seen her since their chat in the park. "Welcome back aboard *Mervie*."

"Won't lie, I was hoping I was done with this ship after we returned to Procyon," Mason said, smiling at Jessica despite what he was saying.

Jessica held up a mechanical hand and flexed her fingers. "Yes, well, our jobs don't mean we get to have what we want all the time."

"I suppose not," Mason said. "How are you holding up?"

"Much the same as last time," Jessica said. "I doubt that will change after a week flying to Sol. And after that? Well, best-case scenario is I get to tough it out a few more days before I make an appointment with a cyberneticist on Centauri Fleet Base."

"Good to see you're in an optimistic mood," Mason said.

"I would be insufferable if I was gloomy the whole flight," Jessica said. "How are you feeling?"

"Oh, you know. Never been more scared to go home," Mason said. "Not sure how I'll react when I see the world I grew up around under enemy occupation."

"You'll be fine, Mason," Jessica said. "You're almost as tough as Colonel Shimura."

"High praise," Mason said.

"It's the truth," Jessica said.

An alarm sounded, a warning that *Mervie* was about to light her engines.

"Guess we're about to head out," Mason said, grabbing a hold of a wall-mounted handhold, Jessica doing the same beside him. The hab rotor's rotation slowed to a stop, leaving Mason weightless until it folded into the hull, the swing creating a moment of light gravity until the rotor locked into place, once again leaving him in null gravity. After one last alarm, the engines lit, and *Mervie's* acceleration gradually built up until a standard gravity pulled them down to the deck. A sense of anxiety gripped Mason as he felt *Mervie* underway.

"What's wrong?" Jessica asked.

Mason sighed, embarrassed that Jessica had noticed. "It's really happening. We're actually going to do it. Operation Autumn Fire is no longer just a crazy plan—it will be our lives for the next week. And possibly our deaths."

"Well, you're in a dark place," Jessica said. "A bit on the late side to back out."

Mason shook his head. "Don't want to back out, believe it or not. I'm just a little overwhelmed where this has all gone."

Jessica shrugged. "Such is life in the Special Purpose Branch. Now, come on. I think it's been too long since you had a proper cup of coffee."

CHAPTER 22

MAGNIFICENT SEVEN WAS fully kitted out when Mason floated out of the airlock into Hangar Bay 10. The space between the engine nacelles and fuselage were packed with torpedoes and stiletto pods. She almost looked too heavy to take off, even though there was no gravity to hold her down. It was a reminder that, whatever waited for him in Jupiter, Mason would only have what he brought with him. There would be no reinforcements, no resupply, and no rescue should things go wrong.

Mason floated into the open canopy, locked himself to the acceleration seat, and began the start-up sequence. In minutes, the war machine came to life around him—flight, sensor, and combat AIs reporting they were ready to accept his commands. Four torpedoes, four stiletto pods, with all the little interceptors they contained, and the eight full-sized interceptors in the weapons bay, and the big gun in the nose all came up green on the weapons display. Whatever they were about to fly into, *Magnificent Seven* was ready for a fight.

"This is the captain. Final jump in fifteen seconds."

Mason felt the slightest tremble through his seat, and the hangar doors parted open.

"Deploying the cloak," Captain Vann said. "All fighters, prepare for launch."

Mason disengaged the maglocks and pushed *Magnificent Seven* out of the hangar with a pulse from the maneuvering thrusters. The cloak had detached from *Mervie's* nose and was floating away. At the same time, FSFV *Cairo*,

FSFV *Houston*, and the three destroyers escorting them, lit up space with the drive glows of their longburn torpedoes. There was a fourth destroyer on Mason's screen, FSFV *Walker Young*, that didn't fire any torpedoes. But that was because *Young* was simply the disguise *Mervie's* mimic array had given her.

Eight Ball 1 took position at the very center of the canopy. The Lightnings formed two rings around the assault shuttles, eight fighters making up the inner ring and the remaining nine forming the outer ring. Mason was positioned in the bottom of the inner ring. While the strike force of Operation Autumn Fire formed up behind the cloak, *Mervie* and all the other starships in the little taskforce started turning away, their torpedoes expended. As one, all the starships disappeared in a single flash of red-shifted emissions, leaving Autumn Spear's strike force alone in their long, hard fall towards Amalthea.

"Tight beam connection established," Colonel Shimura said. "Uploading data from the cloak's sensors."

The universe beyond the reflective inner surface of the cloak resolved into view—the concentric rings of Jupiter's pole, the Galilean moons, and the Second Battle of Jupiter ragging in full force. The reinforced 1st Fleet was engaged in a long-range missile duel with the Cendy invasion fleet. There were no flashes of nukes going off yet, but there were thousands of torpedoes and hundreds of strikecraft marauding around the space between the two fleets. Incoming on the flanks from the Cendy occupation fleet were hundreds more torpedoes. Already, squadrons of Cendy fighters were burning to intercept the converging groups of longburn torpedoes. Squadrons of Lightnings and Conqueror bombers skirmished with the Cendy fighter-screen, roaming between the fleets like packs of wolves. It was too far to see exactly what was going on with the strikecraft, but if they were following the plan, Mason hoped they were baiting away the Cendy strikecraft as far from Amalthea as possible.

Over twenty million klicks out, he was still closer to home than he had been in months and getting closer at a rapid pace. It all seemed unfamiliar. He had never looked down on Jupiter from this high before.

Amalthea was just a speck of dust compared to the planet it orbited. So far, there weren't any signs of activity around the little moon. The lumpy little moon would complete a full orbit of Jupiter in the time Autumn Fire's strike force reached it. Arrival was timed for the closest approach to Io, where the volatile moon's sulfur plumes and the radiation belts would provide some measure of concealment from the Cendy sensors. It wouldn't be enough to avoid detection once they lit their longburn, but it would make it harder for the Cendies to determine the exact makeup of the strike force.

Mason watched and waited during the long, long fall towards the invisible point in Amalthea's orbit where the Autumn Fire strike force would reach the moon. The 1st Fleet and the Cendy occupation fleet continued their slow, deadly dance, throwing torpedoes and strikecraft at each other without either committing to a full engagement. Neither side was willing to risk heavy losses.

"We've got a problem," Colonel Shimura said.

That was not a sentence Mason wanted to hear while hurtling through the Jovian system at 500 kilometers per second.

"What is it, Colonel?" Cade asked.

"Two Cendy starships are orbiting Amalthea. It looks like they've found the shipyard," Colonel Shimura said.

"So, I take it this is no longer a recovery mission, sir?" Wing Commander Cade said.

"We don't know what the status inside the shipyard is yet, Wing Commander," Colonel Shimura said.

"Given there's no signs of weapon fire, sir, I would guess that they've already captured the shipyard," Wing Commander Cade said.

"We don't know that for sure, and I will not sign the death warrant on three thousand Federal citizens just based on the presence of a couple of battlecruisers," Colonel Shimura said. "Your squadron is to engage and eliminate all Cendy vessels in the vicinity of Amalthea. Then we will ascertain the status of the shipyard, *Independence*, and the people down there."

"Roger that, sir,' Wing Commander Cade said. "Beginning braking burn in fifteen minutes. Sir, request your shuttle braking burn early to delay your arrival. My fighters will do a harder, shorter burn to make sure we arrive about twenty minutes ahead of you."

"Understood, Void Knight Leader," Colonel Shimura said.

"All fighters, preparing for deceleration burn. The Cendies will see us as soon as we light, so expect their reaction to be immediate and decisive," Wing Commander Cade said.

Eight Ball 1 fired her maneuvering thrusters and slipped through the gap between Lightnings, drifting out of the cover of the cloak and turning her engines towards Jupiter. The assault shuttle's drive lit, and she started falling away at full burn. The Cendies reacted almost as fast as light lag allowed. A squadron of fighters burned up from Amalthea towards the assault shuttle that had appeared out of nowhere.

Twenty minutes later, Cade gave the order for the fighters to start their braking burn. With a single choreographed movement, seventeen fighters pulsed their maneuvering thrusters and pushed themselves away from behind the canopy, spreading out like the petals of a blooming flower. As one, they flipped over as they drifted away from the cloak, arresting their movements once their engines were pointed towards their destination, and then, as one, they lit the longburn drives.

Twelve gs landed on Mason like an elephant had tripped and fallen on him, pushing his body into the gel layer of his hardsuit and his hardsuit into the back of his acceleration seat as the chair tilted back on its trunnions.

The Cendies reacted quickly to the sudden appearance of seventeen Lightnings. The Cendy fighters burning to intercept the assault shuttle flipped around to arrest their acceleration and burn back down towards Amalthea, clearly not keen on engaging a superior force of Federal fighters on their own. Another squadron of attack craft appeared after launching from the other battlecruiser. They stayed near their mothership as the battlecruiser lit her own drive and started burning up from Amalthea towards the incoming Lightnings. As the minutes ticked down and the relative speed dropped, the fighters remained close to both battlecruisers. The Cendies wanted to meet the Federal fighters with a unified force.

Mason checked on the main Cendy force fighting millions of kilometers away. There wasn't any sign of ships breaking away to deal with the trouble down orbit. As far as he could tell, their primary concern was the 1st Fleet.

"All fighters, enter combat formation. Ready stilettos and interceptors," Wing Commander Cade said. "We'll deal with the fighters first, then we'll torpedo those battlecruisers."

Mason set the combat AI to start cooking up some firing solutions on the Cendy fighters. This would be a high-speed flyby battle, with the complication that they would have to kill every fighter on the first pass. Otherwise, the survivors could go after the Eight Ball 1 while the momentum carried the Lightnings away.

After forty minutes of braking, Cade ordered the drives cut. The remaining velocity was still over 200 kilometers per second and gaining as the Cendy starship accelerated towards them at three gs. With that added velocity, interceptors and kinetic rounds would pack several times their normal punch. Even a glancing hit would be fatal.

When the enemy closed into range, the Lightnings fired first. Interceptors sprouted from the Lightnings, falling away from the accelerating fighters for half a second before their shortburn drives lit and they shot forward. A volley of 136 interceptors burned towards the Cendies, 135 running and tracking their targets. The last one suffered a malfunction that caused it to tumble out of control, its icon blinking red before disappearing. The Cendies replied with a wave of 120 interceptors. Neither side held back. The Cendies would rely on the point defenses of their starship, the Lightnings on their stiletto pods. It would just be a matter of time to see which proved the better shield.

The combat AIs tracked the Cendy interceptors and reverse-engineered the firing solutions to determine who was their most likely targets. The Cendies had not evenly distributed their interceptors but concentrated them against ten of the seventeen Lightnings. Mason had twelve interceptors burning towards his fighter speed closing in on 250 kilometers per second.

"All fighters, follow my vector. Stay close together," Wing Commander Cade said.

Mason followed the order as the Lightnings moved as one, like a flock of starlings evading a hawk, and burned their engines at high thrust, accelerating tangentially to the incoming interceptors. Fifteen gs crushed down on Mason, but his chief concern was the twelve interceptors homing in on him, and the imaginary sphere that represented the range of the stilettos.

The combat AIs of each fighter coordinated with each other, sharing data, refining firing solutions, coming up with ways to counter the incoming interceptors that would give the maximum chance for the survival of the entire squadron.

The moment the Cendy interceptors entered the engagement envelope of the stilettos, they started firing in rapid-fire volleys. The sound of the pods throwing the little missiles into space shook *Magnificent Seven* like she was firing a machine gun. Stilettos hit interceptors and space sizzled with white-hot flashes of hypervelocity impacts.

"Break."

Mason pulled the nose up, his seat rocking forwards as the pull of acceleration changed direction, pointing *Magnificent Seven's* nose almost directly towards Jupiter.

Decoys started flying out of his fighter like a fiery halo. Something exploded close to his fighter, and all the sensors on the right side when dark, leaving a blind spot off his right wing. It wasn't the detonation of a warhead, just the flash of a 1500-kilo interceptor vaporizing as it slammed into a decoy not a hundred meters away.

As sensors came back online, and Mason regained vision on his right side, he saw that there were six fewer Lightnings than there were moments before. Growler, Fat Chance, Hardtop, Laser Brain, Burn Notice, and Whatsit were all gone from the squadron datalink. There wasn't even wreckage left behind, just clouds off rapidly cooling gas on an escape trajectory heading down out of the plane of the ecliptic. In exchange, all twenty fighters were gone. Just broken metal and expanding gas remained.

Mason didn't perceive the moment when they passed the battlecruisers. One second they were in front of him, and the next second they were behind him and receding at 200 kps.

Flipping *Magnificent Seven* over, Mason disabled the safeties and fired the engines at full power. Eighteen g's crashed down on him like a boulder.

The ten other remaining Lightnings did the same, burning as hard as modern physical enhancement allowed. They would all be bruised and hungover from the acceleration drugs later, provided they survived to experience the after-effects. It would take twenty-two minutes to cancel out his speed and start closing with the Cendy starship.

Eight Ball 1 increased her acceleration and changed her vector. With her greater acceleration, neither battlecruiser would be able to force the assault shuttle into range of their point-defense guns. The spinal guns of the battlecruisers were another story. The emissions of both battlecruisers spiked, and hypervelocity projectiles that had enough kinetic energy to knock out a battleship shot past Eight Ball 1, missing the assault shuttle by just a few hundred meters.

Colonel Shimura, Major Hauer and his Raiders, the two starship pilots, and Jessica were on that shuttle. If one of those rounds hit, they'd be reduced to their component atoms, and those atoms would be heated to the point they'd throw off their electron shells, leaving nothing but hot ionized gas behind.

Eight Ball 1 started evading, making sudden changes in acceleration and vector that would not be any fun for the passengers and crew aboard but were mostly preferable to sudden death. The battlecruisers changed their vectors as well, turning to keep their guns trained on the assault shuttle.

Mason fired off a tightbeam towards the assault shuttle. <"Eight Ball 1, this is Void Knight 17. Turn your vector perpendicular to incoming Cendies. They'll have to turn to engage you.">

<"Roger that, Void Knight 17. I'm changing vector,"> the assault shuttle pilot said. She turned the shuttle until the exhaust of her drives was shooting out perpendicular to that of the Cendy battlecruisers. The battlecruisers turned, tracking the assault shuttle, and each fired another shot just seconds after Mason sent his message. Both went wide, shooting past the shuttle's exhaust plume.

As they turned, their relative acceleration decreased, along with the time it would take for the Lightnings to catch up. As the range closed, Eight Ball 1's tangential velocity would increase. Mason wasn't sure how fast the battlecruisers could turn, but those longships would have to have a limit. There would be a point where the assault shuttle would simply be moving too fast for them to track with their main guns. It was just a matter of surviving long enough to reach that range. Otherwise, Mason would have to settle for avenging Jessica and Colonel Shimura.

The battlecruisers spiked again, and again, missing Eight Ball 1 every time. It was clear the main guns were never intended to be used for dealing with strikecraft. That was why battlecruisers carried strikecraft of their own. Which wasn't to say that the assault shuttle and everyone aboard was safe. The Cendies only had to get lucky once to kill the assault shuttle.

He wanted to do more, but there was nothing else he could think of.

All he could do was watch, wait, and try not to lose consciousness from the crushing pressure weighing down on him.

The Cendies kept up their fire, throwing hypervelocity projectiles at the assault shuttle, but the assault shuttle continued to gain velocity, and the shots started to miss by greater and greater margins as the range closed. As the assault shuttle was about to fly by, the tangential velocity was too much for the battlecruisers to track.

In a move that could only come from a desperate desire to kill the assault shuttle, both assault combatants fired their point defenses beyond their effective range. The assault shuttle avoided the streams or rounds and flew past the Cendy warships. The relief Mason felt seeing the assault shuttle reach relative safety almost overpowered the pain of extreme acceleration.

The Cendies were cornered. Not by any physical obstacle, but by the simple mathematics of space combat. Against craft that could push multiple times their own acceleration, there was no escape.

<"Hauler, as the odd man out, launch two torpedoes at each target,"> Wing Commander Cade said. <"I want to evenly share the torpedoes with both combatants.">

<"Roger that, Zero,"> Mason said. He had the combat AI compute a firing solution with both Cendy warships, and waited for the moment to fire.

The assault combatants turned to present their broadsides towards the incoming Lightnings, bringing as many point-defense guns to bears as possible.

<"All fighters, spread out,"> Wing Commander Cade said. <"Circle of Death.">

Mason changed his vector, making sure *Magnificent Seven* would pass outside effective range of either battlecruiser's point defenses, waiting for the combat AI to prompt him to fire his torpedoes.

Eleven Lightnings formed into a rough circle several thousand kilometers across, with the two Cendy battlecruisers in the center. As one, they fired all their torpedoes. The torpedoes converged on the center of the circles, weathering a barrage of point-defense fire, losing more than half their numbers before reaching detonation range. The remaining torpedoes detonated in discreet flashes of light, shooting spears of hot plasma into the hulls of the battlecruisers as the Lightnings passed them by. One battlecruiser went dark, engines gone, while the other continued to burn but had glowing holes gouged into its hull.

Mason turned to re-engage. If the Cendy ship could still maneuver, it could still fight.

Most of the battlecruisers' point-defense turrets were destroyed. The combat AI identified the active ones.

<"Fourth Flight, suppress the point defenses. Everyone else, target the drives,"> Wing Commander Cade said.

The pilots acknowledged and, after a few minutes, had canceled out their speed and were burning towards the remaining Cendy starship.

Mason armed his cannon and prepared to let the combat AI take over the attitude controls. The approach speed would be too fast for him to aim the gun manually.

The battlecruiser fired first, its remaining point-defense turrets sending a preemptive barrage of projectiles towards the Lightnings. Mason turned the control stick to the left, and *Magnificent Seven's* flight AI responded instantly, lurching the fighter to the left, causing the acceleration seat to turn right to keep parallel to the line of thrust.

Another Lightning, piloted by a man with the callsign Flink, disappeared from the tactical screen, ripped apart by a burst of fire. Wipeout's fighter took a hit and went into an uncontrolled spin that tore her fighter apart.

Mason lurched *Magnificent Seven* out of the path of another burst of point-defense fire, then ceded control to the combat AI. The drives cut, *Magnificent Seven* turned toward the battlecruiser and fired the cannon in a series of bursts, the maneuvering thrusters pulsing after each burst as the combat AI adjusted its aim.

The targeted turrets flashed from impacts and stopped firing. Just as the combat AI was about to shoot the last PD turret in the queue, *Magnificent Seven* took a hit to the left engine nacelle. The impact jarred Mason in his seat as alarms filled his ears and frightening icons filled his HUD. The wing was still there, but the nacelle was gutted. The reactor and longburn drive were knocked out. How the structural members survived was beyond Mason. Hot coolant and sublimating fuel leaked out the ragged remains of the nacelle.

Mason still had control—the flight AI had compensated for the asymmetrical thrust instantly. Behind him, the battlecruiser was a drifting wreck with her drive dark and her hull riddled with holes.

<"Hauler, you still alive?"> Crash asked.

<"Yeah, but I think I'm going to break my promise to Chief Rabin,"> Mason said.

<"Can you still maneuver, Hauler?"> Wing Commander Cade asked.

<"Looks like I should have enough delta-v with the remaining longburn drive to burn down to Amalthea and land,"> Mason said.

<"Understood, Hauler. Follow us in,"> Wing Commander Cade said.

<"Roger that, sir,"> Mason said.

Mason turned towards Amalthea. The lumpy, rusty moon barely obscured the bulk of Jupiter behind it. He burned his remaining longburn drive as hard as he could without ripping off pieces of his damaged fighter.

<"Void Knight Leader, what's your status?"> Colonel Shimura asked.

<"We're down to just guns and a few stilettos, Colonel, and one of my fighters is damaged to the point of combat ineffectiveness,"> Wind Commander Cade said. <"He'll be joining you on Amalthea once we get down there.">

<"Which one is it?">

<"Your favorite, Colonel: Flight Lieutenant Grey,"> Wing Commander Cade said.

<"Understood, Void Knight Leader. Be advised, we're picking up movement around the surface complex,"> Colonel Shimura said. <"We'll hold our distance until your strikecraft get here. We'll need you to do a little delousing before we can land.">

<"Roger that, Eight Ball 1,"> Wing Commander Cade said.

There was an explosion of contacts rising over the horizon of Jupiter. Fighters, over a hundred of them, burning hard for Amalthea.

<"Eight Ball 1, be advised, we've got a lot of Cendy strikecraft coming our way. Their vector suggests they're coming from Jupiter Fleet Base,"> Wing Commander Cade said.

<"We see them, Void Knight Leader. I guess it was too much to ask for the Cendies to commit all their attack craft against the 1st Fleet,"> Colonel Shimura said. <"They'll get here twenty minutes after your arrival.">

CHAPTER 23

Eight Ball 1 loitered a thousand kilometers away from Amalthea, staying clear of any hand-held weapons the Cendy soldiers on Amalthea might have. The surface complex was a single rectangular building with a landing pad located adjacent to it. Jupiter permanently fixed above the facility due to Amalthea's tidal lock to the planet.

A few hundred meters away, dwarfing the surface complex itself, was a huge circular door covering the entrance to the construction chamber below.

Scattered all around the surface complex were dozens of landing pods. There had to be a few hundred Cendies on the moon.

Mason brought his fighter to a stop near the assault shuttle.

There weren't any contacts active on the surface, which didn't surprise Mason. Even Cendy soldiers would have to take shelter from the radiation belts of Jupiter, which herself loomed large directly overhead, taking up much of the sky. Mason could make out every swirl of the atmosphere as the belts and zones ground into each other.

Io hovered just above the horizon, a dirty yellow disk in the sky, the plumes of its volcanoes visible without magnification. The volcanic moon was in a period of unusually high activity, and the space around Mason was filled with charged sulfur particles. Enough to cause serious damage to the sensors of all the strikecraft present, given enough time. Time they didn't have. If they didn't find a way into the moon, the retaliatory wave of Cendy fighters would wipe them out.

"We'll cover your landing, Eight Ball 1," Wing Commander Cade said.

"Good, but we'll have to be fast. There's a lot of radiation on the surface. Even with their hardsuits, I don't want to expose Major Hauer's troopers to more radiation than needed," Colonel Shimura said.

"Understood, Colonel," Wing Commander Cade said. "My people will stand by. Major Hauer just needs to make the call and we'll be there."

"Good to hear, Void Knight Leader," Colonel Shimura said. "We're starting our descent now."

"Roger that. Second Flight, you're in close escort. Third Flight, provide overwatch. If anything shoots at Eight Ball 1, I want you to pulverize it," Wing Commander Cade said.

Mason had to remain in orbit. His crippled fighter was little good for providing close support. All he could do was watch the assault shuttle and escorts approach the surface of the moon while the constellation of approaching Cendy attack craft burned hard from above the western Jovian horizon.

Eight Ball 1 did a low-speed flyby of the surface facility, dropping a line of thirty Raiders, who fired up their thruster rigs to land on the surface. The escorting Lightnings loitered nearby, their cannons trained on the surface, ready to blast anything that took a shot at the assault shuttle or the Raiders.

"Well, this is damned peculiar," Major Hauer said.

"What is it, Major?" Colonel Shimura asked.

"Both hatches for the main airlock are blown outward, like from an internal explosion," Major Hauer said.

Colonel Shimura didn't respond immediately. "You think they blew the base?"

"Sir, there's at least a hundred boarding pods on this moon," Major Hauer said. "I have a hard time believing they'd send so many if they intended to blow up the base."

"Maybe there was more resistance than they expected," Colonel Shimura said.

"If *Independence*'s weapons were online, maybe, sir," Major Hauer said. "We're sending drones down now. Find out what's waiting for us down there."

"Understood, Major. We're coming in to land," Colonel Shimura said. "Flight Lieutenant Grey, land your fighter near us."

"Roger that, sir," Mason said.

Eight Ball 1 landed on a clear patch of the surface well away from the Cendy boarding pods. There were puffs of gas as the assault shuttle's harpoon launchers fired into the ground. Amalthea's gravity was too weak to be relied on to hold the assault shuttle in place.

The hit to the left engine nacelle had taken out the landing gear, so Mason didn't bother with lowering the undercarriage. He brought *Magnificent Seven* to a complete stop just a couple meters above the surface, and then cut the drives, letting *Magnificent Seven* settle onto Amalthea's frozen surface like a falling leaf. Mason shut down *Magnificent Seven* for the last time, filled with a sense of sadness. She was a good fighter, and it was a shame to abandon her on the surface where the Cendies would no doubt destroy her. At least she'd die a warrior's death in battle, rather than being scrapped and recycled like unwanted garbage.

He depressurized the cockpit and popped the canopy. Radiation alerts filled his HUD the moment he pulled himself out of the cockpit. He couldn't stay outside for long. Even with the protection of the hardsuit, it would only be a matter of time before he absorbed a dangerous radiation dose. With a push, Mason launched himself into the air and activated his suit thrusters, pushing himself towards the surface facility's blown out airlock, where Colonel Shimura, Jessica, the assault shuttle's crew, and over two dozen troopers waited outside.

Mason landed among them, grabbing a bent railing to keep from bouncing away.

"Glad you can join us, Flight Lieutenant," Shimura said.

"When do we go inside, sir?" Mason said. "It's a bit hot out here."

"Just as soon as Major Hauer gives the all-clear," Colonel Shimura said.

Mason glanced towards Major Hauer, who was almost anonymous among his troopers in his combat hardsuit. Only his name and his rank insignia gave him away.

"I think it's safe to enter, sir," Major Hauer said. "I'm seeing dead Cendies and a lot of thermal damage, but the drones aren't picking up any radiation."

Colonel Shimura looked at the broken airlock. "Do you know what caused all that damage, Major?"

"No, sir," Major Hauer said.

"Let's get inside the surface facility. No point in baking out here," Colonel Shimura said.

The troopers filed in first, their weapons held at the ready. Mason followed them with Colonel Shimura and Jessica.

Inside, he found Major Hauer looking at something on the ground. A slender, muscular arm terminated at the shoulder, a Cendy rifle clutched in its long-fingered hand.

"Huh," Colonel Shimura said.

"Sir, is there anything about this base's security I should know?" Major Hauer asked.

"I'm as surprised as you are, Major," Colonel Shimura said.

"Blimey, look at the elevator," Jessica said.

Mason turned to look where Jessica was pointing. A cylindrical elevator car had smashed into the far wall, crashing through the paneling to embed itself into the foam insulation. Severed arms and legs and broken torsos of Cendy soldiers surrounded it.

Jessica moved over to it and glanced at the shaft. "Something from inside blasted this thing out with a lot of force."

"I don't see any human body parts," Mason said.

"No." Jessica walked up to the elevator shaft.

"Hold, Lieutenant. Let Major Hauer's troopers examine the elevator shaft," Colonel Shimura said.

Major Hauer approached with a couple of troopers, each bearing a drone. They tossed the drones into the shaft, and the little vehicles came to a complete stop under the power of their thrusters.

"Send them down," Major Hauer said. "Let's see what's waiting for us down there."

"Patch my feed into the drones," Colonel Shimura said.

"Me too," Jessica said.

Colonel Shimura nodded. "Her too."

"You got it, sir," Major Hauer's opaque faceplate turned to Mason. "You want in, Flight Lieutenant?"

"If you're offering, sir, sure," Mason said.

Major Hauer nodded, and a window opened on his HUD, showing a feed from the drones.

"Look at the damage to the insulation. The explosion stripped the walls down to bare ice," Jessica said.

Mason checked the radiation gauge. "No radiation."

"And the temperature is the same as the surface," Jessica said.

"I think we can safely rule out a nuke going off inside the base," Colonel Shimura said.

After several minutes descending down the elevator shafts, the drones reached the bottom. The elevator doors were bent outwards, into the elevator shaft. The bottom was littered with debris, including more than a few mangled Cendy bodies.

"No sign of the base's personnel," Mason said.

"I have a theory, Colonel," Jessica said.

"Out with it, Lieutenant," Colonel Shimura said.

"Whatever did this, it was likely caused by the base's crew," Jessica said. "I'm willing to bet that when the Cendies landed, the base's personnel retreated aboard *Independence* and sabotaged something in the base to cause the mess we're seeing now."

"And they were getting *Independence* ready to launch," Colonel Shimura said. "Is there any way to get in contact with *Independence?*"

"Drones aren't picking up any signals, but that could just be because the internal network got taken out by whatever caused the explosion," Major Hauer said. "I could send drones deeper into the base, but we'll lose the direct feed. Their transmitters can't cut through this much ice."

"No, we'll descend into the base directly," Colonel Shimura said. "We need to get the outer doors to the construction chamber open so Wing Commander Cade's Lightnings can shelter before the Cendy reinforcements get here."

"Understood, sir," Major Hauer said. "My troopers will jump down first, just in case there's anything unfriendly still alive down there."

The first squad of Major Hauer's raiders dove head first into the elevator shaft, battle rifles held ready as they fell slowly in the weak gravity.

"Major, once your troopers reach the bottom, secure the operations center and primary access to the construction chamber," Colonel Shimura said. "Lieutenant Sinclair, Flight Lieutenant Grey, follow me."

Colonel Shimura stepped out in the shaft. Before Mason could follow, Jessica jumped in after her.

"Here goes," Mason said, walking over the edge and letting himself tip over in a slow free-fall. With a couple puffs from the suit thrusters, Mason oriented himself face-down. Jessica and Colonel Shimura fell before him, their arms and legs held out like skydivers. Beyond them was a dark shaft, partly illuminated by the helmet lights of the troopers before him. His HUD's altimeter slowly ticked away the meters as he very, very gradually gained speed. It didn't feel like he was falling down an elevator shaft, but simply floating through a tunnel at a leisurely pace.

The troopers landed a minute before he did, their icons disappearing from below as they moved into the elevator lobby at the bottom of the shaft.

"Colonel, my troopers are securing the base proper," Major Hauer said. "So far they're not finding anything but dead Cendies and melted furniture."

"Melted furniture, sir?" Jessica asked. "As in plastic's melted?"

"Yes, Lieutenant," Major Hauer said.

"What about metal, ceramic, or other high-temperature tolerant materials?" Jessica asked.

"There's plenty of broken and bent metal. But no signs that it melted," Major Hauer said.

"Interesting. So the explosion wasn't that hot," Jessica said.

"What's your theory, Lieutenant?" Colonel Shimura asked.

"Everything we're seeing, Colonel, is consistent with a steam explosion," Jessica said. "And I'm willing to bet that it was deliberate."

"You're saying the shipyard's crew vented the cooling system into the base," Mason said.

"That would be my guess," Jessica said. "Think about it. They would've known they'd not be able to hold off a bunch of Cendy soldiers. So, they retreated into the armored protection of *Independence*, waited for the Cendies to get in from the radiation outside, then set off a steam explosion that killed everything in the base."

"If they vented the cooling system, then how are they preventing *Independence* from overheating?" Mason asked.

"I… don't know," Jessica said.

"We'll ask them when we find out," Colonel Shimura said, flipping her feet down and firing her suit thrusters to safely land on the bottom of the shaft.

Jessica mimicked her moments later. Mason himself fired his thrusters and landed on his feet next to her.

"Colonel, sir, I'm in ops, now. It's a mess. Everything's broken all to hell," Major Hauer said.

"What about access to the construction chamber?" Colonel Shimura asked.

"Sergeant Cane's headed there now, sir, but there's a lot of debris and Cendy bodies in the way," Major Hauer said.

"Understood, Colonel. I'm headed to primary access now," Colonel Shimura said. She climbed out of the elevator shaft into the base proper. Mason followed her, the only light coming from suit lights and LED lamps laid out by the troopers. None of the base's internal lighting survived the steam explosion that ripped through the base.

What he saw looked like a great wind had blown through the base, shoving everything towards the elevator shaft. Troopers were busy moving debris to create a clear path. Colonel Shimura followed the cleared path, and headed down a tunnel marked "Construction Chamber Access". The walls were stripped bare of insulation, exposing the dirty ice underneath. All the debris was covered in thick layers of ice.

"Yeah, definitely a steam explosion. The remaining water flash froze as it sublimated into vacuum," Jessica said.

"This is Cane. We've reached primary access. Looks like the main door is intact, but it's covered in ice."

"Start picking it off, Sergeant. We need to get inside that chamber and get line-of-sight with *Independence* asap," Colonel Shimura said.

"On it, sir," Sergeant Cane said.

By the time they arrived, a chain of explosive charges ran across the width of the wall of ice that covered the large metal door. Sergeant Cane's troopers looked like they were making the finishing touches.

"I didn't have explosives in mind when I ordered you to pick the ice off, Sergeant," Colonel Shimura said.

"You wanted the ice clear as soon as possible, sir, and this is the fastest way to do it," Sergeant Cade said. "The charges should be able to shatter the ice without damaging the door."

"How much more time do you need to finish planting the charges?" Colonel Shimura asked.

"No time at all, sir," Sergeant Cane said. "Just need everyone to get into cover."

Mason ducked into a side corridor. "Don't have to tell me twice."

Jessica and Colonel Shimura followed. Sergeant Cane and her troopers didn't join them; they likely had cover of their own.

"Fire in the hole."

A tremble ran through the chamber, and a wave of broken ice flew by. Mason walked out into the chamber with Colonel Shimura, finding the large circular hatch clear of ice. Shimura launched herself towards the hatch, and Mason followed.

"Help me open this, Flight Lieutenant," Colonel Shimura said.

"Roger that, sir," Mason said.

Colonel Shimura pulled a lever on the hatch, then grabbed the handle and planted her feet on the wall, easily holding herself sideways in the low gravity. Mason joined her and pulled. The hatch budged and came open under its own momentum. Mason had to push himself back to keep the lip of the heavy hatch from smacking him in the faceplate. Beyond, the outer hatch of the large airlock looked undamaged. Colonel Shimura moved inside.

"Uh, Colonel, shouldn't we wait for the troopers to clear the construction chamber first?" Mason asked.

"The Cendies didn't make it into the construction chamber, Flight Lieutenant," Colonel Shimura said. "If they knew what was in there, they'd have nuked this place rather than try and capture it."

The inner hatch had to be opened manually, but there was no ice to impede them. Shimura simply pulled a release, and then opened the hatch. Beyond the inner hatch was a wall of solid dark-grey metal.

Mason followed Shimura out of the airlock. "So where is the–"

It wasn't a wall. It was the side of *Independence*, stretching up more than a kilometer above him, higher than most skyscrapers. Layers of tubes and bridges branched off the sides of the ship, connecting it to the sides of the construction chamber.

"Wow," Mason said.

"Never seen a big starship up close before?" Jessica asked.

"Plenty of times, just not inside a construction chamber where I can get a sense of the scale," Mason said.

Shimura took a few steps towards *Independence* and planted her hands on her hips like she was about to shout up to the starship above. "This is Colonel Shimura to anyone who might be aboard *Independence*. If you're listening, please respond on this channel."

Silence greeted them. Mason walked up next to Shimura, right up to the railing at the edge. *Belts and zones*, there was more starship extending below. The bottom of the construction chamber was a yawning chasm below him, filled with the vast grey metal cylinder of *Independence*'s drive section.

"Maybe they don't have the comm system online, sir?" Mason said. "We might have to find a hatch and knock."

"You might be right, Flight Lieutenant." She pointed at a scaffold running along the side of the starship. "We can take that up–"

Colonel Shimura was interrupted by a blast of radio static that quickly resolved into a male voice.

"This is Captain Ferris. Glad to hear your people finally made it, Colonel."

"What's the status of your people, Captain?" Colonel Shimura asked.

"All civilian and military personnel are aboard *Independence*, Colonel," Captain Ferris said.

"I assume blasting the base with steam was your doing?" Colonel Shimura said.

"It was, sir," Captain Ferris said. "Sorry for the mess."

"Better than having to fight our way through a bunch of Cendies," Colonel Shimura said. "What's *Independence*'s status?"

"So, about that, Colonel—I've got some bad news."

"How badly was *Independence* damaged?"

"Not at all, but that's not the problem. After venting the cooling system into the base, we had to shut down *Independence*'s reactors to keep from overheating," Captain Ferris said. "We'll have to do the start-up process from scratch. That will take some time."

Shimura sighed. "We'll deal with that problem later, Captain. Can you open the outer doors of the construction chamber?"

"I can," Captain Ferris said. "Why?"

"Because I have eight Lightnings that need to take shelter before a wave of Cendy fighters get here."

CHAPTER 24

MASON RODE AN elevator running up the side of the construction chamber with Colonel Shimura and Jessica. The elevator stopped at an open bridge just short of one of *Independence*'s largest airlocks. Holding the railings, they bounced across the bridge to the open outer hatch. It closed behind them as soon as they entered. When the inner hatch opened, there was a small crowd packed into the corridor just outside the airlock. It was an even mix of military and civilian personnel—shipyard workers in dirty jumpsuits, enlisted spacers in various colors of pressure suits, and a few officers in clean blue pressure suits, including a short man with dark hair holding a helmet under one arm. On the front of his helmet were the bars of a full captain.

Mason stopped paying them any mind when his attention turned to a tall man and woman in utilitarian pilot jumpsuits. Mason fumbled for his helmet's release.

"What are you doing, Flight Lieutenant?" Colonel Shimura asked.

Mason ignored her. The seals of his helmet hissed as they broke, and he pulled his helmet off. *Independence*'s air was clean, cool, and antiseptic.

On the outside of the open inner hatch of the tubular airlock, Mason's parents stared at him in shock. They looked different. His mom's fair hair was longer than the last time he saw her, and his dad looked more haggard, his face covered in grey-specked brown stubble.

"Mom? Dad?"

"Mason," his mom said.

"Belts and zones, kid. What are you doing here?" his dad asked.

Mason jumped forward, landing outside the airlock to embrace them.

"So much for asking permission to come aboard." Colonel Shimura said behind him.

"Honey, we've missed you, but please don't crush us to death," his mom said.

"That would ruin the moment, kid," his dad said.

Mason let them go. "Sorry. It's, uh, it's been an eventful few months. And I've been worried."

"You hear that, Hedi? The kid missed his parents."

"I know. Isn't he a dear?"

"Oh, blimey, this is so adorable," Jessica said.

"Who's your friend?" Mason's mom asked.

Mason turned around. "Oh, that's Lieutenant Sinclair."

"Most people just call me Jessica. It's a pleasure."

"I've been working with her and Colonel Shimura. They're why I'm here."

"You mean you didn't come to rescue us?" Mason's dad asked.

"Uh, no. I, uh, I didn't know you were here," Mason said. "How are you here?"

"Got caught on the ground when those Ascendency types showed up and started shooting up the 9th Fleet." His dad cast an angry glance towards Captain Ferris. "Your mother and I were getting ready to take off when this guy locked down the base and revoked our takeoff clearance."

"Couldn't risk having you draw attention to this base, Mister Grey," Captain Ferris said.

"Well, that's neither here nor there," Mason said. "We're here to get this big starship out of here. You're welcome to come too."

"Well, that's a relief," his dad said. He turned to Captain Ferris. "I take it you won't need us to fly this tub out, after all."

"What?" Mason asked.

Captain Ferris sighed. "As a precaution, in case we couldn't get outside help, I was going to have your parents try to fly *Independence* out of Amalthea."

"Fortunately, that won't be necessary. I brought a pilot of my own," Colonel Shimura said.

Mason's mom and dad glanced at Mason, then back to Shimura. "Him?" they asked at the same time.

"Not him. I mean a starship pilot. She's on her way up right now," Colonel Shimura said.

"Oh, well, uh. What's your job here, kid?" Mason's dad asked.

"Well, I flew one of the fighters that escorted Colonel Shimura's shuttle here. "Unfortunately, that fighter's no longer serviceable."

Colonel Shimura walked past Mason and his parents, stopping in front of Captain Ferris.

"Is *Independence*'s bridge operational?"

Captain Ferris nodded. "It is, Colonel."

"Then we'll head up there and plan *Independence*'s defense." Shimura turned to Mason. "I know you want to catch up with your parents, Flight Lieutenant, but I could use your help."

Mason nodded and turned to his mom and dad. "I'll catch up with you later. You two have a safe place to stay on the ship?"

"We'll be in one of the galleys on this deck," his dad said. "Your mother and I can wait for you there."

"Okay," Mason said. "Once we get out of this mess, I'll catch you two up on what I've been up to."

"We'll hold you to that, kid," his dad said.

"Come along, Flight Lieutenant," Colonel Shimura said, waving at Mason to follow her and Captain Ferris.

Mason spared his mom and dad one last look before turning to follow Colonel Shimura.

"Well, that was a fortuitous turn of events, wasn't it?" Jessica said as he fell in beside her.

"That my parents are here?"

"Yes. I mean, what were the odds?"

Mason shrugged. "Small universe, I guess."

"And now you get to rescue Earth-Fed's biggest starship and your parents all in one go. Quite a deal."

"That's one way to look at that," Mason said. "Though I can't say I'm in love with the idea of my parents being stuck aboard a ship the Cendies are going to do everything they can to destroy the moment they spot her leaving Amalthea."

"Oh, right," Jessica said. "That does put a bit of a dampener on things."

⁓

Colonel Shimura, Captain Ferris, Wing Commander Cade, and Major Hauer stood before the holotank at the center of *Independence*'s circular bridge, looking at a holographic representation of *Independence* towering inside the construction chamber. Three tiers of control consoles wrapped around the base of the bridge where the holotank was located. All the unoccupied consoles made the bridge feel deserted.

"There are only two ways for the Cendies to get inside the construction chamber." Colonel Shimura's finger traced the line of the elevator tunnel that ran parallel to the construction chamber. "First is by using the elevator tunnel from the surface facility." Her finger moved to the top of the construction chamber. "Or by breaching the big doors above us."

Major Hauer traced a line across the bottom of the elevator shaft. "Colonel, my Raiders have already set up demolition charges. Just give the word, and I'll set them off to collapse the elevator shaft. That should delay any Cendy assault through the surface facility until *Independence* is ready to launch."

"One less thing to worry about. Do it," Colonel Shimura said. "Captain Ferris, is the cooling system vulnerable to external attack?"

On the holotank, the representation of the base zoomed out, revealing the Jupiter-facing half of Amalthea. From the bottom of the construction chamber, cooling pipes descended like roots deep into Amalthea. Captain Ferris traced the points where the pipes were closest to the surface. "Only if they breach the construction chamber itself and damage the pipes carrying coolant to and from *Independence*, Colonel. The rest of the cooling system's buried too deep. They'd have an easier time just blowing up the ship."

"Which they're likely to do if they decide they can't capture her," Colonel Shimura said.

The projection on the holotank zoomed in on the top of the construction chamber, above *Independence*'s pointed bow. Above it was the massive door that capped the top of the construction chamber, resting on a metal ring embedded in the ice at the top.

Captain Ferris pointed at the door. "The door covering the construction chamber is thick, but not very dense. It's designed to conceal the heat given off by *Independence*, not hold off a determined assault. A few big explosive charges could pop it right off."

"So, when the Cendies attack the base, we need to assume they'll breach through the construction chamber's doors," Colonel Shimura said. "How long until we can get *Independence*'s weapon systems online?"

"Theoretically, as soon as we get the first reactor online, but that would mean shunting power away from start-up," Captain Ferris said. "It would take two hours before *Independence* generates enough reserve power that we could activate any of the point-defense guns without delaying ignition of the main engines."

"My fighters can cover the entrance until the point defenses come online, Colonel," Wing Commander Cade said.

"Your pilots won't have a lot of room to maneuver down here," Colonel Shimura said.

"We'll make do, sir," Wing Commander Cade said.

"That's all well and good, sirs, but I think everyone's missing the biggest problem," Jessica said. "All lines connecting the surface sensors to the base were knocked when Captain Ferris flooded the base with hot coolant. We're completely blind to what is happening outside. For all we know, the Cendies could be attaching a nuke at the top of the door big enough to fry anything inside the construction chamber."

"So, what do you propose, Lieutenant?" Colonel Shimura said.

Jessica walked up to the holotank and further expanded the projection of the door. "Someone in a hardsuit needs to go outside and feed their sensor data back to us. Even the relatively small sensor suite built into a hardsuit's helmet should be adequate for detecting any shenanigans going on outside."

"I'll ask for volunteers from one of my Raiders," Major Hauer said.

"No need, sir. I volunteer," Mason said.

Jessica blinked with surprise. "I actually was thinking of Major Hauer's Raiders when I mentioned 'someone' going outside."

"Any Raider that goes outside is one less we have down here defending *Independence* and everyone aboard her," Mason said. "And, besides, I'm most of the way to the door anyway just standing here."

"I can't fault that logic," Colonel Shimura said. "All right, Flight Lieutenant. If you insist on volunteering, I won't say no. Just be careful out there."

"I second that," Jessica said.

"I'll try to stay out of trouble," Mason said. "And, besides, the view will be amazing."

෯

When the outer hatch of *Independence's* top-most airlock swung open, the two main guns of the battlecarrier's A turret towered before Mason. He stepped out onto the small platform that extended from the airlock and looked up at the large doors above. The light-grey door contrasted with the dirty grey of the ice walls and the solid dark grey of *Independence's* hull.

Mason leapt straight up, launching himself off the front of the warship. Firing his suit thrusters, Mason gained speed, passing the muzzles of the main guns, and then the slanted armored nose of the warship. He aimed for the scaffold that lined the bottom of the door.

He landed on the scaffold set just short of the maintenance hatch. On the wall panel, he pulled a heavy lever and pushed the hatch open. Inside was a ladder leading straight up. A ladder seemed of dubious utility in such low gravity, but Mason didn't see reason to dwell on it. He jumped up the ladder and grabbed the last rung just short of the roof hatch. Opening the hatch, Mason found the swirling red and white atmosphere of Jupiter filling the sky above.

An elevated radiation warning popped up on Mason's HUD. He was sheltered from the worst of Jupiter's radiation belt, but what was left was close to the limit of what Mason's hardsuit could protect him from.

Cendy fighters flittered above like motes of dust against Jupiter's face, each one highlighted by a green box on Mason's HUD.

"There's a frightening number of fighters up here," Mason said.

"We see them, Flight Lieutenant," Colonel Shimura said. "Probably means they're up to something. You'll need to examine the door itself."

"Right. Peeking out now, sir," Mason said. He crept up the ladder, sticking his head through the open hatch. He came face to face with a squat conical device. Its rounded tip pointed toward Jupiter while its wide base was adhered to the silo door with translucent resin.

"That's a bomb, isn't it?" Mason said.

"A demolition charge by the looks of it," Colonel Shimura said. "Get out of there, now."

Mason pulled himself up a little further to see over the bomb and looked around. There were more of them, a lot more, arranged in concentric rings radiating from the center of the construction chamber door.

"Oh, shit."

CHAPTER 25

THE BOMBS STARTED detonating in a wave of silent fury that shook the ladder Mason held on to as it crashed towards him. Mason turned his back to the wave and launched himself out of the maintenance hatch with all the force his hardsuit-augmented legs could muster, and fired his suit thrusters to gain more speed and altitude. The wave caught up to him as he flew over the outer ring of bombs, just short of the ridge of regolith that circled the silo door.

Something slammed into Mason, and his left thigh exploded with pain as he went tumbling out of control. A kaleidoscope of ominous icons filled his HUD as he tumbled head over heels. Jupiter, space, regolith, and space again came into view as he spun, the regolith getting closer with each rotation. Mason fired his suit thrusters to stop his spin and turn himself feet-first as Amalthea's weak gravity pulled him back down. His heels hit the regolith and dug in, the impact causing another flash of white-hot pain through his left leg, and Mason blacked out.

When his vision cleared, the face of Jupiter was marred with warning icons and delicate spider-web cracks in his visor. The icons warned of high radiation, damaged sensors, and multiple suit breeches. The most serious being the one in his left thigh plate, the icon reinforced by the sharp, hot pain coming from his left leg.

Mason dismissed the icons clouding his view and sat up. Through his cracked visor, he saw a shard of metal as long as his hand sticking out of his left thigh.

"Belts and zones." Mason reached to pull out the shard but stopped when he realized that was a stupid move. There was no guarantee his suit's inner lay would be able to staunch the bleeding and hold in his suit's air if he ripped it out. He settled for ordering his hardsuit to give him a double-dose of painkillers and lock out its left leg, turning it into an armored leg brace. A wave of cool relief passed through his body like a tender kiss, and the pain dulled.

The shrapnel in his leg was not the only bit of metal embedded in the frontal plating of his hardsuit, but it appeared to be the only piece that punched all the way through. He didn't want to think about how deeply it was stuck into his flesh. No air was leaking from his hardsuit, despite all the breaches. The inner gel-lay was plugging all the leaks like it was supposed to.

Mason took a moment to gather his wits. He had taken the backblast of several hundred shaped-charges to the face and had gotten away with a flesh wound. If that shard had hit him in the chest, he'd be in real trouble. The radiation alarm buzzed with increasing urgency, reminding Mason that he was sitting on the surface of a moon bathed in charged particles.

He got up on his good leg, an easy task in the pitiful gravity. He looked around and found himself in a depression of featureless rusty regolith. The only indication of where he had come from were the twin ruts his heels had dug into the regolith when he landed, pointed back in the direction he had come from. He started hopping back towards the silo door.

There was a painfully bright flash that left Mason blind, with a bright after-image burned in his vision. His damaged visor couldn't polarize anymore, it seemed. When his vision cleared, he saw lines of white-hot kinetic rounds shoot in and out as Cendy fighters above traded shots with the Lightnings below. Holding up a hand to protect his eyes from more kinetic flashes, Mason moved up. When he crested the rise, he saw the door was gone. Completely disintegrated by shaped-charges, leaving only the ring of the door's frame. Below, he saw Lightnings maneuvering between *Independence's* hull and the wall of the silo, firing their weapons. One Lightning took a hit, and spun out of control, smashing against *Independence's* armored hull while it tumbled slowly to the bottom, more kinetic fire ripping into it as it fell.

A movement in his peripheral vision drew his attention. On the far side of the broken door, hundreds of faceless armored Cendy soldiers gathered at the edge, waiting their turn to leap into the construction chamber while gunfire erupted from below.

Leaping into the open silo, while it was filled with weapon fire and enemy soldiers, did not hold much appeal. But it was only a matter of time before one of the Cendy soldiers on the surface, or one of the fighters above, took notice of him. It was a choice between certain death and merely likely death. Mason chose likely death. Making sure his suit transponder was on to discourage having a friendly shoot at him, he jumped.

Weapons fire flashed all around him. Below, *Independence*'s armored hull sparked and flashed from countless hits and Lightnings danced around the space between the walls and the starship's hull, firing their cannons with abandon.

Mason noticed a Lightning covered in Cendy soldiers, the pilot jerking the fighter from side to side to try and throw the attackers off. Cendies fired their weapons into the canopy, and the fighter started to spin out of control, smashing into one of the gantries that ran up the side of the construction silo.

There was an explosion on *Independence*'s hull. The Cendies were breaching one of the airlocks. When the smoke dissipated, Mason saw Cendy soldiers crawling over the hull and into the airlock.

A Lightning slewed around *Independence* and fired into the hull around the airlock, turning Cendies into mist. Some of the Cendies higher on *Independence*'s hull leapt for the fighter, a couple landing on the wings. They started moving towards the cockpit. The Lightning's pilot, either oblivious or indifferent to the enemy soldiers crawling on their fighter, continued to shoot soldiers off *Independence*'s hull.

Mason drew his pistol and fired his suit thrusters, guiding his fall towards the Lightning. He turned his feet towards the Lightning and let his good leg absorb the impact as he landed behind the two Cendies as they leveled their weapons at the cockpit. He aimed his equalizer at the back of one Cendy and put two APEX rockets into its back. The second swung around with impressive speed, but Mason shot it twice in the chest before it could bring its rifle to bear. The Lightning lurched under Mason, and he almost lost hold of his gun as he scrambled for a handhold.

Atop the Lightning, his brainset automatically established a near-field communications link.

<"Hey, stop moving so much. You got a friendly riding your back.">

<"Hauler? What are you doing on my fighter?"> Crash asked.

<"You had a couple of Cendies crawling on your back. Thought I'd deal with them for you.">

<"Oh, nice. I was just going to let them shoot me while I killed as many of their friends as I could.">

<"Well, now you can keep killing Cendies without dying,"> Mason said.

<"Not a bad idea. I think I'll do just that. You got a good grip up there?">

Mason tightened his grip on the hardpoint. <"I'm holding on for dear life.">

<"You'd better.">

The maneuver thrusters of Crash's Lightning erupted with hot gas and the fighter lurched beneath him. Kinetic fire from above rained around Crash's Lightning, gouging holes into ice on one side and bouncing off *Independence*'s armor on the other. Crash's Lightning tilted up, pointed her nose towards the open door of the silo, and vibrated as her main gun fired. Mason saw something flash, and the rain of metal stopped.

<"You still there, Hauler?"> Crash asked.

<"Yep. Good shooting,"> Mason said.

<"Thanks."> Crash tilted her Lightning back down and aimed on a group of Cendies trying to climb down the side of *Independence* where her gun turrets blocked the lines of fire from the troopers below. Crash annihilated them with a burst from her cannon.

<"Crash, you wouldn't happen to know what's going on inside *Independence*?">

<"You don't know?"> Landing asked.

<"My suit radio got damaged by the blast that tore open the silo door. I only have near-field communication from my brainset,"> Mason said.

<"Colonel Shimura just said that the bridge is under attack and is requesting reinforcements,"> Landing said.

<"Well, I guess I count,"> Mason said. <"Drop me off near an airlock and I'll try to help.">

<"Sure. If you want to play trooper, I won't stop you.">

❧

The ruined interior of the large airlock was a slaughterhouse filled with the dismembered remains of several Cendy soldiers. Mason's stomach twisted at the sight of the gore as he tried to move through the airlock while stepping on as few bodies as possible. Leading with his equalizer, Mason started hopping towards the bridge.

He got maybe ten hops into *Independence* when he reached an intersection and found himself staring into the barrels of the battle rifles held by two Raiders.

Mason put up his hands. "Hey, friendly!"

One of the troopers lowered their battle rifle. It was Sergeant Cane, anonymous behind her visor, save for the name stenciled across her helmet.

"What the hell happened to you, sir?" Cane asked.

"Got blown up," Mason said. "What's the situation?"

"Cendies are attacking the bridge, sir. Me and Lopez here are heading there to help clear them out."

"What a coincidence. That's why I'm here too," Mason said. "Lead the way, Sergeant."

"I intend to, sir," Cane said. "Watch our backs."

"Will do, Sergeant," Mason said.

They made their way through the depressurized interior of the warship, making their way up to the bridge, running across the bodies of several Cendy soldiers and a few Raiders who had tried to block their path. Neither Sergeant Cane nor Corporal Lopez commented on their dead comrades. Nearing the bridge, Mason couldn't hear weapons fire, but he could see flashes up ahead and feel the vibration through his boot.

Cane held up her hand, "Hold here." She pushed her back to the wall and used the remote optics on her rifle to peek around the corner.

"Bridge is breached, but it looks like the Cendies are being held off by weapons fire from inside," Cane said.

"This is your area of expertise, Sergeant. What's the plan?" Mason asked.

Cane opened the breech of the underbarrel grenade launcher and loaded an explosive shot. "You might want to get back, sir."

"Right," Mason said.

"Lopez, cover me," Cane said.

"Got it, Sarge," Lopez said.

Cane swung around the corner, leveled her battle rifle and fired. The deck vibrated under Mason's feet as the grenade detonated. Lopez and Cane opened fire with their battle rifles.

"Move up," Cane said.

Mason wasn't sure she meant him too, but he decided to follow behind them as they approached the bridge hatch, covering their backs with his equalizer.

Cane moved up to the edge of the hatch but didn't go around the corner. "Any friendlies in there?"

"There are, Sergeant," Major Hauer said.

Cane looked around the corner, then waved for Mason to follow. Mason walked around the bodies of the dead Cendies who crowded around and inside the bridge hatch, careful not to trip over their long limbs. The bridge was filled with debris, bullet holes riddling consoles and bulkheads, the deck covered with glass from shattered console screens and pools of acceleration gel from punctured seats. The holotank was dark, with chunks torn out of its base. Major Hauer stood behind one of the shattered consoles in the upper tier, his hardsuit covered in scratches and divots.

Jessica stood up from behind the holotank. "You're alive."

"Yeah, looks like it takes more than a few hundred bombs to kill me," Mason said.   "Where's Colonel Shimura?"

"I'm behind the holotank with Lieutenant Sinclair, Flight Lieutenant," Colonel Shimura said, her voice strained and hoarse.

Jessica waved Mason over while Sergeant Cane and Corporal Lopez took position to guard the bridge's hatch. He found Colonel Shimura lying on her back behind it. Her armor was breached in several places.

"You look like hell, sir," Mason said.

"Speak for yourself, Flight Lieutenant," Shimura said.

Mason glanced at the ugly piece of metal sticking out of his thigh. "Yeah, but the hardsuit's keeping me filled with painkillers."

"That's a great feature of hardsuits," Shimura said.

"How bad, sir?" Mason asked.

"Pretty bad," Shimura said. "Suit's doing what it can about the internal bleeding, but I'm going to need medical attention."

"Right," Mason said. "What can I do, sir?"

"Help defend this ship," Colonel Shimura said. "Do whatever you can until *Independence* launches."

Mason nodded and looked towards Captain Ferris. "How long until *Independence* can fly, Captain Ferris?"

"A few more minutes at least, Flight Lieutenant," Captain Ferris said.

"Oh, belts and zones," Mason said.

Jessica looked up at him from Colonel Shimura. "We were just about to get some of the point defenses online when the Cendies breached the bridge. With those, we should be able to hold off their beaching pods."

"Well, let's not waste any time," Mason said.

Shimura patted Jessica's forearm. "I'm not going anywhere, Lieutenant. Get those point defenses online before another wave of Cendies find their way onboard."

Jessica nodded and moved to one of the few undamaged consoles, sitting down and activating it.

"Okay, *Independence* is generating enough reserve power to power a few of the point-defense turrets," Jessica said. "I'll just need to… Shit."

"What?"

"Combat AI's down." Jessica waved her arms around the ruined bridge. "Probably due to all the high-speed metal zipping around here."

"Aren't there backups?" Mason asked.

"Never booted those up. We were cutting all kinds of corners to get guns activated as fast as possible," Jessica said. "It'll take time to get those online."

"Time we don't have," Mason said. "Wing Commander Cade's fighters are going to have to hold the Cendies off by themselves."

Captain Ferris walked up to a console. "The point-defense guns can still fire without the combat AI." He pointed to a bank of unoccupied seats. "We just need a gunner to operate them directly."

"Oh, can I volunteer, sir?" Mason asked.

"Playing gunner not beneath your dignity?" Jessica asked.

"Not today, it's not," Mason said. "Just show me what to do."

"Plant your ass in that seat, Flight Lieutenant," Captain Ferris said.

Mason hopped over to the gunnery station and set himself down in the seat.

Captain Ferris sat down in the seat next to Mason. "You'll get a prompt on your HUD asking you to connect. Accept it, and you'll be able to pick a turret to control."

A prompt appeared on Mason's HUD. He accepted, and a menu came up showing all of *Independence's* point-defense turrets. There were dozens of them, all glowing red, inactive. There were just six showing up green: two on the forward hull and the rest scattered around the drive section, hundreds of meters below the bridge. The gunnery interface was almost identical to the weapon interface of the Lightning. Thank God Earth-Fed used a standardized operating system. Mason accessed external cameras and started scanning the hull, focusing on points where the Cendies could gain access to *Independence.*

There was a constant barrage of fire coming from below, both from the small arms of troopers and from the half-dozen remaining Lightnings flittering around *Independence's* hull like very large, angry hornets defending their hive from swarming invaders. A squad of Cendy soldiers had gathered near one of the large armored doors covering one of the hangar bays, attaching devices to the large hinges. It looked like they were getting ready to breach it, likely intent on going through the hangars to get to the starship's engineering spaces. There was an active point-defense turret not fifty meters from them, set right between Hangar Bays 1 and 3.

Mason connected to the turret, seeing directly through its thermal cameras. In the monochrome vision, the floor and walls of the construction chamber were deep black, while the *Independence's* hull was varying shades of grey. The Cendies were white figures, their body heat standing out against the relatively cool plating of *Independence's* hull. The point-defense guns had an adjustable muzzle velocity and rate of fire. He set the weapon to minimum muzzle velocity, which was more than fast enough to deal with infantry, and maximum rate of fire. He traversed to the right and lowered the aiming reticle right over the Cendies. One of them noticed the movement, and their blank face turned to face the turret.

"Surprise." Mason fired.

There was no sound. The spot where he aimed just started flashing as kinetic rounds impacted the hull at an oblique angle. The Cendies disappeared in a flash. Mason slewed the turret side-to-side, spraywashing the Cendies off the hull with a stream of metal fired at 6000 rounds per minute. When he stopped firing, there was just a white-hot patch on the hull in the thermal imager.

"We've got more boarding pods coming in from above," Captain Ferris said.

Mason switched over to one of the forward point-defense turrets. Jupiter was a dark grey expanse in the background, the approaching Cendy pods white dots filling the hole in the door. Mason fired the point-defense gun in a continuous burst, compensating for his lack of accuracy with volume of fire. He traced the aiming reticle over boarding pods, walking a line of kinetic fire over them like a water hose, shattering them into thousands of pieces. When he destroyed the last boarding pod, all that remained of them were tiny bits of broken metal and composite, falling like snowflakes in the low gravity.

"No more Cendies are trying to push into the chamber," Captain Ferris said.

"Now they know that there's a starship that can shoot at them down here, they'll send something other than soldiers to get chewed up by our point defense," Colonel Shimura said. "What's the status of the backup combat AI, Lieutenant?"

"It's just come online, Colonel. Mason, release manual control of the point-defense turrets," Jessica said.

"Done," Mason said.

Mason was booted out of the direct vision from the turret. Instead, he saw a display of the accumulate data from the sensors mounted on the front of the ship. The face of Jupiter was dotted with Cendy attack craft and a volley of incoming torpedoes. Point defenses fired quick, accurate bursts, and the torpedoes disappeared before they could detonate. Seconds later, the gas and debris flew through the opening and crashed harmlessly against the frontal armor.

"That was close," Mason said.

"Engineering just reported in," Captain Ferris said. "They just got enough reactors online to power the main engines. We can depart."

"Ah, good," Colonel Shimura said through gritted teeth. "Flight Lieutenant York. Be so good as to fly us out of here."

"You got it, sir," Flight Lieutenant York said, flying into the pilot's seat. "Time to see how this big girl moves."

CHAPTER 26

FLIGHT LIEUTENANT YORK fired the starship's rear maneuvering thrusters. Their relatively gentle thrust was more than enough to overcome the pull of Amalthea's gravity and lift the battlecarrier off the pedestal. Debris littering the construction chamber blew around like they were caught in a great wind, swirling around the chamber as *Independence* ascended. When the forward hull pushed through the shattered remains of the construction chamber door, *Independence*'s sensors got their first taste of open space and Mason's tactical overlay started filling with targets.

Over a hundred Cendy fighters swarmed around the Jupiter-facing side of Amalthea. *Independence*'s weapons AI requested permission to fire, and Mason granted it. Point-defense guns started firing as soon as they got a clear shot, snuffing out a score of fighters in the first couple of seconds. The surviving fighters burned hard for Amalthea's horizon, some launching missiles at *Independence* as they did. The point defenses eliminated the missiles with casual ease. By the time *Independence*'s engine bells cleared the silo door, all enemy fighters had either been destroyed or had fled to the far side of the moon.

Independence started tilting towards Jupiter's horizon as Flight Lieutenant York turned her in the direction of Amalthea's low and fast orbit.

"I'm lighting the longburn drives in one minute," Flight Lieutenant York said. "Might want to use that time to get the wounded somewhere comfortable before I start pulling one and a half gs."

Jessica guided Colonel Shimura to an acceleration seat, pulling her down into the cushion and pulling a buckle over her damaged chestplate. "When can we get the bridge repressurized?"

"I've sealed off the breached areas," Captain Ferris said. "Bridge is starting to repressurize."

"I've got medics inbound on the bridge to assist the injured," Major Hauer said.

"You think they could hurry, Major? Colonel Shimura's in bad shape," Lieutenant Sinclair said.

"They're moving as fast as they can, Lieutenant," Major Hauer said, moving over to Colonel Shimura. "You still with us, sir?"

"Not going anywhere just yet, Major," Colonel Shimura said.

A notification appeared on Mason's HUD, a warning that *Independence* was about to start accelerating in one minute. Time enough for any crew to fix themselves to the deck rather than risk a potentially lethal fall when the engines lit. The six remaining Lightnings of the 4th flew out of the construction silo and formed up ahead of *Independence*.

"This is Wing Commander Cade requesting docking clearance."

"Understood, Wing Commander. Opening the doors for hangar bays one through six," Captain Ferris said. "I'll leave it to your discretion which landing pads you touch down on."

"Much appreciated, Captain," Cade said.

The Lightnings folded their wings and ducked into the open doors of each hangar bay.

"All fighters are aboard and maglocked to the landing pads," Captain Ferris said.

"Just in time," Flight Lieutenant York said. "Beginning ignition in five... four... three... two... one." A rumble traveled up the hull of the ship as a one-tenth of a g pulled Mason down into his seat.

"How are the engines looking, Captain?" Flight Lieutenant York asked.

"Green across the board, Flight Lieutenant," Captain Ferris said. "You should be safe to go 100%, but I wouldn't take them past that."

"Understood, sir. Opening up the throttle." Flight Lieutenant York started easing the throttle level forward.

The rumble increased in intensity, and the downward pull started increasing until the accelerometer in Mason's HUD measured 1.5 g, and his wounded left thigh started to throb with renewed intensity. Mason gritted his teeth and tried to distract himself by focusing on the tactical overlay, watching for the Cendies' reaction to *Independence* lighting her drives and announcing her existence to all of Sol. Behind *Independence*, 1st Fleet's fighters hovered a few degrees over Jupiter's horizon, still engaged in their long-range duel with the Cendy occupation fleet. After two minutes, a few of the Cendy battlecruisers broke formation with the rest of the fleet and started burning hard for the jump limit, joined by a swarm of fighters. Given the lightspeed delay, the Cendies' reaction was quick and logical. They knew they'd never beat *Independence's* head start with a direct pursuit using longburn drives. They were going to head outside the jump limit and use their stardrives to cut off their escape.

The 1st Fleet saw that, and formations of Conquers and Lightnings vectored to intercept the fleeing warships.

A notification appeared in Mason's HUD—the bridge had repressurized. Popping the seal of his helmet, Mason pulled it off and held it before him. A gouge ran over the top of the helmet, and there were countless smaller scratches marring its sides. Mason had caught more of the blast to his face than he thought. He was lucky the only thing that had punched through his hardsuit was the bit of metal digging into his thigh.

"Funny how a little gravity can make wounds hurt more," Colonel Shimura said. She had taken her helmet off and handed it to Major Hauer.

"Speaking from experience, sir?" Mason.

"Oh, yes. I'd be screaming if my hardsuit wasn't pumping me full of painkillers," she said.

Major Hauer's medics started arriving on the bridge, troopers with red crosses stenciled onto the shoulders and helmets of their hardsuits.

They swarmed over Mason and Shimura, the two wounded on the bridge. They were both loaded onto stretchers, as was the late Commander Peeters. Once the medics carried them out of the bridge, the medics carrying Peeters broke off, presumably to take his body to storage.

There were more troopers in the corridor, busy stuffing dead Cendies into body bags. Mason suspected they were going to the same place Peeters was.

After an elevator ride one level down, Mason arrived aboard

Independence's med center, which was filled with medics, the wounded, and civilian volunteers.

The medics lay Mason down on an acceleration seat, where he watched Colonel Shimura be carried towards the med bay's surgical section.

Jessica stopped short of following Colonel Shimura and walked up to Mason, laying a gloved hand on top of his. "How are you doing?"

"Not bad, all things considered." He grimaced as a throb of pain shot through his leg.

"Hurts?"

"Oh yeah, but I'm sure it won't be too hard to fix," Mason said.

"Assuming the Cendies don't blow up the ship," Jessica said.

"You and I have a pretty good track-record of keeping the Cendies from blowing up ships we're aboard," Mason said.

Jessica smiled. "Yes, I suppose we do."

A nurse in a red and white jumpsuit approached. "Hello, sir. I'm Ensign Fadel."

"Hello, Ensign Fadel," Mason said.

She kneeled over Mason's leg, getting a close look at the shard of metal sticking out of his thigh plate. "That's quite the piece of shrapnel sticking out of you, sir," she said.

"There's quite a bit of it sticking into me too," Mason said.

"Well, let's see if I can't fix that," she said.

"You're not part of the medical team we brought along," Jessica said.

"No, sir. I'm part of Amalthea's medical staff. The military part, at least," Ensign Fadel said. "Spent most of my time doing regular checkups of shipyard workers and fixing the odd overuse injury."

"Well, I got a genuine battlefield injury for you to play with, Ensign," Mason said.

"I see that, sir," Ensign Fadel said. She pulled on a pair of thick gloves and started prodding the shard. "We'll have to pull this out first, then take off your hardsuit to treat the wound itself. Can I access your hardsuit's health monitor, sir?"

Mason opened the connection for her. "Done."

"Thanks." Fadel's expression became distant as she examined something on her HUD. "You weren't kidding when you said there was quite a bit sticking into you."

"Sounds like you might have some experience with that," Mason said.

"Encountered a few working as an EMT on Starport Leonov, sir," Ensign Fadel said. "Before the war with the League."

"You're from Starport Leonov?" Mason asked.

"Born and raised, sir," Lieutenant Fadel said. "You Jovian too?"

"Starport Armstrong," Mason said.

"Welcome home, sir," she said.

"Thanks," Mason said.

"Okay, this is going to start bleeding bad once I pull it out," Ensign Fadel said. "Hardsuit's gel layer will put pressure on the wound, but once we take it off, I'll need someone to put pressure on the wound."

"I think I can handle that, Ensign," Jessica said.

Ensign Fadel nodded. "Thanks, sir. Okay, Flight Lieutenant, this is going to hurt like hell when it comes out."

Mason gritted his teeth and grabbed a hold of his armrest in one hand, and Jessica's hand in the other. He signaled he was ready with a curt nod. With a pair of forceps, Fadel slowly pulled the shard out of Mason's thigh. The pain overpowered the painkillers, and a moan escaped Mason's lips.

"And it's out," Fadel said, planting the sharp, knife-like piece of blood-ied metal into the tray. "Okay, next step is getting the hardsuit off."

"I'll need to stand up for this, won't I?" Mason said.

"I'm afraid so, sir," Fadel said.

"Belts and zones." Mason took a moment to gather his courage. "Okay, help me up." With Jessica and Fadel under each shoulder, he stood up and locked the legs of his hardsuit so it would stand on its own. He sent the signal, and the hardsuit opened around him. Jessica and Fadel pulled Mason out of the back of his hardsuit. The left leg of his black jumpsuit was a shade darker from all the blood soaking into it.

They sat him back down, and Fadel put a pad on Mason's leg. "Keep pressure on the wound while I cut the pant leg away."

Mason nodded and placed his hand on the wound. Jessica's gloved hand rested on top of his. He looked her in the eyes and nodded, grateful she was there. Fadel produced a large pair of safety shears and made quick work of cutting the pant leg. Setting the shears aside, she started to peel the sticky, blood-soaked cloth off his leg, careful to remove the cloth from around the wound without needing to take the gauze pad off. She disposed of the remains of Mason's pant leg into a plastic bag, and then started tapping on a pad. A robotic arm unfolded from the bulkhead behind Mason's head, the claw at the end opening, each digit sporting a frightening looking tool.

"Okay, Lieutenant, you can take pressure off. I'll get this closed up quickly."

Jessica let go of the bloodied pad, clearing the way for Fadel to get to work. Fadel tapped a screen, and the robot arm descended over Mason's legs. A pair of arms unfolded and squeezed the wound shut, while another ran up his leg, suturing it closed like it was zipping up a bag. The arm finished by covering the sutured wound with a teal pad, held in place by a strong adhesive. The thought of it pulling out his leg hairs when it had to come off turned Mason's stomach. Strange to dread something so petty.

"All right, that will take care of the wound for now," Fadel said. "You'll just need to take it easy."

"Thanks, Ensign Fadel," Mason said.

'My pleasure, sir," Fadel said. "Not to seem like I'm kicking you out, but I have other patients that need tending to, and we can't have non-life-threatening injuries crowding the med bay."

"Right," Mason said. "Can I walk on this safely?"

Fadel nodded. "Those sutures will hold for normal walking, but I wouldn't do any more than necessary, not in this gravity. And anything more strenuous than that should be avoided."

"Understood," Mason said, standing up, feeling more than a bit ridiculous to have his leg bare up to his thigh.

"So, where to?" Jessica asked.

"First, find a pressure suit, and then back to the bridge," Mason said.

"You sure?" she asked.

"This ship's understaffed as it is and, besides, I'm the most experienced gunner on this ship," Mason said.

Jessica chuckled. "Thinking of changing careers?"

"Not a chance. Just want to shoot more Cendies," Mason said.

After riding the elevator back up to the command deck, Mason limped back to the bridge with Jessica. His leg ached, but the pain was manageable now that he no longer had metal sticking out of his thigh.

Captain Ferris glanced at him. "Shouldn't you be in the med bay?"

"Too crowded for walking wounded, sir," Mason said. "Figured I'd return to manning *Independence's* gunnery station."

Ferris shrugged. "If you insist, Flight Lieutenant."

Mason return to the gunnery seat, sighing as he took weight off his wounded leg. Even without his hardsuit pumping painkillers into him, it felt a lot better than it did before Ensign Fadel worked her magic.

"I'm going to handle electronic warfare systems," Jessica said. "That's actually an area I have some experience with. You should spend some time familiarizing yourself with *Independence's* big guns. We'll likely need them."

"Right," Mason said, bringing up the status display of the battlecarrier's main armament. *Independence* had eight main guns in four turrets. Each turret was designated A, B, C, and D. B and D turrets were mounted furthest from the hull and had full 360-degree firing arcs. A and C only had 270, blocked by the barbets of the other two turrets. The magazines were only partly filled, and only with basic ammunition. Quarter-ton command-guided kinetic kill vehicles. The kinetic kill vehicles didn't have seekers of their own, just an antenna on the back and a cluster of maneuvering thrusters for making mid-course corrections. The rounds needed *Independence's* help to home in on their targets, which limited their effective range to inside a light-second. However, they were highly resistant to countermeasures since they relied on *Independence's* big sensors and powerful AI's for guidance. A starship would always have better sensors and smarter computers than could be packed inside a KKV or a missile.

"Captain Ferris, is *Independence* generating enough power for the main guns?" Mason asked.

"More than enough, Flight Lieutenant," Captain Ferris said. "Though those weapons were never test-fired after installation."

"Guess they'll have to be tested in battle, like everything else on this ship," Mason said.

"Wow," Jessica said.

"What?" Mason asked.

"I knew the electronic warfare systems of this ship were first-rate, but actually seeing them working is something else," Jessica said. "I'm picking up Cendy transmissions from all over Outer Sol. It's all encrypted, but I'm willing to bet most of them are about us."

"It's nice to be noticed," Mason said.

"Looks like they're breaking off from the 1st Fleet. Bunch of battlecruisers and arsenal ships are burning hard for us, but with our head start, we'll be clear of the jump limit long before they reach us–"

A launch alarm interrupted her.

"Oh bugger," Jessica said.

The Cendy fleet launched a large volley of torpedoes towards *Independence*, probably whatever they had left over from their long engagement with the 1st Fleet.

"Okay, that's a problem," Mason said. "That's way more torpedoes than *Independence's* point defenses can handle."

"Good thing not all of them are going to make it," Jessica said.

"I take it you got something in mind?" Mason asked.

"It'll take four hours for those torpedoes to reach us," Jessica said. "That's four hours I can use *Independence's* big, powerful ECM systems to fuck with them."

"Well, proceed with the fuckery, Lieutenant Sinclair," Mason.

"I shall," Jessica said. "Torpedoes are mostly going to rely on command-guidance from their launching starships for most of their flight," Jessica said. "So, I'm going to try and jam up the sensors of the starships, while at the same time creating false torpedoes for their systems to try to guide. With luck, they'll have a hard time distinguishing between their real torpedoes and my ghost torpedoes."

"All right," Mason said.

It took a minute for the photons Jessica sent out towards the Cendies to hit the sensor arrays of the launching vessels and the seeker heads of the torpedoes. After Jessica started her electronic fuckery, Mason noticed a change in the torpedoes' courses. It was subtle at first, minor deviations in course that would have huge effects when they reached terminal range. But as soon as torpedoes started to waver, they returned to their original course. All of a sudden, the incoming torpedoes multiplied.

"Dammit," Jessica said.

"What's happening?" Mason asked.

"It wouldn't be called electronic warfare if the enemy couldn't fight back. Cendies are trying to fuck with us back," Jessica said. "Let me unclutter our sensors first."

The false torpedoes disappeared from the tactical screen, but then the Cendy fleet multiplied.

"Oh, that's clever; creating false contacts for me to spoof," Jessica said.

The false starships disappeared as Jessica figured out how to differentiate real contacts from the illusory ones. "Well, *Independence*'s sensors are well hardened. Cendies are pouring a lot of energy into jammers and dazzle lasers. Flight Lieutenant York, please put *Independence* into a clockwise spin. That will make it harder for the Cendies' dazzle lasers to keep focused on us."

"Roger, rolling the ship," Flight Lieutenant York said.

"Okay, that's better," Jessica said.

Mason watched the missiles. They weren't headed directly towards *Independence*, but towards a point ahead of the accelerating carrier. Nothing particularly unusual about that, leading the target was a basic part of any firing solution. Mason noticed their vector would take them close to one of Jupiter's irregular moons, Pasiphae, a captured asteroid about halfway between the highest and lowest points in its orbit.

"Hey, Jessica, those torpedoes are going to pass really close to one of Jupiter's irregular moons," Mason said.

"What of it?" Jessica asked.

"I don't suppose you could try and trick the torpedoes into thinking Pasiphae is us?" Mason asked.

"I don't see how. The torpedoes aren't activity seeking just yet," Jessica said. "They're relying on in-flight guidance from their launch vessels."

"But they're still tracking us, right? Whatever changes in course *Independence* makes, they have to match. What if we adjusted *Independence*'s course so that the torps flew into Pasiphae?"

"Cendy torpedoes almost certainly have built-in collision avoidance," Jessica said. "And the Cendies would just instruct the torpedoes to move around."

"Yeah, but not by a very wide berth," Mason said. "It would waste delta-v, and those torpedoes are probably near the edge of their effective range."

"Yes... let's see. Pasiphae is just under ninety kilometers across and the torpedoes are clustered in a group about... fifty kilometers in radius," Jessica said. "Okay, Flight Lieutenant York, do you think you're up for some highly precise flying?"

"Precision is what starship drivers are trained for, Lieutenant," Flight Lieutenant York said. "What do you need me to do?"

"I need you to adjust *Independence*'s course so that the torpedoes' vector passes through Pasiphae," Jessica said. "I'm going to try and coordinate that with an EM attack to get those torpedoes to ram into the moon."

"Oh, I like that," Flight Lieutenant York said. "Just tell me what you need *Independence* to do."

"The timing for this needs to be perfect," Jessica said. "Can you make the necessary commands to the Flight AI?"

"I'm already on it," Flight Lieutenant York said.

Mason tried not to dig his hands into the armrests of his seat as he waited for Jessica to give the word. From his position in the gunnery station, he could see Flight Lieutenant York's fingers dancing over the controls, plotting the course change.

"I have the maneuver plotted and uploaded to the Flight AI," Flight Lieutenant York said. "It's ready to execute as soon as you're ready."

"Right, begin course change in five... four... three... two... one... now."

"Changing course," Flight Lieutenant York said.

Independence started to change course, her movement so slow and subtle Mason couldn't feel the massive ship turn. After two minutes of lightspeed delay, he saw the torpedoes start to change course, their vector edging ever closer to Pasiphae.

"Executing program now," Jessica said.

Independence's dazzle lasers and jamming arrays burst with activity as Jessica's program overloaded them, shunting a significant portion of the warship's reserve power through them. On a screen, a wave representing the photons carrying Jessica's attack flew from behind *Independence*. The wave split in two as it flew, the leading wave directed towards the Cendy fleet, and the trailing wave directed towards the torpedoes. The lead wave further split into beams of disruptive light focused on each Cendy arsenal ship. The second wave stayed concentrated, an invisible front headed for the clustered Cendy torpedoes, intent on blinding their collision avoidance systems for the crucial second as they closed near Pasiphae. *Independence* stopped maneuvering, and the missiles expected vector passed right through the tiny volume of space that Pasiphae occupied.

Mason held his breath.

The dot representing the torpedoes followed the vector line, getting closer and closer to the icon representing Pasiphae. Then the dots merged. Pasiphae remained, but the torpedoes disappeared.

Jessica's hands shot into the air. "Yes. Yes. Look on my skills at electronic warfare and despair, Cendies! I just flew all your torpedoes into a rock!"

"I flew them into a rock, Lieutenant Sinclair," Flight Lieutenant York said. "You just kept them blind."

"Okay, yes, you helped," Jessica said.

"Hey, it was my idea to crash them into the moon," Mason said.

"No, your idea was to try and get trick them into honing into the moon," Jessica said. "That was a terrible idea that would never work. I just took it and turned it into an idea that would work."

"Whatever you say," Mason said. "So, uh, are we free and clear yet? I don't see any more torpedoes coming from the Cendies."

Jessica let out a sigh. "I think it's pretty safe to say that all the longburn torpedoes the Cendies could throw at us are now at the bottom of a bunch of brand new craters on Pasiphae's surface."

"And there's nothing between us and the jump limit but fifteen million kilometers of open space," Mason said.

"For the moment," Jessica said.

CHAPTER 27

MASON LIMPED DOWN the corridor to the galley, his left leg aching the whole way. *Independence* was an hour from crossing the jump limit. An hour from safety, assuming her stardrive worked. Though *Independence* was still technically inside Jovian space, the Galilean moons, Jupiter fleet base, and the constellation of stations that housed most of Jupiter's population were tens of millions of kilometers behind. As were any enemy contacts. For millions of kilometers in all directions, there was nothing but empty space.

It seemed like a good moment for Mason to head down to the galley, both to try and score some coffee for himself and the other members of the battlecarrier's ad hoc bridge crew, and to check in on his parents.

As he limped out of the elevator and towards the galley, Mason thought about Jupiter's civilian population watching the Federal Space Forces battle it out with the Ascendency, probably thinking and hoping that their liberation had come. He wondered how they would react that they learned that the whole operation was not to save them, but to recover the starship that Mason was walking inside.

He put those thoughts aside when he limped into the crowded galley. Civilian workers from Amalthea filled the tables, some having to sit down on the deck when there was no table space to be found. As far as Mason could tell, he was the only member of the Federal Space Forces inside the compartment.

He found his parents sitting on the deck in one corner of the galley, shoulders touching as they shared a meal pack resting on a paper towel laid out on the deck. His mom said something that made his father chuckle. The sight sent a bloom of warmth through Mason's chest, displacing the cold anxiety that had dwelled there for months.

When they saw him approaching and noticed his limp, their contentment with each other morphed into concern for him. They moved to get up.

"No, please, sit," Mason said.

"What happened to your leg, kid?" his dad asked.

"Flesh wound. Already taken care of it," Mason said.

"You get shot in the fighting?" his mom asked.

"I didn't get shot," Mason said. "It's just a bit of shrapnel."

"'Just a bit of shrapnel,' he says. Kid, no need to act tough with us."

"Not acting tough, Dad." Mason patted his wounded thigh. "This is nothing compared to some of the things I've seen people survive." *Like decapitation*, he didn't add. "It's not something either of you need to worry about."

"Fine. If you say so, we won't worry. Much." His mom gestured to the plate of food resting on the floor between her and Mason's dad. "Want to join us? Been awhile since we last had a picnic."

Mason looked around the crowded galley. "Quite the little spot for a family picnic."

"Isn't it? Even better, there are no ants to get into our food. Or thieving little squirrels running away with a muffin," his dad said.

"Never one to hold a grudge, are you, Dad?" Mason said.

"It was a damn good muffin. Honestly, whoever thought introducing squirrels into Starport Armstrong was a good idea is a goddamn idiot."

"People think squirrels are cute, and they adapt well to living on a station."

"Well, of course they adapt well, kid. They're rats with fluffy tails."

Mason chuckled. It felt good to laugh at one of his dad's little rants.

"So, I heard we're almost clear," his mom said.

"We're closing in on the jump limit. I wouldn't say we're clear just yet," Mason said. "Cendies still have some time to throw something at us before we jump out."

"Word is you managed to trick the Cendies into shooting a rock," his dad said.

"It's not quite how I'd put it, but we did manage to neutralize a Cendy torpedo volley," Mason said.

"You don't seem all that confident," his mom said.

Mason sighed. "I've had enough run-ins with the Cendies to learn not to assume anything about them."

"So, you're saying we shouldn't leave the protected areas of the ship just yet," his mom said.

"No, no. I think you should stay where there's lots of armor between you and space," Mason said.

"Fine by us. This fancy starship Earth-Fed's built has got the best coffee maker I've ever seen embarked on a ship."

"Good that you mentioned that. I came down here in part to grab some coffee for the folks on the bridge."

"You mean you didn't come down here just to see us?" his mom asked.

"They wouldn't have let me off the bridge to check on you two if I didn't promise to return with coffee," Mason said with a smile. "Spacers need their caffeine."

"Well, we won't delay your coffee run any further, sweetheart." His mom nodded towards the coffee makers. "Go ahead."

"Think you could get one for me, kid?"

"You can get one yourself, Morgan," his mom said.

"I'll check in on you two after the jump. Let you know what I've been up to these last few months," Mason said.

"I'll hold you to that, kid," his dad said.

Mason left his parents to their picnic in the corner of the galley and headed for the coffee maker. Grabbing a tray on the way and three of the largest coffee packets, Mason filled them one at a time, and laid them out on the tray. With his prize, he limped out of the galley, and back towards the elevator. From the elevator on the bridge level, he passed the battle damage. Bullet holes, burn marks, torn spall liner, and more than a few bits of red human blood and white Cendy blood.

He walked through the bridge's broken hatch. The bridge itself was quiet save for the low hum of the ventilation system. Flight Lieutenant York sat immobile at her station, eyes fixed on the displays in front of her. Mason placed a coffee packet next to her. She nodded in thanks without moving her eyes off the displays and grabbed the coffee packet, pulling the cap off the straw with her teeth.

Mason approached Captain Ferris. "Coffee. One cream, one sugar, sir."

"Thanks, Flight Lieutenant," Captain Ferris said, accepting the packet.

"How's the ship running, sir?" Mason asked.

"Not to my satisfaction, but still within limits. The radiators aren't evacuating heat as efficiently as I'd like," Captain Ferris said.

"That going to be a problem, sir?" Mason asked.

"In five years, when they have to be replaced early," Captain Ferris said. "But they'll do for now."

"Good to hear. Enjoy your coffee, sir," Mason said.

Captain Ferris nodded and pulled open the straw of his coffee packet.

Mason sat down at his own station, near Jessica, sighing with relief as he gave his injured leg a chance to rest.

"Still hurt?" Jessica asked.

Mason nodded while he pulled the cap off his straw. "Yeah. But not too badly. Anything interesting happen while I was out?"

"1st Fleet's started to withdraw," Jessica said. "We're close enough to the jump limit that the main Cendy fleet won't be able to reach the jump limit themselves and catch us before we jump out."

"So, it's just a question of the picket ships, then," Mason said.

"Yes, and if they're going to try and stop us, it will be within the next hour," Jessica said.

"See any sign of *Mervie* and the other ships?" Mason asked.

Jessica nodded and brought up a sensor display, pointing at a collection of dull red blobs against a black background. "Loitering a few light-minutes out, just as the mission calls for. Assuming nothing happens, they'll jump in to cover us just before we cross the jump limit and start charging our stardrive."

"Good to know there's help out there." Mason took a sip.

"How's the coffee?"

"Good. Dad wasn't kidding when he said this ship had good coffee makers," Mason said.

"Are your parents doing okay?" Jessica asked.

"They're camped out in the galley one deck down," Mason said. "Got a little corner all to themselves."

"I'm sure they are plenty relieved to have you back," Jessica said.

"I don't think you could find a more relieved couple inside the orbit of Pluto. I'm pretty relieved too, for that matter." Mason took another sip of the coffee and relaxed in his seat.

"The way you're enjoying that coffee makes me miss having a stomach," Jessica said. She held up a drained vial. "Certainly better than injecting one of these into my mobility rig every few hours."

"Well, once you get a body more suited to your liking, we can go out to a nice cafe," Mason said. "I know a place on Centauri Fleet Base."

Jessica arched an eyebrow. "Did you just ask me out for coffee?"

"Yes, I think I did," Mason said.

Jessica looked around the bridge. "Your timing is a bit curious."

Mason shrugged. "Seems as good a time as any."

"Fair enough," Jessica said. "Fine, I accept. Once I get a new body with a stomach that can process things like coffee. And, better yet, actual food."

"Well, if the coffee date goes well, we could get dinner aft–"

Something pinged on Jessica's terminal. She turned her attention back towards it. "Oh bugger."

"The Cendies?"

"As expected, their picket force has finally shown up," Jessica said.

Coffee forgotten, Mason dropped the packet into a holder and brought up the tactical display on his HUD. A dozen Cendy battlecruisers had appeared just outside the jump limit, spread out in a loose wall across *Independence's* vector. Their icons spawned more icons as they started launching fighters.

CHAPTER 28

"I'LL BE BLUNT, it is doubtful that *Independence* can survive the combined firepower of twelve battlecruisers, especially with the support of their organic fighter complements," Captain Ferris said. "Our combined closing velocities will give their KKVs enough speed to punch right through the frontal armor."

"So, you're saying the Cendies can kill *Independence* with one shot, Captain?" Wing Commander Cade said.

Captain Ferris nodded. "Yes. And they will be firing twelve shots at us once a minute, every minute, from the moment we enter kinetic range, to when we fly past them and out of the jump limit. From there, our velocity works in our favor. We'll be moving away from them faster than the muzzle velocity of their guns."

"But the battlecruisers are only part of the problem," Wing Commander Cade said. "Their fighters could throw shortburn torpedoes at us. Which, if they're smart, they'll do at the same time we're dealing with their KKVs."

"Would *Independence's* point defense be able to handle both the torpedoes and the KKVs?" Jessica asked.

"If she had some interceptors, three squadrons of Lightnings, and a full gunnery crew directing her point defenses, maybe, Lieutenant," Captain Ferris said. "Unfortunately, she has no interceptors, six Lightnings, and her gunnery crew consists of one grounded fighter pilot." He nodded to Mason. "No offense, Flight Lieutenant."

"None taken, sir," Mason said.

"I'll get my pilots ready to launch," Wing Commander Cade said. "We'll stay close so we can augment *Independence's* point defenses with our own weapons."

"If you do that, sir, I would suggest you slave your gunnery AIs to *Independence's*," Mason said. "Hers will be able to compute fire solutions much faster and cut through Cendy jamming more effectively."

Wing Commander Cade grimaced. "*Independence's* gunnery AI will prioritize her own survival over that of my pilots."

"Yes, sir," Mason said. "Though, truth be told, I doubt *Independence* would survive much longer than your fighters. Six Lightnings just isn't much against that many fighters."

"But thirty-six would be."

All eyes turned to Jessica.

"Remember how we used *Mervie's* mimic array to replicate the signatures of some of the 4th's Lightnings?" she asked. "We could try the same with *Independence* using her ECM systems."

"That doesn't sound easy," Mason said.

Jessica nodded. "It would not be trivial, but it's the best we've got."

"Isn't it a bit of a stretch to assume the Cendies would fall for that trick, Lieutenant?" Wing Commander Cade asked.

"I have some ideas on how to make the illusion more convincing, sir," Jessica said. "Having a few real Lightnings in the mix is one of them."

"You need my pilots to fly out," Wing Commander Cade said.

Jessica nodded. "Yes, sir. And quite promptly too. We'll be in firing range in less than thirty-five minutes."

"In that case, I'll tell my pilots to mount up." Wing Commander Cade pulled his helmet back on.

"I'll coordinate launching your fighters from here, Wing Commander," Captain Ferris said.

"Thank you, Captain." Wing Commander Cade turned around and stomped out of the bridge.

"Good hunting, sir," Mason said.

"You too, Hauler."

Jessica turned to her station and started typing away with furious, rapid strokes.

She paused and turned towards Captain Ferris. "Captain, what I'm about to do is going to require a lot of power."

"What systems will I have to shut down, Lieutenant?" Captain Ferris asked.

"Pretty much everything other than sensors, the AI network, and the longburn drive, sir," Jessica said.

"That include weapons?" Mason asked.

"Yes, and I'll need the computing power of the combat AI to assist," Jessica said.

"We're going to need our guns if we want to break through the Cendy blockade," Mason said.

"But we don't need them right now," Jessica said. "What we need is to get the Cendies to believe that this ship is carrying a full complement of fighters."

"I can direct the power that you need, Lieutenant, but I would like to know why you need that much power to simulate thirty Lightnings," Captain Ferris said.

"It's not just a matter of creating false Lightnings. The Cendies would see through it," Jessica said. "But if I make it look like we're using our ECM to hide the false Lightnings, it might convince the Cendies that they are in fact real."

"Much more convincing when they think they've earned it," Mason said.

"Exactly," Jessica said. "I'll also need all the computational power that can be spared."

"It'd be pointless to have a combat AI with no weapons," Mason said.

"I can keep *Independence* moving in a straight line under manual control," Flight Lieutenant York said.

"I'm afraid I can't spare any computing power," Captain Ferris said.

"I should have enough," Jessica said. "Now it's just a question of instructing the sensor AI to do what I want."

Her fingers danced over the keyboard as she detailed to the sensor AI what she wanted it to do.

On Mason's tactical overlay, *Independence* lit up across the electromagnetic emissions and directed it in a concentrated cone towards the Cendy blocking force. It bore none of the finesse Jessica had used to sever control of the Cendy longburn torpedoes. It was the electronic warfare equivalent of putting a pot over someone's head and walloping it with a ball-peen hammer. The Cendies responded with their own disruptive energies, the glare of dazzle lasers and jammers blinding *Independence's* sensors.

The six remaining Lightnings of the 4th launched during the electro-magnetic bombardment.

"This is Void Knight Leader. It's awfully noisy out here," Wing Commander Cade said over a tightbeam connection.

"It's even worse for the Cendies, Void Night Leader," Jessica said. "Now, please position your fighters in a close ring around *Independence*. That will be the optimal distribution to make this ruse work."

"Understood, Lieutenant Sinclair. I'm positioning my fighters now," Wing Commander Cade said.

"And now the final ingredient." Jessica struck a key.

On the tactual overlay, the remaining Void Knights multiplied by six, forming a tight ring around *Independence*. Jessica sighed, her fingers drumming on the armrest of her seat, and glanced over to Mason with a nervous smile on her face. "Now the waiting game."

Mason watched the tactical overlay, waiting for the Cendies to respond. If Jessica did her job too well, the Cendies wouldn't detect the Lightnings. If she didn't do it well enough, they'd know it was a ruse.

For several agonizing minutes, *Independence's* sensor AI battled it out with the Cendies, trying its hardest to both conjure fake Lightnings out of nothing but light, while at the same time making it really hard for the Cendies to detect them.

Ten minutes before *Independence* entered kinetic range of the Cendy battlecruisers, 120 fighters lit their drives and started burning hard for *Independence*.

"It worked. It worked."

"Congratulations," Mason said. "When do you think you can transfer power back to weapons so I can keep them from killing us?"

"The very last moment," Jessica said. "Captain Ferris, how quickly do you think that can happen?"

"For the point defenses? As little as thirty seconds if I do it right."

Jessica turned to Mason. "You better get ready."

"Yeah," Mason said. He brought up the control overlay for the point defenses, which gave him an error message when it couldn't connect to the combat AI.

"I'm going to need the combat AI if I want to hit anything," Mason said.

"I'll switch it over as soon as the power is restored," Jessica said.

The swarm of Cendy fighters burned towards *Independence*, their time to intercept plummeting. Mason pulled down the visor of his pressure suit, thinking about all the nukes that were about to come flying his way.

"Come on, you bastards. Just keep coming," Jessica said.

The fighters started sprouting missile tracks that rocketed ahead of the strikecraft. The fighters themselves scattered in all directions, flaring their longburn drives and pushing the acceleration into the low twenties, bending their vectors away from *Independence* to stay out of range of her point-defense guns. No matter. They would fly by so fast that they'd never catch *Independence* before she jumped out. Assuming they got past the torpedoes burning down on them. Mason realized most of the missiles weren't torpedoes. Their tracks were consistent with interceptors, homing in on the Lightnings, both real and fake, closely escorting *Independence*. That was good for him, but it was very bad for the Void Knights.

Mason patched into the tightbeam with Wing Commander Cade. "Void Knight Leader, the ruse has done its job. I suggest you take cover behind *Independence* before those interceptors hit us."

"That's awfully nice of you to think of us, Hauler, but our guns can help deal with those torpedoes," Cade said.

"*Independence* can handle the torpedoes, sir. We'll need your fighters to help deal with the KKVs."

"I hope you know what you're doing, Hauler," Cade said.

"*Independence's* combat AI does, sir." Mason looked up to Jessica. "Once it's back online, that is."

"Keep your pants on. I'm returning it to you now," Jessica said.

"Shifting power to point defenses," Captain Ferris said.

The combat AI connected with Mason's tactical overlay, and instantly started prioritizing targets and computing firing solutions. Mason gave the combat AI permission to fire at will and sat back to watch the fireworks. Dozens of rapid-fire kinetic cannons fired all at once, and lines of kinetic fire reached out ahead of *Independence*, plowing through the cloud of missiles bearing down on her. Torpedoes flashed out of existence faster than Mason could keep track of. But the cloud grew closer and closer even as the point defenses thinned it out.

"Come on. Come on. Come on," Mason said, urging on *Independence*'s combat AI and the fantastic number of guns under its control.

As the time neared zero, Mason tensed as if to brace against a physical impact. A deep rumbling boom traveled down the hull, and damage icons filled Mason's HUD.

"A few of the torpedoes detonated at standoff range," Captain Ferris said. "The outer ablative layers of the frontal armor absorbed most of the energy, but looks like several point-defense guns and sensor clusters were knocked out."

Mason opened a channel with Wing Commander Cade. "Void Knight Leader, status?"

"We're still here, Hauler," Wing Commander Cade said. "Those big turrets offer a lot of room to hide behind. Saw a hell of a flash."

"Frontal armor ate a couple of nukes, Void Knight Leader. We lost some point-defense guns in the process," Mason said. "You think you could help fill in the gaps?"

"I think we can do that," Wing Commander Cade said. "We'll link our Combat AIs with yours."

"Roger that, Void Knight Leader," Mason said.

The six remaining Void Knights linked their combat AIs to *Independence*'s while they maneuvered their fighters ahead of the battlecarrier, effectively becoming six remote point-defense guns.

Mason dismissed the damage alert, and shifted his attention to the Cendy battlecruisers, the final obstacle between *Independence* and the relative safety of FTL. The radiators of each battlecruiser glowed in the upper reaches of the visual spectrum as they dumped waste heat from charging the capacitors of their main guns. All the while, they hammered *Independence* with disruptive emissions, trying to blind her before launching their first strike.

Jessica and the sensor AI did a good job of keeping Mason's scope clear of interference, and were giving back as good as they got. But it would be too much to hope that any KKV the Cendies fired would miss *Independence*. Powerful as it was, *Independence*'s ECM system wasn't good enough to make a ship as big and ponderous as *Independence* anything other than an easy target.

"Uh, Captain Ferris, how good is *Independence*'s armor, exactly?" Mason asked.

"It's the best ever installed on a Federal Starship, Flight Lieutenant. Which is not going to be good enough against those KKVs if any of them hit solid. No amount of armor is. Point defenses will have to vaporize all of them. And the clouds of metal vapor we plow through will still cause damage to things that are outside of the main armor layer. Like sensor clusters and point-defense turrets."

Mason grimaced into his display. "I see what you're getting at, sir. Each volley we survive will likely result in reduction of *Independence*'s ability to defend herself. Which is going to be compounded by the fact that, as we get closer, the combat AI will have less time to compute firing solutions against more incoming KKVs."

"Yes, Flight Lieutenant, that's about the size of it," Captain Ferris said.

"Belts and zones." Mason glanced over to Jessica. "Any more tricks to tilt the odds of survival in a favorable direction?"

Jessica glanced over to him. "Afraid I'm fresh out. You?"

Mason shook his head. "I got nothing."

Jessica smiled. "A pity."

Mason's tactical overlay showed five seconds to enemy firing range. A couple of minutes after that, and *Independence* would enter effective range of her own guns. He was doubtful she'd be in any state to shoot back by then.

He sighed. "Guess we won't have that coffee together."

There was a staccato of flashes, and several friendly contacts appeared, including FSFV *Cairo*, FSFV *Houston*, three Churchill-class destroyers and, most surprising of all, FSFV *Sirius*, a Jupiter-class battleship.

"Blimey, it's *Mervie*," Jessica said. "Captain Vann must be pushing the mimic array hard to disguise her ship as a battleship."

That made a lot more sense than a battleship appearing out of nowhere, but the Cendies didn't seem to realize it.

Six of the battlecruisers fired their maneuvering thrusters, swinging around as fast as they could to bring their big guns to bear before the presumed battleship had time to charge her weapons.

"Remind me to buy Captain Vann a drink," Mason said.

"You and me both," Jessica said.

Mervie lit her drive, the output coming up exactly like that of a *Sirius*-class battleship, and started burning for the Cendy fleet at a steady one g.

Mason looked over to Jessica. "How long can Mervie keep up that kind of output?"

"Twenty minutes, maybe," Jessica said. "She'd need to overcharge her systems to give off the emissions of a ship sixteen times her mass. Not that she'll wait that long. I suspect Captain Vann will drop the illusion as soon as the Cendies fire the first shot."

Mason opened up the overlay for the main guns and began charging their capacitors. "Might as well give the Cendies more to worry about, then."

"Hope to draw their attention back towards us?" Jessica asked.

"Hoping they'll see what big guns we have and decide they have better things to do than get caught between two angry Federal capital ships," Mason said.

"Because they've had that much trouble dealing with our capital ships in the past, yeah?" Jessica said.

Mason glanced over to Jessica and sighed. "Fair point."

Jessica shrugged and gave him an apologetic smile.

The emissions of six Cendy battlecruisers spiked on the tactical screen, and six KKV came screaming through the night at *Independence*.

"Well, it was a good thought," Jessica said.

"Not good enough," Mason said

The combat AI started tracking the KKVs, prioritizing the most threatening target for destruction. The battlecruisers increased the intensity of their electronic assault on *Independence's* systems to try and throw off the aim of her point defenses, increasing the chance of one or more of their KKVs striking true. KKVs started moving strangely on Mason's tactical screen as junk data corrupted the firing solutions, while false contacts appeared.

They were quickly wiped away as Jessica and the sensor AI sifted true sensor data from the forgeries, giving Mason a clear view of the incoming KKVs.

The KKVs pulsed as they fired their maneuvering jets, trying to throw off the firing solutions. The combat AI adjusted as quickly as the KKVs changed course.

"Void Knight Leader, you get the first crack at them," Mason said.

"Roger that. Moving to engage."

The Void Knights flared their longburn drives and moved ahead of *Independence*. The combat AI kept them up-to-date on which KKVs were the most likely to score a hit, and they concentrated on those. The Lightnings opened fire barely more than a second before the KKVs passed them, turning two of them into expanding clouds of metallic vapor.

Independence opened fire a second later, atomizing KKVs in rapid succession in the last seconds before impact. What was left of the KKVs, broken fragments and metallic gas, continued as expanding clouds of fast-moving matter.

Independence's armored nose plowed through the clouds like the prow of a seagoing ship crashing through a wave, the outer layers flashing, and damage icons appearing in Mason's HUD.

"We've got spalling in the upper decks. Two more point-defense turrets no longer operational," Captain Ferris said, narrating what the damage icons were telling Mason.

There were more energy spikes, but the KKVs that appeared on the tactical screen were moving away from *Independence*, and towards what the Cendies clearly believed to be a well-armed Federal battleship. *Sirius* disappeared, replaced by a much smaller Federal ship *Independence*'s sensor AI couldn't identify. *Mervie* turned away much faster than any battleship could, and lit her longburn drive at full power, pushing up to three g of acceleration. *Cairo* and *Houston* matched the maneuver to stay in close formation.

If the Cendies were confused by the sudden transformation, they didn't show any sign. Their KKVs adjusted their courses to track *Mervie*.

"Oh, no, we can't have that," Jessica said.

Mason was about to ask what she meant, then he saw the KKVs homing in on *Mervie* flare up as their maneuvering thrusters started firing, and they started changing course.

"What did you do?" Mason asked.

"The KKVs flying after *Mervie* have their guidance antennas facing towards us. I just had *Independence* send them a bunch of spurious commands to waste their propellant," Jessica said. "Oh, and by the way, the Cendies are about to shoot at us again."

Six battlecruisers spiked, throwing more KKVs towards *Independence*. The Void Knights vaporized three KKVs as they flew by, before the point defenses took out the remainder. More damage alarms sounded as the gaseous remains slammed into *Independence*'s hull. Damage icons appeared on Mason's HUD, but he dismissed them. Managing damage wasn't his job. It was inflicting it.

Which was exactly what he was going to do, as *Independence* was about to reach effective range of her own lower velocity, but much more numerous main guns.

Mason picked a battlecruiser in the center of the blocking force and ordered the combat AI to target it. A firing solution for all eight of *Independence*'s guns appeared on a tactical overlay, along with a short countdown to firing.

Two minutes from flyby, a boom traveled through *Independence*'s hull as all eight guns fired in unison. Eight friendly KKVs appeared on the tactical overlay, little blue wedges following the dotted lines of the firing solution like breadcrumbs leading towards the center of the Cendy formation. Jamming intensified, and the Cendy battlecruisers closed ranks around the targeted vessel, keeping the slanted armor of their frontal hulls pointed towards the KKVs.

While the main guns recharged, Mason selected a second armored combatant for the combat AI. Thirty seconds after the first shot, ninety seconds before flyby, *Independence* shuddered again, and eight more KKVs flew towards the Cendies. Mason picked a third target for the combat AI to engage just as the first volley reached point-defense range. The battlecruisers opened fire with their point defenses, vaporizing a KKV in an instant. A second followed shortly after that, followed by a third, and then a fourth. *Independence*'s first volley fired in anger dwindled rapidly as the time to impact counted down.

There was a white-hot flash when the timer hit zero. The combat AI reported one solid hit. The Cendy battlecruiser Mason had targeted broke apart, glowing brightly on the infrared where one KKV had struck it. *Independence* guns fired again, and at the same time, the Cendies spiked and sent KKVs of their own after *Independence*. The combat AI prioritized targets, computed firing solutions, and uploaded them to the turrets and fighters within a second. KKVs started dying as the combat AI worked down the list, from the most threatening to the least. But with her degraded point defenses, one of the Cendy KKVs got through.

There was a distant screech from below and a decrease in the pull of gravity. A flood of damage icons appeared on Mason's display.

"We've lost the number two longburn drive," Captain Ferris said.

Two KKVs from *Independence's* third volley connected with their target, ripping open another battlecruiser, spilling its guts out into space. Maneuvering thrusters fired, and the armored combatants facing *Independence* started to turn away rather than try to get another shot on the battlecarrier.

"*Mervie's* going to need our help," Jessica said. "When we fly by, I won't have an angle to jam their KKVs. They'll be flying true, and I don't think the taskforces interceptors or point defenses will be enough."

Mason looked at the tactical screen, noting *Independence's* vector relative to the combatants firing on *Mervie*.

"Flight Lieutenant York, could you adjust our heading, so we pass closer by the Cendies?" Mason said.

"Adjusting course," Flight Lieutenant York said. *Independence's* vector slowly turned towards the combatants.

Mason ordered the combat AI to lay each main gun turret on one combatant, and compute firing solutions for the secondary guns on the remaining two.

"Will secondaries be enough?" Jessica asked.

"At the speed we're going? I think so," Mason said.

The secondary guns were tiny compared to the main guns, and fired dumb projectiles instead of guided KKVs, but they were rapid-firing weapons that could fire a volley every few seconds and, with the approach velocity, they'd hit with many, many times their rated muzzle energy. There was a rumble as the rapid-fire secondary guns opened fire, sending lines of kinetic projectiles after two battlecruisers. A deeper rumble traveled through the ship, and four separate pairs of KKVs radiated out from *Independence* towards the Cendy battlecruisers.

The Cendies put up an instant wall of point-defense fire, and icons flashed as metal struck metal at hundreds of kilometers per second.

The Cendy blocking force was behind them and receding faster than the muzzle velocity of *Independence's* guns. Mason had scored hits on all six combatants, though none of them solid, and their point defenses had vaporized all his KKVs. But the gaseous metallic remains of the KKVs slammed into the sides and rears of each ship, where their armor was relatively flat and thin. Four Cendy combatants showed signs of serious damage, their drives dark, though still active enough to be considered threats by the combat AI. The two Cendies targeted by the secondary guns were not active threats. The large volume of rapid-fire projectiles perforating their rear hulls left both ships dead in space.

"Preparing to shift power to the stardrive," Captain Ferris said. "Preparing for main drive shutdown."

"Ceding control to astrogation," Flight Lieutenant York said.

There was an alarm and, a few seconds later, gravity disappeared as the longburn drives went dark. "Belts and zones, this is a badass ship," he said.

Mason flipped up his visor and let out a shuddering breath. He noticed his hands were shaking and balled them into fists to try and steady them. A gentle hand rested on his right arm, and Mason looked over to Jessica. Her visor was up, and she had a relieved smile on her face.

"I think we made it," Jessica said.

Mason looked at the tactical overlay, saw the Cendy blocking force in disarray, making no effort to pursue *Mervie's* taskforce or *Independence*. All that lay ahead of *Independence* was open space.

"Yeah, I think you might be right," Mason said. He wrapped his fingers around Jessica's hand and held tight until a vibration traveled through the ship. In an instant, Jupiter was over a hundred billion kilometers behind them.

EPILOGUE

A TASKFORCE OF 2nd Fleet ships was waiting for *Independence* just outside the jump limit. A swarm of shuttles and tugs descended upon the damaged battlecarrier, the former to carry her mishmash of a crew, and the latter to tow the warship to Alpha Centauri Fleet Base's drydock.

Mason lost track of Jessica after the shuttles dropped them off at Alpha Centauri Fleet Base. He was taken to the station's main hospital to repair the deep wound in his leg, while she headed to a facility more appropriate to her needs. What followed were days of debriefings while his wound healed up.

The news was dominated by reports of Operation Autumn Fire, which Federal Command had given out at a press conference. Far from the clandestine nature typical of Special Purpose Branch operations, Operation Autumn Fire was played up as Earth-Fed's first real victory against the Ascendency, which Mason thought was fair enough, even if it cost the lives of hundreds of Federal spacers.

The 1st Fleet lost thirty ships during its diversionary battle against the Cendy occupation fleet, but the keenest losses were those by the 4th Fighter Squadron. Only six out of sixteen of some of the Earth Federation's most elite fighter pilots had survived. Wing Commander Cade and his five remaining pilots were instant war heroes, their names and faces appearing in broadcasts on multiple channels.

Mason was glad their valor was being recognized, but also a little sad. Earth-Fed didn't like losing heroes, which meant that the careers of the remaining Void Knights as combat pilots were over. At best, they could serve as instructors and perhaps as test pilots, but they would never be assigned to a combat squadron, either regular or special forces. Mason, at least, got to keep his anonymity, and all the freedom that allowed.

He knew something was up when they took him in for fast healing. After applying a local anesthetic, the doctors sat Mason down in an autodoc, which proceeded to jam a nightmarishly large needle into his wounded thigh. For the rest of the day, Mason was convalescent as his wound burned from healing faster than nature intended. Generally, doctors only used fast healing on non-life-threatening injuries when the patient in question needed to get back to duty as fast as possible. Which meant Mason wasn't going to get that leave he was hoping for. His suspicions were confirmed when Colonel Shimura walked into his room, supporting herself with a cane.

"Sir," Mason said. "Good to see you back on your feet."

"Thank you, Flight Lieutenant," Shimura said. "How's the leg feel?"

"Like it's been cauterized with a plasma torch, sir," Mason said. "Which I'm guessing you have something to do with."

"A fair assumption, though not actually the case, Flight Lieutenant," Colonel Shimura said as she limped towards him. "It seems you've attracted some attention from higher-up."

"Oh, joy," Mason said.

Shimura smiled and sat down in the seat next to his bed. She let out a sigh of relief as she settled her weight, balancing her cane between her legs with her left hand. It was then he noticed the robust-looking black box clutched in her right.

"What's that, sir?"

Shimura glanced down at the box. "Oh, this? This is just a bit of recognition for your fine service." She held up the box and opened it. Inside, resting on the box's red satin interior, was a set of Squadron Leader bars.

"Huh, not a lot of ceremony as far as promotions go," Mason said.

Shimura pulled the box back. "Well, in that case, I'll just take this..."

Mason held up his hand. "No, no, this is fine. I gladly accept."

Shimura chuckled. "That's better." She held the box out.

Mason took the box in his fingers. It felt heavy, and solid. Made of high-quality materials. He glanced down at the bars, seeing his reflection in the polished metal.

"So, Colonel, what kind of mission do you have in mind that requires a fast-heal and a bump in paygrade?"

"Oh, it's not my mission. If I had my way, you'd be getting a long leave of absence," Colonel Shimura said.

"Well, I'm sorry you didn't, sir," Mason said. "So, what mission is it that the powers-that-be have in store for me?"

"You'll be building a new fighter squadron, both as a replacement for the 4th Fighter Squadron and to serve as a template for future special forces squadrons," Colonel Shimura said.

"That's quite the mission, sir," Mason said.

"The reward for good work, Flight Lieutenant," Colonel Shimura said.

"Guess I shouldn't work so hard, then," Mason said. "So, I take it I'll be working with you and Lieutenant Sinclair, then? How's her new body coming along, by the way?"

Colonel Shimura's smile faded. "Unfortunately, Lieutenant Sinclair is no longer under my command. She's been reassigned."

"To where, sir?"

"I don't know. All I know is that she's no longer on-station. Might not even be in the Alpha Centauri system anymore."

Mason sighed and sank into his bed. "Reward for good work, huh, sir?"

"That's right, Squadron Leader."

"So, what's your reward for good work, sir?"

"I will work with you selecting pilots to recruit to your new squadron, Squadron Leader," Shimura said.

"Not getting rid of me any time soon, are you, sir?" Mason said.

Shimura chuckled. "No, I'm not, Squadron Leader. That's something I think the Cendies are going to come to regret, don't you?"

Mason smiled with all the warmth of the icy dwarf planet the Cendies had left him stranded on after his first encounter with them. "Yes, sir. I would think so."

⁐

It was a bloody boring flight to Procyon, but it gave Jessica time to acclimate to her new body. She had forgotten what an irritating process that could be as her brain adjusted to her new body's artificial nervous system.

One day, her senses were so dialed up she had to float inside a sensory deprivation chamber just to keep from being overwhelmed by something as simple as air blowing over her skin. Other times, her body was as numb as a side of frozen vitro-beef.

When FSFV *Arlington* jumped into Procyon, she had mostly finished adjusting to her new body. It was a lot like her older body, with the same face and largely the same proportions, but about twenty percent taller. Her brief experience seeing through Mason's eyes had given her an appreciation for the virtues of height.

Jessica felt a twinge of regret thinking of Mason. The orders to board *Arlington* and travel to Procyon immediately left no time for her to visit him, and she was under strict orders not to send any personal messages before she departed Alpha Centauri.

Such was the life of an intelligence officer. No one told her what her new assignment was, but it wasn't hard to guess. Her destination made it pretty clear who she was going to work for.

The space around Procyon Fleet Base was crowded with warships, the scattered survivors of the 9th and 10th Fleets joining forces with the 7th Fleet to protect Earth-Fed's best-developed fuel infrastructure while the Ascendency continued to occupy Outer Sol.

The shuttle ride from *Arlington* to the Special Purpose Branch's private dock in Procyon Fleet Base was uneventful, and the group of humorless officers waiting for her after as she disembarked was unsurprising.

After a tram ride, she passed through multiple security checkpoints until she arrived at Admiral Julia Mobius' office at the top level of Procyon Fleet Base's command center. The expansive windows making up the back wall of the office gave a spectacular view of the interior of the fleet base's main cylinder, the station's greys and greens contrasting sharply with the dark wood of the admiral's desk.

Jessica wondered if that desk was there before Mobius was appointed Supreme Commander, or if Mobius had lugged the thing all the way from 1st Fleet headquarters in Inner Sol. Knowing what she did about Admiral Mobius, she suspected the latter.

Mobius sat behind her desk straight-backed, her long ponytail draped over the epaulette covering her right shoulder.

Jessica moved to salute.

"No need to stand on ceremony, Lieutenant. Sit. We have much to discuss." The admiral gestured to one of the seats before her desk.

"Yes, sir," Jessica said, taking the offered seat.

"How is your new body, by the way?" Mobius asked.

"More or less broken in after my flight from Alpha Centauri, sir."

Mobius nodded. "You did fine work recovering *Independence* despite the complications that arose. You should be commended."

"Thank you, sir. Though, at the risk of being trite, I should point out that it was a team effort," Jessica said.

"Nothing trite about giving credit where it's due," Mobius said. "*Independence* will go a long way toward offsetting the losses we've taken. And news of her recovery is already resulting in a major boost to morale across the fleet. Everyone involved is being rewarded."

"Does that include Colonel Shimura and Flight Lieutenant Grey, sir?" Jessica asked.

Mobius nodded. "Colonel Shimura will continue to do what she does best, working as a field officer for Special Purpose Branch. As for Flight Lieutenant Grey, he's now Squadron Leader Grey. I sent the promotion through on the same drone that ordered you here."

"I do still wonder why you ordered me away from Colonel Shimura," Jessica said. "She and I have done good work together."

"I know it must seem like I'm breaking apart the Branch's star team, but the best place for you is not with Colonel Shimura in the field."

"Then what is the best place for me, sir?" Jessica said.

"On the trail that leads to where the Ascendency came from, Lieutenant."

The End.